THEIR OWN LITTLE MIRACLE

CAROLINE ANDERSON

SURPRISE TWINS FOR THE SURGEON

SUE MacKAY

D1076552

MILLS & BOON

First Published in Great Britain 2018
by Mills & Boon, an imprint of HarperCollins*Publishers*
1 London Bridge Street, London, SE1 9GF

Their Own Little Miracle © 2018 by Caroline Anderson

Surprise Twins for the Surgeon © 2018 by Sue MacKay

ISBN: 978-0-263-93365-9

MIX
Paper from
responsible sources
FSC® C007454

This book is produced from independently certified FSC™ paper
to ensure responsible forest management.
For more information visit www.harpercollins.co.uk/green.

Printed and bound in Spain
by CPI, Barcelona

THEIR OWN
LITTLE MIRACLE

CAROLINE ANDERSON

MILLS & BOON

For everyone who's struggled with infertility or faced the anguish of childlessness, and for those who've had the courage to act as surrogate or donor and given such a priceless gift.

CHAPTER ONE

'ED TRAUMA CALL, ten minutes.'

Iona's heart sank. Another one? The previous trauma patient had only just arrived, and they were seriously short-staffed. Andy Gallagher was on holiday, Sam Ryder had gone for lunch five minutes ago at three thirty, they were rushed off their feet and she was virtually on her own because James Slater, the clinical lead, was already up to his eyes in Resus with the trauma patient who'd just arrived, a construction worker with severe crush injuries to his chest who from what she could gather was resisting all attempts to resuscitate him.

Which made her, a brand new registrar, the most senior doctor available, so it wasn't a surprise when she was called into Resus. James didn't pause what he was doing. 'Iona, can you take the trauma call, please? I can't leave my patient but I'll be right here, so you can run things by me if you need to.'

'Sure.'

She went back to her patient, handed her over to the F2 junior doctor she was with, found out as much detail as possible about the incoming casualty, went into Resus and put on a lead apron. Their patient had been hit by a car and had suspected pelvic injuries, which she really

hadn't wanted to hear, so he'd need X-rays to check for
fractures. She hoped they wouldn't be too serious because James was still tied up and looking at him she
was fairly sure he would be for some time, because he
and his team were now opening the patient's chest and
it wasn't looking pretty.

Around her a new team was assembling: Tim, an F1
junior doctor fresh out of medical school who was totally
out of his depth, Jenny, thankfully a highly competent
nurse, Sue, a radiographer she trusted, ready with the
portable X-ray and ultrasound, another nurse who she'd
worked with in the past and who seemed OK, and a recently qualified health care assistant as the scribe.

Well, she just hoped the patient wasn't too bad, because as teams went, this one was inadequate on several
fronts. Not Sue, though, who was already surrounding
the bay with lead screens, and not Jenny. Just her, Tim
and the HCA, then. It was a good job James was right
beside them, even if he was up to his eyes.

She briefed them quickly on what little she knew, allo-
cated them their positions in the team and made sure they
were ready. 'Right, lead and plastic aprons, please, everyone, and you all know what you're doing?' she checked,
then it was too late to worry because the patient was
being wheeled in and they were given the handover by
the paramedics.

'This is Jim Brown, age fifty-six, hit on his right-hand
side by a large van about forty minutes ago, suspected
pelvic injury. We put a pelvic binder on and secured
his spine at the scene. BP one-twenty over eighty, sats
ninety-eight per cent, we've given him ten of morphine
and started him on saline. No apparent head or chest

trauma but he's complaining of pain in the right wrist so we've splinted it.'

The pelvic injury wasn't good news, but at least his blood pressure was all right so hopefully he could be transferred to Orthopaedics shortly. 'OK, everybody, can we get these clothes off so I can do a primary survey, please? Sue, we need a FAST scan, and somebody book an urgent CT? Jenny, take bloods, cross match for four units, and we'll have packed cells and FFP on standby, please. Sue, after the FAST scan I'd like X-rays of C-spine, chest and pelvis. And make a note of the time. Fifteen forty-six.'

The team went into action and she bent over the patient so she was in his line of sight; he was conscious but in obvious pain and distress, and she smiled reassuringly at him. 'Hello, Jim. My name is Iona, I'm a doctor and I'm going to be looking after you. Can you tell me where it hurts?'

'All down there—don't know, it's all blurred together.'

'Anything else? Head? Chest?'

'No, they're fine. My right wrist hurts, that's all.'

'OK.' She looked up at the monitor to check his blood pressure. One-ten over seventy, slightly down. She'd need to keep a close eye on it. 'How's the FAST scan, Sue?'

'Some free fluid in the abdomen,' Sue murmured softly. Which was highly suggestive of a pelvic fracture. And his blood pressure had dropped since the paramedics had reported it.

They stepped back briefly so Sue could X-ray his pelvis for confirmation, then Iona shut her mind to everything else and concentrated on Jim. Pupils equal and reactive, airway clear, good bilateral breath sounds, no significant pain when she felt his chest, no obvious bumps on his head, but his right wrist was almost certainly fractured.

And so was his pelvis. The X-ray showed multiple fractures of the pelvic ring, some displaced. No wonder he was bleeding, but hopefully his neck and chest were clear and he still had circulation to both feet. Small mercies, she thought.

'Right, Jenny, can we start the PRBC and FFP, and can someone page Orthopaedics please? Multiple pelvic fractures. Sue, can you get the neck and chest shots, please.'

'If he's got pelvic fractures you need to page IR,' James said over his shoulder, and she took a breath and nodded. At least he was listening and keeping her on track. She could do this.

'OK. Can someone page Interventional Radiology as well, please? How about CT, James?'

'No, wait for IR. They'll probably take him straight to the IR suite to embolise the damaged arteries.'

If she was lucky...

She was scanning the X-rays when she heard the swish of the door opening and closing behind her. She glanced round to see who it was, and her heart did a funny little hitch. The interventional radiologist? He didn't look old enough to be a consultant, but he had the firm tread of someone who knew what he was doing. She could only hope—

'Hi. I'm Joe Baker, IR Specialist Registrar. You've got a pelvic fracture for me?'

She met his eyes and her head emptied. Framed by the longest, darkest lashes, they were very pale blue, almost azure, with a dark rim. Utterly gorgeous and curiously penetrating. Mesmerising, in fact...

She gave herself a mental kick and tried to focus. 'Yes.

Hi. I'm Iona Murray, Registrar. This is Jim Brown, fifty-six years old, hit by a car on the right, BP one-twenty over eighty on admission, now…' her eyes flicked to the monitor, and her heart sank '…ninety-five over sixty. Sats were ninety-eight per cent, now ninety-six. FAST scan shows free fluid, X-ray confirms multiple fractures of the pelvic ring. I think the chest and neck are clear but they haven't been checked by a radiologist.'

He nodded and held out his hand. 'May I?' He took the tablet from her, scrolled through the images and frowned. 'Right, they are clear but the pelvis is a mess and I'll need to embolise him. Has he had a CT yet?'

'No. We haven't had time.'

'How's his airway? Any obvious chest trauma or signs of head injury? Cardiac tamponade? Pleural effusion?'

'No.'

'Are you leading?' he asked, and she nodded.

'Right, I'll take over from here. Go on.'

She didn't know whether to be relieved or furious, because frankly it was a close-run thing. She went for relieved.

'He's also got a query fracture of right radius and ulna, but good cap refill and sensation.'

'OK, that can wait, then, so can the CT. Can you cancel the slot, please, if you've booked it, and alert IR?'

Joe reached for his neck, then frowned. 'Stethoscope?' he said briskly, holding out his hand, and she lifted her stethoscope over her head and handed it to him reluctantly.

'You're dead meat if anything happens to it, it was a graduation present from my sister,' she muttered darkly, and he rolled his eyes, introduced himself to Jim and checked his chest.

'OK, his chest's clear so I'll take him straight to IR—'

'BP falling. Sixty-five over forty.'

Jim was crashing. He groaned, and Iona took his hand.

'It's OK, Jim, we're here, we've got you,' she said, squeezing his hand for reassurance. But it was cold and lifeless, clammy now as well, and she felt her pulse spike.

'Right, can we have the REBOA kit, please, we need to do this now,' Joe said. 'And get me an arterial kit before we lose the femoral artery.'

He was going to insert a balloon into his aorta in *Resus*? Her eyes widened. She'd never seen it done, far less assisted, and she felt a moment of panic.

'I can page Sam,' Iona said hopefully. Sam, who was an ex-army medic, had done it dozens of times in the field and would know exactly what to do, but Joe Baker wasn't waiting.

'No time. Can I have a pair of scissors? The first thing we need to do is cut a chunk out of the pelvic binder to give me access.'

He cut a slit above the femoral artery on Jim's left leg and removed a V from the fabric with a deft snip of the scissors. 'First I'm going to secure access to the CFA so we don't lose it. I'm going in on the left because the fractures are worse on the right, so this is our best chance,' he explained, searching for the artery with his gloved fingertips, his hands rock steady. 'OK, Jim, sharp scratch coming,' he warned as he inserted the needle, but Jim was beyond noticing.

'Right, we're in. Someone open the REBOA pack and cover him in the sterile drapes. Just leave the site accessible, please. Iona, you're assisting, come and scrub.'

She felt her pulse rate go up another notch. The IR was already scrubbing and she followed him, joining him at the sink. 'Isn't it dangerous without imaging?' she asked under her breath as she scrubbed. 'You can't see what's going on in there. Wouldn't it be safer in the IR suite?'

He skewered her with those mesmerising eyes, and they'd turned to ice. 'Are you questioning my clinical competence?'

She held the icy stare with difficulty and shook her head. 'No, no, not at all! I'm questioning mine. I've never assisted with one of these—'

'Well, here's your chance, because he won't make it to IR and if we don't do this now, we'll lose him, so I suggest you take a deep breath and get on with it, because frankly he doesn't have time for this and nor do I. What do you know about a Zone III REBOA?'

She searched her brain, her heart hammering. 'It stands for Resuscitative Endovascular Balloon Occlusion of the Aorta, and it's a balloon catheter inserted via the common femoral artery to cut off the blood supply from the aorta below the balloon. Zone III occlusion is below the renal and mesenteric vessels, and it stops the bleeding from the damaged arteries in the pelvis, so it'll keep his heart and brain alive until you can get him into the IR suite or Theatre and stop the bleeding.'

'Contraindications?'

'Chest trauma, cardiac tamponade, pneumothorax, haemothorax, pleural effusion, aortic dissection—'

'OK, we've ruled them out, so what are the dangers?'

'Damage to the femoral artery or aorta, and reperfusion injury from cutting off the blood supply for too long.'

He nodded. 'Exactly, so time is of the essence. Right, let's get on with this.'

She swallowed and sucked in a breath and reached for

a paper towel as someone helped him into a sterile gown. 'What do you want me to do?'

'Get gowned up.' He crossed to the bed, snapping on gloves as he went. 'OK, we're ready. Let's go.' Jim was completely covered with the sterile drapes, leaving just the small area with the cannula sticking out uncovered for access. He glanced at the team as he reached for the REBOA trolley and injected a local around the site of the cannula, then flushed it with heparinised saline and inserted a fine guide wire.

'Someone phone the IR suite and get them on standby for immediate transfer as soon as I'm done,' he said as he was working. 'Tell them I'll be ten minutes. OK, Iona, watch and learn.'

She watched, and she learned how wrong she'd been to doubt him. His hands were steady and confident, sensitive as he removed the cannula from the guide wire and inserted the large bore introducer with great care. 'This is the tricky bit,' he said. 'You don't want to tear the artery, and the Twelve French makes a damn great hole, so you have to be subtle. OK, that's good.' He pulled out the fine wire and threaded the stiff guide wire in to the mark he'd made by holding it up against Jim's body. Hence the gowns and extensive drapes, she realised, so he could do that without risk of contamination of the wire.

'Right, it's in. Can you hold that steady, please, Iona, I don't want it to move. Keep an eye on the mark on it. Good. X-ray check, please, around T4.' He watched the screen, then nodded. 'OK, that's good. Then I slide the balloon catheter in over it, up to the mark, which is below the end of the guide wire, and then I inflate—like that, until I feel the resistance change,' he said, squeezing the syringe steadily to fill the balloon with saline.

'OK, that should be it. X-ray check here, please,' he said, indicating the level.

His eyes flicked to the clock, then the monitor, then the X-ray screen, and she saw the tension go out of his shoulders. 'Good. His BP's picking up. Time sixteen seventeen. Make sure that's on the notes, please. Right, secure this lot with a grip-lock dressing so nothing moves, and let's go. The clock's ticking and we've got an hour, max.'

Moments later the doors swished shut behind them, and as the team dispersed Iona stood there amid the litter of the procedure, staring after them in a mixture of bewilderment and awe.

Had all that only taken thirty-one minutes? It had been the longest half-hour of her life, but Joe Baker seemed to have taken it in his stride, not seeming even slightly fazed by it.

Good luck, or good judgement? Maybe a bit of both, but Jim was still alive and she knew if it hadn't been for Joe they would have lost him.

It wasn't going so well for James and his team, though, from what she could hear, and definitely not his patient.

Then she heard James sigh heavily. 'OK, everyone, I'm calling it. Are we all agreed?' There was a low murmur, followed by silence. 'Time of death, sixteen twenty-one. Can somebody cover him, please, but leave everything in place for the post mortem. I'll go and talk to his family.'

Her eyes flicked to James, and he was stripping off his gloves and gown and coming over to her.

She smiled at him sympathetically. 'Thanks for your support. I'm sorry about your patient.'

'Yeah, me, too, but that's life. You did well, by the way. Are you OK?'

She smiled properly this time, slightly surprised to find that she was, even though she was shaking from head to foot. 'Yes, I am. He was quite hard on me, but I probably deserved it. I was freaking out a bit, but he made it look so easy.'

James smiled. 'I've heard great things about Joe. He's only been here a few weeks, but his clinical lead says he's red hot, and he thinks he'll go far.'

'Unlike me. I was like a rabbit in headlights.'

'No, you weren't, you were just faced with a dying patient and no real way of dealing with it, even though you were doing everything right. Sam couldn't have got here in time, and if Joe hadn't been here you would have lost him, or I would have had to abandon my patient to save yours. Not that it would have mattered, as it turns out. Sometimes we just can't save them.'

She swallowed. 'I know.' She stripped off her gown and gloves, dumped them in the bin, took off the heavy lead apron and realised her stethoscope, her anchor that reminded her on an hourly basis that she really was a doctor and it wasn't just a dream, wasn't there. And Joe had already mislaid his own.

'Rats. He's still got my stethoscope.'

'They'll have one on the desk. You'll get it back.'

She smiled grimly. 'Too right I will. Thanks, James.'

He pushed open the door. 'You're welcome. Right, I need to talk to my patient's family, and you need to talk to yours. Ah, here comes the cavalry. You've just missed Iona's first REBOA, Sam.'

Sam's eyes widened and he looked at Iona. '*You* did it?'

'No, of course I didn't, I just assisted. Joe Baker came

down and he was going to take him to IR, but then the patient crashed and it was—he did it, just like that.'

'Of course he did. That's all they do in IR, stick things in blood vessels. It's their job. I should damn well hope he was good at it. Did he talk you through it?'

'Yes—once he'd lectured me for doubting him.'

Sam laughed. 'Yeah, that wouldn't have gone down well.'

'It didn't. He got his own back, though. He's nicked my stethoscope.'

'The one your sister gave you?' He chuckled. 'He's a brave man. I suggest you go and look for a nice quiet in-growing toenail until it's time to go home. That should keep you out of mischief. And don't worry, you'll get it back.'

He still had her stethoscope.

The graduation present from her sister, the one he'd been told in no uncertain terms not to lose or damage. He could see why, it was a really expensive one, although it had to be a few years old now. No wonder she'd been precious about it. His own was only slightly better, and he'd bought it last year because he'd mislaid the one identical to this.

That was getting to be a habit.

He changed out of his scrubs, pulled on his clothes, clipped his watch on his wrist and checked the time. Seven thirty. She'd be long gone, unless she was on a late shift, but it was worth a try. He might even invite her out for dinner—assuming she'd speak to him. He'd been a bit tough on her, but he felt a grudging admiration for a junior registrar who'd had the guts to stand up to him in defence of her patient.

He headed down to the ED, found the nurse who'd been with them in Resus and asked her where Iona was.

She folded her arms and looked him straight in the eye, and he had the distinct feeling he was in trouble. 'She's gone.'

'Do you know where I can find her? I borrowed her stethoscope and forgot to give it back.'

'Yes, she mentioned that. She wasn't happy about it.'

He laughed softly. 'No, I'm sure she wasn't.'

'You can leave it with me.'

'I can't do that. She told me I'd be dead meat if anything happened to it and I don't think it was an empty threat. I'll hang onto it and give it to her tomorrow.'

'She's away this weekend. She's not back in till Monday.'

'And I'm on a course next week. Great.' He hesitated. 'I don't suppose you know her address or mobile number?'

Jenny raised an eyebrow. 'Now, you don't seriously expect me to give it to you? I do know where you can find her, though. She's at the Queens Hotel just round the corner. There's a charity speed-dating event raising money for the new IR angio-surgical suite. I'm surprised you aren't going anyway as it's in aid of your department, but here's your chance to support it. Out of the drive, turn left, five hundred yards on the right. You can't miss it.'

Speed-dating? Seriously? She was gorgeous! Why would she need to go speed-dating, of all things? And then he realised she'd be helping with the organisation. Idiot.

'OK. Thanks.' He headed for his car, followed the directions and parked on the road opposite the hotel. The speed-dating event was signposted from Reception, and he headed towards the door. It shouldn't be hard to find her—

'Oh, excellent, we're short of men, especially good-looking young doctors. That'll be ten pounds, please. Can I take your name?'

He frowned. 'How do you know I'm a doctor?'

'The stethoscope?'

'Ah. Yes. Actually—' He was about to tell the woman why he was there, and then spotted Iona at one of the tables that were arranged in a circle, a man sitting opposite her. OK, she wasn't just helping, she was actually doing it as well, and if he wanted to see her, he'd have to pay up and queue for his slot. That was fine. It meant she'd have to listen to him for three minutes or whatever it was, which meant he'd have time to apologise for pushing her so far out of her comfort zone in Resus. And having three minutes to look at her was no hardship. He might even persuade her to go out for dinner—

'Name, please?'

'Sorry. Joe Baker. I've only got a twenty-pound note,' he said, but the woman just smiled, said, 'That'll do perfectly,' plucked it out of his fingers, stuck a label with 'JOE' written on it on his chest and handed him a printed card and a pencil.

So he could score the ladies? Good grief. He wrote her name and ten out of ten, and waited.

There was a gap before Iona, maybe because of the lack of men, so he hovered and then pounced when the bell rang and the man at her table got up and moved on.

He sat down in front of her, and she looked up from her score card and did a mild double take, her eyes widening.

'What are *you* doing here?'

He took the stethoscope from round his neck and

handed it to her with a rueful smile. 'I forgot to return this, and when I refused to give it to the nurse who was in Resus because you'd told me in no uncertain terms what you'd do to me, she told me where to find you.'

Her mouth flickered in a smile. 'Ah. Jenny.'

'Yeah, that's right. She wouldn't give me your address.'

Her eyes widened. 'I should hope not!'

He gave a little huff of laughter at the outrage in her voice. 'I might have been insulted if I hadn't been glad she was so protective of your privacy, but I also wanted to apologise for pushing you out of your comfort zone in Resus.'

'You don't need to apologise,' she said, her clear and really rather lovely green eyes clouding, 'even though you were rude and patronising—'

'Rude and patronising?' he asked, pretending to be outraged, but she held his eyes and a little smile tugged at her mouth, drawing his attention to it. Soft, full, and very expressive. Like her eyes. He wondered what it would be like to kiss her—

'You were a teeny bit. I was way out of my comfort zone, because I thought you'd need more from me than I could give you. I've never led before on a case that critical and I should have appreciated you'd only do what you knew you could, but I was afraid Jim was going to die and I was freaking out a bit. I'm sorry you took it wrong, it really wasn't meant like that.'

'Don't apologise,' he said wryly. 'Standing up to me took guts, and you were quite right about the risks. Without image guidance there were no guarantees I could get the guide wire in without causing more damage, but I'd had a good look at the X-rays and I was pretty sure I could do it, and anyway, as I think I pointed out fairly succinctly, Jim had run out of options. He's OK, by the way. I sorted the bleeds, repaired the entry site and shipped him off to the orthos with a nice healthy reperfusion and well within the time limit. They've put an ex-fix on in Theatre and he's doing OK.'

He saw her shoulders sag slightly with relief. 'Oh, good. Thanks for the update. I've been worrying about him.'

'No need to worry, he's sore, he's broken but he'll make it. Good stethoscope, by the way. Very good. Your sister must think a lot of you.'

She smiled, her eyes softening. 'She does. That's why I was worried about you walking off with it, knowing you'd already lost yours. It didn't bode well.'

He laughed at that little dig. 'I hadn't *lost* it, it was in my locker, I just failed to pick it up—but I did lose the last one, so you weren't wide of the mark. You did well, by the way,' he added, sliding his score sheet across the table to her. 'It was a tricky case to manage and you'd done everything right. You should be proud of yourself.'

She glanced down at the paper and her eyes widened. 'Ten out of ten? That's very generous. You must be feeling guilty.'

'No, I just give credit where it's due, even if I *am* rude and patronising. And I did return your stethoscope, so hopefully that'll earn me a few Brownie points.'

'Maybe the odd one.'

Her lips twitched, and he sat back with a smile, folded his arms and held her eyes, trying not to think about kissing her. Or peeling off that clingy little top and—

'So, anyway, that's why I'm here. What about you?'

'Me?' She looked slightly flustered. 'Because it's a good cause?'

He raised an eyebrow at her, deeply unconvinced, and she smiled and shrugged and took him completely by surprise. 'OK. You asked. I'm looking for a sperm donor.'

Joe felt his jaw drop, and he stifled the laugh in the nick of time. Of all the unlikely things for her to say, and to him, of all people…

'You're kidding.'

'No. No, I'm not kidding. I'm looking for a tall Nordic type with white-blond hair, blue eyes and good bone structure, so you can relax, you don't qualify.'

'I might feel a bit insulted by that,' he said, still trying to work out if she was joking.

She smiled, her eyes mocking. 'Oh, don't be, it's not personal. I have very specific criteria and you don't fit them.'

He frowned at her, but she was so deadpan he didn't know whether she was completely off her trolley or winding him up. He turned and scanned the men in the room and this time he didn't stifle the laugh.

'OK,' he murmured in a low undertone. 'Nor does anyone else in this room. So far you've written zero out of ten against everyone, and the nearest candidate is white-blond because he's twice your age. He's also about three inches shorter than you and twice as heavy. And the lady on the next table looks *utterly* terrifying, so frankly I reckon we're done here. I'm starving, I haven't eaten since breakfast and I don't suppose you have, either, so why don't we get the hell out of here, go and find a nice pub and have something to eat? And that way I can apologise properly for being *rude and patronising*.'

'Won't your wife mind?' she asked, clearly fishing, and he raised an eyebrow and gave her the short answer.

'I don't have one. So—dinner?'

She hesitated for so long he thought she was going to say no, but then the bell rang, the lady at the next table was eyeing him hungrily, and she looked at the man heading to take his place, grabbed her bag and stethoscope and got to her feet.

'Sorry. We have to go,' she said, squeezing round from behind the table, and they headed for the door amid a chorus of protests. From both sexes. He stifled a smile.

'Right, where to?' he asked, and she shrugged.

'What do you fancy? Thai, Chinese, Mexican, Indian, Asian fusion, pub grub, Italian, modern British—'

'Good grief. All of those in Yoxburgh?'

She chuckled. 'Oh, yes. They might be busy, though, it's Friday night.'

He had a much better idea. 'How about a nice, cosy gastro-pub? There's one right round the corner from my house that comes highly recommended, and we'll definitely get a table there.'

'Is it far? Can I walk back? My car's at home.'

'No, it's a bit out of town, but that's fine, I'll drive you home. Look on it as a hire charge for the use of your stethoscope.'

Again she hesitated, a wary look in her eyes, but then she nodded as if she'd finally decided she could trust him. 'OK. That sounds good.'

To her surprise—and slight consternation—he headed out of town and turned off the main road down a lane so small it didn't even have a signpost.

'Where are we going?' she asked, wondering if she

should be worried and trying to convince herself that she shouldn't, that he was a doctor, he was hardly going to harm her—

'Glemsfield,' he said. 'It's a tiny village, but it has a great pub and a thriving little community.'

'It's in the middle of nowhere,' she said. Even quieter than where her parents lived, and that was pretty isolated. And it was getting dark. Was she mad? Or just unable to trust any man to have a shred of decency?

'It is. It's lovely, and it's only three miles from Yoxburgh and much more peaceful. Well, apart from the barking muntjac deer at night. They get a bit annoying sometimes but I threaten them with the freezer.'

That made her laugh. 'And does it work?'

'Not so you'd notice,' he said drily, but she could hear the smile in his voice.

They passed a few houses and dropped down into what she assumed must be the centre of the village, but then he drove past the brightly lit pub on the corner, turned onto a drive and cut the engine.

Although it was only dusk the area was in darkness, shrouded by the overgrown shrubs each side of the drive, and the whole place had a slight air of neglect. She suppressed a shudder of apprehension as she got out of the car and looked around.

'I thought we were going to the pub? You just drove past it.'

'I know, but the car park'll be heaving on a Friday night so I thought it was easier to park at my house— well, actually my aunt's house. She's in a home and I'm caretaking it for her and trying to get it back into some sort of order. It's going to take me a while.'

'Yes, I think it might,' she murmured, eyeing the weeds that had taken over the gravel drive.

'I'll get there. Come on, my stomach's starting to make its presence felt.'

He ushered her across the road, and as they walked back towards the corner she could hear the hubbub of voices growing louder.

'Gosh, it's busy!' she said as they went in.

'It always is. I'll see if we can get a table, otherwise we might have to get them to cook for us and take it back to mine.' He leant on the bar and attracted the eye of a middle-aged woman. 'Hi, Maureen. Can you squeeze us in?'

'Oh, I think so. If you don't mind waiting a minute, I've got a couple just about to leave. Here, have a menu and don't forget the specials board. Can I get you a drink while you wait?'

'I'm going to splash out and have tap water, but I'm driving. Iona? How about a glass of Prosecco to celebrate your first REBOA?'

'It was hardly mine.'

'Ah, well, that's just splitting hairs. Prosecco? Or gin and tonic? They have some interesting gins. And tonics.'

She wrestled with her common sense, and it lost. She smiled at him. 'A small glass of Prosecco would be lovely. Thank you.'

'And some bread, Maureen, please, before I keel over.'

'Poor baby,' Maureen said with a motherly but mildly mocking smile, and handed them their drinks before she disappeared into the kitchen.

'So, the menu. The twice baked Cromer crab soufflé with crayfish cream is fabulous. It's a starter but it makes a great main with one of the vegetable sides.'

'Is that what you're having?'

'No. I'm having the beer-battered fish and chips, because it's absolutely massive and I'm starving.' He grinned wickedly, and it made him look like a naughty boy. A very grown-up naughty boy. Her pulse did a little hiccup.

Maureen put the bread down in front of him. 'Is that your order, Joe? Fish and chips and mushy peas?'

'Please. Iona?'

'I'll go with the crab soufflé, please. It sounds lovely.'

'Have sweet potato fries,' he suggested. 'They're amazing.'

'I don't suppose they've got a single calorie in them, either,' she said, laughing.

'Calorie? No. Ridiculous idea. They do great puds, as well,' he added with another mischievous grin, and sank his teeth into a slice of fresh, warm baguette slathered with butter.

She couldn't help but smile.

CHAPTER TWO

'Wow. THAT WAS so tasty.'

'Mmm. And positively good for you.'

She used the last sweet potato fry to mop up the remains of the crayfish cream. 'Really?' she said sceptically.

He laughed and speared a fat, juicy flake of fish. 'I doubt it, but one can live in hope. So, what *were* you doing at the speed dating gig?' he asked, and she frowned, hugely reluctant to go back to that and wondering why she'd opened her mouth and blurted it out.

'I told you.'

His eyes widened, the fish on his fork frozen in mid-air. 'You were serious? I thought you were winding me up.'

'No. You probably deserved it, but I wasn't.'

He laughed, then looked back at her, those incredible eyes searching hers thoughtfully. 'You're genuinely serious, aren't you?'

'Yes. I genuinely am, but it's not why I was there, not really. I was helping set it up, and they talked me into taking a table, but a bit of me was wondering if anyone appropriate might rock up.'

'Iona.' His voice dropped, becoming quieter but somehow urgent and his eyes were suddenly deadly serious. 'Sorry, I know it's really none of my business—'

'No, it isn't, and I don't think this is really the time or the place.'

He frowned, nodded and let it go, but only with obvious reluctance. 'Yeah, you're right. OK. So—tell me about yourself. Apart from that.'

No way. 'I'd rather talk about you,' she said, smiling to soften it. 'What brings you to Yoxburgh?'

'Oh, that's easy. As I said, my aunt lives here in a home and I spent a lot of time here as a child, the hospital has an expanding IR department, they were looking for a specialist registrar, I wanted to broaden my experience and it seemed like a perfect fit. Plus I get a free house to live in,' he added with a little quirk of his lips that drew her attention back to them.

She wondered what it would be like to kiss them…

'So, why are you here?' he asked, and she hauled her mind back into order and edited her answer because the truth was too messy.

'Oh—similar reasons, really, work-wise. They've got a great ED department, I was looking for my first registrar's job, I'd worked in Bristol up to now but frankly I'd seen enough of it—' That was putting it mildly, but she wasn't going into that. 'And my family are based in Norfolk so it's not too far from them, and it's a great hospital, and I love the seaside. Not that I've seen much of it because the summer's been rubbish and, anyway, my shift pattern's pretty crazy and I haven't had a lot of time because I've been studying, too.'

'All work and no play, eh? Don't do that, Iona. Keep your work/life balance. It's really important.'

She tilted her head slightly and searched his eyes, because there'd been something in his voice…

'That sounded like personal experience,' she said, and his eyes changed again.

'Yeah, kind of. I know what it's like. My shift pattern's crazy, too, and on top of that I've got a mass of courses and exams coming up in the next year, but that's IR for you. It doesn't matter how hard I work, how much I learn, there'll always be more.'

'Is that "Do as I say, not as I do"?' she asked, and he laughed and nodded.

'Pretty much. Work can easily take over—not that I'm the best person to tell anybody how to run their life since I seem to have trashed my own, but there you go. You could always learn from my experience,' he said, and went back to his fish and chips.

'They look tasty. Can I pinch a chip?'

'Be my guest,' he said, and she took the last one off the plate as a shadow fell over the table.

'Was everything OK for you both?'

'Great, thanks.' He looked up at Maureen and smiled. 'Filling. I've eaten myself to a standstill.'

'So you don't want dessert? That's not like you.'

'Not tonight, I don't think. Iona?'

She would have loved a dessert. She'd spotted one on the specials board, but Joe didn't seem inclined.

'I don't suppose you'd like to share the baked chocolate fondant?' she asked wistfully, and he just groaned and laughed.

'There's my resolve going down the drain.'

'That's a yes, then,' Maureen said with a smile. 'One, or two? And do you want coffee with it?'

He shook his head. 'Just one, and no coffee for me, Maureen. Iona?'

'No, I'm fine, thanks. The fondant will be more than enough.'

It took ten minutes to come, but it was worth the wait and she was enjoying the view and the company.

Maureen put the plate down between them, they picked up their spoons and Iona waited for him to cut it in half, but he didn't, just dug his spoon in, so she joined in and kept eating until their spoons clashed in the middle.

She glanced up, their eyes locked and he smiled and put his spoon down. 'Go on. Finish it. It was your idea.'

She didn't argue, just pulled the plate closer, scraped it clean and put the spoon down a little sadly.

'That was delicious. All of it. Thank you.'

'You're welcome. Shall we go?'

She nodded, and he got to his feet, dropped a pile of notes on the bar in front of Maureen and they headed out into the darkness and a light drizzle.

'Oh. I didn't know it was going to do that,' she said with a rueful laugh, but he just reached out and took her hand in a firm, warm grip and they ran, guided by the light of his phone, and got back to the house before they were more than slightly damp.

'Coffee?' he asked, heading for the porch and standing under the shelter.

She hesitated on the drive. 'I thought you didn't want coffee?'

'No, I didn't want coffee *there*. I prefer mine, but I can't say that to Maureen, can I? It would break her heart.'

It made her laugh, as it was meant to, and she suddenly realised she did want a coffee, and she was also curious about the house, and his aunt, and—well, him, really.

And she was getting wet.

She stepped under the shelter of the porch and smiled. 'Coffee would be lovely. Thank you.'

He put the key in the door, turned it and pushed it open, flicking a switch that flooded the hall with light.

'Welcome to the seventies,' he said wryly, and stepped back to let her in.

It was stunning, and completely unexpected.

The walls were a pale acid green, but that wasn't what caught her eye, it was the way the ceiling sloped steeply up from right to left, rising along the line of the stairs and over the landing, creating a wonderful, open vaulted entrance hall.

'Wow! I love this!'

'Me, too. It goes downhill a bit from now on, mind,' he said with a low chuckle that did something odd to her insides. 'Come into the kitchen, I'll make you a coffee.'

She followed him through a glass door into a large rectangular room that ran away to the right across the back of the house. To the left were double doors into another room, in front of her beyond a large dining table was a set of bi-fold doors, opening she assumed to the garden, and on her right at the far end of the room was the kitchen area.

Not that there was much kitchen.

'Ahh. I see what you mean.'

He chuckled again. 'Yeah. It's a mess. I got the bi-folds put in and the dividing wall taken out, so I lost most of the units, but to be honest I haven't got the time or energy to decide what I want in here and it's a big job, starting with taking the floor up and re-screeding it because they weren't quite level. So I'm learning to love the tiny scraps of seventies worktop and the ridiculously huge sink and the utter lack of storage, but it's only me so it's fine. And the pub's handy when I get desperate,' he added with a grin. 'So, coffee. Caf, decaf, black, white, frothy?'

She stared at him, slightly mesmerised by the sight of him propped against the sink with his arms folded, relaxed and at ease. It was gradually dawning on her just how incredibly attractive he was, how well put together, how confident, caring, thoughtful, sexy—

'Hello?'

She pulled herself together and tried to smile. 'Sorry. I was just a bit stunned by the kitchen,' she lied. 'Um— can you do a decaf frothy?'

'Sure, that's what I'm having.' He flipped a capsule into the machine, put a mug under the spout and pressed a button, put milk into the frother and then propped himself up again and frowned thoughtfully at her.

'What?'

'Nothing. Well, nothing you want to hear. You told me to butt out.'

'Are we back to that?' she said with a sigh.

'Yes, we are, because…Iona, if you want a baby, why wouldn't you look for a partner?'

'I've tried that,' she said, really not wanting to go there. 'And, anyway, that's not what it's about.'

He looked puzzled, then shrugged. 'OK, so why not go through a proper sperm bank or clinic? The risks to you are *huge* if you don't use a donor regulated by the Human Fertilisation and Embryology Authority. They won't have had genetic testing, no sperm quality check— it's a minefield, even if you don't take into account the risk of picking up a life-changing infection such as Hepatitis or HIV. The screening process is so thorough, so intensive, the physical and mental health screening, sperm quality, family medical history, motivation—and the children have the right to trace their fathers now once they're eighteen, so nobody's going to be doing it for anything other than the right reasons. Why on earth would you go anywhere else?'

'I wouldn't. I haven't. I'm not that stupid, so you can relax and stop fretting. I wasn't serious about picking up a random stranger, I was winding you up, really, but I am looking for a sperm donor. That much was true.' She studied him thoughtfully. 'You seem to know an awful lot about it,' she added, searching his eyes, and something in them changed again.

He looked away briefly, then back, the silence between them somehow deafening in the quiet room.

'Yeah. I do,' he said finally, as if it had been dragged out of him. 'I've done it, but that was years ago, before I properly understood the knock-on effect of it.'

Wow. 'Knock-on effect?' she asked, still processing the fact that he'd been a donor. Ironic, since she'd mentally given him ten out of ten, but he didn't need to know that.

'Yes. Wondering—you know—about the children, if there are any, if they're OK? That sort of stuff.'

'Can they contact you?'

'No, because I did it before the law changed, but I can still provide contact details if I want to via the HFEA, and I could also find out how many children there are, their ages, their genders, but I can't contact them to find out if they're OK, and that troubles me. Are they happy? Are they safe? What are their parents like? Are they still together? Are they well? I just don't know, and it's unlikely I ever will, and it bugs me.'

'But it's not your worry, surely?'

'Yes, it is,' he said emphatically. 'I know they aren't technically my children, but in a way they are because without me they wouldn't exist, so morally I feel responsible. What if they're unhappy? What if someone's hurting them? It's unlikely, I know that, but still I worry. Of course I worry.'

'But as you said, it's highly unlikely and, anyway, you've signed over that right, that responsibility. They're not your children, any more than this would be my child. I'm doing it for my sister, and I won't have any rights, I know that because I'll sign them all over to Isla and Steve when they adopt it, but I'm fine with that. That's why I'm doing it, not because I want a child.'

His eyes widened and his jaw dropped a fraction. 'You're going to *give it away*?' he said. 'Iona, that's— Will you be able to do that? It's going to take so much courage. What if you change your mind when it comes to it? Are you able to change your mind?'

Her heart gave a little hiccup, but she ignored it. 'I won't change my mind, because there's no room in my life for a child now, and I don't know if there ever will be, and this is something I can do for Isla and Steve, and I want to help them because I love them.'

'Yes, of course you do, but—' He rammed a hand through his hair, his eyes troubled. 'I only gave away my DNA and that feels hard enough sometimes. You're talking about cradling your own baby inside your body for *nine months*! How will you be able to give it away, even if it is to your sister? I know you love her and you know her very well, so you know the baby will be safe and loved, but—what about *you*, Iona? How will *you* feel? And what if they split up? What if their marriage breaks down?'

'It won't! And this is my sister, Joe—my *identical twin* sister, so genetically it would be identical to a child of her own. It could *be* her own. It'll be just like being the incubator for their own baby, and I want to do it for her because I love her and I want to help her—'

'I know you do, but...?'

'But? How many siblings do you have?'

'None.'

'None?' She laughed disbelievingly. 'None. So how can you *possibly* judge my motives?'

'I can't. I'm not judging your motives, I wouldn't presume to do that and I'm sure you're doing it for the all right reasons. I have immense respect for your courage in even contemplating it. I'm only thinking of the impact it would have on you, knowing how hard it's been for me, and what I've done is *nothing* compared to what you're talking about. Please tell me you've thought it through.'

'I thought you were making me a coffee?' she said, changing the subject abruptly, and he swore softly, threw away the one he'd made ages ago and dropped another capsule in the machine. Then he scrubbed a hand through his hair again and sighed as he turned back to her.

'Sorry.'

'Are you?'

He sighed again. 'Yes and no. I know I keep banging the same old drum, Iona, but I'm really worried about you now.'

'You really don't need to be, Joe, I do know what I'm doing. It's not an idle thought. I've researched it, I've considered it at length, discussed it endlessly— I'm not stupid.'

'I never said you were. Just maybe too kind for your own good. Whose idea was it?'

'Mine. All mine.'

'And they said yes?'

She rolled her eyes. 'Yes, they said yes, but not until they'd tried to talk me out of it, but I could tell they didn't really want to do that, they just wanted to be sure that I was sure, and I am.'

'Have you ever been pregnant?'

She shook her head, feeling a pang of regret because they'd tried and failed. 'No. Have you?' she asked, and he laughed.

'I don't believe so.'

'Then how can you lecture me on what it'll feel like?'

'Because I have imagination? Because I have empathy? Because I know how hard I've found even doing what I did?'

'But it's different to your situation. I *know* who the baby's going to, and I know it'll be loved and cherished and brought up with my values. Did you have any control over who had your sperm?'

He shook his head. 'No. And that's at the root of my worries, I have to admit, because I can never be utterly sure my ch—' He cut himself off. 'My *offspring* will be loved and cared for as I would have loved and cared for them.'

She searched his eyes—those gorgeous, penetrating, honest eyes—and she could read them clearly, could see the genuine worry he felt for his unknown children, the responsibility he felt for their happiness over which he had no control.

'You're a good man, do you know that?' she said

softly, and he laughed and turned away, making a production of spooning out the froth onto her new coffee.

'Chocolate sprinkles?'

'Is it powder?'

'No, it's flakes of real chocolate.'

'Oh, yes, please. I love those.'

'Me, too. Here.'

He handed it to her, and she went up on tiptoe and brushed a kiss against his cheek.

'Thank you.'

He looked slightly startled. 'It's only a coffee.'

'It's not for the coffee, it's for caring—about the children you don't know, about me—just—for caring.'

He hesitated, staring down into her eyes, and then he gave a fleeting smile.

'You're welcome. I didn't mean to interfere, but I can't stand by and watch a friend sleepwalk into potential unhappiness without saying anything.'

'Am I a friend?' she asked, and he gave her a thoughtful half-smile.

'I think you could be. I'm not in the habit of spilling my guts to people who aren't.'

He turned back to the coffee maker, and she perched on a chair at the big old table, a funny warm feeling inside, and watched him make his own coffee, his movements as deft and sure as they'd been in Resus. He rinsed out the milk frother, sat down opposite her and met her eyes.

'Talking about spilling my guts, it's a bit late to worry about this, but you're the only person outside my family who I've ever told about any of this stuff, so I'd be grateful if you'd keep it to yourself.'

She nodded, surprised that he'd even felt he had to

ask her. 'Of course I will. I'm amazed you told me. It's not the sort of thing people talk about—and snap, by the way. Only my sister and brother-in-law know. We haven't even told the rest of the family.'

'Yes, I can understand that.' He gave a wry chuckle. 'I didn't mean to tell you, by the way, it just sort of came out, but—Iona, please be careful, and if you do decide to do it, do it properly? Don't go and have some unpremeditated random one-night stand with someone just because they're tall and blond and have good bone structure.'

That made her laugh. 'I was sort of joking, but it's what my brother-in-law looks like, and we've been trying to find a sperm donor who at least has some of his physical characteristics. They tried IVF and got a few live embryos, but the quality wasn't great and none of them implanted, although nobody could say why for certain. Steve's sperm quality isn't good, so she's tried AI with a tall, blue-eyed blond donor, which didn't work, and I've tried AI three times with Steve's semen and not got pregnant.'

A little frown appeared fleetingly between his brows. 'I didn't realise you'd got that far down the line,' he said slowly.

'Oh, yes. This isn't a spur-of-the-moment thing, Joe. We've been talking about it for ages. That's part of the reason I took this job, to be nearer to them. So, anyway, it needs to be another sperm donor since the one she tried has reached his limit of donations, and we can't find another one that ticks all the boxes on any of the donor sites, at least not the physical appearance boxes. And, yes, I know that's the least important thing in a way, but it's tough enough for them without the child looking like a cuckoo in the nest. Maybe I need to go on a cruise up the fjords and try and find a Viking,' she added lightly, winding him up again, and he spluttered into his coffee and wiped the froth off his lip, his eyes brimming with laughter.

'Do you know who goes on fjord cruises? Tourists, Iona. People like my parents. And, believe me, they don't look like Vikings.'

'Oh, well, there goes that idea, then.' She laughed, then sat back, cradling her coffee. 'Tell me about them—your parents.'

'My parents? What can I tell you? My dad's called Bill, my mother's Mary, they're in their late sixties. Dad's an ex-army officer, invalided out after an explosives accident that left him with—well, let's call them life-changing injuries, for want of a better description. And as if that wasn't enough, my mother, who was pregnant at the time, lost her baby.'

'Oh, Joe, that's awful. That's so sad.'

He nodded. 'They think it was probably the shock of the severity of his injuries that caused her miscarriage. It might have been, or it might not, but because of his injuries it was their last chance and they lost it. Hence why I'm an only child. And despite his best efforts to get rid of her, my mother's stuck by him and they have a great relationship, but underlying it all is this sadness, a sort of grief I guess for the baby they lost and the children they never had.'

'Hence why you were a sperm donor,' she said slowly, understanding him now at last. 'To help people like them.'

'Yes. Or at least partly. I was four when the accident happened, and I spent a lot of that year living with my aunt and uncle here, and it was the nearest they got to having their own children and we're still really close.

Elizabeth, my aunt, is my father's much older sister, and she's widowed now, but she and her husband built this house in their thirties as their family home, and the family never happened. She's never got over that.'

'Does she know what you've done?'

'Oh, yes. She was the first person I told and she's been hugely supportive.' He smiled fondly. 'Oddly, I can talk to her about things I could never tell my parents.'

'I don't think that's odd. I feel the same. There are things I can tell my aunt I'd never tell my mother.' She looked up at him again, watching his face carefully as she spoke because she'd just had a crazy idea and she didn't know how it was going to land.

'Talking of families—are you busy this weekend?'

'Why?' he asked warily, turning his head slightly to the side and eyeing her suspiciously.

'Because I need a plus one. My baby brother's getting married tomorrow, and I have to go to his wedding, and I really, really don't want to go on my own.'

He frowned. 'Are you suggesting I should come with you? Because there's no way in hell I'm going to another wedding as long as I live, not after my catastrophic car crash of a marriage.'

She laughed wryly, even though it wasn't funny. 'I can understand that. It's exactly why I don't want to go, except I never got to the altar. I found out three days before my wedding that he'd slept with the stripper on his stag weekend, and when I challenged him he said something about it just being drunken high spirits, so when I asked him if he'd still been drunk on the subsequent four occasions he started grovelling, but I'd had enough so I called it off, and then he went round slagging me off to all our friends, saying I'd dumped him without hearing his side of it.'

'What *side*? It sounds to me like you're well off out of it.'

'Oh, tell me about it, but I still don't want to go to Johnnie's wedding on my own with all the friends and relatives who would have been at mine, who'll feel morally obliged to come and tell me how sorry they were and try and get all the juicy details. Especially not since it's also the same church I should have got married in less than two years ago.'

'Where is it?' he asked, surprising her.

'Where? Norfolk. A village just west of Norwich, not all that different to this one, but at least it's a nice, easy drive.'

He grunted. 'It's not the drive I have issues with, it's the wedding. Watching someone making their vows and wondering if they have the *slightest* idea what they've let themselves in for.'

'What, like your parents, who by the sound of it are devoted to each other? Or your uncle and aunt?'

He gave a sharp sigh. 'They're different.'

'No, they're not. They sound like my sister and brother-in-law, and my parents, and my uncle and aunt. And Johnnie and Kate love each other to bits. They always have. They're childhood sweethearts, and they're wonderful together, but I just know I'm going to cry and make an idiot of myself and everybody'll think it's because of…'

'So you want me there to—what? Pass you tissues?'

She laughed at that, at the thought of him handing her tissues like a production line as she sobbed her way through the ceremony that she'd been denied.

'Well, I think you need to do something fairly mega to make up for being arrogant and then stealing my stethoscope. Is it really too much to ask?'

She was only joking, never for a moment thinking he'd agree, not now she knew he'd had an apparently disastrous marriage, and he stared at her slightly openmouthed for a moment.

'I didn't *steal* it. I just forgot to give it back.'

'So you're not denying you were arrogant?' she said with a little coaxing smile, and to her surprise he groaned and rolled his eyes. Was he weakening?

'I'm not staying over,' he said, jabbing his finger at her to add emphasis to every word. 'I don't want to stay over.'

So he'd go? 'Nor do I, but it goes on until midnight so it's a bit late to drive back. I should be there now, as well, but I lied and told them I was on call.'

He gave her an odd look. 'Why would you do that?'

'To get out of the family dinner, so they didn't have to tiptoe round the elephant in the room? But I don't really have a choice about tomorrow night. They'll be expecting me to stay, and I'm sure there'll be room for you somewhere. You can have my room if it comes to that. And you'd get to meet my sister and brother-in-law, too, and see why I want to make them happy.'

She left it there, hanging, holding her breath, and he said nothing for an age, just stared into his coffee, swirling it round and watching the froth, then he lifted it to his mouth, drained it and put it down with exaggerated care.

'OK. I'll do it,' he said, his eyes deadly serious now. 'As much as anything so I can meet them, and find out what kind of people would let you do this for them, because they'd have to be pretty special for you to make that kind of sacrifice.'

She felt her eyes fill and grabbed his hand, squeezing it hard. 'They are—and thank you! You're a life-saver.'

'Don't bother to thank me. I'll probably spend most of the journey there and back trying to talk sense into you. So, what's the dress code, and when do we need to leave?'

He picked her up at eleven, and she took one look at him in a blinding white dress shirt, black bow tie and immaculately cut black dress trousers, and felt her heart rate pick up.

He took her bag, put it in the back of the car and held the door for her, then slid behind the wheel and clipped on his seat belt, drawing her attention to his hands. He had beautiful hands. Clever hands.

'OK?'

'Yes. You scrub up quite nicely,' she said rashly, and he turned his head and met her eyes.

'You don't do too badly yourself,' he said, and then turned away before she could analyse the expression in them, but he'd looked...

'What's the postcode?' he asked, and he keyed it into his satnav, started the engine and pulled away.

She swallowed, fastened her seat belt and took a deep breath, and he turned the radio on, saving her from the need to break the silence.

'So, why interventional radiology?' she asked after an hour interspersed with the odd comment about landmarks and idle chat.

He gave her a wry look and laughed as he turned his attention back to the road. 'Are you afraid I'll start lecturing you again or something?'

She felt her mouth twitch. 'No, I'm not. I doubt if I

could stop you, anyway, you're like a dog with a bone. I'm just genuinely curious. It's seems a bit...'

'Dry?' he offered.

'Exactly. Or maybe not, not after what I saw you do yesterday.'

He laughed again. 'Oh, that was pure theatre. Most of it's much more mundane and measured. And the amount of learning, the sheer volume of what you have to know, is staggering. There are so many uses for it, so many different conditions that can be cured or alleviated by what is essentially a very minimal intervention. Every part of the body has a blood supply, and by using the blood vessels we can deliver life-saving interventions directly where they're needed—stents, cancer treatments, clearing blockages, making blockages to stop bleeding—it's endless.

'We used to think that keyhole surgery was the holy grail, but IR is expanding so fast and there are so many potential uses for it it's mind-boggling. I spend most of my waking hours either practising it or studying it, because if I don't, I won't know enough and I'll make an error and someone will suffer when it could have been avoided.'

'Is that what went wrong with your marriage?' she asked without thinking, and he flashed her a glance.

'What, that it suffered because I didn't study it enough?' he asked drily, and she laughed.

'No, I meant you being a workaholic, but that wouldn't have helped, either.'

He gave a soft snort, and nodded. 'Probably not. No, she fancied the idea of being a doctor's wife—the money, the social status—she had no idea what being married to a junior hospital doctor actually meant.'

'She can't have been that clueless.'

'Oh, she wasn't—far from it. She just hated her job and thought I'd be a good meal ticket, but then she realised that it wasn't just for a year or two, it was going to be like it for at least a decade, and so...'

'So?'

'She found a way to deal with it. I didn't know about it, but I knew she was unhappy, and one day I thought, To hell with it, I won't stay at work practising in the skills lab, I'll go home, take her out for dinner. And I caught her in bed—*our* bed—with her lover.'

She sucked in a breath. 'Oh, Joe, that's awful.'

His hands tightened on the wheel. 'Yeah, tell me about it. He wasn't the first, either, apparently, but it was my fault as much as hers. I was neglecting her, I was constantly tired, we hardly had a social life to speak of—it was no wonder, really, that she'd got bored with waiting for me to notice her and turned to other men.'

'You still don't do it like that,' she said, furious on his behalf. 'You stay, or you leave. You don't cheat.'

'Exactly, and especially not as many times as she told me she had, or for as long. So I left. And then, even though technically she was the one in the wrong, she got half the equity from the house. And we lived in London, so she did very nicely out of it because I'd bought it two years before I met her and pushed myself to the limit, and by the time the divorce settlement was through I'd been priced out of the market.'

She reached out and laid her hand lightly over his on the steering wheel. 'I'm sorry, Joe.'

His head turned and his mouth flickered into a wry smile. 'Don't be sorry. It was a lesson learned. I won't make the same mistake again.'

He drew in a slow breath, let it out on a huff and smiled again. 'So, tell me about your family so I don't put my foot in it.'

'Oh, there's not much to tell. My father's an accountant, my mother was a nurse, my sister's a town planner, her husband's an architect, my brother's a solicitor and Kate, his fiancée, is a legal executive. We're all boring normal, except that Isla and Steve can't seem to make a baby, and to put the cherry on top, Kate's just found out she's pregnant.'

'Ouch.'

'Yes. Ouch. And ignore your satnav, you need to turn left here.'

CHAPTER THREE

'YOU DIDN'T CRY. There I was, with tissues at the ready—'

'Oh, I nearly did, but only for the right reasons, and it was a lovely wedding.'

He laughed softly. 'I suppose it was, as weddings go.'

They were sitting at one of the round tables in the marquee that had housed the reception, alone now because the others had gone off to mingle, and he absently unwrapped another of the heart-shaped chocolates covered in red foil and offered it to her.

She reached over and took it out of his fingers and put it in her mouth. 'Thank you for coming with me. I know you didn't want to.'

He unwrapped another chocolate, balled up the foil and flicked it idly into the middle of the table. 'No, I didn't, but hey. We've survived, and the band's starting up, judging by the sound of it. Fancy a dance?'

'Really? You want to dance?'

'Not really, I'd rather sit here and eat chocolates, but if it'll keep you out of mischief and stop you crawling off into the bushes with the best man, then I guess I probably should.'

'Why would I do that?' she asked, half laughing, half shocked, and he just rolled his eyes and smiled.

'I was joking—but he is tall and blond and vaguely Nordic.'

'And happily married to a very pregnant woman, in case you hadn't noticed. Anyway, I wouldn't do that!'

'Good. One less thing for me to worry about,' he teased.

Iona stood up, wobbled slightly and grabbed his hand, hauling him to his feet. 'You're very rude. I'm beginning to regret inviting you. Come on, Johnnie and Kate are going to have the first dance, and then, since you're so keen, you can dance with me, but you'd better not tread on my toes.'

'I wouldn't dream of it.' He looked down into her eyes, soft and almost luminous, touched with stardust from the thousands of tiny fairy lights strung around the marquee, and had a sudden, burning urge to kiss her.

Which he was *not going to do.*

Then she took a step and saved herself by grabbing him. 'Oh, these stupid shoes. I knew they were too high, they keep catching on the matting.'

She kicked them off under the table, and he slung an arm round her waist, steered her to the dance floor and then endured watching her loved-up brother and his new bride dancing a shamelessly sentimental waltz. Then it was over, and Iona stepped onto the dance floor and started to move, and his heart revved up a gear.

Oh, this was not good. His tongue glued itself to the roof of his mouth, his body roared to life and he kicked himself for agreeing to come with her. Because she was incredibly sexy, in a quietly sensual way that he hadn't really registered before, and he wanted her. Right here, right now. She moved with sinuous grace, her body seeming to flow as she swayed to the beat of the music, and when she reached out and grabbed his hands and drew him in he didn't know whether to laugh or cry.

Or kiss her...

But in the end he did none of them, he just danced, and to his surprise he enjoyed it, despite the cheesy wedding music and the spotlight that was circulating round the dancers and picking the couples out one by one. Including them, of course, and she played up to it, twirling and twisting like a candle flame, her face alight with laughter as she whirled into his arms and kissed him.

For show, to prove to everyone that she was so over her feckless ex? Either that or she was tipsy, and he didn't think she was. Not that he would have blamed her, he would have been in her shoes, but then the light moved on and she was still pressed against him, her body warm and soft and lithe, tantalising him.

Not good. He still wanted to kiss her—*needed* to kiss her, properly this time and definitely not in public—but then to his relief the band launched into 'YMCA' and she straightened up and started to sing along with everyone else, trying and failing to get the actions right.

'You're hopeless,' he said, laughing at her, and spent the next few minutes face to face with her, reminding her of the actions and singing at the top of his voice along with all the others. Not that he wanted to, but it knocked spots off watching her with his tongue hanging out and his libido running riot.

He was a good dancer. An amazing dancer, actually. And you could tell a lot about what kind of lover a man was by the way he danced.

And she couldn't believe she was thinking that.

'Come on,' she said, grabbing his hand and towing him off the dance floor before she did something inappropriate. 'I need air and water. Or maybe coffee.'

They went back to their table, she recovered her shoes and took one step before she kicked them off again.

'Right, grab that bottle of wine off the table and follow me,' she said, scooping up the shoes and a handful of the chocolate hearts that still littered the table.

He followed her out of the marquee and into the house via the front door, and she threw her shoes onto the stairs and headed down the hall to the kitchen.

'Are you all right with dogs?' she asked over her shoulder, but it was too late to worry because the dogs had sneaked past her and were already mugging him.

'Hello, dogs, did you think you'd been forgotten?' he said softly, and to her amazement he was fondling their ears and rubbing their tummies.

'Come on, you two hussies, back in here.' She ushered them all—him and the dogs—into the kitchen, filled the kettle and put it on, then plonked herself down at the kitchen table and put her feet up on the edge. 'I hate those shoes,' she grumbled, inspecting her feet, and she heard a dry chuckle from Joe.

'What? Why are you laughing?'

'Well, it isn't rocket science to know that putting your feet into instruments of torture is going to hurt. Is there any chance of a proper coffee?' he asked, dumping his jacket and undoing his bow tie.

How could he possibly look even sexier?

'A proper coffee?' she croaked.

'Yeah, as in a mug, rather than a delicate little bone china thimble? I'm guessing it's going to be a long night.'

'Oh, I don't doubt it, but Kate and Johnnie aren't leaving, they're staying here, so we can quit when we like. I need to find out where we're sleeping, though— Ah, Mum. Perfect timing. Can we find a bed for Joe, please?'

'Not until I get these shoes off.' Her mother plonked herself down and winced. 'Ooh, that's better. Right. Bedrooms. I've put you in the little single room, darling, I hope you don't mind, because Kate's parents are in your room. Mike, where are we going to put Joe? The study?'

'Could do. It's got the sofa bed. It's that or in here with the dogs unless you want to bunk up with Iona. Oh, well done, you picked up some of the chocolates. I'm Mike, by the way, Iona's father. I don't think we've been properly introduced.'

Joe got to his feet and shook hands. 'Joe Baker. I'm a colleague of Iona's.'

Her father searched his eyes. 'Just a colleague? That's a shame.'

'Dad! Joe, I'm so sorry, just ignore him.'

But Joe was laughing, and he sent her a tiny, almost unnoticeable wink as he sat down again.

'So, what do you do?' her father asked, like a dog with a bone. 'Are you in the ED with Iona?'

'No. No, we have worked together,' he said, stretching the point so far she nearly laughed out loud, 'but I'm an interventional radiologist.'

'What in the heck is that?' her father asked, and so Joe blessedly launched into a long-winded explanation that kept them all neatly off the subject of how long they'd known each other and exactly what their relationship was.

She could have kissed him. Maybe it was just as well she really, really couldn't…

* * *

They left the following morning after an early brunch, and as they drove away she rested her head back with a sigh and shut her eyes.

He glanced across at her. She looked tired. Maybe she needed to go home to bed.

With him? He felt his mouth tip into a rueful smile. No. Too soon—although it didn't feel it, not after dancing with her last night…

'Hangover?' he asked, glancing across at her again, and she shook her head.

'No, just a relieved-it's-all-over-over. And, actually, it wasn't nearly as bad as it could have been.' She rolled her head towards him and rested a hand lightly on his shoulder. 'Thank you so much for doing this, Joe. I know it can't have been easy, but it made so much difference to me having you there. It just deflected all that sympathy I was expecting, so thank you.'

'You're welcome,' he said, and realised he meant it. 'As you said, it wasn't as bad as it could have been, and some of it was quite fun. So how come it was at your parents' house and not Kate's parents'?'

'They live abroad, so it was easier and cheaper to do it here. They all split the cost, I think, and let's face it, it had already been planned for me so they all knew what was involved and it made it fairly simple. They all liked you, by the way. My father's desperately match-making, and Isla even asked how well I knew you and if there was any way I could persuade you to be the sperm donor.'

What? 'Tell me you didn't tell her?'

'Well, no, of course I didn't. I promised I wouldn't. I don't think she was serious, but I put her off, anyway. I told her there was no way I could ask you, I didn't know you nearly well enough, and she said that was a shame because you'd be perfect. Which you're not, because A, you don't want to do it, and, B, you don't look like a Viking.'

All of which sounded reasonably plausible, but he had still a gut feeling he'd been played. Thank God he hadn't given in to his instincts and found a way to sleep with her last night.

'So why on earth would she ask? I thought the Viking thing was set in stone?'

'No, not any more, apparently. Since the law changed there are far fewer donors, so they've realised that they have to compromise because other things are much more important. And, anyway, the baby stands a fair chance of looking like me and Isla, so it's not really that big an issue.'

'So is this why you really asked me to the wedding?' he asked bluntly. 'So she could size me up as a sperm donor now they've changed their criteria?'

She stared at him open-mouthed. 'No! Absolutely not! It hadn't even *occurred* to me to ask you. Well, no, that's not strictly true, it *had* occurred to me, but that was before you told me how you felt about it and I realised it would be pointless asking you anyway, so I dismissed it. I certainly didn't ask you to the wedding with that in mind, because apart from anything else she's only just told me about their changed priorities. I just wanted someone with me to deflect all the sympathy, and it was a way for you to meet them and realise how nice they are so you could maybe understand why I want to do it, and get off my case a bit.'

'They are nice,' he agreed, still not quite convinced of her motive for inviting him. 'They're lovely. I'm sure they'll be great parents. But it doesn't change how I feel,

Iona—either about me doing it again, which I never will
so please *don't* ask me, or about what it'll do to you to
give up your child, which you can't know until the time
comes. And it doesn't matter how worthy the intended
parents might be, that's irrelevant to me because I'm
not worried about them, I'm worried about you. I have
huge sympathy for their situation, but you're my concern, not them.'

'I realise that, but they are mine, and it's in my power
to make them happy, and I don't see why I shouldn't do
that—and, anyway, when did I ask you to worry about
me?'

'You haven't—'

'No, I haven't. And how you could even *think* I'd trick
you into coming to the wedding so they could assess your
donor potential, for goodness' sake? I'd *never* do that
without discussing it with you first. It just shows how
little you know about me if you think I could possibly
be that devious. I wish I'd never told you…'

She turned her face away and he let his breath out on
a long, quiet sigh, pulled over into a handy layby behind
a lorry and switched off the engine.

The driver got out and walked past them, heading no
doubt for the tea hut behind them, and Joe reached for
her with a sigh.

'Come here.'

'Why?' she asked, her voice choked.

'So I can give you a hug,' he said, his voice softer now,
but she shrugged off his hands and he dropped them back
in his lap with another sigh. 'I'm sorry. I didn't mean to
upset you, it was just a knee-jerk reaction, and you're
right, I don't really know you, Iona, but it doesn't stop
me caring deeply about what happens to you or worry-

ing that you're going to do something that could hurt you so badly. I just didn't want you sleepwalking into it.'

'I know, you keep saying that,' she said, her voice sounding clogged with tears, 'but you don't have to worry about me. I'm a big girl, Joe. I can do this. I don't need counselling, and certainly not from someone who doubts my motives about everything!'

She straightened up, swiping her cheeks with the backs of her hands, and he reached into his pocket and pulled out a tissue.

'Here.'

She took it with a little hiccupping laugh. 'You always knew you were going to end up doing this, didn't you?'

'Not like this. I'm sorry, I truly am. I don't want to fight with you, but I just had a horrible sinking feeling you might have engineered the whole situation.'

She looked up at him, yesterday's mascara smudging onto the fine skin beneath her wounded eyes. 'How could I have done that? Even if I was that kind of person, how could I have done it? I only met you on Friday!'

'May I remind you that you told me in words of one syllable that you were on the look-out for a sperm donor, so it's not like it's a huge leap.'

She glared at him, her eyes red-rimmed and filled with disgust. 'I so shouldn't have told you. It's got nothing to do with you anyway, and just because you've been a sperm donor doesn't give you the right to tell me what to do, but trust me, if I'd seriously considered you or anyone else as a potential donor, I would have asked openly, not resorted to subterfuge.'

'So if it had been some other wedding and they were going to be there, you wouldn't have asked me to go with you?'

'No. Why would I? I wouldn't have needed you there, but it wasn't, it was Johnnie's wedding and I had to go, I had no choice. He's my baby brother, and with Kate pregnant and rubbing salt into the wound, I had to be there for Isla and Steve, too. And it was a chance for you to meet them.'

'Are you absolutely sure that wasn't my real role, even subconsciously? To be dangled in front of them to make them think there was some hope you'd found a suitable victim?' he asked, hating himself but feeling gutted at the same time that yet again, he might have been used, not for himself but for what he could offer. 'Because you seemed to me to be fine at the wedding, and I'm not convinced you needed my support at all.'

She glared at him, her face a riot of emotions, none of them good. 'Of course I did, I was hanging by a thread! For heaven's sake, listen to me, you're not hearing what I'm saying! You were just my plus one. No ulterior motive. And what do you mean, *victim*? You make me sound like a black widow spider—'

'OK, victim was a bad choice of word—'

'Tell me about it!'

'But if you knew you didn't want to go alone, why not ask someone else to go with you? You surely have friends you could have asked, and you must have known about it for months.'

'Of course I have, but I've been putting it out of my mind, refusing to face up to it, trying not to think about it. And suddenly it was Friday night and there it was, right in front of my nose, and I realised I couldn't do it. And then there you were, and I thought maybe, if I could twist your arm—'

'I don't buy it. It just all seems too convenient when you've only just met me and you're looking for—'

'How big *is* your ego? For the last time, Joe, I don't *want* your bloody sperm!' she yelled, and the truck driver on his way back to his cab jerked to a halt and slopped coffee on his hand, his mouth open.

'Well, that's me told,' he said mildly. 'Shall I wind the windows down so you can repeat it, just in case there was anyone else who didn't hear?'

'No! Just take me home,' she mumbled, sliding down into her seat, and he fired up the engine and dropped the window.

'Don't worry, mate, she wasn't talking to you,' he said grimly to the wary truck driver, and gunning the engine he pulled back out onto the road and shot her a glance.

She was staring straight ahead, her face a mask, and he turned the radio on and drove the rest of the way without another word, furious with himself for allowing her to dupe him. And to think he'd been contemplating taking her to bed!

But his thoughts were in turmoil, and by the time they'd reached Yoxburgh and he'd dropped her off and driven halfway home, he'd got his battered ego back in its box where it belonged and had the sickening realisation that he'd made a dreadful mistake, and that somewhere along the way he'd lost something infinitely precious that he hadn't even known he'd had.

He was on a course all week, he'd told her, so at least she'd be spared the agony of bumping into him again after that humiliating fiasco in the layby.

Not that it was all her fault, not at all. How could he possibly have thought she was that conniving? But he'd dropped her off, leaving the engine running as he'd lifted her bag out of the back, and she'd taken it from him and gone inside without a word, and now the next time she saw him it would be unbearably awkward.

She shouldn't have yelled at him like that, even if he'd deserved it, but she'd been so hurt, so distraught that he could have thought so little of her that she'd just lashed out.

Frankly she never wanted to speak to him again as long as she lived, but hospitals were too small to get away with that, and he'd already proved his worth in the ED so he was bound to be back. She had to clear the air, but how?

She didn't have his mobile number so she couldn't even text him. But she did know where he lived. She'd write a card and put it through his letterbox so he'd get it when he came back. Better late than never, and there was no way she wanted to bump into him in the hospital with a cloud like that hanging over them. She just hoped she could find his house in daylight—but not today. Not until he was out of the way because she wasn't sure she could trust herself not to say something awful.

As if she hadn't already.

Damn...

Damn.

Why had he said that? Any of it? Why had he believed even for a second that she could have tricked him into going to the wedding?

And she hadn't been all right. She'd been silent and withdrawn until they'd got to the church, then she'd plastered on a brave smile and dazzled him and everyone else. Except during the vows, and because they'd been packed closely together in the pews, he'd felt a shudder run through her when the priest had said the words, 'and forsaking all others'.

Not surprising, under the circumstances. The image of Natalie and her lover locked together on the tangled bedding was burned on his memory for all time.

It was all he'd been able to see for the rest of the service, so wrapped up in his own bitterness and regret he'd been oblivious to Iona. How had she taken it? She hadn't cried, he knew that, but he'd seen nothing of the inner turmoil that she'd undoubtedly been feeling. He'd been too preoccupied with his own.

He swore and pulled over to the side of the road. He had to go back, to do something to repair the damage he'd caused, because he had to leave shortly and head for Manchester for the course he was booked on, and then he'd have no way of contacting her until he was back.

He'd be gone for days, and he couldn't leave it that long without apologising. Not even he was that much of an egotistical bastard.

So he swung the car round, headed back and pulled up outside her house and rang the doorbell.

Nothing. Not a sound, not a flicker of movement through the frosted glass in the door—nothing. He rang it again, and then again, but she didn't come to the door, so he stepped back to the edge of the pavement and looked up, but there was no sign of her at the windows, and he had no idea where her flat was in the house.

He could leave her a note—except he had nothing with him to write with or on, so that wouldn't work. One last try?

No. If she was going to answer, she would have done it. He let out a heavy sigh, turned on his heel and went

back to the car, slammed the door and rested his head
on the steering wheel.

Idiot. Stupid, stupid idiot. How could he ever have
considered that she'd use that kind of subterfuge? She
couldn't lie to save her life, and when he'd asked her
why she was at the speed-dating event, she'd told him
the truth. Not the whole truth, not until later, but probably nothing but the truth.

It was him who'd brought up the sperm donor thing,
him who'd taken her back to his house, given her coffee
and spilled his guts about his marriage. Why, he had no
idea. It was so unlike him he still couldn't understand
why he'd done it, but there was just something about
Iona that seemed to drag the truth out of him, whether
he wanted it out or not.

Oh, well. She didn't want it now. Didn't want anything
from him, if she wasn't answering the door. Maybe it was
as well. He had things to do before he left, like more re-
search into the topic of the course, and a quick visit to
his aunt. And it wouldn't hurt to muck out the fridge and
get rid of the things that were past their use-by date so
the house didn't reek when he got home after the course.

Angry, dispirited and utterly disgusted at himself, he
straightened up, reached for the key and saw her there,
standing by the car with her arms wrapped defensively
round her and her eyes red-rimmed and wary.

He got out, shut the car door and stood there in silence
facing her. *What the hell had he done?*

'I don't know where to start,' he said eventually.
'There's nothing I can say to make it better, except to
say I'm sorry. So sorry. You didn't deserve that. You
didn't deserve any of it.'

Her arms tightened round her waist but her eyes didn't

leave his. 'No, I didn't. She did a real number on you, didn't she? Your ex?'

'Yes.' He nodded slowly. 'Yes, she did. But you know what? I'm a grown man, I shouldn't be letting the actions of someone in the past affect the way I interact with people now, but sometimes I think I can't trust my own judgement, and then if I think I've been lied to I lash out, but I shouldn't have done that, I shouldn't have said the things I said and hurt you like that. I never meant to, and if I'd stopped to think about it for a second, I would have known you weren't lying to me.'

She nodded. 'I know. But I shouldn't have yelled at you like that, either. That poor lorry driver.' Her mouth twitched, and she gave a tiny ripple of laughter that was verging on tears and pressed her fingers to her lips. 'I don't know what he thought was going on.'

Joe felt a reluctant smile tug at his mouth. 'I have no idea, but I'd love to know what he told his mates.'

He saw her eyes soften, and he took a step forward and wrapped his arms gently round her and hugged her, resting his head against hers. 'I'm so, so sorry I hurt you.'

'Me, too. Can we start again? Forget any of these conversations happened and just be nice to each other?'

He lifted his head and looked down into her eyes.

'I don't know if I *can* forget that easily. You've told me too much, and whatever you say I'm going to worry about you now.'

'Don't. I'm not going to do anything rash, I'm honestly not that stupid, and I'll think really seriously about what you've said before I go any further, I promise. And I'll have another look at the donor sites.'

'No fjord cruises?' he teased, and she laughed and shook her head.

'No fjord cruises. No random one-nighters with tall blond strangers or sneaking off into the bushes with the best man.' Her eyes were smiling now, teasing him back, and he felt himself relax. At least she wasn't still furious with him, even if the hurt he'd caused would take a while to fade.

'Good. Right, I need to go, I've got things to do before I leave.' He hesitated, then threw out his reservations and bent his head and kissed her.

Just a fleeting kiss, or it was meant to be, but then she kissed him back, her lips soft but supple, their warmth melting something deep inside him that he'd long forgotten. And so he lingered, not heating it up, but not letting her go, either. Not yet. Not for a moment…

With a mammoth effort he lifted his head, brushed his knuckles slowly over her cheek and stepped away before it was too late. 'Take care, Iona. Stay safe.'

'I will. You, too. I'll see you next week.'

He nodded, turned away, then turned back again. 'Have you got your phone on you?'

'Yes.'

'Take my number. I know what it's like when there's nobody to bounce stuff off, and if I know nothing else, I know about sperm donation.'

She nodded, gave him a fleeting smile and keyed in his number. 'Thank you.'

'Don't thank me. Just call me if you need to.'

And with that he got back into his car, started the engine and drove away, watching her in the rear view mirror. As he got to the junction, he glanced back and she was still there, her hand raised in a little gesture of farewell.

He lifted his hand and pulled away reluctantly.

* * *

'What's happened? You look different.'

'Different?'

He bent and kissed his aunt's cheek, and she reached up and took his hand.

'Yes, different,' she said thoughtfully. 'And you didn't come yesterday.'

'I know, I'm sorry. I did let you know.'

'I know that, I got your cryptic message, but you never change your plans unless it's for work, and I knew you weren't working.'

He chuckled and sat down beside her. 'You don't miss a trick, do you?'

'No, I don't, so don't try and pull the wool over my eyes. What's going on?'

He smiled wryly and gave up. 'I've had a rather interesting weekend, what with one thing and another.'

'Have you?' she asked thoughtfully.

'Yes. I met someone on Friday. At work. A very junior registrar. She—um—she challenged my ability to do a REBOA.'

'Oh, dear—I can't imagine that went down well,' she said with a chuckle, and he gave a wry smile.

'No, not exactly. But then I borrowed her stethoscope and forgot to give it back, and when I returned it to her—well, we got talking, and to cut a long story short she's thinking about being a surrogate for her identical twin sister.'

'What—having a baby for her? Well, bless her heart. What a very brave thing to do.' She dabbed her eyes with a tissue, then tucked it back up her sleeve. 'Goodness. I can't imagine how she'll be able to do that. She must really love her sister. I could never have done anything as brave or selfless as that, even if I'd been able to.'

'No, nor me,' he said, still unconvinced she could do it without being destroyed. 'Anyway, it was her brother's wedding yesterday, and she talked me into going with her, and her sister was there and—well, basically the sister asked her if there was any way she could convince me to be their sperm donor.'

Elizabeth's eyes widened. 'Oh! What did you say?'

He gave a wry laugh. 'All the wrong things? I accused her of inviting me to the wedding just to meet her sister—'

'Why *did* she invite you?'

'Because she found out three days before her own wedding that her fiancé was sleeping with the stripper from his stag weekend, so weddings aren't really her thing. And it was in the same church as her wedding would have been, with a lot of the same people, and she wanted me with her to deflect the sympathy. She really didn't want to go.'

She sucked in a breath and put her hand over her chest. 'Oh, the poor girl. No, I should think not. No wonder she didn't want to go alone. I'm also surprised you went.'

He laughed without humour. 'So was I.'

She plucked an imaginary bit of fluff off her sleeve, and rearranged her cardigan. 'So—are you going to do it?'

'Do what?'

'Be their sperm donor?'

'No! Elizabeth, you know how I feel about it.'

'Yes, I do, but—that's because you had no idea who the parents would be. This way, you'd know, because you've met them, so it would be different.'

'No, it wouldn't. And anyway I don't care about them. I care about Iona, and I know she thinks she's thought it through, but I'm so worried that's she's not grasped the enormity of what she's doing, that her love for Isla is blinding her to what she herself stands to lose. What if it destroys her?'

'Maybe it won't. If her sister's an identical twin, they share exactly the same genes, so it would make sense, wouldn't it, for her to be the one to carry the baby if her sister can't? Then the sister will have a child who could have been her own, and Iona will have a child she'll have a lifelong relationship with, without running the risk of another potentially messy relationship before she's ready. I can see why she's thinking like that, and it's quite unlike your situation.

'I know what you feel about your children—and, yes, before you say it, I know they're not your children, but you know what I mean. She would know the answers to all the questions you constantly ask yourself. And there's nothing to stop her further down the line meeting someone and falling in love with them and having a family of her own—someone like you, maybe?'

His aunt had the most eloquent eyes in the universe, he thought, and wouldn't hesitate to give him her opinion if she felt he'd invited it. Which he had, just by telling her. Didn't mean he liked it, especially when her eyes were saying what they were saying.

'Elizabeth, we've barely met! She's not in love with me, and I'm certainly not in love with her, and I'm not going to be.'

'No, I don't suppose you are, not after such a short time, you're much too wary. But I knew about Owen the moment I met him. It was love at first sight—'

'That doesn't exist.'

'Says the boy who couldn't work out why a woman like Natalie would be unfaithful if she was left alone for long enough.'

'I'm not a boy, Elizabeth.'

'No, you're not. You're a man, and it's high time you stopped running away from it and having meaningless affairs and allowed yourself to be happy.'

He sighed. 'I'm not in the market for it. I'm too busy, I'm not ready for it yet, not until I've got a consultancy, if then. I'm not going to risk trashing another relationship like I did the last one.'

'Well, hopefully it wouldn't be like the last one. Hopefully she'd be rather more level headed and less egocentric, and if Iona's prepared to have a baby for her sister, I think that qualifies her quite nicely. I'd like to meet her.'

He laughed. 'Over my dead body. You know way too much about me.'

'Not if she's going to be carrying your child. She should know the kind of man you are.'

'She's not going to be carrying my child, either! And if we were in love, which we aren't, not by a country mile because we know next to nothing about each other, why would we have a baby and give it away?'

She smiled gently at him, her eyes softening. 'I wasn't suggesting that. It was a sort of either/or. I know how hurt you are, how much Natalie destroyed your faith in women, and because of that, because I know you can't trust easily and don't want another relationship, it might be the only chance you have to bring a child into the world that you could have a relationship with.'

'No! I'm not going to do it!' And especially not now,

after their row. She'd made that quite clear, and it was a miracle she'd even spoken to him again.

'Never say never. Tell me about her. What's she like?'

'Lovely. She's gorgeous,' he said honestly. 'Almost too good to be true. She's caring, very fond of all her family, but she's also spontaneous and emotional. That's why I'm worried for her, in case she's suggested this out of pity and now doesn't quite know how to retract it.'

'Maybe she doesn't want to. Maybe she'd be happy doing. And you used to be spontaneous and emotional.'

'I know. And I learned by my mistake, and I don't want Iona to have to do the same, because as well as spontaneous and emotional, she's also either immensely brave or she's totally missed the point of what it could do to her.'

'Don't underestimate her. Women are strong, Joseph. Yes, it could hurt her, but so would not giving her sister the joy of being a mother if it's in her power. Maybe she really is that selfless. Oh, and that's the gong for tea. Lucky you, you get to run away,' she said with a twinkle in her eye that made him laugh in spite of himself.

'I need to go anyway. I've got a lot to do, I'm leaving for Manchester shortly, for this course. Would you like me to walk you along to the dining room on my way out?'

'That would be lovely, my darling. And you drive carefully, now. That car of yours has got far too much power.'

She kissed him goodbye at the dining room door, but she couldn't resist a parting shot as he walked away.

'Bring her to see me!'

He laughed. As he'd already said, over his dead body...

CHAPTER FOUR

'SO DID HE manage to track you down at the speed dating?'

Iona stared at Jenny, taking a second or two to work out what she was talking about because it seemed like a lifetime ago.

'Oh—yes. Yes, he did. Thanks for sending him there.'

'I hope he apologised for being rude in Resus as well as running off with your beloved stethoscope?'

She laughed softly. 'Yes, he apologised.' For that, and for all the things he'd said in the car, too, which had been much more hurtful. They'd come totally out of the blue and had seemed really out of character from what little she knew of him—which, she realised, was precious little, so maybe it wasn't out of character. But then he'd kissed her...

'So where am I today?'

'Oh, I think James has put you in Minors, keeping an eye on Tim. Between you and me, I think he's a bit worried about him.'

She rolled her eyes. 'He's not alone. OK, Jenny, thanks.'

She made her way to Minors, relieved in some ways that it would be a relatively easy day, but she should have realised nothing was ever as straightforward as it seemed. And Tim, with his lack of experience and apparently no gut instinct, was at the root of it.

'How are you getting on?' she asked him after a while.

'OK. I've got someone with migraine I'm just about to discharge with codeine.'

She frowned. 'Do they have a history?'

'No. It's the first time, but he said it was very bad with a roaring in his head and he was very shaky for a few minutes, so his wife brought him in.'

Iona frowned again. 'Shaky?'

'Yes—she said he was shaking all over. I assume it was from the pain.'

'Don't assume,' she said, red flags appearing all over the place. 'Ask. Follow up. When did this start?'

'About half an hour ago, I think, or a bit more. I've done some basic neuro obs and his strength is fine.'

'Right, where is he?'

She went in, introduced herself, skipped the basic neurological strength tests and made him close his eyes and touch the tip of his nose with his index finger, first right, then left.

And he missed with the left.

'OK, it's just a precaution, but I'd like you to have a CT scan. I'll go and arrange it now.'

'A CT? Really? For a headache?' Tim asked, following her to the desk.

'Or a stroke,' she said quietly, and picked up the phone. 'Hi, I need an urgent CT on a query CVA, but he's coming up to the hour and he's got some neurological deficit. Can we send him down now?'

She put the phone down, and Tim looked shocked. 'But he's too young. He's only thirty-seven.'

'Nobody's ever too young. Let's just see what the CT comes up with.'

* * *

She was right. He had a clot in his right parietal lobe and another in the cerebellum, and was immediately whisked into the stroke unit for treatment with anticoagulants.

Tim, predictably, was shaken. 'I thought he just had a headache. His wife said it was a migraine—'

'Is she a doctor?'

'No—no, she's not. And I'm not sure I am, either.'

Iona sighed. 'Yes, you are, Tim. You just need to question everything, take nothing at face value and don't overlook the obvious. His wife said he was shaking. You should have asked what kind of shaking, because when she demonstrated it to me, it looked like a Parkinsonian tremor and that can be symptomatic of a brain injury. It's OK, I picked up on it and no harm was done, so go and get a coffee, take a break, and come back and find me. We'll work together. OK?'

He nodded, and she watched him go and let out a quiet sigh.

'Trouble in paradise?' Jenny asked, and she nodded.

'Tim misdiagnosed a stroke patient. It's OK, I picked it up in time. He's in the stroke unit.'

'Well done. So how was the wedding?'

She smiled wryly. 'OK, thanks. I went with a…friend, in the end,' she said, wondering if she would have picked up on that slight hesitation, but the red phone rang and Jenny answered it, and she escaped without any further interrogation.

Not that Jenny would really have interrogated her, but somehow she didn't want the fact that Joe had gone with her to come out, because without a doubt it would unleash a barrage of questions she didn't want to answer. She wasn't even sure she *could* answer them.

Not until she knew him better, and she suddenly realised how much she wanted that. She'd gone from thinking he was arrogant to friend to arch enemy and back to friend in the course of less than forty-eight hours, and next weekend when she'd see him again seemed a long, long way away.

The course was tough.

Tough, challenging and utterly fascinating. Or it should have been, but for some reason he couldn't get Iona out of his mind. Iona, and her hunt for the elusive donor.

He wondered how her week was going, and if she'd looked at any more donor sites. If so, she hadn't contacted him, and he wondered if it was because she was still feeling hurt and insulted and didn't want to talk to him.

He wouldn't blame her. What an idiot. If he'd only engaged his heart instead of his mouth, he would have realised she could never have done anything that devious, but no, he'd gone straight in with all guns blazing like an arrogant idiot. Serve him right if she didn't want to speak to him again—far less ask him to be her sperm donor. Although he'd got that message, loud and clear, and so had half of East Anglia.

Damn Elizabeth for making him even consider it. There was no way—

He dragged his attention back to the lecture, forced himself to concentrate and put Iona and her surrogacy project firmly out of his mind.

* * *

The week came and went without a word from him, but then again because she'd been letting the dust settle she hadn't contacted him, either. Which meant he didn't have her phone number, she realised, because although he'd given her his, she hadn't reciprocated.

Oh, well. It was too late to ring him at ten on a Friday night, and he might be driving, or even coming back to-morrow. Or he might have been back days ago. She had no idea how long the course had been, he hadn't said, but he should be home by tomorrow. She'd call him then before her night shift and ask—just casually—how the course had gone.

Except when it came to it she didn't, because he'd said call if she needed to talk about the donor thing, and that wasn't it at all. She just wanted to hear his voice.

So she didn't call him.

And then she was in Majors on Saturday night and a patient came in with sudden acute abdominal pain, and was crippled by it. Appendix was the obvious, but she'd had it removed some years before, and she was post-menopausal so it wasn't an ectopic pregnancy, and when Iona had listened to her heart, the beat had been slightly irregular. Atrial fibrillation? Maybe, which meant she might have a clot that had been thrown out of the heart and lodged in her mesenteric artery, and that could be fatal.

She was about to arrange an urgent CT when she heard Joe's voice outside Resus, and stuck her head round the door.

'Hi. I don't suppose you've got a minute to chat about a patient, have you?'

'Sure. What's up?'

She ran through the symptoms, and he nodded. 'So what are you thinking? Acute mesenteric ischaemia from a thrombosis?'

'Maybe, and if it is I don't want to miss it.'

'No, absolutely not,' he murmured. 'CT?'

'I was about to call them when I heard your voice.'

'Let's do that now, then, if the scanner's free, and I'll take her straight to IR and sort it if you're right.'

'Call me when you have the answer.'

He grinned. 'That would be easier if I had your number,' he said, and so she rang him and heard his phone buzz in his pocket.

'OK, got it. Phone CT and tell them I'm on my way.'

'I'll get you a porter.'

'I'm sure I can manage. I'm not too posh to push,' he said with another wry grin.

'I thought that was elective Caesareans?' she retorted, and he chuckled and wheeled the patient out, taking the nurse and the notes with him.

'Good spot,' he said when he rang her twenty-five minutes later. 'She's just being wheeled into the IR suite. What time do you finish?'

'Seven thirty.'

'Me, too, technically speaking, although we both know how that goes. How do you fancy breakfast? I had a food delivery on Friday, including dry-cured bacon and massively squashy bread rolls.'

'Ooh, now... Are you offering me a bacon buttie?' she asked, her heart beating just a little faster.

'Of course.'

'Well, it's a rhetorical question then, isn't it?' she said with a laugh. 'Call me when you're done. I'll drive over.'

'I will,' he promised, and she could hear the smile in his voice and feel its echo in her lips.

'Wow. I had no idea the doors opened onto a veranda. That's fabulous!'

'It is. I love it. I sit out here whenever I can—which isn't nearly often enough, because I'm normally shut away in the study, working.'

'Can't you work out here?' she asked, peering through the doors, but he shook his head.

'Look at it. Would you do any work if you were out there?'

She laughed and turned away. 'I guess the view would be a bit of a distraction.'

'Not to mention the wildlife. The hazel tree's covered in nuts and the other day a squirrel carrying one ran from end to end of the veranda, practically over my feet. Then it dug up the lawn to bury it.'

She smiled. 'How cheeky. How are the muntjacs?'

'Noisy,' he said drily, 'but I prefer them to endless traffic noise and screaming sirens on emergency vehicles.'

She pulled out a chair and sat down at the table to watch him while he cooked. 'I'm guessing that was London?'

'And Manchester, where I was last week. The hotel was triple glazed but I could still hear it, just a dull roar in the background. Not to mention the doors slamming all night on the corridor. I don't know why people can't shut them quietly.'

He flipped the bacon under the grill and grabbed a couple of mugs from the shelf over the cooker. 'Tea or coffee?'

'Oh—tea, please. I've had so much coffee overnight I'm wired.'

'Am I keeping you up?'

She shook her head. 'No, I need to wind down. This is perfect. So, how was the course, apart from noisy?'

'Good. Here, slit these open and butter them, the bacon's nearly done,' he added, sliding the rolls and a knife across the table. 'It was about advances in IR procedures for stroke patients. Direct access thrombolisation of the clots.'

'I had a stroke patient last week. A thirty-seven-year-old. Your course would have come in handy.'

'It would. I could have thrombolised him in IR, which I probably wouldn't have done before this week.'

'I'll bear you in mind if I have another one. This guy nearly slipped through the net, but I rescued him from Tim, who was about to send him home on codeine.'

'Oh, dear,' he sighed, pulling a face. 'Well done, you, though. Another good spot.'

'Yes. This diagnosis thing is almost getting to be a habit,' she said lightly, and he winced.

'Was I patronising again?'

'Only slightly. I'll forgive you.'

He gave a wry laugh and stirred the tea. 'Is he OK, your patient?'

'I hope so, because we caught it within the hour so hopefully he'll be fine. No long-lasting neurological deficit, with any luck. You ought to look up his notes, see if you could have done anything.'

'Yes, I will. Good idea.' He put two mugs of tea and a plate piled with bacon down on the dining table and eyed the doors. 'Outside or in? It's chilly, but it's going to be a gorgeous day.'

'Out,' she said promptly. 'I want to meet your cheeky squirrel.'

* * *

They ate their bacon rolls on the wicker sofa outside, but the squirrel didn't show. It was still worth it, worth grabbing every moment before the Indian summer ended, and he loved it. Loved the veranda, loved the garden, loved the tranquillity after the chaos of London and his divorce.

And sharing it with Iona just made it better.

'This weather's just gorgeous,' she murmured from beside him, her feet propped on the edge of the coffee table next to his, nursing her tea in her hands. 'I can't believe it's mid-September.'

'I know, it's crazy. July and August were awful, but on the plus side I got the wall down and the doors in and the bedrooms decorated in July before the new carpets went down and I started my job.'

She turned her head and studied his face, her eyes thoughtful as if she was trying to read his mind. 'So how come you're doing all this work to your aunt's house?'

He shrugged. 'Good question. I suppose because it'll make it easier for her to let when I get a consultancy elsewhere, and ultimately it'll come to me, anyway, so I don't mind the investment. I'm her only surviving relative apart from my father, and she doesn't think he needs it. They're in a purpose-built house and he had hefty compensation for the accident, so she's probably right. And anyway, after Natalie's asset-stripping efforts, I think she feels sorry for me.'

She laughed. 'Lucky you. I'm struggling to save a deposit so I'm sharing a two-bedroomed rented flat in that converted Victorian heap. And I don't have a garden, so I'm jealous.'

He frowned. 'No access to it, or a balcony or anything?'

'No. It's the top floor, so technically I could say I live

in a penthouse flat, but in reality it's an attic,' she said, her eyes crinkling in a rueful smile. 'I do have roof lights that open up to make a kind of balcony, but it's not big enough to sit there really. You ought to come and see it. I should cook for you—make a change from supermarket ready meals or the pub. Assuming we're still friends, that is?'

Her eyes were wary now, and he shook his head slowly and sighed, the memory of their argument still all too fresh in his mind. 'That's down to you, Iona, I was the one out of order, but I really hope so. Am I forgiven yet?'

A slow, teasing smile dawned on her face, lighting her eyes and bringing him an element of relief. 'Oh, I think so. You've made me bacon butties, so it would be churlish not to. And anyway,' she added, the smile fading, 'I'm blaming it on your ex.'

'Yeah, and I still do, but I'm nearly thirty-five, Iona. It's time I got over myself and stopped using her as an excuse for being suspicious about everyone's motives.'

'That's easy to say, not so easy to do. I don't want a relationship ever again, not one built on false promises and lies at any rate, and how can you possibly know until it happens? And how can you trust anyone after that? I thought Dan loved me in the way I loved him, but clearly he didn't, or he wouldn't have been shagging the stripper right before our wedding.'

'Or the umpteenth lover eighteen months after the wedding, in your own bed,' he said grimly. 'Believe me, I know exactly where you're coming from. I have no urge to get myself tied down to anyone ever again—despite my aunt's best efforts.'

She blinked at that, and laughed. 'Is she trying to set you up with one of the carers in the home?'

He chuckled and shook his head. 'No. But she wants to meet you.'

Her eyes widened. 'She knows about me?'

'Yes. I told her about you,' he admitted, 'about you wanting to have a baby for Isla. And, yes, I know I said I'd keep it to myself, but I was worried about you, and she's a doctor. She understands confidentiality, she understands childlessness, and anyway, who would she tell?'

'That's OK, I'm fine with that,' she said, to his relief. 'So what did she say?'

'She said she thought you were immensely brave. So do I, or I would if I wasn't afraid you'd get badly hurt.'

She sighed and rolled her eyes. 'Joe, I know what I'm doing, and why I'm doing it. I'm not stupid, I understand the implications, but it really won't be my baby. It'll be exactly the same as carrying Isla's embryo and a donor's. If I can ever find one, that is. I did what you said, by the way. I looked again at all the sites, read all the profiles, scoured the information given.'

'And?'

She looked back at him, then looked away again. 'There's nobody who springs out. Nobody who sounds right.'

'Isn't that for Isla and Steve to decide?'

She nodded slowly. 'Yes, I suppose it is, but they've got the same problem I have, they can't seem to find anyone that fits what they're looking for, nobody who shouts "Me!" regardless of what they look like. They've even talked about going to one of the sites where you get to meet the donors, but they're unregulated so that's not a goer, and—I know I'm dragging my heels on this, but I have so many reservations about it. Just the idea of a stranger's baby growing in my body unsettles me,' she confessed.

'If it was Steve's, it would have been a bit weird, but he's a lovely guy and I could have coped with it because it would have been giving them essentially their own baby, but that didn't work and—I don't know. Some random stranger's semen, regardless of how well screened, just makes me shudder,' she added, pulling a face, and he gave a wry laugh.

'Yeah, I can understand that it might, but if you're going to do this, there isn't really any other way apart from IVF. Have you considered trying that with Steve's sperm as the AI didn't work?'

She shook her head. 'No. I think Isla found it quite gruelling and all the embryos failed anyway, so they decided it wouldn't be fair to put me through IVF, and when the AI failed with me as well, the clinic thought it must be something to do with Steve so they suggested a sperm donor. And I hit a brick wall, and I don't know what to do or how to tell them.'

'I'm not surprised, it's a big decision.'

'I know. I just need to get over myself. Or find a donor I like the sound of, but there's only so much that information can tell you and they never seem to say enough.'

'No, I'm sure, but the profiles are hard to write. What on earth do you say about yourself that doesn't make you sound arrogant?'

'What did you say about yourself, when you did it?'

'Oh—I can't remember, I just know it was difficult.' He stood up. 'I've got a copy of it somewhere, I'll find it for you.'

He scooped up the plates and mugs, refilled the kettle and went into the study, rummaging through the filing cabinet.

'So is this where you hide out?' she asked from right behind him, making him jump.

'Are you trying to scare the pants off me?' he said with a laugh. 'Yes, it's where I hide out. I keep the blind down so I'm not distracted, and it turns it into a gloomy hole but it helps me concentrate. Here we go.'

He pulled the profile out of the file and handed it to her. 'Bear in mind I was only twenty and probably fairly full of myself.'

She took it from his hand, headed outside onto the veranda and sat down to read it, and he made more tea and went back to her.

'Well?'

'Well, you'd definitely make the short list. You give good, decent reasons for wanting to do it, you share lots of information about yourself, you aren't arrogant about your academic success or stunning good looks or physical attributes—'

'Stunning good looks? Physical attributes?' he said, preening himself a little, and she shot him a dirty look that would have worked better if she hadn't been laughing.

'Stop fishing. I didn't mean it like that. I meant some of them are, and you aren't. You almost don't say enough to sell yourself.'

'I'll take that as a compliment,' he said with a chuckle, and took it away from her. 'Drink your tea, and then I'm going to take you home. I need sleep.'

He didn't sleep.

He couldn't, because still, as it had been all week,

Iona's dilemma was playing on his mind, and so was the fact that Isla had asked her about him and said he'd be perfect.

Not that she really knew anything about him, of course, so he was sure it hadn't in any way been a serious suggestion, but—what if it had been? What if she really did mean it?

He didn't want to do it again, but as Elizabeth had said, this was different, because he'd met Steve and Isla and could maybe even have a relationship with the child. And that was tugging at him in a way he hadn't expected.

Then there was the question of Iona, who'd made it quite clear what she thought of his sperm—although she'd said he'd be on the short list. Would she baulk at carrying his child?

He shut his eyes and turned over, thumping the pillow. Not *his* child. Just as none of the others out there were *his* child.

Which reminded him exactly why he wasn't going to do it again. Ever.

Not even for Iona. Assuming she'd have him.

He gave up trying to sleep, pulled on his clothes and went down to the study, and there on the desk waiting to be filed was his donor profile.

He went back upstairs, changed into shorts and trainers, plugged his ear buds into his phone and went for a ten mile run.

She didn't see him again for over a week, and then on Tuesday he sent her a text and asked if she was busy after her shift, because he wanted to discuss something. And he had food in his fridge. The last was a PS, and made her smile.

She rang him, got his answer-machine and left a message saying she'd come at seven and supper would be lovely, and then she spent the rest of her shift wondering what he wanted to talk about. Not the sperm donor thing, she knew that with absolute certainty, but what?

Was he going to suggest they have a relationship? No, he'd been clear about that. Never again. So—a no-strings affair?

No, she thought, squashing the little leap of hope. Not even he would be that premeditated. Pity...

Maybe it was work related? Something about referrals, perhaps? But then he'd do it at work. So—what, then?

She left work late, had the fastest shower on record and got to his house just after seven. He gave her a hug, then led her into the kitchen and opened the fridge.

'What do you want to drink? I've got juice, squash, cola, sparkling water, pomegranate and elderflower cordial, or I can make tea or coffee?'

'Fizzy water with a splash of cordial,' she said, dropping her bag on the table and propping herself up against the sink. 'Got any nibbles? I'm starving.'

He handed her a bag of olive breadsticks and a pot of hummus, then picked up their drinks and went out to the veranda to watch the last rays of the sunset.

'So what is it, then?' she asked, settling herself at the table and ripping the top off the hummus, and he gave a wry laugh.

'Am I that transparent?'

She crunched on a breadstick. 'Well, I haven't heard anything from you for days, and then you text me and say you want to discuss something—not did I fancy supper or you'd had an interesting case or anything like that. So it must be something else—or am I reading you wrong?' she added, studying his face.

He sighed, turned to meet her eyes and shook his head. 'Not really. I just wondered how you were getting on with the donor sites.'

'Oh, that.' She stifled her disappointment and blew on her coffee, watching the way the froth moved, creasing the pattern in the chocolate sprinkles. 'I don't know, Joe,' she sighed. 'I've still got this mental block about the stranger thing, and I'm going to have to tell Isla and Steve because I just don't think I can do it this way.'

'What if it was a friend?' he asked, his voice low, measured. Laden with meaning?

She turned her head slowly and met his eyes again, searching them in the twilight. His gaze was steady, serious. Did he…?

'I thought you said…?'

'I know, I did, but—do you think Isla was serious? About me?'

He *did* mean that. 'I'm sure she was. I didn't really think so at the time, but she's mentioned it again, and I told her about our row in the layby and the lorry driver because I thought she'd laugh, but she was gutted that she'd caused a rift between us.'

He shook his head. 'It wasn't a rift, it was me being overly defensive and running scared, feeling I'd been tricked when I thought I'd gone to the wedding to help you out of a fix that I could understand and empathise with. And I know you didn't trick me, I know you wouldn't do that, to me or to anyone. And the more I know you, the more I realise what a fool I was. I can't believe I was that stupid or that unkind.'

'So—have you seriously changed your mind about doing it again? Because you were so emphatic—'

'Not as emphatic as you. "I don't want your bloody sperm" is pretty emphatic,' he said drily. 'And maybe you meant it, but when you read my profile you said you'd put me on the shortlist, so I thought it was worth asking if you'd even contemplate carrying my baby for them, because it certainly didn't sound like it in the layby.'

Carry his baby? Her heart gave a sudden little hitch. 'I didn't mean it—not like that. I just meant I wouldn't ask you because I realised after we talked about it that you'd say no, so I never really even considered it after that, but now it seems you've changed your mind, so if you're asking me how I feel about that, then, yes, of course I would, because I know you're a really decent human being and you care about people. So the answer is, yes, I would happily carry a baby if you were the father—even if you are a bit of an idiot at times and inclined to be arrogant and patronising,' she added, smiling to soften it, 'but hey. Nobody's perfect.'

He gave a soft huff of laughter. 'Thanks—I think.'

She smiled fleetingly, then snapped a breadstick in half and dipped it in the hummus, trying to take in what he'd said and what the implications were. 'So why the change of heart? You've been so against me doing this, spent hours trying to convince me I was making a huge mistake, and now apparently you want to be part of it? What made you think again?'

He sighed and took a breadstick from her and dunked it in the hummus. 'I don't know. Your desperation? Or, as my aunt said, because this would be different to what I did before, and it might be my only chance of having a child whose life I could have some feedback about, or maybe some involvement in? Not contact necessarily, but the odd photo, progress reports, snippets of information, that sort of thing.'

But she wasn't listening any more, she was stuck on 'only chance' because it sounded so sad, and so empty. 'Why your only chance? Did she really hurt you that badly?'

He met her eyes fleetingly and looked away, but not before she'd seen the desolation in them. 'You really need to ask that, after what you've been through and what I told you? I'm not putting myself in harm's way again, Iona. I was devastated when I caught Natalie with that guy, and to learn that he wasn't the first—no way. I'm happy to have an affair with someone who doesn't expect anything else of me, but anything that could remotely be called a relationship is definitely off limits. And I wouldn't want to have a child of my own if I wasn't in a strong, solid relationship with a woman I could trust absolutely, and I can't trust anyone, because I can't trust my own judgement—and I know you can understand that, you said it yourself the other day.

'And besides, I don't have time. I need to be able to work, to concentrate on my studies, to secure a consultancy. That's as far ahead as I'm looking at the moment, and there's no way a child features in that. So my aunt could be right. It might be my only chance to have a child and follow its progress, however remotely. And if Isla and Steve were happy with that and you felt OK with it, then—I don't know. Maybe we could meet up, get to know each other better, find out if we think it could work for us all, with any of us able to walk away if we didn't feel it could.'

She stared at him, speechless, almost overwhelmed

at what he'd just said. Then she put her breadstick down,
leant over and hugged him. Hard.

'Thank you. Thank you so much. I'll talk to them—
ask them how they feel. They're actually coming down
this weekend. How about coming to mine? They'll be
staying with me because my flatmate, Libby, is away for
the weekend. I could cook for us.'

'Is it big enough, or do you all want to come to me?
They can see more of me, then, find out how I live, what
I'm really like. You could all stay, if you wanted to. I've
got plenty of room and we'd have more privacy.'

'How can you cook for four in that kitchen?'

He smiled. 'Easy. I told you, the pub does takeaways.
Or we could go to the pub—neutral territory, public
place, no awkward questions, just friends having a meal
and a chat.' He stood up. 'Think about it. Don't say anything to them today, just think about it and talk to me
again before you speak to them. You never know, you
might decide you meant what you yelled at me in the
layby.'

But his eyes were smiling, and he bent and brushed her
cheek with his lips before he turned and walked back into
the kitchen, leaving her there in turmoil, because she'd
just realised that the slender hope she'd been cherishing
that this might blossom into something more intimate
between them had been nixed by this new development.

Sure, she was delighted for Steve and Isla, but it meant
putting her own needs on the back burner, and for the
first time ever, she felt a tiny twinge of resentment.

No. That was just selfish. She'd been fantasising
about a bit of fun, a bit of hot sex and lazy Sunday morn-
ings, and he'd offered her something else altogether,

something much more fundamental, and possibly even more intimate.

The chance to have a child for Isla. How could she put anything above that?

CHAPTER FIVE

HE'D ASKED HER to think about it, and she did.

Constantly, for the next twenty-four hours.

She couldn't think about anything else, and the more she thought, the more convinced she was that they should do it. So she rang him as soon as she got home on Wednesday evening.

'Did you mean it?' she asked without preamble.

He didn't pretend not to understand. 'Yes, I meant it. And before you ask, yes, I'm sure. How about you?'

'Yes. I want to talk to Isla and Steve. Is that OK?'

'It's fine. Oh, and there's something you might want to tell them. I contacted the HFEA and found out about... the children.' She heard a little pause in there, almost as if he'd been about to say '*my* children' and thought better of it, but then he went on. 'Apparently there are six boys and five girls, in five families. One egg split so two of the boys are twins and they already had a daughter. The others are pairs.'

Eleven children. She felt suddenly a little breathless. 'Gosh. So they all worked. How did you feel when you found out?'

'A bit stunned? It made it all much more real. The oldest is fourteen, the youngest is eight.'

'Wow. So everything's working, then.'

'It would seem so. Anyway, feel free to pass that on. They might want to know—oh, and if they say yes, I'll go and get all the necessary checks done again to make sure everything's still all right. OK?'

'Very OK. Thank you, Joe. Thank you so much.'

'You're welcome. Right, I'm working so I need to get on. Let me know what they say.'

They were stunned.

'He said yes? But I thought—?'

'So did I, Isla, but for some reason he's changed his mind and he wants to see you again for longer, so you can get to know him and vice versa, and he suggested we all stay at his house instead of mine this weekend if you're up for that? It's out in the country, and it's lovely, and there's a great pub right on the doorstep, but if you'd rather not, if you don't feel comfortable with that, we can do it at mine—or not at all. It's up to you. There is something I haven't told you, as well, that you need to know,' she said, and told Isla all about him, his donor history, his children, then added, 'He said he'll have all the appropriate tests again before we did anything, assuming you decide you want to go ahead.'

'Wow. I had no idea. I don't know what to say. How would you feel about him being our donor?'

Her heart thumped. 'Me? I'm fine with it,' she said, trying not to think about what it might cost her in terms of a relationship with Joe, instead of what it could give her sister, which was far more important. And anyway, what relationship? He hadn't said anything about them having any other sort of relationship...

'Great. Let me talk to Steve and come back to you.'

It didn't take her long. Steve said yes immediately, and Iona rang Joe straight back as soon as they were off the phone.

'They said yes, they'd love to meet up. Are you sure about it being at yours?'

'Yes, that's fine, but I'm working on Friday night so if you all come over at say two on Saturday, after lunch? That should give me a few hours to sleep, but I'm off all day Friday so I can sort out the house and do a food order. If I book it now we can go to the pub on Saturday evening and I'll do breakfast.'

'Let me pay for the food.'

'No. This was my idea. Right, back to the paper-work— Ah. Any dietary things I need to know?'

'No. Totally omnivorous, like me. They're not fussy.'

'Great. Right, well, I'll see you on Saturday,' he said.

After he'd hung up she sat motionless, staring blindly out of the window, her thoughts in freefall.

It was going to happen. If they all got on, and she couldn't see why they wouldn't, she might end up having a baby. Unless she didn't get pregnant with Joe, either. Maybe there was something wrong with her, too?

Well, it looked like she was going to find out—assuming the weekend was a success.

There was a strange, tight feeling in her chest.

Fear?

No. Not fear. There was nothing to fear. It would be fine.

Maybe—anticipation?

Ten to two.

Would they be early? Late? Right on time? Iona had been late once, but that was because of work. Would they bring two cars? He'd put his in the garage out of the way, so there was room for two just in case.

The fridge was full, the house was clean, the beds were made, the dishwasher, his only concession to a new kitchen, was on. He glanced at the clock again.

Seven minutes to two.

His palms prickled, and he realised he was nervous. Nervous that they wouldn't like him, or nervous that they would? He felt as if he was about to be interviewed, but he'd been through that process before and passed the clinic's test. Not with the intended parents, though. Although they would have seen his—

Profile. Damn. He'd updated it last night at work in an oddly quiet interlude, but he hadn't printed it.

Too late. He heard the crunch of tyres on gravel, doors slamming, voices, and he unclenched his fists, walked into the hall and opened the front door.

Iona was there, Isla and Steve beside her, and they all looked as nervous as he felt.

He stifled the laugh, stepped back and welcomed them in. He had a weird moment when he didn't know how to greet them, but Isla took the decision out of his hands and gave him a quick, warm hug and kissed his cheek.

'This is so kind of you, Joe,' she said softly, her eyes so like Iona's that he felt he could read every emotion in them—and there were plenty.

'I just felt it would be easier for all of us. We've got more space here, room to get away from each other if necessary.'

Isla returned his smile, her face relaxing slightly. 'I'm sure it won't be.'

'I hope not. Steve—good to see you again.' He shook his hand, felt the firm, warm grip, met the clear blue

eyes that searched his and maybe found what they were
looking for, because he smiled, his face relaxing just as
Isla's had.

'You, too. And thank you so much for inviting us here.'

'You're welcome. Hi, Iona. You OK?'

She nodded, hesitated a moment and then gave him
a quick hug. 'You?'

'I'm fine. Come on through.'

He made coffee, and they took it in the sitting room and
he answered all their questions, and they answered his.
So many questions, Iona thought, and the more openly
they talked, the more she realised what a good fit he was
with them.

They felt so much the same about so many things,
and whether you believed in nature or nurture, that was
important. Biologically his role, like hers, was clearly
defined, to provide Isla and Steve with a child as genetically close to their own as possible. OK, he wasn't a dead
ringer for Steve, but apart from his hair colour he wasn't
a million miles off and other things were more important. And, as Joe had so succinctly put it, they were both
just a means to an end—and that end was now in sight.
So she took herself off into the kitchen, put the kettle on
again and made a pot of tea.

She'd baked a cake this morning while she'd waited for
them to arrive, and she went out to the car and brought it
in, just as Joe came out of the sitting room.

'Wow, that looks good.'

'I hope so. It's my mother's apple cake recipe and it's
usually pretty reliable. So how's it going?'

He shrugged. 'OK, I think. They haven't got back in
the car yet, at least.'

That was said with a slight lift to his lips, not quite a smile, but his eyes were gentle and she put the cake down, put her arms around him and hugged him.

'I'm so grateful to you for doing this,' she mumbled into his chest.

'They haven't said yes yet.'

'They will. Cake?'

'Definitely. I haven't eaten since last night.'

'No lunch?'

He shook his head. 'I wasn't hungry. The nights mess with my body clock.'

She felt her mouth tilt. 'I reckon you're saving yourself for Maureen's fish and chips. Did you book a table for tonight or did you forget?'

He laughed and got some plates out. 'No, I didn't forget. Our table's booked for seven thirty. Is that OK?'

'Sounds fine. We've brought walking shoes, by the way. I thought maybe we could go for a stroll after we've had cake?'

He nodded. 'Great idea. It's easier to talk while you're walking. No eye contact. You can say the things that are harder to say face to face.'

'What, like "no"?'

He laughed again. 'Hopefully not, although it's down to them. Shall we have tea on the veranda?'

'So, did I pass?'

They were standing in the hall, bags packed and ready to go, after what he hoped had been a good and constructive weekend. He'd meant to leave it up to them to tell him how they felt after they'd had time to consider it, but the suspense had got the better of him.

Isla's jaw dropped, and then her eyes filled. 'Did *you* pass? I thought you were vetting us? Did *we* pass?'

He laughed, the tension going out of him like air out of a punctured balloon. 'Of course you passed. That was never in question. And—if you decide to go ahead, I just hope it works for you, because I've seen the grief of childlessness at first hand, and I wouldn't wish it on anyone,' he added quietly.

'Thank you. Thank you so much.' Steve hesitated a second, then wrapped his arms around Joe and hugged him hard. 'You're a good man.'

Steve let him go, and he caught Iona's eye and she winked at him and turned to the others. 'Well, if you've all finished your mutual love-in, maybe we'd better get on the road because you've got a long journey back and I'm absolutely sure Joe has a heap of work he wants to do before tomorrow.'

They said their goodbyes, Iona kissed his cheek and whispered, 'Thank you,' and he closed the door, turned around and leant on it with a sigh of relief.

He was drained. Physically, mentally and emotionally exhausted, and oddly flat, because—ah, no point thinking about what might have been with Iona. This was far more important than scratching an itch, and she was turning into a cherished friend. He should concentrate on that, be there for her, not worry about what he might or might not be missing. And anyway, he wasn't ready for that and she deserved better than what he could offer. He'd already proved that with his stupid accusations after the wedding.

He levered himself away from the door and went into the kitchen. It was a mess, strewn with the remains of brunch. He emptied and reloaded the dishwasher, switched it on and went out onto the veranda, too tired to think about working.

The Indian summer seemed to be lingering indefinitely, and it was a beautiful early October day. He lay down on the wicker sofa, shifted the cushions until he was comfortable and closed his eyes. Just five minutes…

He was fast asleep.

He hadn't answered the doorbell, so she'd walked round the side and there he was, sprawled out across the sofa, one foot on the ground, his other leg draped over the end, sleeping like a baby.

She perched on the chair by his feet and waited, but it wasn't until the squirrel ran along the veranda and its tail whisked past his trailing hand that he woke with a start.

'Iona? I didn't know you were here. What was that?'

She was laughing. 'The squirrel. Its tail brushed you.'

He yawned hugely and sat up, stretching, and she sat down beside him on a nice warm patch. 'Are you OK?'

He nodded, his eyes still looking a little bleary. 'Yeah. I'm just exhausted. It was a long night at work on Friday, and it was quite tough being on my best behaviour all weekend. How are they?'

'They love you. They think you're amazing. So do I.'

'So—are we going to do this? Subject to my test results coming back OK?'

'It looks like it. When are you having them done?'

'I did it on Friday. I thought I'd get ahead of the game, just make sure, you know? Since Natalie—well, I've been a bit phobic, so I had a sexual health screen straight away and another one six months later just to be sure nothing had been missed, but they were all clear, so I guess I got away lightly. And before you ask, no, I haven't had sex

with anyone, unprotected or otherwise, since then. It was
the semen analysis I wanted to check to make sure all
the little swimmers are up to speed, just so I don't waste
anybody's time.'

'So when will you know that?'

'Couple of days? It shouldn't be long. What about you?
Have you had any screening ever?'

She laughed a little unsteadily. 'Oh, I got checked out
eighteen months ago after I dumped Dan, and again before I started this process, just to be on the safe side. And,
no, neither have I, before you ask,' she added with a smile.

He smiled back understandingly. 'Good. So, if we get
a definite yes from Isla and Steve, I guess we wait for you
to ovulate—if you're absolutely sure you want to do this?'

'I'm sure. For what it's worth, you might want to put
Saturday week into your calendar,' she said, feeling
suddenly a little embarrassed and not quite meeting his
eyes—which in the great scheme of things was ridiculous, as they'd just been talking about his little swimmers.
She stood up and headed for the kitchen.

'I don't suppose there's any cake left? It's a long time
since we had brunch.'

She heard the wicker sofa creak, and he followed her
into the kitchen, coming up behind her and putting his
hands on her shoulders. She turned into his arms and
rested her head on his chest, listening to the steady beat of
his heart under her ear, feeling the warmth seep through
her. She wanted more, so much more, but he hadn't ever
suggested it, and now with this new relationship, it would
be crazy to contemplate—

'Stay for dinner,' he said softly. 'I've hardly seen you
recently.'

'You've been working.'

'I'm always working. Stay anyway.'

She lifted her head and looked up at him, noticing the slight stubble coming through, wondering how it would feel against her skin...

'You just want me to cook for you,' she said accusingly, trying not to smile, and she felt his chest vibrate slightly as he chuckled.

'Rumbled. Why don't we go to the pub? They do a great Sunday roast. And they clear up their own kitchen.'

'Sold. And I'm buying.'

They said yes. An unequivocal, definite, gold-plated yes.

His results were good—his sperm quality was excellent, apparently—and then came the wait, and she found it almost unbearable.

Would it happen this time? Would she, in the next few weeks, find out that she was pregnant?

She was due to ovulate on Saturday, a fortnight after Isla and Steve had left, but where and how they were going to do this hadn't been decided. It wasn't going to be made any easier to schedule it as she was supposed to be working on that Saturday, and yet again in the week before they were both busy and working conflicting shifts, so there didn't seem to be a good time to meet and discuss it. And then, on the Thursday night before *that weekend*, she rang him.

'Are you still OK for this weekend?' she asked, and she heard a grunt of what could have been laughter.

'Yes, I'm fine. I was thinking we should do it here. It's easier than at your flat with Libby there. Much more privacy, and we'll probably both be more relaxed. So— what time do you finish work on Saturday?'

'I don't know. Hopefully before seven.'

'So how about straight afterwards? You could come here and I'll cook us a meal and then afterwards when it's done you can stay over. Unless you've got a better idea?'

'No, that sounds fine. Are you sure about this? All of it?' she asked again, and he said yes without hesitation.

'Sure?'

'Yes, Iona. I'm sure. You're right, they're great people, and I'm less worried about you than I was because you're really close to them, so you'll have lots of contact with the child and you'll be able to see the huge difference it'll make to their lives. They were adamant about that, about wanting you to be a big part of the child's life, and that takes away a lot of my concerns. So, yes, I am sure, not only for you or me, but for the child, too. They'll be the perfect family. I couldn't ask for more than that. So stop worrying, and I'll see you on Saturday evening.'

She was nervous.

Nervous, awkward and a little embarrassed, for him as much as for herself. She packed a few things—including, for no good reason, a pretty raspberry pink silk nightie with shoestring straps and little lace inserts. She'd never worn it, but for some reason it seemed appropriate, and it would be the only touch of romance in a soulless clinical procedure, so she threw it into the bag, zipped it up and headed over to his.

He opened the door before she was out of the car, and she met his eyes through the windscreen and felt a flicker of panic. Not doubt, it wasn't that, she'd never doubted for a minute that this was the right thing to do, but getting through the next hour or two might be a bit of a challenge.

She got out of the car, locked it and headed towards him, trying to smile. 'Hi.'

'Hi,' he said, his voice soft and low and slightly gravelly. 'You OK?'

'Yes, I'm fine,' she lied. 'Something smells good.'

'I made lamb shanks. They've been in the slow cooker for hours, they'll be ready soon. Do you want to put your bag upstairs and settle in? I've put you in the room you had before.'

Her heart thumped a little, and she nodded. 'Thanks. I'll do that now.'

She ran upstairs, opened the door and paused. He'd closed the curtains and turned on the bedside lights, bathing the room in a soft, golden glow. He'd even changed the bedding, although she'd only slept in it for one night. She put her bag down, then sat on the edge of the bed and ran her hand absently over the soft cotton. So this was where it would happen, the thing that hopefully would change Isla and Steve's lives and give them what they wanted more than anything in the world.

Fingers crossed.

She could hear music playing downstairs, soft and relaxing, and she went down again and found him in the kitchen. He turned and smiled at her.

'Glass of wine?'

'Oh—that would be lovely,' she said, and he handed her a glass.

'Try that. It's a nice smooth Rioja. Or if you don't like it, I've got others, but I thought it would go well with the lamb.'

She sipped, nodded and smiled. 'That's really nice.'

'Good. Come on, let's go and sit down and chill for a minute before we eat. There's no rush.'

There were crisps in a bowl on the coffee table, and she scooped up a few, kicked off her shoes and settled into a corner of the sofa with her legs curled under her. 'So are you going to give me the third degree again?' she asked after a silence that stretched out too long for her comfort, and he laughed.

'No, Iona, I'm not going to give you the third degree. I've told you I'm fine with it. This is your decision, you've obviously all thought it through carefully and sensibly, and I'm just here to provide the means.'

'That's a big "just",' she pointed out, and his eyes softened in another smile.

'Let's face it, you're the one who's got the tough job. I'm just going to have a couple of minutes of fun.'

She felt a faint brush of colour sweep over her face, and she dropped her eyes and twiddled her wine glass between her fingers for a moment. 'It's more than that— much more. I know you had huge reservations about doing this again—'

'I'm over them. This is different, and I'm sure Isla and Steve will be amazing parents. I have no reservations about that at all. My only concern is you—'

'Joe, I'm fine—'

'Right now you are, but I want you to know that you can always talk to me about it, whenever you need to, day or night, and if you need any help while you're pregnant, if it happens, then I'll be here for you. You won't be alone.'

She felt her eyes fill, and swallowed. 'Thank you,' she said, her voice little more than a whisper. Not because she felt she'd need help, but because he'd offered it unsolicited when he really hadn't needed to.

A beeping noise sounded from the kitchen, and he went through, telling her to stay where she was, but she was restless, so she uncurled herself and got to her feet, studying the books on the bookshelf, the CDs and DVDs in the rack, the photographs she'd never looked at before.

His parents, she realised, seeing a man in a wheelchair with a woman leaning over the back of it and laughing down at him. They looked the picture of happiness, but she knew that that happiness was the bedrock of a marriage that had been tried to its limit.

There was another photo, the woman looking strikingly similar to his father, and to Joe. His aunt? The man beside her was tall and gaunt and unsmiling, but his arm was curled protectively around her and she was leaning into him with a contented smile on her face.

What a contrast his own marriage had been. It must have been such a shock to discover that not everyone was so happy, so committed, so much in love. She knew exactly how that felt...

'Ready when you are,' he said, sticking his head round the door, and then he saw what she was looking at and came over to her. 'My parents, Bill and Mary, and my aunt and uncle, Elizabeth and Owen.'

'I'd worked that out.'

'Had you, Sherlock?'

'I had. It took some deduction, but it was the strong family resemblance that gave me the clue.' She smiled up at him, and he laughed softly and steered her out of the sitting room into the kitchen.

The food was delicious, the lamb meltingly tender, the rainbow of vegetables clean and fresh, a perfect foil for the rich sauce. He'd served it on a bed of crushed baby potatoes drizzled in olive oil, and she ate every bite.

'That was amazing. You're a really good cook—or else

you got it from the pub and reheated it,' she teased, and he laughed despairingly and rolled his eyes.

'Oh, ye of little faith. I cooked it from scratch, I'll have you know. I am housetrained. It's Elizabeth's recipe. She's the one who taught me to cook.'

'Your aunt, not your mother?'

He nodded. 'My mother was too busy looking after my father then, so I spent a lot of time here with my aunt and uncle while I was growing up, and it was a happy time. There's a playground on the other side of the stream that runs down the side, and my uncle made a little makeshift bridge over it so I could go there. I spent hours there, either on my own or playing with the other children in the village.'

'Is that why you took the job in Yoxburgh? So you could come back to the place where you'd been so happy?'

He nodded again, thoughtfully this time. 'Yes—I suppose it was. I wanted to be near for her anyway, but I have very fond memories of my time here, and it was a no-brainer when the job came up at the right time. And I might even get a consultancy if they expand the department.'

'When will you finish all your exams?'

'By next summer, and then I'll be looking for a post, but fingers crossed I get one near enough so I can still see her regularly. If it wasn't for her it wouldn't matter where I went, but I think it comforts her to know I'm near so I don't want to go far. My parents are younger and they've got each other, but since Owen died she's been alone and I think she finds losing her independence difficult, too. And she likes the intellectual stimulation of discussing medical issues with me—says it keeps her brain on its toes. Whatever, she's always pleased to see me.'

'I'm sure she is. I'd love to meet her. She sounds a wonderful woman.'

'She is. She was a GP before women doctors were the norm, and she had to fight hard to get where she did. But I'm not sure I'm going to introduce you. She knows way too much about me and I have no doubt she'd be more than happy to share. Pudding?'

'You've got pudding? I'm stuffed!' she said regretfully.

'That's a shame. I've made chocolate mousse, and I've picked the last fresh raspberries from the garden.'

'Ooh. Well, in that case it would be rude not to...'

And then finally there was nothing else to talk about, nothing more to do but face the reason they were there together.

He put his glass down on the table, met her eyes and smiled gently, as if he understood how she was feeling. 'Why don't you go upstairs and have a nice hot shower and get ready?' he said softly, and she nodded and went up, unpacked her bag and took out the little pot and the syringe she'd bought in readiness. Then she found her wash things and went into the bathroom.

There was a clean towel on the side of the bath, and she locked the door—crazy, really, because there was no way he'd come in—then stripped off, twisted her hair up out of the way and stepped under the steaming water.

For a long moment she just stood there letting it wash over her, and then slowly, as if she was preparing herself for some fertility ritual, she reached for the shower gel and lathered herself carefully, paying attention to every square inch of her body, readying herself for the momentous thing she was about to do.

It seemed curiously important that she should do this

right, should prepare herself, body and mind, as if it would make her body more receptive.

She knew she was ovulating. She'd felt a tugging pain low down on the left earlier that day, so her body was ready.

All she needed now was Joe…

She stepped out of the shower onto the thick, fluffy bathmat and wrapped herself in the towel. Egyptian cotton? Probably. He liked the good things in life.

Then she gathered up her things, went back to the bedroom and dried herself, then slipped on the hopelessly romantic silk nightie that she'd never worn before, stifling a pang of regret that he wouldn't see her in it, that they wouldn't do this thing the way her heart and her body were crying out to do it. There was a fluffy towelling robe on the back of the door and she put it on and belted it firmly over the nightie, took a steadying breath and opened the door.

CHAPTER SIX

HE'D SHOWERED DOWNSTAIRS, towel-dried his hair and pulled on clean lounge pants and a T-shirt, and now he was waiting.

How was she feeling?

Weird, probably. He certainly felt weird. This was so different to doing it anonymously in a clinic, but he'd just have to shut his mind to all the tumbling thoughts and do the job.

He glanced down at his body. 'You'd better co-operate,' he told it, and then he heard her door open and her voice calling him.

He took a deep breath, let it out slowly and walked out of his room.

She was perched on the edge of the bed wrapped in the robe, but he could see a sliver of thigh at the hem and in the gaping neck he could make out a flimsy bit of dark pink silk and lace above a shadowed cleavage, and his body leapt to life. Well, that would make things easier, he thought wryly, but she wasn't looking at him, just sitting there on the edge of the bed staring at the floor, and beside her on the bedside table was a little pot and a syringe.

He swallowed. 'Are you OK?'

She nodded, but she didn't look up and he wondered

if she was embarrassed. Or if she'd changed her mind about him?

He dropped down onto his haunches in front of her and put his hands on her knees over the robe. 'What's wrong? Is it still making you shudder?'

'No. No, it's nothing. It just—it all seems a little soulless, that's all. I know it's stupid because it couldn't possibly know, but—it just seems such a clinical and loveless way to make a baby…'

She glanced at the pot, then away again, and he put a finger under her chin and lifted her head gently until he could see her eyes.

They were soft and luminous in the light from the lamp, shimmering with unshed tears.

'It isn't loveless,' he said softly. 'You're doing this out of love for your sister and your brother-in-law. Just think of that, of them.'

She swallowed and nodded. 'Yes. Yes, you're right, I'm only being silly, but it just seems so cold—'

She broke off, took a deep breath and looked him in the eye. 'Go on, then. Go and do your stuff. I'll be all right.'

He picked up the pot and straightened up, then glanced back at her. She was hugging herself, her arms wrapped tightly round her waist as if she was holding herself together, and he replaced the pot, sat down beside her and put his arm round her.

She was as taut as a bowstring, and he shook his head and dropped a kiss on her hair.

'Hey, Iona, it's OK. We don't have to do this if you're not sure.'

'I am,' she said, her voice small and clogged with tears. 'I'm just being ridiculous.'

'It's not ridiculous, it's a huge step. Or is it me? Am I the problem?'

She looked up at him again, her eyes like windows. 'No—no, it's not you. Definitely not you.' She sighed wistfully and looked away. 'I always used to dream of falling in love and getting married and having babies, and I don't ever seem to have got past the first one, and maybe there's a bit of me that wants to do this for them because like you it might be my only chance to have a baby. And at least I won't have to change nappies.'

She was laughing at that, but it was such a sad little laugh it tore him in two, because he'd had the same dream of happy-ever-after once, and Natalie had snatched it from him and turned it into a nightmare.

'I can understand that,' he said. 'I had that dream, and it was destroyed. It's like she took my innocence and burnt it alive in front of my eyes and left me unable to trust or love anyone.'

She looked up at that, reached up, cradled his jaw with her hand, a little frown creasing her brow. 'I'm so sorry she hurt you.' Her fingers were icy, and he realised she was shivering, although it wasn't cold. He turned his head a fraction, pressed his lips into her palm.

'Let's go downstairs and talk about it, hmm?'

'No. No, Joe, I want to do this now,' she said, her voice much firmer. 'I'm just being a drama queen, but you're right, I'm doing it for love, and it's not as if the baby's going to notice how it gets there, is it?'

He looked at the pot, looked at her determined but wistful face, and threw his sanity out of the window.

'There is an easier way,' he said softly, and she turned and looked up at him, her eyes confused as they searched his.

'Easier—?' And then her eyes widened, her lips parted, her soft gasp barely audible. 'You'd do that?'

'Why not? I'm not in a relationship, neither are you, and neither of us has any reason to want one at this time in our lives, but that doesn't mean we aren't still normal, healthy adults, and there's no way I'm going to deny that I want you, Iona. I have done, right from day one. You're beautiful, in every way, so, yes, I'd do that, without hesitation. So long as you don't expect anything else from me, and so long as you don't do anything crazy like imagine you're in love with me, then I'm more than happy to have a no-strings affair with you.

'But you do need to understand the rules. This isn't happy-ever-after, Iona. This is just what it is, an honest, straightforward physical relationship between two like-minded people, and if it leads to a baby for your sister, that's good. If it doesn't, I'm still happy, but it's not for ever and you need to know that up front. I'm not and I never will be again in the market for happy-ever-after, so it's entirely your call.'

She searched his eyes, felt a shiver of need run through her and her breath caught in her throat.

'OK. And—yes.'

'Are you absolutely sure?'

She nodded. 'I'm sure.'

He stood up, pulled her to her feet and cupped her shoulders in his hands, staring down into her eyes. He must have seen what he was looking for, because he lowered his head—slowly, as if he was giving her time to back away—and then she went up on tiptoe and closed the gap.

Her mouth met his and it felt—hot. So hot, soft yet

firm, and hungry. So hungry. Flames shot through her and she parted her lips for him, her tongue meeting his and searching, exploring the taste and feel of him as he kissed her back.

Mint, cool and clean, contrasting with the heat of his tongue, the warmth of his hands on her back. He slid one down, cradled her bottom and she tasted his groan as he lifted her against him.

She felt the hard ridge of his erection, the tautness of his spine beneath her hands, the softness of his hair as she threaded her fingers into it and pulled his head down towards her. He hadn't shaved, and she felt the slight rasp of his beard against her skin, the sensation sending fire dancing through her veins.

He eased away, sliding the gown off her shoulders. She heard the sharp hiss of his indrawn breath, then his hands traced her body through the silk and lace, the heat of his palms setting fire to her everywhere they touched.

'I want you,' he breathed, his lips leaving hers, teasing her throat, his breath drifting hot and urgent over her skin.

His hands cupped her bottom and he rocked against her, making her gasp and clench her legs together against the sudden blizzard of sensations. She'd never felt—

'You're shivering,' he said, and letting go of her he flicked back the covers. 'Get into bed, you're freezing,' he said, his voice gruff, and she lay down, staring up at him, seeing the need raw in his eyes as he stripped off his clothes and rested one knee on the edge of the bed, his body taut and proud, aroused.

Her heart pounded, her breathing short and tight, and then he reached out a hand and ran it lightly over her breast, and she thought her heart would stop.

The nipple peaked instantly under the silk and his eyes darkened, the ice turning to fire. 'You're beautiful, do you know that? So beautiful,' he said rawly, and then he was there beside her, wrapping the covers over them and reaching for her again.

His mouth found hers, then moved on, trailing fire over her throat, her collar bones, down between her breasts. He turned his head a fraction, caught her nipple between his lips, flicked it with his tongue through the fine silk and then blew on it, cooling it again.

A shudder ran through her and her hands plucked at him, running over his hot, smooth skin, down his back, up again and round, her fingers trailing over his hip, down, across a board-flat abdomen, finding their target.

He gave a shuddering groan as her fingers closed around the hot, straining shaft of his erection, and his hand found the edge of lace and slid under it, his hot palm flat against the bowl of her pelvis. She rocked, arching up towards him, and his hand moved down, one knee nudging her legs apart to give his skilful fingers access.

She should have known. She'd seen how sensitive his fingers were, almost instinctive, and his touch was unerring as he gently explored the delicate folds. How did he know how to touch her, to turn her body into liquid fire? 'Joe—!'

'Shh. I'm here. I've got you,' he breathed, and then his mouth found hers again and he moved over her, their bodies merging into one. She could feel his heart beat against her chest, breathed his air as he held his face just over hers, their eyes locked as he started to move, picking up the rhythm of the silent drumbeat of their bodies.

She felt the beat quicken, felt his instant response, the driving, thrusting urgency of his movement as his body surged against hers over and over again as she rose to meet him, and then he found her mouth again, his teeth nipping gently, his tongue thrusting, faster and faster as her body exploded into a million shards of light.

She felt him stiffen, felt the deep, pulsing shudder of his climax, felt the groan torn from deep inside his chest, his head dropping against her shoulder. His body went limp for a moment as he caught his breath, and then he propped himself up on his elbows and stared down into her eyes.

He looked as shocked as she felt, stunned by the force of what they'd unleashed, but then he lowered his head and touched a gentle kiss to her mouth before rolling to his side and gathering her tenderly into his arms, while the aftershocks rolled through them and their hearts slowed.

'Wow,' he murmured softly, brushing a hand lightly over her hair and sifting the fine, silky strands through his fingers. 'Where did that come from?'

'I don't know, but I'm not complaining.'

Her voice sounded stunned, and he chuckled. 'Me neither,' he murmured, hugging her closer and trying to work out what had happened.

And then she laughed a little unsteadily. 'I know one thing, if I am pregnant it's a good job the baby won't know how it got there,' she said, and his gut clenched.

The baby. He'd forgotten about the baby.

He'd started out with the best intentions, but then somewhere along the line he'd forgotten why they were doing it, what it was all about, and concentrated on wringing every last ounce of exquisite pleasure out of it for both of them.

Well, he'd certainly done that, and whatever else it might have been, it certainly hadn't been soulless.

'I think maybe some things are best left unsaid,' he told her, his voice sounding rusty, and then sucked in his breath as another shockwave rippled through his body. He felt blindsided, totally confused. He'd never felt like this in his life, so right, so connected, so—perfectly in tune. And it had come out of nowhere, just when he'd committed himself to looking after her.

And it was too late to change his mind, too late to re-alise that making love to her was a big mistake. Because it had felt like making love, not having sex, and if it hadn't been for his commitment to her he would have run a mile.

But he couldn't do that, because he'd made her a prom-ise, and he didn't break his promises. There was no way he could walk away from her, not now, and he realised he didn't really want to. He wanted to stay with her, see her through her pregnancy, if there was one, enjoy the next few months, and then move on as planned.

They could still have the relationship he'd outlined to her, based on a mutual understanding, and then when the time was right they'd both move on, her to handing over the baby if there was one and getting her life back on track, him to furthering his career.

But he knew, in his heart of hearts, that she would be a hard act to follow, and suddenly nine months didn't seem anything like long enough.

Better make the most of it…

She stirred, waking slowly from a heavy sleep, and then blinked, confused for a moment until it all came back to her.

The room was in semi-darkness, the only light coming from the landing through the slightly open door. Joe must have turned off the lights, she realised, and reached for him, only to find he'd gone.

Gone some time ago, as well, if the cool sheets were anything to go by, and she felt oddly bereft. Stupid, really. It was only sex, he'd made that clear enough, and the only reason she was there at all was because he'd offered to help her sister.

She had no hold over him, no rights to any expectations, and she knew that. She'd agreed to it, but it hadn't taken her long to work out how little her promise to him had registered with her heart.

Where was he? Not her business, but she needed the bathroom. Maybe that was where he was?

She lay there for a while, but the house was silent, and she turned on the light and rummaged for her phone.

Four thirty-eight. Had he woken and gone back to his own room? She slipped out of bed, pulled on the robe and crept out of the door, trying not to disturb him, but his bedroom door was open, the bed untouched. And the light was on in the hall below.

She used the bathroom and then went downstairs, followed the light and found him in his study, sitting on the sofa with the laptop on his lap and a mug in his hand. He'd pulled his clothes back on, but his feet were bare and curiously sexy, and she felt a little awkward. Was she supposed to feel that? Or was she out of line, following him down here to see what he was doing? Maybe he hadn't wanted her to. Was that what he'd meant by not getting any ideas? She didn't have a clue.

She hovered there in the doorway for a moment, not knowing what to say and wondering if she should quietly slip back upstairs and pretend she hadn't been down, but he looked up and met her eyes a little warily.

'Hi. You OK?'

She nodded. 'I wondered where you were. I might have known you'd be working. Is the kettle still hot?'

'I doubt it. Do you want tea?'

'I can make it,' she said, and he held the mug out to her. 'Is that "Please can I have another one"?' she asked lightly, going over to take it, and he grinned and put the mug down and caught her hand.

'It could be,' he said, closing his laptop. 'Or we could get a glass of water and go back up to bed, which is my preferred option.'

She felt the tension go out of her like a punctured balloon, and he pulled her onto his lap so that she straddled him, threaded his fingers through her hair and drew her head down so he could kiss her. She felt his body change instantly, felt hers responding, then without warning he stood up, cradling her bottom in his hands, and carried her upstairs to bed.

'Right, where were we?' he asked gruffly, sitting down on the bed. She was still straddling him, the contact intimate and yet not—until his hands slid up under the gown, under the nightie, shifting her as he tugged down his trousers. Then he settled her back down and rocked against her, just gently, just enough to drive her wild.

He shifted again, his fingers—those clever, wicked fingers—stroking, searching until she thought she was going to die if he made her wait another second—

And then he was there, filling her, making her gasp and fall forward, her hair tumbling across his chest as he lay back and tunnelled his fingers through it, tilted her face and kissed her.

So much for her doubts, she thought, and then felt herself tighten, felt sensation crashing through her as he rolled her onto her back and drove into her one last time, and then she lost all coherent thought...

They woke up starving, and he showered quickly and went down to start breakfast while she followed him through the bathroom.

It seemed a lifetime ago that she'd showered in there, in preparation for what had turned out to be the most amazing night of her life. She smiled and hummed to herself as she washed, a little part of her wondering if deep within her body a tiny life was starting.

No. It would be too soon—wouldn't it? Better not to think about it yet. She'd done that before and it hadn't worked.

She turned off the water, towelled herself quickly dry, pulled on her jeans and a light sweater and ran downstairs in bare feet.

'Perfect timing. Veranda?'

'Lovely. I'll get socks,' she said, and ran back up to get them. She put her trainers on, too, and threw her things back into her bag and took it down with her, dumping it by the front door.

'Right, breakfast,' she said, going out onto the veranda, and he touched his finger to his lips and pointed down the garden.

A small deer was there, nuzzling the ground under the sweet chestnut tree at the bottom of the garden, and as she took a step forward it lifted its head, turned and vanished into the shrubs.

'Does chestnut stuffing go with venison?' she asked, tucking into a bacon roll, and he chuckled.

'I don't know, but it woke me last night so I might yet find out. That was when I got up, a little after three. I was awake, and—well, there's always work to do.'

'There is—for you, anyway. I'm all packed. I'll eat this and head off, leave you to get on.'

'I won't do much, I need to go to bed at some point. I'm on nights all week, starting tonight, so I'll work in the quiet spells. It's not usually that busy, it's just for covering the out of hours stuff, so it might be fairly useful because I've got an exam at the end of next week.'

'I don't suppose I'll see much of you in the next few days, then,' she said, trying to keep it light and not sound needy, but he shrugged.

'I don't know. I would say if you were going to get pregnant this weekend we've probably done enough, unless you want to wake me up at five,' he murmured with a lazy, wicked twinkle.

Her heart thumped at that reminder of why they were doing this, and although she wanted to say yes, she knew that she had to keep some distance for the sake of her sanity. So she said no. 'I'm tempted, but I think you probably need to concentrate on work and sleep for the rest of the week,' she told him with a smile to soften it.

'Maybe next weekend, then? We'll have to see how it goes. If I haven't got enough work done for the exam, I'll need to study all weekend as well. Want another?' he offered, and she took another bacon roll.

'You make the best bacon butties in the world,' she mumbled round a mouthful, and he chuckled.

'I do, don't I?' he agreed, and sank his teeth into another one.

* * *

She didn't see him again that day, although she was tempted to go back and wake him as he'd suggested, but she thought better of it and it was just as well because it turned out he'd gone and visited his aunt and wouldn't have been there anyway.

And the nights that followed apparently weren't as quiet as he'd hoped, so he ended up having to work all the following weekend.

Did she mind? Yes. Did it matter? No. She had no rights, no claim on his time or attention, and she had no urge to distract him from his work, but she began to get a glimmer of how Natalie might have felt left alone so much.

Not that she was much better. She had study of her own to do over the weekend after a one-day course down in London that Thursday, and apart from sporadic texts and emails they didn't talk.

She caught up with him finally in the ED on Tuesday afternoon of the week of his exam, when she was struggling to get a line into a very sick little girl. She'd been brought in by her anxious parents and not a minute too soon. She was floppy and pale, seriously dehydrated after forty eight hours of gastroenteritis, and Iona couldn't get a line in anywhere.

She'd tried to find a vein, so had Jenny, there wasn't a paediatrician free to come and do it and she was about to call Sam to put an intra-osseous cannula in her tibia when she heard Joe's voice and stuck her head out of the cubicle.

'Joe, have you got a minute?'

'For you, always,' he said softly. 'What's up?'

'Three-year-old girl, Lily, severe gastroenteritis, she's

dehydrated and becoming slightly delirious and I cannot for the life of me find a vein I can get into. I found one and it's blown, Jenny's tried and failed—I don't think it's possible. Can you do an IO for me?'

'Let me have a look. Have you got a very fine cannula in case I can find a vein?'

'Yes, I've got a handful,' she said wryly, and took him in.

'Hi, I'm Joe,' he said to the parents, then crouched down to Lily's level. 'Hi, Lily. My name's Joe. Do you mind if I have a look at you, poppet?'

Her lip wobbled, and he smiled reassuringly. 'It's OK. Don't worry, sweetheart. You just lie there for a minute, I'm not going to hurt you.'

He turned her little hands over, checked the veins, moved down to her elbows, and smiled. 'Got one,' he said softly. 'Right, Lily, I'm going to rub some lovely magic cream on your arm, and then I'm going to put a funny little tube in it to give your body a drink, OK?'

Her lip wobbled again but her mother cuddled her and he smeared on a little local anaesthetic, chatted to them for a moment to give it time to work and then he put a soft tourniquet round her arm, gave the skin a little wipe to remove the cream and before Lily could protest, the line was in, taped down and ready to go.

They left Jenny setting it up and went out into the corridor.

'You're quite good at this vein-finding thing, aren't you?' Iona said with a little twinge of envy.

'You're only jealous,' he teased. 'And, yes, I am good at it but then I need to be. In another world I probably would have been a water diviner,' he added with a grin. 'So how's it going otherwise?'

'OK. Busy. How's the revision going?'

'Oh, don't. It's a nightmare. I'll never pass. There's just so much to know and my head feels as if it's going to burst, but hey. This time on Friday it'll all be over.'

'Are you back on Friday night?' she asked hopefully, but he shook his head.

'No, I won't be home until Sunday, probably early afternoon? I promised my parents I'd go and see them. I've been neglecting them, but I'll leave after breakfast. Stay the night on Sunday?' he added, in a murmur, and she felt a little surge of happiness.

'Yes, that'll be nice.'

'Nice?'

She felt herself colour. 'You know what I mean.'

'I do. I'll look forward to it,' he said softly, and grinning that mischievous grin he sauntered off and she went back to little Lily, trying to suppress her smile.

She shouldn't have done it.

She should have waited until after the weekend, but she hadn't been able to wait. And now there it was, the little white wand, saying 'Not Pregnant'.

Her period wasn't even due yet, not until Saturday, but the tests were good these days and she'd so hoped—

She bit her lips. She'd have to tell Joe, of course, when she saw him. She'd probably know by then for sure anyway, because her period would have started. And maybe he wouldn't want to see her, if she was out of action? Not much fun for him, and he hadn't had a lot of fun of any sort recently. And tomorrow was his exam.

She'd sent him a text wishing him luck, but she hadn't heard back. Too busy, probably.

She threw the wand in the bin, washed her hands and

went back to work, but she felt sick. Pregnant sick? No. Really sick.

Little Lily's bug? She'd had gastroenteritis really badly and would have been shedding viruses all over the place, including on her.

She turned back to the cloakroom, lost her lunch and went home. No point in giving it to anyone else, she thought, but then after a few hours of slight stomach cramps, it all settled down again and she woke up on Friday morning still slightly queasy but feeling much better.

And then, against her better judgement and because she'd bought a two-pack, she did another pregnancy test.

Just in case.

Not Pregnant.

And still queasy. She phoned work, told them she still felt unwell and was advised to stay off for forty eight hours for staff and patient safety, so she tackled her laundry, tidied the flat—long overdue because it had been Libby's turn—changed the sheets and then dug out her notes on the course she'd done the previous week and did some extra study.

And then on Friday night she had a call from Joe.

'Hi. I'm on my way home. My mother's not feeling very well, she's got a horrible cold apparently so they've told me not to come. Fancy coming over? I'll be home in about an hour.'

She closed her eyes, relief flooding her, because she really, really needed him. 'That would be great.'

'Good. Pack a bag, come for the weekend.'

She opened her mouth to tell him, then changed her mind. 'OK. Ring me when you're back, I'll come straight over.'

* * *

She arrived fifteen minutes after he called, and he let her in, took one look at her and frowned. She looked pale, and definitely not her usual bouncy self.

'Hey, what's up?' he asked gently.

'I think I've had a touch of Lily's bug—that little girl? I was sick once and I've felt a bit queasy but nothing much.'

'Yeah, I've been feeling queasy, too. I reckon we've both had a touch of it, but I'm not surprised, she was shedding viruses all over us. Come on, come and sit down and have something to drink. You're probably dehydrated and that won't help the nausea. Electrolyte replacement?'

'Oh, no, it's disgusting. Can I smell toast? Because I'm suddenly ravenous, and tea and toast would be just amazing.'

He laughed. 'I'm glad that's what you fancy, because all there is in the house is the remains of a stale loaf and some out of date milk, but it passed the sniff test. That do you?'

She chuckled. 'Sounds fine to me.'

He made them both tea while she buttered the toast, then they took it through to the sitting room and ate it on the sofa.

'So how was your exam?' she asked.

'Gruelling and very, very hard. I'm sure I will have failed. Still, I can resit.'

'You might have to have another go at getting me pregnant, as well,' she said, and put the toast down, her face crumpling.

Oh, no. He put his arm round her and hugged her

gently against his side. 'Oh, sweetheart. When did you find out?'

'Today. I did a test. I know it's stupid of me, but I did it and it was negative.'

He frowned. 'Isn't it too early to tell?'

She shook her head. 'No. Apparently not, and I've done it twice now. Joe, what if I can't get pregnant? What if I'm like Isla? Then I'll never be able to give her a baby—'

Her face crumpled, and he drew her gently into his arms and cradled her against his chest while she cried. It was so like her that her first thought had been for her sister, not for herself, and his heart ached for her.

'Hey,' he murmured, rocking her gently. 'Come on, it'll be all right.'

'But what if it isn't, Joe? What if I *can't* get pregnant? We're identical twins, so I guess it's possible we have the same body chemistry, if that's the problem, or the same anatomical issues—although she didn't have any, come to that, and—'

'Your period isn't due until tomorrow, is it?'

She shook her head.

'So don't borrow trouble. Pregnancy tests can be wrong. Maybe it's too early.'

'Or maybe I hadn't ovulated after all, maybe that happened later, too late. Or earlier. We only had one night.'

He sighed. 'I know, and that's my fault—'

'It's not your fault, you were busy. And you were pretty dedicated to the task on the Saturday night,' she added with a wobbly smile.

He could have hugged her for that. Well, for that and a whole host of other reasons that he'd rather not analyse, so he stuck the mug back in her hand instead. 'Here. Drink this and finish your toast, and then let's go to bed. I'm shattered, and you look as if you could do with a good night's sleep, too.'

She nodded, drank the tea, finished the toast and then closed her eyes. 'That's better. Thank you.'

'It's OK. Come on, bed for you.'

She wasn't going to argue.

He took her upstairs, undressed her, sent her into the bathroom first and then tucked her into bed.

'I'll be two minutes,' he said, and she snuggled down under his duvet, breathed in the scent of him on the sheets and sighed in disappointment. No scent of him. He must have changed the sheets.

For her? She smiled slightly at her silliness. Why would he do that for her? He was probably just fastidious.

Then he walked back in, stripped, turned off the light and got into bed beside her, folding her into his arms. 'OK?'

She breathed in the scent of him, rested her head on his chest and smiled. 'I am now,' she said softly, and drifted off to sleep in seconds.

CHAPTER SEVEN

SOMETHING WOKE HER.

A noise? It was utterly silent, apart from the soft sound of Joe breathing by her side, but then it came again, a short, sharp bark, and he swore under his breath and she laughed.

'It's not funny. I'm going to kill it one of these nights,' he growled, and she chuckled, knowing it was an empty threat.

'I can't see you as a hunter-gatherer type, somehow,' she murmured, and he rolled towards her, his mouth finding hers in the dark. He was still smiling. She could feel it in the shape of his lips, the creases round his eye as she laid her hand against his face.

But then the smile faded as his lips tasted hers, nibbling, tormenting, moving out along the line of her jaw to that ticklish place below her ear, his warm breath drifting over the skin and making her arch her neck to give him better access. She felt his tongue flick her earlobe, then the cooling as he blew softly on it and then moved on, down, over her throat, pausing in the little hollow where her pulse was beating, to do the same again.

She felt his hands on her body, searching, smoothing, stroking, felt the soft sighs of his breath against her skin as he found something he liked—her hip, the curve of her bottom, the inside of her thigh.

And then he moved on, up over her ribs, cradling her breast with a warm, dry palm, his fingers teasing her nipple. His mouth found the other one, his tongue flicking, and she moaned and arched against him.

'Joe—'

'I'm here.'

'I know. I want…'

'Shh. All in good time.'

She threaded her fingers through his hair, her body writhing as he found endless ways to torment her with those wicked hands that seemed to understand her so well, the mouth that had no boundaries.

She tried to touch him, to reach down between them but he stopped her, his hands taking hers and shackling them loosely above her head as his mouth claimed hers. His knee nudged her legs apart, his thigh moving rhythmically. She could feel the firm jut of his erection on her hip as he rocked against her, feel the pounding of his heart against her own, his breath faster now as he moved over her, freeing her hands at last to touch him as he sank into her and went still.

'Don't move,' he groaned, his body taut, his breath brushing her face as he fought for control, but she couldn't wait, couldn't lie still when she knew all he'd do was torment her more, and she was done with that. She rocked against him, her hands moving urgently down his back, finding his taut, firm buttocks and urging him closer, deeper, beyond reason now.

'Ah, dammit, Iona,' he hissed, half laughing, and then he started to move, thrusting deep into her, all humour gone now, totally focused on wringing every last drop of sensation out of their bodies. She felt her body rising to meet his, the coiled need inside her spiralling tighter and tighter until it shattered and she sobbed his name and took him with her into oblivion...

They spent the weekend together doing nothing but eating, sleeping and making love, and he taught her more about her body than she'd ever known existed.

They showered together, cooked together after his food order was delivered, played chess—he won, of course—and then went back to bed and did it all over again. And again.

And then, early on Sunday afternoon, he sent her home.

'I have to visit my aunt.'

She searched his eyes. 'Can I come?'

She saw humour there, as well as alarm. 'Absolutely not. Not after this weekend.'

'What's so special about this weekend? She won't know if we don't tell her.'

He laughed. 'You reckon? You've got stubble burn on your top lip, you look like the cat that got the cream and the woman's not stupid, so, no. She knows more about me than anyone else on earth, but there are some things that I won't tell even her, and this is one of them.' He was serious now, his voice dropping. 'I don't want her to know—not about this, not about us. She'd only start matchmaking and she's bad enough without encouragement, and neither of us are in this for the long haul, so— no. At least, not today, when a blind man could see what we've been doing. Maybe another time. Perhaps when you're pregnant.'

He kissed her again—to soften the blow? It wasn't a

blow, not really, and she could see where he was coming from, but the word 'pregnant' had stopped her thoughts in their tracks.

'OK. You win,' she said, and gathering her things up, she kissed him goodbye, got into the car and drove to the nearest supermarket, picked up another pregnancy test and went home.

'Hello, darling! You're looking very chipper. What have you been up to?'

'Nothing,' he lied. 'I'm just glad the exam's over.'

'You didn't come yesterday.'

He just stopped the laugh. If she only knew…

'You weren't expecting me because I was supposed to be with my parents, and—anyway, I had things to do, so I thought I'd stick to what we'd arranged.'

'You're an appalling liar. It's Iona, isn't it? You spent the weekend with her.'

'No. I didn't.'

She just smiled. 'Such a pedant. All right, *she* spent the weekend with *you*. I hope you didn't set my house on fire.'

He closed his eyes, groaned in despair and gave up the unequal struggle. 'Look, it's nothing. It's not going to go anywhere, neither of us is looking for happy-ever-after, it's just a bit of fun, so don't get excited. It's not good for your heart.'

'On the contrary. Seeing you happily settled with a decent woman would be very good for my heart.'

'Well, it's not going to be Iona, and it's probably not going to be anyone ever, so you need to find another way to entertain yourself apart from meddling in my love life.'

'So it is love, then?'

Why was she so quick to pick up on the minutiae?

'It's just a euphemism, Elizabeth. And my *sex* life is none of your business. I am, as you pointed out very recently, a grown man. I am allowed my privacy. And, no, we did not set your house on fire,' he added wryly.

She just smiled, patted his knee as if he was five and sat back with a smug expression on her face. 'I knew it the moment I saw you. You look like the cat that got the cream. So how was the exam?'

His phone tinged as he got into the car, and he pulled it out of his pocket and opened the text.

It was from Iona, just one word.

Pregnant.

He stared at it, his emotions in freefall. It was happening. She was going to have a baby, and give it to Isla and Steve.

His baby.

He swallowed, dropped his head back against the head restraint and closed his eyes. *Not his baby. Not, not, not his baby.* Not hers, either, but a gift for Isla. Better remember that.

He started the car, drove home, walked into the house, shut himself in the study and worked until he couldn't see straight. Then, a little after midnight, he ate some toast, went up to bed and found a tangled mess that still carried the scent of her body. He breathed it in, his body roared to life and he stripped the bed, changed the sheets, had a shower and tried again.

Better—until he closed his eyes, and then the memories flooded back anyway. All the things he'd done to her, the things she'd done to him, the things they'd done together right here in his bed. And the shower. And the sitting room. The only room apart from two of the bedrooms that was free from memories was the study, but he'd spent enough time in there in the last two weeks to last him a lifetime, and he wasn't going back there now.

So he lay awake, in the bed where they'd—no. Not made love—had sex. Glorious, extensive, mind-blowing, all-consuming sex. Just as they'd done two weeks ago in the other room, the night he'd apparently made her pregnant.

And he missed her. Missed her body, but also her warmth, her mischievous sense of humour, her gentleness, her kindness.

He was not in love with her! And he wasn't going to be.

Ever.

He didn't reply.

Maybe he hadn't got her text. The signal in the village was a bit patchy. Maybe he was in the study and his phone couldn't pick up the signal there.

Or he didn't know what to say? Was she not meant to have told him?

She phoned Isla, who burst into tears at the news and made her cry as well, then she put the phone on hands free and Steve joined in, and eventually they stopped sniffing and asked questions. When was it due? How was she feeling?

'Early July—it's really, really early days, and you know, it might not happen,' she warned, trying not to let them build their hopes up, but she'd had to tell *some-*

one, and as Joe didn't seem interested, she'd done the next best thing.

They talked some more, and then Isla asked what Joe's reaction had been.

'I haven't spoken to him yet,' she said, not entirely untruthfully, and they seemed happy with that, which got her off the hook, but after she'd hung up she thought about work, about seeing him and maybe having to tell him there, in a public place.

Not that there was any urgency. As she'd told Isla and Steve, it was very early days, but—she wished he'd ring her. Just so she knew he knew, and was OK with it. Too late if he wasn't, but hey. He'd signed up for it, known exactly what he was doing because he'd done it before, for heaven's sake!

Only not like this. Not so intimately, or with so much passion and feeling.

Not in person.

Whatever, there was nothing either of them could do about it now, so there was no point worrying. And he might simply not have picked up the text.

Or decided that since they'd achieved their objective, his job was done and he could step back and forget her?

She had a shower and went to bed because there was nothing more she could do tonight. She'd talk to him tomorrow and get some answers, hopefully before she went crazy.

'Hi.'

She looked up from her coffee—decaf—and searched his eyes warily, not sure what she'd see there. Not a lot, for once. 'Did you get my text yesterday?'

He nodded but then looked away. 'Yes. I'm sorry I didn't reply, I was working. Mind if I sit down?'

She nearly laughed. After what they'd done at the weekend, he had to ask?

'Be my guest.'

He sat down on the other chair at the little table by the café window, stirred his coffee—black, no sugar, hence no need to stir—and then finally met her eyes again. 'So,' he said, his voice so soft she almost had to lipread. 'It happened.'

'Yes, it happened. Isla and Steve are delighted.'

'Good. Does it—change anything?'

Her heart thumped. 'In what way?'

'This…' he gestured between them '…whatever it is.'

'I don't know. I hope not. Not as far as I'm concerned, anyway. One is a—business arrangement. The other, this friends-with-benefits thing—'

'Is strictly pleasure,' he murmured, his voice low and laden with meaning, his eyes smouldering now and easy to read. A smile touched them. 'Good. I was hoping you'd say that.'

She smiled back, feeling her body flood with relief because when he hadn't replied she hadn't known what to think, and she'd been so afraid that she'd lost him. 'Yes. Thank you for the weekend, by the way. It was…' She couldn't find a word to sum it up, so she just shrugged and smiled again.

'Yes, it was, wasn't it?' he said, his answering smile flickering behind the fire in his eyes and telling her everything she needed to know.

'So how was your aunt?' she asked, scrabbling for her sanity.

He rolled his eyes and groaned. 'She took one look

at me and knew. I denied it, but apparently I'm a useless liar.'

'You are.'

He grinned at that. 'Well, it takes one to know one.'

He picked up her glass of water, put a splash of it in his coffee and drained it, then got to his feet. 'Gotta go. Stuff to do.'

'Isn't there always. So—will you call me?'

He nodded. 'Of course. You know where I am in the meantime, if you need me for anything. I meant what I said.'

His eyes were serious now, and she nodded.

'I know. Thank you—for that and for everything. I'm so grateful.' Grateful for what he'd given her—well, Isla and Steve, really—and grateful for his promise to stand by her, even more so because it had been unsolicited. That, more than anything, spoke volumes about him, and as she watched him walk away, she thought what a shame it was that she'd met him after Natalie had destroyed his trust and—how had he put it? Taken his innocence and burned it alive before his eyes? Something like that. Powerful image, and one she could easily identify with. Dan had done much the same to her.

She picked up her cup, took a sip of the tepid coffee and put it down, drank the water instead and headed back to work. She'd slipped out in a quiet moment, but no doubt that had all gone haywire by now. Time to get back to the real world.

Their 'friends with benefits' arrangement, as she'd described it, worked well for the next few weeks.

He didn't ask her to move in, she didn't suggest it. Sometimes she stayed over, sometimes she didn't, and when morning sickness hit—why morning, when it was all day, every day?—she stayed in her flat when she wasn't working and slept and ate carbs like they were going out of fashion.

It was short-lived, and by the time she was ten weeks pregnant, she was starting to feel better, and so instead of hiding out and feeling sorry for herself, whenever they were both free their evenings and weekends were spent curled up in front of the wood burner in the sitting room, reading and talking and binge-watching box sets on catch-up TV.

It was blissful, but a little bit of her had to keep reminding herself that they were only playing happy families and it wasn't for real.

She went home to her parents' for Christmas with Isla and Steve, and on Christmas morning they told their parents that she was pregnant with their baby. Her mother cried. Her father patted her shoulder and frowned, but either way, hers or Isla's, they were going to have a second grandchild. Johnnie and Kate were in Geneva with her parents, but they made a video call and broke the news, and Johnnie was speechless for a moment.

'Wow,' he said after a long pause. 'That's mega, Iona. Are you OK?'

She smiled at him, her little brother worrying about her. 'Yes, I'm fine, it's all good. How are you?'

They chatted for a bit, then she left their parents to speak to him and took herself off to the kitchen to raid the fridge.

'Hey, we're eating soon,' Isla said, following her into the kitchen, but she just laughed.

'Not soon enough. I am seriously short of carbs and

I'm not waiting until the Aga's decided it's warmed up enough to finish the turkey. I've been here before.'

She found the remains of last night's rice pudding and hauled it out. Her mother made the most amazing rice pudding. Only Steve's presence prevented her from sticking her face in the dish and licking it out. She scraped up the last bit, put the enamelled pan on the floor for the dogs to lick and sat back.

'So, I have my twelve-week scan appointment at ten on Wednesday. Can you come?'

Isla sat forward, her face filled with longing. 'Can we?'

'Well, yes, of course. I was expecting you would.'

'Won't you be back at work?'

She nodded. 'Yes, but I'll have time off for the scan.'

And she'd have to tell James, she realised. Or HR. Both, probably. Whether she did or not, it'd be all round the hospital in a flash if she was spotted in the waiting room.

Her phone rang, and she pulled it out of her jeans— new, with stretch to accommodate the carbs—and it was Joe. 'Sorry, I need to take this,' she told them, and went out into the study. 'Hi. Happy Christmas.'

'Happy Christmas. How's it going?'

'OK. We told them. Mum got a bit teary, Dad was just Dad, and Johnnie was shocked, but all in all, OK. How's work?'

'Busy, but not too bad so far. When are you back?'

'I'm working tomorrow night, so I'll leave after breakfast and sleep when I get back, if I can. Then I'm off on Tuesday, the normal rota Wednesday onwards.'

Except for the scan, which she didn't mention. She'd rather do that face to face.

'That's a shame. I'm working tomorrow and Tuesday, so I won't see you until Tuesday evening, if then. Depends when I get away. Oh, I had a great Christmas present, by the way. I passed my exam.'

'Seriously? Well done, you. I thought you were convinced you'd failed?'

'I was. Apparently they set the bar low.'

'Did they say that?'

'No, of course not, but *I* wouldn't have passed me if I'd done the examining.'

She laughed at him. 'You're so hard on yourself. So—maybe see you on Tuesday evening?'

'Yes, hopefully, if I get off in time. Drive carefully.'

'Anybody would think you cared.'

'I do. I don't want to end up embolising your mangled blood vessels after they pick you out of the wreckage,' he said candidly, but there was an underlying thread of what sounded very like affection, and she chuckled.

'I'll try not to ruin your day.'

'ED trauma call, ten minutes.'

Really? She'd been at work eleven hours, and this was the fifth call in the last two. What was wrong with everyone? Why weren't they asleep in their beds at six in the morning?

She went to the desk. 'Do you want me to take this?'

'If you could, please. Elderly lady in a care home. She's had a fall, query fractured neck of femur. Elizabeth Williamson, aged eighty four. I'll get her notes up.'

'Thank you,' she murmured, her mind working. Elizabeth, care home, eighties—and then the ambulance arrived and she was wheeled in and Iona knew without looking at the notes. The paramedic did the handover, and she waited until he'd gone and introduced herself with a smile.

'Hello, my name's Iona, I'm a doctor and I'm going to be looking after you today.'

'So, I finally get to meet the mystery woman,' she murmured, so quietly that only Iona heard. She smiled warmly, a mischievous twinkle in the eyes so like his. 'I'm Joseph's aunt, Elizabeth.' She held out her frail hand, and Iona took it gently.

'I know. The eyes are a bit of a giveaway,' she said with a wry smile. 'I'm very pleased to meet you, too. I've heard so much about you.'

'Oh, dear. I interfere, so I'm sure none of it was good.'

She laughed at that. 'It was. He's very, very fond of you.' She turned to the nurse who was with her, hoping she hadn't heard the conversation. 'Could you please call Dr Baker and tell him his aunt's here?'

'Oh, do you really need to, Iona? He'll only lecture me.'

'I'm sure you can take it. So what happened, then, Dr Williamson? Did you fall?'

'Elizabeth. And, yes, I was in the bathroom, and I just—well, to be honest, I think I must have passed out. I have postural hypotension, so it's quite likely.'

'And how long were you there before you had help?'

'I don't know. Quite a while. Two or three hours?'

She frowned. That was a long time to be on the floor alone. 'OK, let's try and get to the bottom of this, then. Can we get a monitor on please, and do a twelve-lead ECG, and we'll take some blood. You might be a bit anaemic or have an infection.' She reeled off a list for the bloods, turned back to Elizabeth and smiled. 'I think we'll wait for Joe before we order any X-rays. He's bound to have an opinion. I take it you're happy for me to share your medical details with him?'

'Of course. He'd only get it out of me anyway, so you might as well tell him.' She tilted her head on one side. 'You're a very lovely young woman, Iona,' she murmured softly. 'I wish Joe wasn't so set on self-destruct. He could do a lot worse than you—has done, of course, with that dreadful Natalie woman. I wish he'd met you first. You've put a twinkle in his eye and a spring in his step I haven't seen in years.'

'Well, that's as maybe, but we probably shouldn't be talking about him here,' she said with a wry smile. 'Do you mind if I have a look at you, Elizabeth?'

'No, of course I don't. I know you have to do your job.'

She was a mass of bruises. There was a bruise forming already on the point of her hip, where she'd gone down, and she had several others, which was a bit worrying.

'Do you always bruise so easily?' she asked, covering her again, and Elizabeth shrugged.

'Only if I fall.'

'And do you fall often?'

Her smile was wise and tired. 'More often than I should. I feel very tired these days.'

'Well, we'll check all that while we've got you here— Oh, look who it is. That was quick.'

'I was here, the home phoned me. What on earth have you done to yourself?' he asked fondly, stooping to kiss his aunt.

'I fell in the bathroom.'

'Oh, that's such a cliché. I would have expected something a little bit more imaginative from you. So, any injuries?' he asked, turning to Iona, and she could see the worry in his eyes.

'Query neck of femur,' Iona told him. 'Bruising over the left trochanter consistent with a fall on her side, other bruising on the same side and also some older bruising elsewhere. I've ordered a whole raft of bloods, but I haven't ordered any X-rays yet because I know you'll have a better idea than me of what you want.'

He tried to smile. 'You must have read my mind. OK, Elizabeth, can you put any weight on that leg?'

'I haven't tried, but possibly not. It's quite sore.'

'Right, let's get a CT of the pelvis, just in case. I don't want to miss anything, I'd never hear the end of it.'

The CT was clear, to everyone's relief, but the bloods showed she was anaemic. Iona stayed with her past the end of her shift because Joe had to leave, but he came back and she told him about the other falls, out of earshot.

'She hasn't told me about this.'

'No. I'm sure she hasn't. She may not have told the home. I spoke briefly to the lady who came in with her, but she's gone back to the home now. Maybe you need to call them.'

He nodded. 'So what's the plan?'

'They're putting her in a side ward while the geriatrician has a look at the bloods, then he's going to work out what to do and call you. I gave him your number, and he knows you're here.'

'Good. Thank you. Now you need to go home and get some sleep. I'm sure your shift ended ages ago.'

She nodded. 'OK.' She hesitated a moment, then added quietly, 'Isla and Steve are coming down tomorrow morning. I've got my first scan at ten. Do you want to come?'

He shook his head. 'No. Of course not, it's nothing to do with me.'

She smiled her understanding. 'I thought so, but I wanted you to have the option. So I'll see you whenever, then. Probably not tonight if she's kept in.'

He gave a rueful smile. 'Probably not. I hope it all goes well tomorrow. Thanks for looking after Elizabeth.'

The scan was incredible.

She'd seen hundreds of scan photos when she'd done her obstetrics rotation, but this was *her* baby. *Hers and Joe's, so small, so perfect, so incredible. Her baby—*

'Oh, Steve, it's beautiful—look at that little nose!' Isla said, her voice cutting through the dream and turning it to dust.

No. Not her baby, and not Joe's. It was Isla's baby, Isla and Steve's.

She swallowed, turned her face away from the screen and willed it all to be over.

'There we are, all done and it's all looking good. Do you want a photo?'

'Yes—oh, yes, please,' Isla said, and then asked for two.

They went out to collect them from the reception desk, and she straightened her clothes, got off the couch and met the sonographer's curious eyes.

'I'm a surrogate for them. She's my twin sister, so it's sort of her baby.'

She nodded, the curiosity turning to sympathy. 'Take care,' she said gently, and Iona tried to smile, gave up and walked out.

'Here—your photo. Thank you so much for letting us come. That was just amazing.'

She stared at the square white envelope, didn't quite know what to do with it but took it anyway. 'Thanks.

And you're welcome. Right, I need to get back to work. Love you lots.'

She hugged them both and walked away, suddenly conscious of the tiny life growing inside her, and her need to protect it. She'd been dodging Resus recently because of the X-rays, and she knew it was time to tell James.

Not that she had a choice, now, because she hadn't taken her bag and had nowhere to put the envelope, so when she got back and ran into James and Sam in the locker room, they took one look at the envelope, familiar from scans of their own small children, and Sam made an excuse to leave, closing the door behind him.

'Yes,' she said to James, without waiting for his question. 'I'm having a baby—for my sister. It's due on the eighth of July, and I'll work as long as I can, hopefully to my due date, then I'll be back two weeks afterwards.'

James stared at her, slightly open-mouthed, and then shut his mouth, waited until she'd put the envelope in her locker and then ushered her to his office and sat her down.

'Iona, I don't really know what to say.'

She laughed softly. 'You don't have to say anything, James. I don't want any special concessions, I don't want a fuss made, and I'd rather nobody knew about it until they have to.'

'I don't think it's a secret. You've been looking peaky, said you weren't feeling well and making excuses not to work in Resus. It's not that, it's what you said about your sister. So is this an implanted embryo?'

She could have lied, could have said yes, but he'd been so good with her from day one she couldn't bring herself to do it, so she told him the severely edited truth. 'And

I'm not going to take any annual leave,' she added, 'so you won't be short-staffed.'

'I don't care about that, I care about you. If there's anything you need, anything you want, time off without notice, anything—just ask me, OK? And you will take annual leave, and as much maternity leave as you need to. I don't want you getting stressed and exhausted.'

'I don't want any concessions—'

'Tough. And if anyone gives you a hard time, refer them to me.' He stood up, came round the desk, pulled her gently to her feet and gave her a little hug. 'I always knew you were a kind and generous person. I didn't realise you were this brave. For what it's worth, I think what you're doing for your sister is amazing. Now go and find something safe to do, and remember, my door's always open.'

She felt her eyes fill, blinked hard and nodded. 'Thank you.'

He wasted every free minute of the day wondering how the scan had gone, if she'd been all right, how she was dealing with it. She came over in the evening after he'd called her to say he was home, and she walked in and handed him an envelope.

'Here,' she said. 'Just in case you wanted to see it.'

He held it in his fingers like an unexploded bomb, staring at it in horrified fascination. 'How did it go?'

'Fine. Everything looks good. It's due on the eighth of July.'

He dropped the envelope on the hall table like a hot brick and went into the kitchen, desperate to change the subject. 'I made a curry.'

'Not turkey, I hope.'

'No. Not turkey. It's venison.'

'You didn't shoot it!'

He laughed and pulled her into his arms, relenting. 'No, of course I didn't shoot it. I don't have a gun and, anyway, I don't particularly like venison. It's a Goan fish curry, very mild, so it shouldn't give you acid reflux.'

He bent his head and kissed her lingeringly, then let her go, laid the table and dished up.

'I saw James,' she told him. 'He'd worked out weeks ago that I'm pregnant because I was avoiding Resus because of the radiation risk, but I explained the situation and he was brilliant about it.'

He froze. 'Did you tell him I was the donor?' he asked, and she looked horrified.

'No, of course not! I won't tell anyone that. It's nobody's business but ours. This curry's lovely, by the way. Thank you. How's your aunt doing?'

'OK. She's back in the home, on iron supplements. They're going to monitor her. It might be gastric erosion from painkillers, so they've switched her to something gentler on the stomach and put her on omeprazole. She's not happy. She says the painkillers are useless.'

They chatted more about her, then about his plans for the kitchen, his work schedule, but he wasn't really concentrating because out of the corner of his eye he could see the envelope sitting on the hall table, and he didn't know what to do with it.

He should have thrown it out. Should have done something with it—lit the fire with it, anything—because on New Year's Day he took Elizabeth home for a festive lunch, turned his back to hang up their coats, and the first thing she did was pick it up.

'You haven't opened your card,' she said, and before

he could stop her she'd opened the envelope and pulled it out.

'Don't—'

But he was too late. She opened the card, saw the grainy ultrasound photo and gasped softly. 'Joe?'

'Do you have no boundaries?' he asked, snatching it out of her hand and stuffing it back in the envelope without looking at it, and she put her hand over her mouth and her eyes filled.

'It's Iona's, isn't it?' she asked, ignoring his comment.

'No. It's her sister's.'

'But the name said Iona—'

'It's her sister's baby,' he said firmly. 'She's not keeping it.'

'And yours.'

'No!' he denied, and then softened. 'No. It's not *my* baby, Elizabeth, it's not *her* baby, either, and it's definitely not *our* baby. She's having it for Isla, so don't get any ideas and start knitting, because it's not going to happen.'

'Oh, Joseph,' she murmured sadly, and took his hand, a tear trickling down her cheek. 'Dear boy—'

He retrieved his hand. 'I'm not a boy, Elizabeth. I'm a man, and I know my own mind, and I can make decisions for myself. And this was my decision, to do this for her, for them. So don't waste sympathy on me, because I'm fine with it, so's Iona. It's all good.'

'Is it? Then why are you so angry?'

He had no answer for that, at least not one he was prepared to voice, so he led her through to the kitchen, parked her at the table and put the vegetables on to steam while he made the gravy and tried to get his emotions under control.

CHAPTER EIGHT

THE WEATHER CHANGED, growing much colder as winter got into its stride, and Iona thought she felt a cooling in Joe, as well.

The roads were icy, he didn't want her risking an accident, and anyway he had work to do, another course to go on, another exam coming up...

Excuses? It felt like it, but then out of the blue he'd pick her up, take her home, feed her, make love to her as if she was the most precious thing in the world, and then return her to her flat. Even then, he seemed distracted. The only emotion she felt from him was when they were making love, and otherwise he seemed to be trying to distance himself from her.

Or from the baby?

No. She didn't think so, because when he made love to her, he'd caress her bump, lay kisses on it. Was that the action of a man who was trying to distance himself from it? Not that he could avoid it. She was noticeably pregnant now, the small bump above her pelvis appearing at fourteen weeks and continuing to grow. Her waist thickened, her breasts grew heavier, and her scrubs were barely hiding it.

Maybe he was genuinely busy, and concerned for her

on the icy roads? She didn't know, but she needed to, so the next time he phoned and asked if she was free, she drove over to his house an hour earlier than planned and found the house in darkness.

Stupid. He might be anywhere, expecting to pick her up on his way home. Or maybe he was in his study. She rang the doorbell, and the hall light came on and he opened the door.

'Iona? I thought I was picking you up?'

'You were. I thought I'd save you the job.' She went in without waiting for him to ask, and turned to him, meeting his puzzled eyes with determination.

'Is this some kind of test?' she asked him bluntly.

He frowned. 'Test? Is what a test? I don't understand.'

'Leaving me in suspense from day to day, picking me up when it suits you, then dropping me again until the next time you can fit me into your schedule? Is it because you're bored with me, or is it to see if I get bored like Natalie—?'

'No! Iona, no, absolutely not! You're nothing like her and I'm not in the slightest bit bored with you!' He took her hands, unknotting them from each other and wrapping them tightly in his. 'I just need to work and, believe me, I'd far rather not. And it's not that I don't want to see you. I do. I just can't concentrate if you're here, and I *have* to.'

'Why? Why push yourself so hard if you don't want to?'

'Because there's…' He hesitated, clearly torn, then met her eyes again. 'There's a consultancy in the offing, totally unofficial and it may not happen, but my boss wants me for it, and I can't blow this because I want it, too. I want it—need it—so badly I can taste it, but if you're here

I know I won't work because I'll want to be with you, I'll get distracted, and I can't afford to let that happen, not now, not with so much at stake, but that doesn't mean I don't want you. You must know how much I want you, God knows, I can't disguise it, but I have to pass these exams if I'm going to stand a chance of the consultancy if it comes up.'

She felt stupid. Needy, whinging, pathetic—

'I'm sorry. I didn't realise the pressure you were under. Of course you have to work. I'll go—'

'No! No, stay. I was nearly done. Make yourself a drink, let me just finish off what I was doing and then I'll stop.'

'Are you sure?'

He pulled her into his arms and kissed her lingeringly, then let her go, strode down the hall to the study, turned off the light and came back. 'I'm sure. I'm done. It'll still be there tomorrow. Come in the sitting room and talk to me about anything you like except medicine.'

They didn't talk. Not for long. She ended up lying in his arms on the sofa while he kissed her tenderly, his fingers sifting through her hair. 'I've missed you,' she said, and he kissed her again.

'I've missed you, too. The only thing that's getting me through the work is knowing you're there when I come up for air.'

'Which isn't often enough.' She stroked his face. 'You sound exhausted, Joe.'

'I am. I could sleep for a week, but there'll be time for that in the summer, when it's all over.'

It? The work—or the baby? Because by midsummer, the baby would be Isla's… She sucked in a breath. 'So— tell me about this consultancy. Is it a new post?'

He nodded. 'They're trying to get funding. They've raised nearly all the money for the new angio-surgical suite, and my boss is going to be running it, which leaves the IR suite a bit in the lurch.'

'Hence the job.'

'Hence the job. So I need to make sure I'm ready for it. It could be my only chance to work here for years, by which time Elizabeth won't be here any longer and I will have missed my opportunity to spend time with her. And I owe her that time, for all she's done for me.'

She smiled, just so he knew she was teasing. 'So does she see you more than I do?'

He laughed a little ruefully. 'She does, but not for long, and she's *much* less distracting,' he added, trailing a fingertip down her throat and under the V of her jumper to linger tantalisingly in her cleavage.

'What about your parents?' she asked, retrieving his hand. 'Don't you owe them?'

He sighed. 'I guess, but they're younger, they've got each other, so there's time for them later. And this...' He shifted, dropped a slow, lingering kiss in her cleavage and disentangled himself from her. 'I need to go and cook. Or we could go to the pub.'

'Or I could cook and you could go and finish whatever you were doing.'

He searched her eyes. 'Don't you mind?' he asked, and she had to laugh.

'No, silly. I don't mind at all. Go and do it, and I'll investigate the fridge.'

It set a new pattern, one in which she took care of him instead of the other way round. She kept out of his way for most of the week and then when it fitted with their shifts, she went to him, taking food already prepared so he didn't have to do it, and they spent the night together, talking, eating, making love.

And then one day in February, she felt something— a tiny flutter? It could have been anything, a movement of her gut, a muscle twitch—but then the next day she felt it again, stronger, so that if she laid her hand over it, she could feel the faintest movement under her palm.

Her baby was moving.

She felt a surge of joy, and then reined it back. Not her baby, Isla's baby. And in less than two weeks, they'd be coming down for the twenty-week anomaly scan.

Except they didn't. Isla had had been ill with a tummy bug in early January, and she phoned the day before the scan and said she still wasn't right and couldn't face the long journey from Northampton to Yoxburgh, so she'd made an appointment to see the doctor.

'You should have told me you were still ill,' she told Isla with a pang of guilt. 'It's been weeks since that bug, you shouldn't still be feeling funny, so I'm glad you're getting it checked out.'

'But I'll miss the scan, and I was so excited. I'm really sorry.'

'Don't be sorry. You take care, let me know what they say, and don't worry about not being here, it doesn't matter. I'll get you photos. You just get well.'

She put the phone down and smoothed her hand absently over her bump. It was a shame they couldn't make it, but the most important thing was that Isla went to the doctor and found out what was wrong.

She thought of all the things it could be. Hepatitis of some sort? Pancreatitis? A food intolerance, like dairy?

That could happen after a tummy bug, so when she got to Joe's that evening she ran it by him.

'That's unusual,' he said, frowning slightly. 'Did you tell her to get it checked out?'

'She's already got an appointment with the doctor. Joe, what if something's really wrong?'

'It won't be. Lots of gastric bugs can trash you for weeks,' he said firmly, wrapping his arms round her and holding her close, rocking her against his chest. 'It'll be something simple like a lactose intolerance after the bug. Don't worry.'

'I know you're right, but I can't help worrying. And they're going to miss the scan. She sounded gutted about that.'

'Do you need me to come with you?' he said after a beat.

Need? Or want? He sounded reluctant, and as far as she knew he hadn't even looked at the first scan photo. The envelope was still lying on the hall table, gathering dust.

'No, I'll be fine—unless you want to come? You're welcome.'

Very welcome, and for a second she thought he hesitated, but then he shook his head and she knew she'd imagined it.

'No, I'll be busy, you know what it's like. There's a lot of elective stuff tomorrow, as well, so it'll be like a production line. What time is it?'

'Ten thirty.'

'No. That's right in the middle of it. Sorry.'

Was that a tinge of regret in his voice? Could be. Or just her imagination. She buried her needy side and moved out of his arms, smiling up at him as she cradled his jaw and went up on tiptoe to kiss him. 'Don't worry. So, what's for supper? I'm ravenous.'

He spent all day trying not to think about Iona and her scan, but the day was hell on wheels as he'd expected and of course nothing was easy, things went wrong— one patient arrested, another had such tight kinks in the radial artery he had to start again using the femoral artery, someone else reacted to the contrast medium and almost died—and just when he thought it couldn't get any worse, he had a call from Iona and her voice sounded odd.

'Are you going to be long?'

'No. I'm done—why?'

'We need to talk. Can you come to mine?'

His heart thudded against his chest. Was it Isla? The baby? 'I'm on my way.' He ran to his car, drove to hers and rang the doorbell, and she came straight down, her face ashen.

'Right, let's get you home,' he said, slinging an arm around her and holding her close, and he led her to his car, drove her home, took her into the kitchen and sat her down. 'Right, talk to me, Iona. Tell me what's wrong. Is it the baby? Did they find something on the scan?'

She closed her eyes briefly, shook her head, and his heart speeded up.

'Is it Isla, then? Have they found something?'

She nodded, and gave what could have been a strangled laugh, but it was more of a sob.

'She's…' Her voice trailed off, but then she tried again. 'She's pregnant.'

The blood drained from his head. *What?*

'I know. I've spent all day convincing myself she's got

something awful, and it turns out she's pregnant, and I don't know whether to laugh or cry.'

He stared at her, stunned. 'That's impossible. I don't understand. How can she be pregnant?'

Iona shrugged. 'I don't know, but apparently she is.'

He stood up, his legs shaking, and put the kettle on, stuck a carton of soup in the microwave while the kettle boiled, and then made them tea, plonking it down on the table in front of her and dropping back into his chair.

'So, what exactly did she say?'

She ignored the tea, using it as a hand warmer instead. 'She's thirteen weeks, give or take. She had no idea. She had a period, a bit light, a bit late, which she thought was odd, and then she got this horrible gastric bug which she thought was definitely a bug because she had diarrhoea, too, but she didn't get better. And she started to worry, so she went to the doctor today, which is why she couldn't come down, and it was a locum who'd never seen her and didn't know her history, and she said she thought it sounded as if she was pregnant, sent her off to produce a urine sample and it tested positive, but she couldn't hear a heartbeat so because of her history they thought it might be a molar pregnancy and sent her straight to hospital for a scan, and they found a perfectly normal thirteen-week foetus. So she rang me,' she ended, finally coming to a halt and taking a breath.

'So—what happens now? With...' *No, not our.* 'With this baby?'

Her eyes looked dazed. 'I don't know. We didn't talk about our baby, just hers, but she said she didn't know how to tell me. They'd only just found out, and she was a bit stunned. And of course there's no guarantee their baby will survive. She had a miscarriage years ago, with

Steve, but nothing since and they've been trying everything for the last five years, so this is completely unexpected and she's convinced she'll lose it, but—what if she doesn't lose it, Joe?

'What if she goes to term and they don't want our baby? I mean, I know it sounds selfish and obviously I don't want them to lose it, that would be tragic, and I'm overjoyed for them, but neither of us signed up for this. I can't have a baby now, not at this stage in my career. And on the other hand, if they lose theirs and then still want ours, will they be able to love her? Will she be as precious, as loved, as the baby they lost? I don't think so, and I couldn't bear that, and I don't know what to do—'

'There's nothing you need to do,' he said, his heart pounding, because this was his worst nightmare come true, the fact that things had changed when she was already pregnant, and now there was no way back. 'You don't know what's going to happen, whether she's going to lose it or not, but even if they do lose their baby and have this one as planned, it will be precious and of course they'll love it.'

Except there was no 'of course' about it. Yes, they'd love it, but—as much as their own? No. How could they? Would they say they wanted it just as an insurance policy, in case their own baby died? That wasn't why he'd agreed to this, to give Isla and Steve a backup baby! There was no way back, no way out of it, and he had to remind himself it wasn't his mess. Iona was pregnant, she was having a baby for her sister, and his only role in this was support for her. How they'd sort it all between them wasn't his business.

Unless they changed their minds and left Iona literally holding the baby.

Did that make it his business? Did the fact that his baby might not be loved and cherished as it surely deserved—did *that* make it his business? Should he—*could* he—try and make a go of it with Iona? Because for all his denial, this *was* his baby. His own flesh and blood. His...

He filtered the conversation through his head again, and found what he was looking for. 'Did you say "she"?'

She looked up and met his eyes, and they welled with tears. 'Yes. It's a girl,' she said with a hitch in her voice, her free hand curling protectively over her bump. 'Our baby's a girl.'

A girl, a tiny little girl, who might end up with parents who did love her, but not quite as much as they would their own baby. Not nearly as much as he would...

Tears stinging his eyes, he got to his feet, walked to the other end of the kitchen and poured out the soup on autopilot.

'Here. You need to eat this. I'll butter some bread.'

'I don't want it—'

'Tough. You need to eat and so do I. Come on.'

She sat up straighter, arching her back a little as if it was aching, and he stared at the smooth, rounded curve of her abdomen. Their baby was in there. Their daughter...

He sat down abruptly at the table, cajoled Iona into eating, and then when she was done he led her upstairs, tucked her up in bed and headed for the shower.

The water was steaming hot, sluicing over him in a torrent, and he stood under it and let it wash away all the things that didn't matter. By the time he turned it off, the only thing left in his mind was Iona, and she needed him now as she'd never needed him before. The rest he could deal with when he knew what he was dealing with.

He towelled himself roughly dry, gave his hair another rub and got into bed behind her, wrapping himself around her and holding her close. She turned in his arms and he realised she was crying, and it made his chest ache with sadness.

He stroked her hair soothingly, pressing his lips to her wet face. 'It's all right, Iona, I'm here, I've got you, I'm going nowhere. It'll be OK,' he murmured, and he didn't know who he was trying to reassure—her, or himself...

She'd hoped the morning would bring clarity, but it didn't. It brought more worry, more stress, more uncertainty.

And a million 'what ifs'.

'It'll be OK,' he said again, after she'd poured out all her fears and worries all over him in a torrent. 'Just give it time. It'll work itself out.'

His hand cradled her cheek, his mouth finding hers, tenderly at first and then hungrily as she responded. His hand left her face, traced her body, his leg easing between hers as he stroked the taut skin over their baby. And then she felt a movement, and he froze.

'Was that—?'

She nodded, smiling wistfully. 'Yes. I felt it a week or two ago. She's a wriggler.'

'She is,' he said softly, his hand splayed over her bump. He shifted, his breath teasing over her skin as he bent and touched his lips to the place where his hand had been. 'Hello, you,' he murmured, and he sounded odd.

Awestruck?

Maybe. That was how she'd felt, but then she'd always been more ready for this than him. Until now, when she had no idea how it was going to end—

His mouth came back to hers, picking up where he'd left off, but his touch was gentler, more tender. More loving?

* * *

He had to start work before her, so he dropped her off at home en route to the hospital, parked the car and went to IR via the Park Café to pick up breakfast. A cappuccino with an extra shot, an almond croissant, and a banana, to redress the balance.

And while he was walking, he gave himself a stiff talking to. OK, so the baby had kicked and he'd felt it. So? Babies kicked. Any woman who'd ever been pregnant would tell you that. It didn't change anything. It still wasn't his baby, it didn't matter what Isla and Steve did, or what Iona did, come to that. She'd cope. Women did. She'd give her baby up to them, or she'd put her in child care, and go to work, and he'd press on with his life plan. Just a few more months down the line and it would all be over, for him at least, because it wasn't and never had been on his agenda for him to have a family at this point in his life and he wasn't going to be swayed by this sudden kink in life's direction.

Except that he wanted to see it—her. To maintain contact with her, follow her progress, maybe sometimes go to a Nativity play or school sports or something like that.

Things a father would do, he realised with a shock. Things he'd wanted to do for his other children, things he'd been denied, both by the donor process and then by Natalie.

So—did he want to be a father? Was that it?

Absolutely not. He'd get these exams out of the way, finish his training and hopefully get the consultancy. Failing that, he'd look elsewhere.

And the baby, whoever she ended up being parented

by, would be loved, he was sure of that. It just wouldn't be him because, apart from any other consideration, he'd given up that right. And he was shocked at how much it hurt…

CHAPTER NINE

JOE WAS WORKING AGAIN.

Well, still working, really, but the pace seemed to have picked up again. He worked gruelling hours in the hospital as it was, never clocked off on time, and then would go home and work until he couldn't see straight.

Not that he told her this, but she'd seen enough of the pattern, and so she left him to it because she realised how important it was to him that he should succeed. And not just for himself, but so that he could stay near Elizabeth for what time she had left.

If he was simply being driven by that urge to succeed, she would have found it harder to accept, but she knew he wasn't, so she left him alone rather than unloading all her angst on him when he really, really didn't need it.

This was between her and Isla, who still hadn't said what their plans were. March came and went, then April, with the safe arrival of Johnnie and Kate's baby boy, and then in the first week of May Isla phoned her in the middle of her shift to say she'd had a bleed—nothing drastic, but it had triggered more scans, further tests, and Iona knew they were worried something might be wrong and they might lose it. And they still hadn't said what they wanted to do about her baby. They probably hadn't given it any more thought, not yet, not when their own baby's life seemed to hang in the balance.

And Iona found herself willing their little baby to stay safe, to be fine, because that would mean they wouldn't want *her* baby. Which was silly. So silly, because how could she give her anything like the life that they would do? She'd be on her own—how could she ask Joe to help her? That wasn't fair, not what he'd signed up for. And he'd made his attitude to relationships perfectly clear on many occasions.

'Take care,' she said gently. 'And keep in touch, Isla. Let me know how you are. Love you.'

'Love you, too. Iona? Pray for us.'

Pray for them? She hadn't prayed in years, yet she found herself doing it over and over again, a kind of mantra.

Please let it be all right. Please don't let them lose the baby. Please let it be—

'Iona?'

She looked up, blinking away tears, and James steered her into his office and shut the door.

'What's up?'

So she told him, all of it except the bit about Joe, and he listened in silence and then shook his head slowly.

'That's a lot to deal with. Do you need time off?'

'To do what? Sit at home and fret? No, absolutely not. I want to be busy. I don't want to have time to think, because it's pointless until I know what's happening.'

'If it all goes well and they don't want it—'

'Then I'll keep it, which is unfair on the baby, and career suicide, but what else can I do? I can't give her up for adoption, James—'

Her eyes welled, and she swiped the tears away angrily.

Don't cry! Don't give in!

'No, of course you can't, I can see that, but you'll cope, Iona. Women have always coped with this, even chosen it. There are ways, and I'll do everything I can to support you if it comes to that. Starting with you having a year off for maternity leave.'

'But—that would leave you in the lurch, and what do I do then? After a year? What do I do, James? It's not like I can take a staff grade, I'm not qualified.'

'Go into general practice? At least you'd get regular hours and you've worked in all the right fields. Just bear it in mind, and in the meantime go and have a lunch break and come back when you're ready.'

She wanted to hug him, but she made do with a wordless nod of thanks, and went to the Park Café, grabbing a decaf coffee and a sandwich and taking them out in the park.

She'd never thought of being a GP, but—could she? And keep her baby? She felt a leap of hope, and then squashed it, because she still hadn't heard from Isla and it might all change again in an instant.

There was a boy, he couldn't have been more than seven or eight, standing on the other side of the ditch staring at something in his garden. He was looking worried, and as Joe watched, the boy climbed over the fence and onto the rotten bridge that his uncle had made him nearly thirty years ago.

'No, no, no, you'll fall in the nettles,' he muttered. He'd meant to cut them back—meant to do all sorts of things, but between work and the baby business he'd had no time for anything.

He shot his chair back and went outside, reaching the edge of the ditch at the same time as the boy.

He wobbled and would have fallen if Joe hadn't caught him by his T-shirt and hauled him to safety off the rickety bridge.

'Are you OK?' he asked, and the boy nodded, looking worried and a bit scared.

'I didn't mean to disturb you. I was just worried about the squirrel.'

'Squirrel?'

'Yes—it's stuck in the bird feeder. I've been watching it for ages, and it can't get out, so I was going to climb up the tree and help it.'

He shook his head. 'No. They bite. Let's have a look.'

They went round to the other side of the tree to the hugely expensive fat ball feeder that he'd restocked only that morning. Supposedly squirrel proof, only not, apparently, and most of the fat balls seemed to be inside the squirrel. It had worked its way half-out, but was stuck and struggling through a hole that seemed impossibly small.

'Hello, squirrel,' he said softly. 'You're in a bit of a mess, aren't you? It's a good job this young man spotted you. I'm Joe, by the way,' he said, turning back to the boy.

'I'm Oscar. Will you kill it?'

'No, of course not. We'll have to get it out, won't we?'

It took thick gloves, a pair of pliers and some doing, but by the time he'd unhooked the feeder, taken the lid off and dodged the teeth of the hissing, terrified squirrel, it had managed to wriggle its way free and shot off across the lawn and up the oak tree.

He pulled off his gloves, turned to Oscar and gave him a high five. 'Well, done, you. I'm glad you found him. Now I'd better get you home to your mother.'

'She's at work,' he said glumly. 'She works from home, but sometimes she has to go to the office but that's OK, I can look after myself. I've got a key and she's not out for long.'

'Shouldn't you be at school?'

He shook his head. 'No. It's a training day for the teachers.'

He nodded. His aunt had worked part time, too, but he'd gone with her to her surgery and played in the waiting room under the eye of the reception staff when he'd been young. Not everyone had that opportunity. 'Have you got any brothers or sisters?'

'No. Just me.'

And he was lonely, just as Joe had been lonely. He'd spent hours alone in the playground across the ditch, idly kicking a ball around or pretending to be an explorer, and he could see that loneliness in Oscar's eyes. At least he knew his donor children all had siblings. That was one of the fears he'd nurtured needlessly all these years. Except his little daughter, safe inside Iona for now, but what would become of her? Would she go to Isla, or would Iona bring her up as an only child?

His heart squeezed, and he looked down at Oscar and smiled gently.

'I tell you what, it's lunchtime. Why don't we make a sandwich and go and eat it in the playground? And maybe someone will come who you can play with. You can tell them all about the squirrel.'

He went back to work, but the look in Oscar's eyes stayed with him for the rest of the day. Was that what was in store for Iona's baby? To be the only child of a working mother? He couldn't stand back and let that happen, and maybe it wasn't necessary. Maybe—if he could just shelve his doubts and dare to trust himself not to let her down as he had Natalie, to love her and cherish her and care for her as she deserved—they could do this together?

Keep the baby, and maybe have another one further down the line?

Was that too much to hope for? Right then it seemed like an impossible dream, such an outside chance that even the most desperate gambler wouldn't bet on it.

And he didn't believe in miracles.

They wanted it.

Isla and Steve's baby was all right, the bleed had been very minor and was nothing to worry about, just a slightly low placenta, but it was fine, she should go to term, and they'd made the decision to have Iona's baby, too.

'We'll bring them up as twins,' Isla said, her voice filled with enthusiasm. 'It'll be amazing. This baby was such an outside chance, and who knows if I'll ever have another, so twins would be just perfect and we'd never have to worry about having another one or it being an only child. And neither of us wants that. Does that make sense to you? I can't imagine growing up without you there by my side every step of the way, and our babies will have that. It'll be perfect!'

Perfect? Iona waited for the flood of relief, but it didn't come. Instead there was a wrenching feeling of loss, and she had to swallow hard.

'Are you sure? It's a lot to take on, two babies at the same time—and of course they won't really be twins, not like we were. We knew each other long before we were born, and these two won't. They won't even share a birthday, yours will be born after mine.'

Mine? Could she still say that?

'Only a little, just a few weeks, and they'll share everything. He'll soon catch up.'

He...

Her breath caught. 'It's a boy?'

'Yes—yes, we didn't want to find out, really, but they did a 4D scan, a video, and he was wiggling around and it was so clear—he's gorgeous, Iona. It's such a miracle.'

Iona shut her eyes, and a tear squeezed out and ran down her face. She swiped it away. 'It is. It's wonderful. I'm so happy for you.' Another tear, another wipe. 'Look, I'm at work right now. Can I call you later?'

'Yes, of course. I've sent you a picture. He's the image of Steve.'

Oh, lord. She hung up, just as her phone pinged, and she opened the picture. Isla was right. Even as tiny as he was, she could see Steve in him.

Does my baby look like Joe?

'It's not my baby,' she gritted under her breath, and then she heard Joe's voice in the corridor and walked out of the locker room.

'Can we talk?' He searched her face and she avoided his eyes.

'Here?'

She shook her head. 'No. Yours, later?'

He nodded. 'I'll call when I'm finished.'

They wanted the baby, to bring them up as twins.

He waited for the flood of relief, and it didn't come, its place taken by a hollow ache that took his breath away for a moment.

'Are you OK with that?' he asked gruffly, struggling with a lump in his throat.

She shrugged. 'I have to be. What else can I do?'

'Keep it?'

She shook her head. 'No. It would be career suicide. I don't want to be a GP, I want to work in hospital medicine and they're not compatible, not at my level. I'm years from being able to do that.'

He nodded, knowing she was right, knowing it made sense as far as her career was concerned, and at least his fear about the baby being the only child of a working mother was put to bed, but she didn't look convinced.

'So what's wrong, then?' he asked, and she shrugged.

'They won't be twins like we were, she won't be theirs, they won't love her the same as him, they can't…'

He pulled her into his arms, cradling her against his chest. 'They'll nearly be twins, and you were twins. It's better than her being an only child. She won't be lonely.' *Like me. Like Oscar. But would she truly be loved?* 'It'll be fine, Iona,' he said firmly, as much to himself as to her, 'and the baby will be part of you, so how could they fail to love her? Of course they will.'

But not as much as he and Iona would have done. How could they? But it wasn't his business. He'd told himself that over and over again, and although he couldn't have stood by and seen her struggle alone, that wasn't going to happen now, so it was back to what he'd signed up to, giving her a baby for Isla and Steve. That job was done, and it wasn't his job to worry about how they'd cope with two tiny babies at once.

Not my baby, and definitely not our *baby.*

But then the baby kicked him and he dropped his arms and stepped away. 'Are you OK with pizza? I think it's about the only thing left in the freezer—or we could go to the pub.'

Except they hadn't been to the pub since she'd had a bump, and he didn't want to have to explain their complicated arrangement to Maureen.

'Pizza's fine,' she said, to his relief.

'Are you staying over?'

She met his eyes then, for the first time in minutes, and he could see the wariness, the doubt in them.

'Am I welcome?'

'Of course you're welcome,' he said, although it wasn't strictly true. He wasn't sure he could cope with taking her to bed and making love to her, not with three of them in the bed. And the baby was really impossible to ignore now. But he'd missed her.

Missed her company, her sassiness, her warmth. Her body, but that wasn't really his for the taking any longer. It was weeks since he'd touched her, but to touch her was to remind himself over and over of the baby whose fate had seemed so uncertain and insecure. It had been easier to ignore it, but he'd made it harder for Iona and that was wrong of him. She needed his support now more than ever, and he hadn't given it to her.

'Of course you're welcome,' he repeated, his voice softer now. 'Come here.' He held out his arms and she moved into them, resting her head on his chest with a ragged sigh.

'I thought you didn't want me anymore.'

She'd said it lightly, but he felt a stab of guilt and tightened his arms around her, dropping a kiss on her hair. 'Of course I want you. I've just been buried in work. I'm sorry. I didn't mean to neglect you.'

She straightened up and smiled at him, her hand cradling his jaw, her fingers gentle. 'Don't apologise. Just talk to me from time to time, keep me in the loop. I do understand about your work.'

Even if she didn't like it. She didn't say that, but then she didn't need to, and he realised that without the baby she wouldn't have needed to contact him and he could have lost her, driven her away. And he didn't want to lose her. Ever...

Where had that come from?

He sucked in a breath, took a step away from her and opened the freezer door.

Did he really want her? She didn't know, but then after they'd eaten they sat out on the veranda, and he put his arm around her and she rested her head on his chest as they watched the sun set in a cloudless blue sky.

Summer was coming. She only had nine weeks now until her baby was due, and she felt a shiver of dread because that would be the end for her, the last act, the last time she'd have with her baby before she gave her to Isla.

She felt a little shudder go through her, and Joe must have picked it up because he looked down at her. 'You're cold. Let's go to bed.'

It wasn't late—positively early by his standards—but she wasn't going to argue. Her feet ached, the ligaments in her pelvis were starting to soften and bed seemed like a fine idea.

Especially with Joe.

Would he make love to her?

Yes. She knew that as soon as he closed the bedroom door and reached for her, his hands gentle as he undressed her. He frowned slightly but it was touched with a smile, a sort of wonder. 'Your body's changed.'

'Well, it will have done. I'm thirty one weeks now, Joe.'

The smile went, leaving just the frown. 'So soon? Where did it go?'

She laughed at that. 'Joe, you've buried yourself alive for the last few weeks. I've hardly even seen you at work.'

'I know. I'm sorry, I didn't mean to do that, it just sort of happened.'

His hands traced her body, cupping her breasts gently, feeling the weight of them, his thumbs brushing her nipples lightly, making them peak. A tiny bead appeared at the tip of one, and his thumb brushed it away.

'Wow.'

She swallowed. 'I know. I'll have to have drugs to dry up the milk.'

'Oh, Iona.' He drew her into his arms, his hug gentle, and then he let her go, threw back the covers and walked to the door. 'Get into bed. I'll be back in a minute.'

'Where are you going?'

He hesitated, and she suddenly realised what he was doing. Taking care of the need she could see in his eyes.

'Don't,' she whispered, and patted the bed beside her. 'Don't do that. Stay. Make love to me.'

'Really?'

'Really.'

He swallowed, then closed the door again, pulled off his clothes and lay down, drawing the bedclothes over them. 'I don't want to hurt you.'

'You won't hurt me. You've never hurt me.'

She shifted closer, reaching out her hand and cradling his jaw in her palm. She could feel the muscle there working, the clenching of his jaw, and she slid her hand behind his neck and drew his face down to hers, meeting his mouth with a tender kiss. 'Touch me, Joe. I won't break, and I need you. Make love to me.'

* * *

He lay awake long after she'd fallen asleep in his arms.

He'd been gentle, taken it slowly, but even so the passion, the need, had swamped him, culminating in a climax so intense that it had shaken him to his foundations.

Because he loved her.

He blinked away the tears that welled suddenly in his eyes. No. He couldn't love her—and he certainly couldn't tell her. Not now, now her baby was destined for another life that didn't include him.

Or could he? Was it too late to stop her giving the baby away? Could they halt the whole process and keep it? Keep her, their tiny, precious daughter?

No. Not because of Isla, but because of Iona herself. She'd been worried for the child, of course, because that was who and what she was, but she'd said so many times that there was no place for a child in her life now, and not for years. He'd said the same, meant it just as much, but now, faced with this, he knew he'd been wrong.

He wanted this, wanted Iona. Wanted the baby, more than he'd ever known he could want anything, but he couldn't have her. She wasn't his to want or need, and in just a few short weeks she'd be out of his life for ever, barring the odd photograph or Christmas card. Out of Iona's, too, and any dreams he might have cherished of them becoming a family had just gone out of the window.

I can't lose both my girls...

He felt a wave of grief so intense he almost cried out. Maybe he did, because Iona stirred beside him, shifting her body slightly so that her leg lay over his, pinning him down and cutting off any hope of slipping out of bed and escaping to the study to immerse himself in something he could cope with, something he had a hope of influencing.

And so he lay there, and he held her in his arms and tried to imprint the memory on his heart, and eventually she rolled away and he made his escape.

'Have you been here all night?'

He was sprawled on the sofa in the study, his laptop upside down on the floor where it must have landed, and he opened his eyes, blinked, and sat up, stretching stiffly.

'Yeah—maybe. I don't know, I can't remember. Where's my laptop?'

'On the floor.'

He picked it up, swore softly and opened it, then sighed and closed it again.

'It looks all right. It's solid state, so dropping it shouldn't have messed it up.' He scrubbed a hand through his hair and looked at his wrist.

'It's six o'clock. I thought I should wake you. I'm going to go home and get ready for work and you probably need to do the same.' She hesitated, then said, 'Will I see you later?'

His eyes met hers, and she could see a whole world of conflicting emotions in them.

'Don't worry. Just let me know.'

'No. Come. Stay. I'll do a food order.'

She smiled. 'Well, that might be an idea if we aren't going to starve to death. I've left you the last two bits of bread so you can have breakfast.'

She walked over to him and he stood up, put his arms round her and hugged her gently.

'Thanks,' he mumbled through her hair. 'I'm sorry you felt abandoned. I should have realised. I won't let it happen again.'

'Don't be silly. I'm fine. I'll see you later.' She eased

away from him, pressed a kiss to his stubbled cheek and left him to it, wishing she could believe that guilty promise.

She found out she could believe it, and although he was still ridiculously busy, he made time for her whenever he could. They got into a pattern, then, of getting together when their shifts aligned, and the weeks ticked slowly by.

She was getting more awkward, finding work more tiring, but the closer she got to her due date, the less she wanted to stop because then she'd have nothing to do but think about what was to come.

And she didn't want to think about it. Didn't want to think about the time when the baby was gone and she couldn't play happy families with Joe any longer. Couldn't pretend to herself that she was going to bring her baby home to him, to the little room beside his bedroom that would make a perfect nursery.

Couldn't pretend that she'd sit on the veranda rocking the baby to sleep in her pram, or take her for walks along the country lanes, or take her to the playground to explore the sand in the sandpit or crawl over the grass in the garden and discover the smell and the taste and the feel of it beneath her chubby fingers.

That was for Isla to do, Isla and Steve and their little miracle baby.

And she—she had her career to focus on, her future to plan, her life to map out. A life without Joe, without the baby. She could hardly bring herself to think about it, but she didn't have to now.

Not yet. For now she had them both, and she was going to cherish every moment of it.

And then, when she was thirty nine weeks pregnant, everything changed.

CHAPTER TEN

HE'D MISSED A call from Iona, but she'd left a voicemail.

'I've had a show. Call me when you get this.'

He felt his heart kick into overdrive and rang her instantly.

'Where are you?'

'At work, so I can't talk for long. I'm fine, it wasn't much, but I think I'm getting close. I've called Isla and Steve and warned them. They're coming down. I thought they could stay at my flat and I could stay with you. Is that OK? Just until—you know.'

He did know. He knew only too well, and it was all he'd been able to think about for weeks, but at least he'd got the last course out of the way, and he'd sat the final exam a week ago. Anything else could wait because there was no way he could abandon her now.

'Yes, of course it's OK,' he said, although his head was screaming *No!* at the top of its voice, but that was just self-preservation and he ignored it. 'Do you think you should go home now?'

'No, I haven't even had a twinge yet. It could be days. I've told James I'll be on mat leave from the end of today, so I'll finish my shift and go and sort the flat. They won't be down here till this evening, Steve's got a meeting with a client at three and then they'll set off.'

He swallowed. 'OK. Well, ring me if anything changes. I'll be home by six.'

'Are you sure? That's early for you.'

'Yes, I'm sure.' He'd make damn sure, because this wasn't something that could wait. When Iona went into labour, she would have Isla with her and maybe Steve, but not now, while she was waiting. Not yet.

For now, she'd only have him, and he'd have her. What happened after that only time would tell, but he was going to be here for her now if it was the last thing he did.

He went and found his consultant and told him he needed a week off, starting now.

'Now?'

'Yes—well, from six this evening. I'm sorry, I know it's difficult, but—there's something I have to do. Something personal. And it won't happen again.'

His boss searched his eyes, then nodded as if he'd found what he was looking for. 'OK. Well, if you must.'

'I must.'

'Fine. Keep in touch.'

'Of course.'

She wasn't sure how she got through the rest of the day, but when she went off at the end of her shift, it felt surreal.

How could she go off on maternity leave when she wasn't going to be a mother? There should be another word…

Isla and Steve arrived at six thirty, and she let them in, hugged them and gave them keys. 'Libby's away on holiday at the moment so you'll have the place to yourselves and you can come and go whenever you like. There's unrestricted parking on the street, and if you can't find anything, just ring me and I can probably tell you where you might find it. And there's milk and butter in the fridge, and some bread on the side there, and various other bits and pieces. Just help yourselves.'

She hugged them again, kissed Isla goodbye and walked carefully down the stairs. Steve carried her bag down and put it in the car, and hugged her again.

'We're so excited,' he said. 'Our first baby. We can't believe it's actually happening.'

'No, nor can I,' she murmured, dredged up a smile, got awkwardly behind the wheel and drove away before she did something stupid like cry.

Joe was home when she arrived, and she walked through the door and straight into his arms.

'Are you OK?'

She nodded, even though she wasn't. 'Mmm. They're here, in my flat. I've told them to ring if they need me for anything.'

'Where's your bag?'

'In the car.'

'I'll get it. Go and sit down and put your feet up. You look done in.'

Did she? She didn't feel it—didn't feel much of anything, except edgy. But she did as he said, kicking off her shoes and settling down in the corner of the sofa with her feet up. The baby wriggled, settling herself into a better position, and she stroked her lovingly, feeling the curve of the baby's spine, the little bump of her bottom, the jut of her heel.

'It's OK, baby,' she murmured. 'You stay there, you hear me? There's no hurry. You take as long as you like.'

'Cup of tea?'

She looked up and saw Joe standing in the doorway, watching her with a strange expression on his face. And for the first time in ages she couldn't read his eyes.

'That would be lovely. Decaf, please.'

He rolled his eyes and walked into the kitchen. She could see him through the double doors, pottering quietly. Emptying the dishwasher, finding mugs, putting shopping away. He must have done an internet order, she realised, or a lightning trolley-dash.

'I ordered some food, things with longish dates so we don't have to worry about shopping,' he said, coming in with the tea and settling down at the other end of the sofa. 'How are you feeling? Any change?'

She shook her head. 'No, not really. I don't feel any different. I hope it's not a false alarm and Isla and Steve aren't hanging around indefinitely.' Which was a lie, because the longer it was, the longer the baby would be with her, the longer she could pretend...

He picked up his tea and rested his other hand over her feet, stroking them absently. 'How's Isla?'

'Oh, OK, I think. She looks a bit thin. I think pregnancy's been tough on her. She hasn't felt great. It makes me realise I've come off lightly.' Except of course at the end of it Isla would have two babies, and she'd have none...

He was watching her thoughtfully, as if he could see straight through her, and she turned her attention to the tea. 'So what's for supper?' she asked, changing the subject.

'Whatever you fancy. I got a fish pie and some sugar snap peas, or you could have pea and ham risotto, or—'

'Fish pie sounds nice. Does it need long in the oven?'

He shook his head and got to his feet. 'I'll put it in

now. I might as well feed you up while you're not in active labour.'

That again. She felt the baby kick and her hand went instinctively to the bump, soothing her with gentle strokes.

Joe turned on the oven, took the fish pie back out of the fridge and glanced at Iona through the glass doors. She was stroking the baby, and her expression twisted something deep inside him. He'd seen it before, on the faces of women stoically tending their loved ones when all hope was gone. Grief—carefully masked, hidden from everyone except those who knew, every caress a tender farewell.

He rested his hands on the edge of the worktop, dropped his head forward and took several long, slow deep breaths.

He was dreading this. Dreading the moment when she'd tell him that she was in labour, dreading the moment of birth—dreading the moment their child ceased to be theirs, and became someone else's daughter.

Breathe...

He sent her to bed early before it was even dark, and she had a shower and washed and dried her hair, just in case. He followed her up shortly afterwards, and as he got into bed she turned to face him and snuggled up close, resting her top leg over his to ease the ache in her pelvis, her head on his chest, his heart beating steadily under her ear.

'You OK?' he asked, his voice a rumble in his chest.

'Mmm. Just—you know.'

Maybe he did, because his grip tightened and he held her closer. 'Oh, sweetheart. Are you going to be OK?'

She shrugged helplessly. 'I don't know. I don't know how I'll feel when I—you know. Hand her over...'

Her voice cracked and she sucked in a breath, and his lips touched her forehead. 'I'll be there for you. You know that.'

'I do. Thank you. I just wish...'

'Wish?'

'That I'd met you before.'

'Before—?'

'Before Natalie. Before Dan, when we were both bright and shiny and fresh out of the box instead of—I don't know. Tarnished.'

'Tarnished. That's a good word for it.' He let out a long, slow breath, his chest sinking beneath her ear. 'Do you think—?'

'What?'

'No, it's just a crazy dream. Only—when we first found out they were having a baby, I thought maybe we—well, whatever, they're having her so it doesn't matter anymore.'

His voice seemed to break a little on that last word, and she tilted her head and studied his face in the dim light filtering through the blind. His jaw was clenched, his eyes open and staring fixedly at the ceiling, and the light caught a tiny trickle running from the outer corner of his eye.

'Oh, Joe. Do you think we could have made it work? You, me, our baby? Or would I just have held you back?'

'You wouldn't have held me back. Never think that. You've been amazing, this whole hellish year, but I've got there, I've done everything I needed to do, and now I just have to wait—so, no, you wouldn't have held me back. You haven't. And—I don't know, maybe it's still just a crazy dream, but perhaps, when this is all over and we're in a better place, maybe we can give ourselves a chance.'

Could they? Was there really a chance for them when this was done, when their little girl had been handed over and they'd got over the wrenching loss she knew they'd feel—would there be a chance for them?

She squeezed her eyes tight shut. Oh, she hoped so. But in the meantime he was here with her, and so was their baby, and she needed rest. She was exhausted, and the next few days and weeks would be an emotional rollercoaster.

'Go to sleep, my love,' he murmured, as if he'd read her mind.

His hand stroked her back slowly, rhythmically, soothing away her tangled feelings, and feeling safe, cocooned from reality, she drifted off to sleep.

Her phone woke them a few hours later, and he reached over her and picked it up.

'It's Steve,' he said, handing it to her, and her heart started to pound.

'Hi, Steve, what's up?'

'Isla's waters have broken and she's having really strong contractions, so I've called an ambulance,' he said, his voice shaking. 'Can you come to the hospital? I wouldn't ask but we don't know anyone there and it's too soon and—'

'Steve, it's fine, I'm on my way. I'll meet you there. Call me when you arrive and give her my love. It'll be OK.'

She pressed the phone to her chest and turned to Joe, but he was out of bed, getting dressed.

'Did you hear that?'

He nodded. 'Get dressed, I'm coming with you.'

'Are you sure? What about work tomorrow—today, whatever it is?'

'I'm not working the weekend anyway, and I've taken a week off so I could be there for you, and I will, no matter what happens. Come on. It's OK. She'll be all right.'

'You can't know that,' she said, struggling into her underwear. 'What if—?'

'Don't do the what-ifs, Iona. Just deal with it as it comes, hour by hour, day by day.'

She pulled her dress over her head and searched his eyes. 'Is that what you're doing?'

He looked away. 'Yes. I've been doing it for weeks—months. How do you think I got through all the revision and courses?'

He was talking about work. Or was he...?

She found her shoes, wriggled her feet into them and stood up, grabbing her phone off the bed.

'OK, let's go.'

Isla's baby was born half an hour after they arrived at the hospital, weighing a mere three and a half pounds, and he was taken immediately to NICU.

'Go with him,' Isla begged, so Steve went, and Joe went with him, leaving Iona with Isla.

'You'll have to wait until the paediatrician's assessed him,' they were told, so Joe told Steve to go back to Isla.

'I'll call you the minute you can go in,' he promised, and as soon as Steve was gone, he buzzed and they let him in. No point in not pulling rank. He'd see what he could find out...

'How is he?'

'OK.' He sat down beside her, and he looked drained.

'What's wrong? Is there something wrong?'

'No. Not now, but he needed two umbilical lines.'

'And?'

'And the consultant was busy with another baby, the IR was tied up as well and the registrar was struggling and about to put in two peripheral lines instead.'

'So you did it?'

He nodded. 'Well, I have just done a refresher course on venous and arterial access in neonates, and it was only building on what I already know and do all the time, but I was feeling the stress by the end of it. They couldn't measure his blood gases without it, though, or get any drugs into him, so it was pretty critical, but it's so delicate, the tissues are really fragile and he seems so tiny. Still, it was working, so hopefully he'll be all right now. How's Isla?'

'In bits. She hardly had time to hold him before he was whisked away. I don't think she's stopped crying.' She closed her eyes and rested her head against him. 'Is he going to be all right?'

'I hope so. He's small, but he's holding his own at the moment and breathing by himself so it's looking hopeful. And thirty two weeks isn't that young, not in the great scheme of things. How are you?'

His voice was soft, his arm around her shoulders, and she wanted to lean into him and cry, but she didn't. She straightened up and met his eyes. 'I'm shattered. I really need to go back to bed, but I don't like to leave them.'

'They're in good hands, and we won't be far away,' he pointed out, and she nodded.

'Yes, you're right.' She rubbed her arms with her hands, not because she was cold but just—

'Hey, come on. Let's get you back to bed. You can call

them from the car. The staff will look after them, they're used to this. You need to rest.'

Over the next forty eight hours baby William made slow but steady progress, with Isla and Steve spending all day with him, taking it in turns to sleep.

Iona visited them again on Monday morning, but they were so focused, so preoccupied by their tiny, frail son that they barely noticed she was there. It was as if they'd forgotten why they were there in the first place, and Isla's fears about her own baby being second best were starting to overwhelm her.

But what could she do? They'd been so adamant about having both, bringing them up as twins. She couldn't turn round to them now, just because things hadn't gone according to plan, and tell them they couldn't have their baby.

Although if Joe had shown the slightest sign of wanting to keep her, had said or done anything to indicate he had any feelings for her, then she might have voiced her fears. But he hadn't, almost the opposite—apart from that one occasion, when he'd felt the baby move for the first time and had scooted down the bed and kissed her bump and murmured, 'Hello, you,' his voice so full of tenderness and wonder. And the night Isla had gone into labour, when he'd held her and wondered if they could have made a go of it, or if they might have a chance together later on, when they were in a better place.

That didn't mean he was ready to sign up for parenthood now, though, and without his support she wouldn't be able to keep her baby. What kind of a life would that be for either of them? And if Isla and Steve had her, she'd still be able to see her, to love her, to shower her with gifts and cuddles and kisses, but she'd have two loving, supportive parents instead of one stressed mother who was trying to juggle her work and childcare commitments against ridiculous odds.

That surely was the better option—at least for the baby?

She rubbed her bump, hoping she would stay tucked up there inside her for a little while longer, just until William was out of the woods and his parents had the time and the emotion to cope with the arrival of another baby. And maybe by then, she'd be ready to do what she knew in her heart she had to do...

Her agonising wait wasn't lost on Joe. She looked strained and exhausted, so strung out by the knowledge of what was to come that he was worried about her. And he knew what she was feeling. It was in her eyes, in her body language—and in his heart, slowly shredding it to pieces.

Please let the baby stay there a bit longer, just until William's stronger and they can do this. Please don't make it harder than it already is.

But whoever was in charge obviously wasn't listening, because she went into labour that night.

He drove her to the hospital at three on Tuesday morning, when her contractions were coming every three minutes and getting so strong she could hardly breathe through them.

'I can't do this,' she said when he'd parked the car, and he took her hand and squeezed it gently.

'Yes, you can. You've come this far, you can make it.'

She shook her head. 'I can't, Joe. I'm not brave enough. Everyone tells me I'm brave, but I'm not, not at all.'

'Of course you are,' he murmured, his voice full of a conviction she didn't feel. 'You're doing something most women would find impossible, and through it all you've been strong. If that isn't courage, I don't know what is.'

She didn't know, either, but it wasn't courage. She felt trapped, trapped into a situation they'd never foreseen, trapped into giving away a daughter she already loved more than anything in the world when it didn't seem necessary any more. At least not for Isla and Steve, and maybe not for her. Would being a GP be worse than giving away her child? No, of course it wouldn't, but how could she tell them she'd changed her mind?

And it wouldn't be fair on Joe, who she knew would feel obliged to support her even though she'd never ever ask him to.

Another contraction gripped her body, bringing the moment of truth closer, and she bit her lips and tried to breathe through it.

'OK?'

'No. I'm not OK, and I don't feel strong now, not at all. I feel scared.' Not of the physical pain. That paled into insignificance compared to what was coming.

'Oh, Iona.' He held her silently in his arms, not even trying to comfort her, because he must realise that nothing he could say could change any of what was coming, and she knew he was feeling it, too. Poor Joe. It was never meant to be like this…

She had another contraction, stronger than the others, and when it passed he got out of the car, went round and opened her door. 'Come on, we need to get you inside,' he said gently, but when they got up to Maternity they were told Isla was sleeping in the parents' room off the ward, and Steve had just gone home to Iona's flat to catch a couple of hours, so they were alone.

And she couldn't do this alone.

'Stay with me?' she asked, and he hesitated because that had never been the plan and she'd given him no warning, no time to shore up his defences.

Not that it would have worked. And she was trying so hard not to beg, but he searched her eyes and she was sure he could see it, the fear, the desperation. Not of the labour, but of that moment afterwards when she gave away the most precious thing in the world...

She saw the moment he caved, saw the moment the shutters came down in his eyes, and she almost wished she hadn't asked him.

'Of course I will,' he said, burying his feelings and hoping he could do this, could stay with her and support her while she gave birth to the child they couldn't keep.

This is wrong! his heart was screaming, but he stayed by her side, held her, rocked her, talked to her in between contractions, trying to reassure her and support her in doing what she'd set out to do, to help to make it easier for her. So he parroted all the old mantras he'd been drumming into himself for weeks.

Lies, all of it.

It'll be all right. They'll love her, of course they will. You'll be fine. She'll be fine. I'm here, I'm not going anywhere.

That last bit was the only one that was true, the only promise he could guarantee.

And then at last their daughter was born, tiny and perfect, and he stepped back away from the bed, the heart-stopping sound as she gave her first cry tearing him apart, and he knew that promise, too, had been a lie. He wouldn't be there. He couldn't. Not for her, or for the baby. Not when she gave their perfect, beautiful little daughter away.

It was Liv, the midwife who'd been so supportive, so understanding, who picked her up, Liv who laid her on Iona's chest, Liv who smiled and patted the baby dry with a warm towel.

He couldn't take his eyes off her, off the shock of dark hair, the tiny fingers, the skinny little legs, but he couldn't watch, either, and he took another step back and hit the wall.

He sucked in a breath. How could it hurt so much?

'I'll get Isla,' he said, his voice strangled, but Iona reached out her hand.

'No! Not yet, please. Stay with me. Liv can get her later, Joe. Stay with me now, please? Just for a little longer...'

So he stayed, against his better judgement, while Liv did her job quietly and unobtrusively, and he watched as Iona held her baby and stroked her tenderly, every touch, every stroke cutting him to the quick. What was it doing to her, this brave, beautiful woman who could sacrifice herself like this?

Then finally everything was done, and Liv turned to them, her face full of compassion.

'Do you want me to fetch them yet, or would you like some time alone together?'

'Please,' he said, because he wasn't ready. He'd never be ready. But Iona shook her head.

'Get them, please. We have to do this, and the longer we wait, the harder it'll be.'

The door closed softly behind Liv, and Iona looked up at him, her eyes welling with tears.

'Stay with me, Joe? Help me do this? I can't do it on my own—'

She was crying now, tears streaming down her cheeks, and he had to blink really hard to focus.

'I can't,' he said, every word feeling as if it was wrenched from him. 'I can't watch you give our daughter away, Iona, I just can't. I know you have to, I know you've promised and you'll never break that promise, no matter how much it hurts you, but I'm not as brave as you. Don't make me part of it, please.'

He couldn't see now, his tears welling too fast, but then he blinked, his head bent, and the baby's eyes were fixed on him. Her little arm moved, lifting up—reaching out to him?—and the last piece of his heart cracked and fell in two.

'Oh, baby…' He held out his hand to her, and her tiny fingers curled around his fingertip, her grip strong and fierce. So like her mother. So brave, so strong. Blinded by tears, and carefully, so as not to hurt her, he unfurled those tiny fingers one by one and pulled his hand away.

It was breaking his heart.

She could see it in every line of his body, every word he spoke, the pain in his eyes so raw it was flaying her alive, and she caught his hand, gripping it tightly.

'Oh, Joe. I'm so, so sorry. I never meant this to hurt you. It was supposed to be simple, but it isn't, is it? None of it. I've got no choice, but I can't do this to you, too, so of course you can go, my love. Just promise me one thing. Come back to me, when I've done it?' she begged, her voice cracking as she gave up the fight to hide her feelings. 'It's going to kill me to give her away, and I can't lose you, too. Don't do that to me.'

He lifted her hand to his lips, clinging to it like a life-line.

'I won't leave you,' he promised, his voice as unsteady as hers. 'I can't, I love you far too much and I never expected to feel like that. If I'd only done what I was meant to do that night, if I hadn't made love to you, then maybe this wouldn't have happened, maybe I wouldn't have let myself fall in love with you and pretend that it was all going to be all right, because it isn't...'

His voice cracked, and he ground to a halt, squeezing his eyes shut to stop the tears from falling, but they were falling anyway and she watched them and realised everything he'd said was true. He wasn't lying, he wasn't saying what he thought she'd want to hear to make it possible for her to keep their baby.

He was telling her the raw, unvarnished truth, and it was killing him.

'Why didn't you tell me?' Iona asked, her heart breaking for him. 'I've loved you for so long now. Why didn't you tell me that you love me?'

'Because I didn't know! I didn't dare to let myself think about it, but now I have it's so blindingly obvious, and I know it doesn't change anything, because I know you won't break your promise to Isla. And they'll be great parents, I know that, and I know she'll be happy, and I know she'll be loved, and we can still see her, maybe later when it's stopped hurting quite so much. And maybe then, when we're both ready, when you've finished your training and I've got my consultancy and the pain isn't so raw still, maybe we can do this again—start our own family. Have another baby, just for us.

'And I won't go now. I can't. I'll stay with you, and I'll watch while the thing I want most in the world is taken away from us, because I can't let you do that alone, and especially not when they don't even need her. It just seems so wrong...'

He ground to a halt and heard a faint sound behind him, a quiet sob. A hand touched his shoulder and he turned his head, to find Isla and Steve standing behind him, arms round each other, their faces drenched with tears.

'It is wrong,' Isla said brokenly, stumbling to Iona's side and taking her hand, gripping it with both of hers. 'Of course it's wrong, and we wouldn't *dream* of taking her from you now, not now we know how you feel. We didn't know you were in love, we thought you were just friends, and if we'd had the slightest clue that you wanted her so much, we'd never have said we'd still take her, even without me being pregnant. How could we hurt you like that?

'When we talked about it first we had no idea what it meant to love a child, and then when we found out I was pregnant, how could we tell you we didn't want your baby when you done all this just for us? But now—now we've had William, just the thought of losing him, of giving him away—it would break our hearts, Iona, just like it's breaking yours. We couldn't do that to you. To either of you.'

'But—I thought you wanted twins?' Iona said, but Joe could see the hope dawning in her face, the love for her baby shining in her eyes, and he pressed his hand over his mouth, holding down the emotion that was threatening to swamp him, not daring to believe that it might all come right.

Isla shook her head. 'No. It was the only solution we could think of, and we would have done it willingly. That's why we're here. We were coming to tell you we'd take her if that was what you really wanted, but it's so obvious you both love her, and she belongs with you—with both of you, and that's where she should be, with her own mother and father, and I can't think of any two people who deserve it more than you. So keep her, and love her, and I know you'll be happy.'

She kissed Iona, touched the baby with a loving hand and then left in Steve's arms, and Joe gave up the fight against his tears, gathered Iona and the baby up against his heart and wept.

Be happy?

Iona, sitting outside on the veranda while Joe fiddled in the kitchen, didn't know when she'd ever been this happy. And she'd never, ever seen Joe smile the way he was today.

It might have been because he'd had a phone call from his clinical lead offering him the consultancy, but she didn't think so. Or, at least, not just because of that.

He brought out a cake—her mother's apple cake recipe, which he'd stolen—and put it and a pot of tea safely out of the way on the table.

'She's got your eyes,' she told him, and he smiled and sat down beside her, looking down at his daughter with so much love it made her heart squeeze.

'Yes, I noticed. It's like looking in a mirror, only rather prettier.'

'Well, that's not hard,' she teased, and he gave a quiet chuckle and hugged her to his side. Then he gave her a thoughtful look and shifted so he could see her better.

'I want to ask you something, but I'm only going to ask it if you'll say yes,' he said.

'Will I regret it?'

He smiled a little sadly. 'I hope not.' And then before she realised what he was doing, he was kneeling in front of her, holding her hand in his and staring intently into her eyes.

She stared back, searching them and seeing everything she'd ever dreamed of, and she felt the smile start deep inside her and spread until she was smiling everywhere.

'Yes,' she said, before he could open his mouth.

'Yes, what?'

'Yes, I'll marry you,' she said softly. 'Will you marry me? Will you love, honour, and cherish me, and keep yourself only for me, as long as we both live?'

'Yes,' he said, his voice gruff and uneven. 'Oh, Iona— yes, I will. Now and for ever. I love you so much—'

'I love you, too,' she murmured gently, her hand reaching up and caressing his rugged cheek as he wrapped her and the baby carefully in his arms. 'I never thought I'd feel like this again. Well, no, not again, perhaps, because I've never felt like this before. It's as if suddenly everything that was wrong in my life has just shifted a bit and fallen into place, and it's all down to her—that tiny little girl, and my silly idea that babies should be conceived in love.'

He smiled and let go, sitting back down beside her again. 'I don't think it was a silly idea at all, and without it this might never have happened. And it was certainly true in her case because I fell in love with you that night,' he said softly, staring down at the baby in her arms. He reached over and lifted her carefully into his arms, his face filled with wonder. 'And look at her. Our baby. I can't believe she's here with us. I never dreamed—no, that's not true. I used to dream sometimes that we could keep her, try and convince myself we could find a way, and all the time I knew it was hopeless, but it wasn't.'

His finger traced her cheek, the line of her tiny little nose, the rosebud lips with such tenderness she felt her eyes filling just to see it.

'She's ours, Iona. She's our own little miracle, and we owe her everything, and when she's old enough, maybe we can tell her the story of how we fell in love.'

'Maybe not all of it,' she said with a smile, and he chuckled softly.

'No. Maybe not quite all…'

* * * * *

SURPRISE TWINS
FOR THE SURGEON

SUE MacKAY

MILLS & BOON

To all my wonderful readers.
Without you I wouldn't have this wonderful career.

CHAPTER ONE

'IT'S PERFECT.' Or it would've been. Alesha Milligan spun around on her toes, arms wide as she scoped the spacious apartment she was going to spend the next week enjoying. She *would* enjoy it. *Thank you very much, Luke.* Her arms fell to her sides, her chin dropped, and all pretence at how exciting a holiday in Dubrovnik would be evaporated.

This was supposed to be seven whole, luxurious days and nights seeing the sights, hitting the clubs, forgetting all about work and patients, having an amazing time with Luke. Instead she was here alone, dumped a fortnight ago. He apparently was now headed for Paris instead of Croatia as they'd planned. Her stomach squeezed painfully. Paris where he was hooking up with another woman he'd met at an accountants' conference last month.

'Hope it rains every day in Paris.'

'Pardon?' The proprietor, who'd introduced herself as Karolina, looked concerned. As if she'd let her apartment to a madwoman.

'Sorry. I was meant to be here with a man, only he changed his mind.' Should've seen it coming. It wasn't as though she was a stranger to men cooling towards her just when she finally relaxed into a relationship and

Luke hadn't exactly been rushing to spend time with her every night lately.

Karolina's face fell. 'That's terrible. You still want to stay?'

She was here, wasn't she? If she went home she wouldn't be able to face her girlfriends after all their nagging for her to go to Dubrovnik and have a great time despite Luke. Cherry had even had the audacity to suggest she have a sizzling fling, burn out the angst in her veins. Her? Sex with another man other than Luke? She wasn't ready. That'd make her seem fickle, and fickle she wasn't. Desperate for love, yes. She was all of that, and once again had tried too hard and set herself up to be dumped. And now here she was. Alone. Might as well soak up the sun lazing by that beautiful pool beckoning from metres away on the vast deck the apartment opened onto. Throw in some sightseeing. Alone.

'Yes. I do.' If right this moment she wanted to run for the hills she could see in the distance, common sense would soon prevail and she'd make the most of this opportunity to learn something about another country she'd always wanted to visit. Finding a smile for Karolina wasn't easy, but slowly her lips tipped upward. None of this was her hostess's fault. 'You have a beautiful spot here.'

'Glad you're happy with it.' The tension that had started racking up in the other woman backed off and she pointed to an expensive bottle of champagne on the table. 'There's wine for you to drink.'

Alesha's smile widened. There were some things on her side, then. Luke was so tight he must've forgotten to cancel that. If she knew where he was staying in Paris she'd send him a bottle of lemon juice, no sugar added.

This wouldn't have been a gesture brought on by guilt. He'd been in a hurry to get rid of her, saying the accountant he'd hooked up with was *the one*. At least he hadn't demanded she reimburse him for his share of this accommodation. Was it possible it was a consolation prize in his mind? It hadn't worked, but, yes, 'I'm going to enjoy it.' Mouthful by delicious mouthful, swallowing the anger and disappointment that was her latest ex, she would enjoy it as a precursor to having a wonderful holiday.

A holiday alone. Pain blurred her sight, removed her smile. What was wrong with her that men didn't stay around for ever? Not only men. Her parents hadn't either.

'There are plastic glasses in that cupboard if you want to enjoy a drink by the pool.'

Alesha snatched up the bottle, ready for a glass now. 'It should be in the fridge.' And she should be acting outwardly strong, if broken on the inside. After all, it wasn't as though this had never happened to her before. Not a cancelled romantic holiday. *That* was new, but broken relationships were becoming her speciality.

'I want you to have a lovely stay. There is a lot to do in and around Dubrovnik.' Karolina handed her a card. 'If there's anything you need, call me. I recommend you put my number on your phone. I don't live on the premises but I'm available any time.'

'Will do.' Alesha slid the card into her shorts' pocket. She'd deal with that shortly. First she'd go stick her toes in that sparkling, crystal-clear water.

Karolina removed a metal ring from the door, and waved keys at her. 'Front door, laundry, and the gate off the street, which must be kept locked at all times for everyone's security.'

'No problem.' They also went into her pocket. 'Do you have a map of the town?'

'All the information you'll need is on that shelf above the table. Restaurants and grocery shops are highlighted. Bus stops, the way to the Old City if you want to walk. Anything else just ask around. Most locals are very friendly.'

'I will, and thanks. I am going to have a wonderful time.' She really was, as soon as she'd banished Luke's haughty face from behind her eyelids. Haughty? Yes, he had been, especially as he'd said she'd got too serious too soon. Hello? Hadn't he also said he'd fallen for the accountant woman instantly? Alesha's stomach tightened. He could've just said it wasn't working for him, not layer in how wonderful this other woman was—at everything.

A bird tweet in her pocket had her tugging her phone out fast. He'd changed his mind.

He hadn't.

'Hi, Cherry. You on break?' She wandered out to the pool's edge as she listened to her friend back in London.

'No, but I wanted to give you the heads up. There's a six-month position coming up on the paediatric ward starting in four weeks. One of the nurses is taking maternity leave, but she's told me it's unlikely she'll come back at all. This'd be the ideal job for you. I've flicked the application form through to your email.'

A couple of weeks ago she'd have jumped at the opportunity. Probably still would once her head and bruised heart settled back into the 'being single' groove. But right now? Alesha didn't want to make any plans for the future other than getting out of bed every morning to go discover this wonderland. 'Thanks for letting me know. I'll think about it over the next few days.'

'Don't take too long. Rumour has it nurses from all over London will be queuing up for the chance to join our team. It'd be cool to work together. So, how's Dubrovnik?'

Alesha hadn't really taken much in yet—she had been too busy feeling sorry for herself on the drive from the airport, instead thinking Luke should've been with her. Wandering over to the wall at the front of the deck, she stared out and around. 'It's beautiful,' she gasped. 'There's an awesome bridge in the background, and hills, and almost right beneath where I'm standing is the harbour where the cruise ships tie up.'

'There'll be nightclubs and the like there, surely? You can be out all night, and lounging by the pool during the day.' Cherry sounded excited for her.

Down, girl. 'Yeah, well, I'm sure there'll be some dancing and drinking going on. Not so sure about having that fling though. I do know there're lots of places I want to visit during the day.'

'You Kiwis and your sightseeing. Can't you visit a town without spending the days walking for miles, taking photos and making yourself too tired to go out at night?' Cherry laughed. 'Oh-oh, dragon on the warpath. Got to go. Put your CV in for that job. Bye.'

Click. Gone.

Alesha sank onto a lounger. The heat was softening her muscles, moistening her skin, draining what little energy she had left. The temptation to fall into the water fully clothed was strong. *There's a phone in my pocket.* Could remove it, but if she was going to do that she might as well get into her bikini. The tiny red creation made to cover the essentials and cause havoc in a man's brain. In his shorts. Instead she'd wear it for a swim on her own.

She'd also pour a glass of bubbles as soon as they were remotely chilled. Right about now.

Dressed, make that just decent, in her new bikini and with a glass of lukewarm champagne, Alesha tossed her phone on the bed and returned to the poolside to stretch out on the lounger to soak up some sun. Already hot, it was nice to feel the heat pushing her down into the cushions. Talk about the life. If she had to be alone then this was the way to go.

How some fun, maybe get laid. Put Luke behind you. He doesn't deserve you anyway.

Leap into bed with just any guy she met? As if she were a tramp? Would that make her a more interesting person? When she'd be uptight and stressed about meeting men in bars on her own? They'd have a different agenda from hers. Theirs would be to head straight to bed, while she was far more cautious. If that made her dull, then dull she was.

I can't deal with this. I've been dumped. Like yesterday's news. A fling doesn't require getting to know the other person too much.

Forget the fling and just have fun doing the things she enjoyed.

I enjoy sex.

The thought made her start. Sitting up, she stared around the beautiful complex with its stunning pool. Was she broken-hearted over Luke's defection? Or hurt because once again she'd failed to find love?

So? It wasn't as if she were incapacitated. Basically she was used to being on her own. Alesha hadn't moved all the way from the other side of the world because she was a wuss. No, she'd shifted to a humongous city where she knew no one, had found jobs, accommodation, a man who'd enjoyed her company for the past few months—or so she'd thought.

Her hands clenched as sweat trickled between her breasts, down her back. The sun beat down relentlessly, heating her skin while internally her blood was frozen and her stomach a lump of ice. Love was an intangible, and always out of her reach. She'd been searching for love since the day her brother got sick and her parents no longer had time for her. She'd been trying too hard to be loved by someone special. It might be time to accept it wasn't going to happen and she should just get on with her life. Get busy so she didn't notice no one was there for her, with her.

Or maybe she should relax, have some uncomplicated fun as Cherry and Shelley suggested and see where that took her.

Alesha gulped a mouthful of champagne, spluttered as it went down the wrong way.

Stop feeling sorry for yourself.

'Yeah,' she sighed. She did have a darned good life living in London, sharing a house with other nurses she got on well with and often contracted to work in some of the best hospitals. Much more exciting and interesting than living in Christchurch, New Zealand, where she'd grown up.

Taking a small sip of the champagne this time, she groaned out loud in exasperation. Her clenched hand pounded the mattress at her side. What a fantastic way to start a holiday. She was not going to spend the week lying on the bed feeling sorry for herself. She *was* not.

Okay. Message received. She'd start enjoying the sun, the blue sky that went for ever, the view of hills and the harbour below. Even the champagne that in all honesty wasn't flash in its warmish state. There was a whole world out there waiting to be explored. Alesha would not leave here next weekend without knowing the sights and sounds and smells of Dubrovnik. But first she was going to get into that pool and cool off, physically and mentally. Then she'd go for a walk and see what was nearby for eating out. If her appetite returned by the end of the week, that was.

Luke could go to hell in a wheelbarrow. A rusty one with a flat tyre. There were other men out there.

Exhaustion pulled at her.

A sad sigh escaped. She would have a great time despite going solo. She really, really would, as soon as she'd had a snooze. Yeah, sure. Her eyes stung, proving she wasn't quite ready to let go the hurt. But crying was not happening. Rarely since the day when she was ten, and stood at her brother's graveside to drop onto the coffin the silver clock shaped like a Labrador and small enough to fit in the palm of Ryan's hand, had Alesha given into tears. The clock had been bought out of hard-earned pocket money mowing lawns for Dad and the people next door. Ryan had been meant to get better and take it with him wherever he went in the future.

She laid back and closed her eyes, savouring the sun as she'd done so often on family holidays a good many years ago. Sun, sea, surf. It was what Kiwis made the most of every summer around Christmas and New Year. A relaxed, exciting time with family and friends, just mucking about in the water, catching fish…

A light breeze tightened her skin. Alesha dragged her eyes open and rolled onto her back. 'Ouch.' Sitting up, she looked over her shoulder, got an eyeful of red skin.

The tube of sunscreen was still inside her case. Probably where her brain was too. Protecting her skin from the sun was always a priority. Not today. The sun was disappearing behind the hills. And she'd wasted the afternoon getting sunburnt.

A gust of wind swished across the pool and deck, and behind her a door slammed. Her fiery skin was intensely cold for a moment then back to flaming. She shivered. Time to put on some clothes.

That door that banged shut must've been hers. But it was all right. It wouldn't be locked. Not when she stood in her bikini with only a towel to wrap around her and the keys still in the pocket of her shorts lying on the floor inside.

The door didn't budge when she turned the handle, nor when she pressed a shoulder against the wood. Seriously? No way. Someone was playing a joke on her.

She was not locked out of her apartment without clothes, money or her phone. When her stomach was complaining about lack of food. Her day had just gone from average to worse. What else could go wrong? Tipping her head back, Alesha made to shout her frustration, but hauled on the brakes at the last second. What was the point? Screaming wouldn't miraculously unlock the door, or hand her phone over with Karolina's number. Had she got around to putting the woman's number in her database? She couldn't remember. Too much emotion had been whirling around in her mind.

Looking up at the apartment above, Alesha saw a light on in the lounge. Relief was instant. Whoever was in there would have the phone number she needed to resolve this glitch.

Loud knocking on that door brought no more success

than trying to open her own. The light was on but no one was home. Nor was there anyone in the other apartments when she banged on their doors. Seemed she wasn't only alone but she might be sleeping on the lounger if she didn't find a way of contacting Karolina.

This would be hilarious if it hadn't happened to her. It might even be funny in a few days' time when she recounted it to her flatmates back in London, but right now it was downright scary. Another shiver wracked her while her sunburnt skin burned and chilled equally. 'I can't sleep outside.' Her stomach rumbled. 'Yeah, and you can wait and all. There's no dinner coming your way until this is sorted.'

Looking around the complex, she smothered the panic threatening to overwhelm her. Think. She was safe in here, cold and hungry, yes, but no one was going to get through the outside door leading from the road. Waiting until other guests came home was her only option, although who knew when that would be? Down on the narrow road cars went by slowly. From the far end of the pool she stared out at the view, which would have looked beautiful if she weren't just a tiny bit afraid she was going to spend the whole night out here.

Lights flickered on in the next-door house. Of course. Neighbours.

Wrapping the towel tight around her, she headed for the gate and out onto the footpath. The gate snipped shut behind her. Her stomach nudged her toes. How stupid could she get? She was out on the street in a bikini and it was getting dark. Lying on the lounger by the pool all night suddenly seemed almost like fun.

Neighbours, remember. Someone would know the owner of the apartments. They had to.

They might've but they didn't speak English. No one at the four houses she tried understood a word she said; instead they looked at her as though she was a madwoman gibbering away in a foreign language—she was fast approaching becoming one—and closed their doors in her face. She should've learnt a few more words of Croatian other than hello and thank you, though it would never have occurred to her to learn 'how do I get in touch with Karolina?' or 'I need a locksmith'.

Back on the street Alesha blinked away the irritant in her eyes. Crying was not happening. This was a holiday, shambolic yes, but a holiday in a beautiful place, and meant to be enjoyed. All she had to do was find a way back into her apartment. How hard could it be?

A couple was walking up the road, talking and laughing.

Relief lifted her heart. 'Hello. Do you speak English? Can you help me, please?'

They did stop and look at her, before shaking their heads in bewilderment and carrying on up the hill.

That had to be a no, then.

A woman came around the corner, a phone plastered to her ear.

'Excuse me. Do you speak English?'

Apparently not. The woman didn't even slow down.

Alesha walked down the road a hundred metres, asking everyone she saw the same questions, getting the same result.

The night stretched ahead interminably. What she wouldn't give to be back in her flat eating yesterday's leftovers and throwing darts at the board after she'd pinned a photo of Luke to it. It had all started with him, hadn't it?

No, it went way further back than him.

Kristof Montfort strolled up the hill, hands in pockets, glad the day was done and the temperature was dropping to something near bearable. Once in a rare year London might get as hot. Might. A cold beer beckoned, and his feet moved faster.

The little girl found curled up, shivering, in the bushes by the Dubrovnik Bridge had been brought in to his mother at the Croatian Children's Home during the night and had stolen into his heart when he hadn't been looking as he worked with her. He must be getting soft because the tiny child's big fear-filled eyes, her gaunt cheeks, and scrawny body had angered him, destroyed his usually well-controlled emotions and let her in where he never let anyone. It had taken all day to get his equilibrium back. How could a parent abandon their child to the vagaries of street thieves and child porn operators? His father might've made a mockery of all he taught Kristof about being an honest, reputable gentleman, but he'd never physically hurt him, and the emotional slam dunk had happened when he was old enough to fend for himself.

They were yet to learn the child's name so in the meantime everyone was calling her Capeka—little stork—for her inclination to stand on one leg with the other twisted behind her knee as she huddled in a corner.

He'd done all he could for Capeka today; operating to fix an arm with multiple fractures, stitching deep, badly infected cuts on her thighs and forearms, putting her back together physically. Food, clean clothes and a warm bed had been priorities. The mental stuff would be taken care of by his mother and her colleagues, and would take a lot longer to resolve, if ever. The counsellors and the nurses at the Croatian Children's Home spent hours with their little patients and lost souls, but there was a gross shortage of caring nurses, the pay being minimum on a good day. Even the most fervent care-giver had to eat and find shelter and wear clothes.

'Excuse me.' A young woman dressed in a towel appeared in front of him, looking wary although desperation was rippling off her.

'Yes?'

'You speak English?' Surprise warred with disbelief.

'I am English.' And Croatian, but that was another story. 'What's your problem?' There went that cold beer. Somehow he just knew this wasn't going to be a quick question and answer session. There was something about those earthy coloured eyes that strummed him, and warned him. The woman was in trouble.

Or *was* trouble.

She jerked a thumb over her shoulder. 'I've gone and got myself locked out of the apartment I'm staying in. As well as the complex,' she added in a rush. 'I need to get hold of the owner but I don't have a phone.' Her cheeks pinked. 'Or her number.'

'You'd be talking about Karolina.'

Hope flared. 'You know her?'

He didn't want to dampen that hope; it made her look less drawn, beautiful even. 'A little, but, better than that, my mother is friends with Karolina's.' Tapping his mother's number, he held his phone to his ear. He listened to the dial tone while studying the woman before him. Temptation in a towel. 'Fingers crossed my mother has her phone with her. She has a habit of leaving it all over town.'

Her shoulders drooped. 'Oh.'

'Is that you, Kristof?'

Kristof raised a thumb in his distraction's direction. 'Yes, Mum, it's me. And before you start in on me about not taking a partner to the fundraiser dinner tomorrow, I've got someone here who's got herself locked out of the Jelinski Apartments and needs to get in touch with Karolina.' As in the lady he was *not* taking to the dinner even if his mother had begged him to.

'She came here to pick up her mother and left five minutes ago. I've tried to give you Karolina's number so many times.'

So you have. Your persistence is admirable, but please use it on more important issues.

He liked Karolina. He didn't have the hots for her, or love her, or want to get to know her better, though he'd do anything for her if she asked because that was who he was these days, and she felt the same about him. Though she might not do anything he asked. Their respective mothers had other ideas and wouldn't listen to them. What did they know? Kristof's mother, in particular, refused to accept that he'd decided not to marry again, ever. Why would he when his ex-wife had cheated on him more times than he could count? Had laughed when he'd told her he loved her and that monogamy was part of their relationship. A deal breaker for him, but her idea of love included adventurous affairs on the side.

The woman before him was looking at him as though he was her saviour, and shivering, wrapped only in that towel and who knew what underneath? Nothing? 'Mum, please let Karolina know she's needed at the apartments urgently.'

Now he noticed red, string-like straps running over her shoulders. A bikini? Or a bra? Whichever, no better than nothing for warmth. But slightly easier on his overactive libido, which did not have a role to play here. It might've been a few months since he'd seen to that need but he would not be scratching it with this woman, despite the heat starting to flow into his blood. Shoving the phone into his back pocket, he told her, 'You shouldn't have to wait long. Karolina lives four streets over.' As long as she'd gone straight home after dropping her mother off.

'Thanks so much. I appreciate your help. I was beginning to think I'd be spending the night out here and there's nothing other than cold concrete or tarmac.' Now that her problem was being fixed her mouth lifted into an ironic smile. 'It's been one of those days.'

Don't smile at me like that. It goes straight to places I don't want to acknowledge.

That bow-shaped upper lip and full lower one would be magic on his skin. He slapped his hand against his thigh, instantly regretting the action when she jerked backwards. 'Well, we've dealt with this problem. Glad I came along.' He was off the hook, had helped her out of a bind and could walk on with a clear conscience. Couldn't he? Kristof sucked in a breath. She wasn't as young as he'd first thought. Mid-twenties? Older? What did it matter? He wasn't interested. It was time for that beer and to forget a particularly difficult day dealing with Capeka. But his hormones got in the way and he asked, 'Why are you cold when the temperature is still warm?'

'I fell asleep by the pool for a little while and got

some sunburn. Now my skin is fluctuating between hot and cold.'

Kristof looked over her shoulder and whistled. 'That's going to sting under the shower.' An image filled his brain of her tall, slim body under the water. He wasn't seeing red, more cream-coloured skin and lots of curves. Forget an itch. Muscles tightened in places they had no right.

His phone rang. Relief at the interruption was quick but didn't loosen the tension plaguing him. 'Mum? Don't tell me you couldn't get hold of Karolina?' His eyes were fixed on the woman in front of him so he didn't miss the way her body momentarily folded inward.

When she saw him watching she was quick to straighten to full height, bringing the top of her head to align with his chin, while struggling to banish the disappointment sparking in her eyes.

His mother harrumphed. 'Of course I did. Karolina will be at least half an hour though. It's something unavoidable.' In other words don't ask.

He wouldn't. 'Okay. I'll tell—' What was her name? They hadn't got around to introducing themselves. He almost didn't want to in case that made her real. Huh? How not real was this stunning female? 'We'll be waiting.' There went that beer. He explained the situation to the woman. 'By the way, I'm Kristof Montfort.' He held his hand out. 'I'm a doctor from London over here helping my mother for a week.' That was added to reassure her he wasn't an axe murderer, not to show off. He didn't need to tell her he owed his mother for hurting her for many years. That was his guilt, not to be shared.

She put her slim hand out to shake his and the towel slid to the ground, giving him an eyeful of her body. Definitely lots of enticing curves and her skin was creamy and smooth. Got that right, then. The moisture on his tongue dried. Her breasts more than filled the ridiculously small red-and-white-fabric cups supposedly holding them in place. He couldn't breathe. Or move. But his eyes roamed. She was a stunner. From top to toes. His eyes cruised down her legs to those toes just to make sure he was right. Of course he was. This woman was hot, beautiful, a magnet for his manhood. He stepped back. Away from temptation. She'd have him locked up in a flash if he acted on the heat ramping through his body, language difficulties or not. Why had he gone and said he was hanging around until Karolina turned up?

Snatching her hand free, she bent to retrieve her only cover, quickly tying it back in place. 'Alesha Milligan, fool extraordinaire. I can't believe I left my phone and keys inside.'

'Pleased to meet you.'

Then she smiled, reminding him of sunny days on the briny in his runabout, and his stomach hit his feet. Her voice was so feminine and warm. 'Actually I'm lying. Yes, I can believe it. I'd been distracted big time. It's a surprise I remembered to take a towel outside.'

It would've been better for him if she'd remembered to take her clothes out to the poolside. Of course only someone who knew they were going to lock themselves outside would do that. 'We all stuff up at times.' As he was now, with his body still reminding him that all parts below his belt were in full working order, despite a recent lack of practice due to long hours working at the private practice in Harley Street hindering a social life. But he had to be grateful for towels. The one wound around that exquisite body was hiding even the curves. Except now

he knew what was under there. Knew, and wanted another glimpse, wanted to touch and get to know.

No, he did not.

'Feel like a beer while you wait?' At least that would
mean a quick break while he went home to get said liquid libation.

Her scrutiny of him seemed haughty. 'You don't appear to have any with you and as I don't intend going to
a bar dressed like this I'll say no. B-but thank you for
offering.' The shivering was back, her skin lifting in
goosebumps.

Inviting her back to the house might be kinder than
letting her stand out here, but then they wouldn't know
when Karolina turned up. Also, his mother was still at
the children's home so there was no one else at the house.
Alesha might not feel comfortable spending time alone
with a stranger while dressed in next to nothing. 'Give
me five and I'll be back with beer and a jersey and some
pants to keep you warm. They'll be too big but better
than nothing.' And just might make that amazing body
look as if it were hanging out in a sack.

But you'd still know what was in the sack.

Again surprise appeared in her face. Kristof liked surprising her for some reason. Maybe because green flecks
appeared in the brown of her eyes? 'Th-thanks, I'd appreciate that.'

'If you're sure you're all right, I'll go now.' She'd be
safe but not comfortable. He'd be fast. She was also a
visitor to his second country, and visitors were meant to
be treated kindly. Yes, that was what this was all about.
Taking care of a visitor. Nothing to do with this hissing
and fizzing in his veins. 'Be right back.'

He'd have that flare of excitement going on in his groin

under control by the time he returned. Hopefully hanging out here in the dark only lightened by low-quality street lamps he'd be safe from those deep, alluring pools blinking at him from under long eyelashes. Safe from the array of emotions darting in and out of her less than steady gaze.

CHAPTER TWO

'HERE, PUT THESE ON.' Alesha's dark-blond, good-looking saviour handed her one of the bags swinging from his large hand.

'Thanks,' she muttered. How embarrassing to be stuck out on the street pulling on a complete stranger's clothes. Lots better than dropping the towel though. His eyes had popped right out of his head, embarrassing her. Had he thought she'd done it on purpose? If so he must think her a bit loose. He wouldn't know that according to Luke she was the dead opposite. If only she'd been thinking straight when she went outside the apartment without keys after Karolina had specifically told her to keep them with her at all times. But she wouldn't have got an eyeful of Mr Handsome. Cherry would probably say he was fling material, but she wasn't going there. It was too soon.

Shoving her arms into the lightweight jersey, Alesha pulled it over her head, down to just above her knees. And she'd thought she was tall. The sleeves needed rolling up, but at least she felt warm and cosy. The fabric smelled of man: good-looking, intriguing man. Yes, well, she wasn't interested. As for the jeans, they were ridiculous. Even with the lengthy belt on its tightest notch they were going to slide down whenever she moved. 'Just as well I'm not going anywhere,' she quipped as she bent down to roll up the hems several turns.

'Sorry I didn't bring some shoes.'

His smile touched her deeply, dodging the lump that was Luke's defection. A genuine, not wanting anything from her smile that went some way to warming the chill gnawing at her. When was the last time a man had smiled at her like that? Had anyone ever? Finding a smile of her own, Alesha glanced down at his enormous feet. 'I doubt you have a pair of size seven high heels stashed in your wardrobe.'

His laugh was light and added to the warmth his jersey was creating. Soon she'd be roasting. 'I've never been into cross-dressing.'

'Again, thank you for everything. I don't know what I'd have done if you hadn't come along.'

'You'd have got a little colder before Karolina came to do her night round.' Kristof dug into another bag and retrieved two beers. 'I promised you one of these.'

Accepting the bottle, Alesha dug deep not to react outwardly to the zip of heat the touch of his fingers on hers created. 'What do you mean? Night round?'

His eyes had flared at that touch. Was he feeling hot too? 'Karolina checks on the apartments every morning and night, and a couple of times in between, often cleaning the pool, pulling the rare weed that dares to pop up in the gardens, making sure everyone staying here is happy. She's very particular about her apartments and wants her guests to get the most out of their time with her.'

The admiration in his voice had Alesha wondering if there was more to his relationship with this woman than he was letting on. 'The place is immaculate, and she was so welcoming that I feel terrible causing trouble.

She told me to put her number in my phone, but it never crossed my mind I'd need to have it with me while I was only a few metres from my room taking a dip.' Or falling asleep. What was done was done, and there was no point bemoaning the fact she'd stuffed up.

'Karolina'll be fine. Bet it's not the first time it's happened.' Kristof broke a short bread stick in half and handed a piece over, then placed a small wedge of cheese on top of his bag along with a knife. 'Here's some nourishment. I hope you like it.'

'I'd like over-boiled cabbage at the moment.' Her gnawing stomach was doing somersaults. 'When you said you help your mother out were you referring to your medical skills?'

'I'm a general surgeon and she runs a shelter and home for children who haven't got anywhere to go, or anyone to look after them. There's a small hospital annexe attached for treating those children and others who don't make it to the main hospital. I come over for a few weeks throughout the year. I'm needed less for my surgical skills and more for general medicine, though we do some simple surgeries.'

'So it's back to basics for you when you're here.' Interesting. His mother must be important to him. Or was it those children that drew him?

'It reminds me of how I can help people in dire circumstances.' He didn't sound too happy about that. 'I also cajole colleagues in London to donate some time to help out whenever possible.' His lips pursed around the rim of his bottle. Unfortunately when he tipped his head back his Adam's apple became very prominent, and sent her stomach into squeeze-release mode, adding heat to her system, which had to be good considering how cold she'd got standing out here.

Looking away, Alesha gulped at her bottle, focusing on what his problem was, not on *him*. Didn't he like working alongside his mother? But if he got involved with organising other medical people to come across to take a turn helping then he must care about what went on in the shelter. 'You didn't mention the mental trauma some of those children must suffer. Who takes care of that?'

'My mother is a psychologist who first trained as a nurse. She also employs counsellors and other medical staff. Her hours are endless because she's driven to helping every kid that turns up on her doorstep.' Kristof's pride was tangible, but there was a chill behind it. As if he didn't approve, which wasn't making sense. 'Sometimes I wish she'd take a break, look out for herself, but it's never going to happen so I've learned to keep quiet.'

'You assist her at the home. She must be pleased about that, working with her son.'

The pride slipped. 'Yes, she is.' This time the words were clipped and there was a definite 'don't go there' warning hanging between them.

Who was she to upset the man who'd had his plans for the evening disrupted because she'd been careless? 'London's amazing. I've been living and working there for nearly two years and I still haven't had enough.' Though she was starting to think the men in London mightn't be good for her if the way they dumped her was an indication. Another gulp of beer went down her throat. She'd survive. She always did. She was about looking after herself, had never been needy, and wasn't about to start. She took another gulp. At least the beer was refreshing.

'Where are you from? I'm picking Australia or New Zealand.'

'Kiwi through and through.' And before he thought to ask questions Alesha had no intention of answering, she went with, 'I came over on my OE after I finished training as a nurse. Living in England and visiting lots of places in Europe is what many of us like to do before settling down.' Of course, settling down meant finding someone who'd love her regardless.

'Why are you here on your own, staying at an apartment? Most single people come with a crowd of friends to stay at a cheap hotel, do the sightseeing, hit the bars and nightclubs like there's no tomorrow.'

'Now there's a thought.' The bottle was empty. Where was Karolina when an open bottle of champagne was cooling in the fridge? Food. She needed to eat, despite having already devoured her share of what Kristof had brought. The bread was soft and delicious, and the cheese to die for. The dairy companies back home didn't make cheese like this.

'You really are alone?' Disbelief echoed between them.

'What of it?' she growled. 'Not everyone has to be with someone.'

'Hey.' Kristof put his hand up. 'If I've offended you, then my apologies. Just making conversation.' He paused and a teasing smile appeared. 'I have learned you don't like carrying keys and a phone when you go out to the pool.' Did he have to sound so sexy when she wasn't interested?

'I was angry.' She was still angry. 'This is supposed

to be the perfect holiday for me and my partner in a gorgeous location.' Bile rose, bitter and ghastly. Jumping up, she stomped to the roadside and peered through the gloom in both directions looking for Karolina.

'He's been held up?' came the logical question.

Spinning around, Alesha lost balance. It took some quick steps to stay upright. 'He's had a better offer.' Sex, kisses, laughter, fun. All of which he could've had with her.

'That's the pits.'

Give the man credit. He hadn't spewed sympathy when he knew nothing of the circumstances. 'It sucks.' She huffed out the air stalled in her lungs. 'I'll look on the bright side. I'm here and there's a whole town to explore out there.' She waved her hand in the general direction of the harbour, knowing full well a lot more of the city was behind the hill she was on.

'This is your first visit to Dubrovnik? I hope you have a wonderful time despite your setback. There's so much to see and do if you put your mind to it.'

A setback? Kristof didn't have a clue, or had the heart of a cold fish. But he'd already proven that particular organ was at least warm by going out of his way to help her. 'I'm sure I'll manage,' she snapped just as a car pulled into the parking bay beside them. The woman getting out of the car was Karolina. Phew. She shot across to her. 'I'm so sorry for being a nuisance. I fell asleep by the pool and the wind came up, blew my door shut.'

'It's okay. Now you'll be careful to take your keys and phone everywhere, eh?' At least her smile was friendly, as was the arm she threw around Alesha's shoulder. 'I'm glad Kristof found you.'

Ignoring how her burned skin stung under that arm,

she smiled at Kristof. 'He couldn't avoid me when I attacked him in the street like a woman possessed.'

Kristof gathered up his bags. 'I think you're prone to exaggeration.' He turned to Karolina with a cute smile. 'Alesha was only slightly crazy when she charged at me demanding that I speak English and get her out of her predicament.'

'Who exaggerates?' Alesha spluttered.

'Let's go inside and retrieve those keys,' Karolina said. Then to Kristof, 'You found anyone to go with you tomorrow night?'

'No,' he growled.

'Have you been asking around? I'm sure there are plenty of girls who'd love nothing better than to go to a formal dinner with *you*.'

'Leave it, Karolina.'

Alesha grimaced. If anyone spoke to her so sharply she'd be heading for the hills. The gate was now unlocked so she slipped free to charge up the stairs. She couldn't get to her apartment and a hot shower quick enough. Too quickly. She missed seeing the final step and tripped, sprawling on the concrete, bruising her elbows and knees.

'Careful.' Strong, masculine hands reached for her, took her hands to tug her to her feet, giving her the odd sensation of being cared about. 'You really are having a bad day.'

He could've pointed out it was her own fault, that running up unfamiliar steps in clothes many sizes too big was right up there with leaping off the tenth floor of a hotel in the hope she'd make the swimming pool beneath. 'Yes, I am, and this one's on me.' She tried to pull free but Kristof held her elbow as he led her to the apartment

Karolina was unlocking. Her head spun so she stopped, remained still, waiting for it to get back to normal.

'Are you all right?'

'I'm good.'

'When did you last eat a proper meal? I saw the way you hoed into that bread and cheese.'

'I had a sandwich while waiting for my flight first thing this morning.'

His sigh was full of exasperation. 'You've got to look after yourself.'

'There you go.' Karolina stepped back from unlocking the door to Alesha's apartment. 'Anything else I can do?'

Glad of the interruption from that annoying look on Kristof's face, Alesha gave Karolina the biggest smile she could dredge up. 'Nothing. I'm truly sorry about this. From now on I'm not even having a shower without my phone in the bathroom so I can call you if needed.'

Karolina slapped her forehead. 'I'd say that was a good idea but—'

'But the idea of hauling me out of the shower isn't.' This time her smile was genuine. 'I get it.' Then she had a brainwave. Going inside, she opened the fridge and grabbed the champagne. 'Would you both like a glass? My way of saying thanks.' Opening the small cupboard above the fridge, she reached for glasses, finding only one. Of course. There was one out on the decking. She'd have hers in a mug if necessary.

'Not for me. I have to be somewhere.' Karolina was already beating a fast retreat, adding to Alesha's guilt about messing up her evening. 'I'll see you tomorrow probably.' She hesitated. 'Add Kristof's number to your phone as well just in case.'

'Just in case what?' Alesha asked Karolina's retreating back.

'In case I'm unavailable,' she called over her shoulder before disappearing around the corner.

'What did I say?' The cork popped with that delightful sound that meant delicious wine. At least she'd pushed it back in tight. One thing in her favour.

'Nothing wrong. She's a busy lady.' Kristof took the bottle from her unsteady fingers. 'Let me.' He filled the glass she'd found and handed it back to her.

'You're not joining me?' A jolt of disappointment rocked her when it shouldn't. Had to be because she was feeling so down.

'I haven't finished my beer, and I've got another bottle in the bag.'

Okay, she'd go with that. But her tongue got away from her. After all, she was exhausted. 'You prefer beer to this?' She held her glass up after taking a long sip.

'Different drinks for different occasions. I was hot and frazzled walking home, and looking forward to a cold one.'

'What are you frazzled about now?' Her tongue had loosened up over the last few minutes. The tiredness was taking over, making her body ache and her head light. She should really say goodbye to Kristof and take that shower she was hanging out for before climbing into bed and catching up on sleep.

Kristof downed the rest of the beer in the first bottle and placed it in the bin under the sink. 'I'm going to get you something more than bread and cheese for dinner. Why don't you have a shower while I'm out, get into clothes that fit?'

That made sense. She had to change, give his gear back. 'Good idea. I'll get you some money for my food.'

'That won't be necessary. Anything you don't like?'

Alesha didn't expect strangers to shout her dinner. But were they still strangers? She was wearing Kristof's clothes, had drunk his beer, and he was here in her apartment. 'I eat most things.' Now he'd buy something she couldn't stand. 'I hope.' The champagne was going down nicely, untying some of the knots in her stomach. Not a bad medicine. Especially now that it was chilled to perfection.

'Relax. I won't buy anything unusual.' He was already at the door. 'I'll be about half an hour.'

'How are you going to get into the complex?'

When his eyes widened his eyebrows almost disappeared under the thick dark-blond waves lying on his forehead. 'What's your number?'

She rattled it off. First night in Dubrovnik and she was already giving out her details. She spluttered into her wine. Not bad at all for an uptight, *I don't do overly friendly* woman. Then, 'Take my keys. If you're a friend of Karolina's I'm sure I'll be safe.'

His eyebrows disappeared completely this time. But he did take the keys.

When the door closed behind Kristof she took her glass and headed for the small bathroom off to the side. One look in the mirror had her gaping. Red cheeks, sunken eyes, hair that looked as if she'd been dragged through a gorse bush backwards, and skin on her neck and shoulders the colour of strawberries. Very pretty. Her skin matched the bikini, which was something positive, she supposed.

Taking a deep drink of her champagne, she stripped

away Kristof's jersey and jeans, then folded them to put in a bag for him to take home. Bringing her, a stranger, clothes had been kind. But kindness might be his middle name. He hadn't hesitated to help her out when he was apparently in a hurry to get home.

And changed circumstances or not, she shouldn't be hesitating over getting on with her holiday despite everything, should instead turn it into an opportunity. She had to stop overthinking the hurt going on in her heart.

But was the hurt *really* in her heart? Or was it her pride smarting because once again she'd got it wrong? She hadn't been good enough for a guy she'd been halfway to being in love with? Her shoulders drooped. She was trying too hard to find someone to love her unequivocally.

A sip of champagne didn't bring any answers, only the reminder that she needed to be busy and make the most of what she *did* have. Starting with another mouthful of champagne and then washing her hair. Those bruises from tripping over that step were already colouring up. Serve her right for not watching where she was going. What a day. Suddenly Alesha was ravenous. Hopefully her saviour wouldn't be too long with the food. Another glimpse of him wouldn't go astray either. So much for being unhappy about Luke.

Kristof stared at the shapely butt in front of him as Alesha reached up into the cupboard for plates. His jeans and jersey had been covering a figure that had his blood thickening and his manhood tightening. Now wearing fitted white jeans with a sleeveless turquoise top and thin-strapped sandals, Alesha looked stunning. Beyond beautiful. There were curves in all the right places, making his mouth water. But he already knew what those curves looked like, had felt their power on his libido. He could imagine those long legs wrapped around him when he should not be imagining anything of the sort. They didn't know each other. How long did it take to be attracted to a woman? Especially one as beautiful as Alesha?

She's a Kiwi; we're from different hemispheres. It wouldn't work even if I tried.

Mixed relationships, as in each partner being from a different country, did not work. Hadn't for his parents, or for him and his German wife.

'What did you get?' the woman causing his body all sorts of problems turned to ask.

'Deep fried squid and salad.'

'Yum. Exactly what I need.'

'Glad to oblige.' He looked away to gather his equilibrium around his overheated body. He did not want Alesha noticing his reaction to her. She wouldn't thank him. In the circumstances, she might find it disrespectful, if not down and out lecherous. He didn't do lecherous, thought it despicable. Women should be respected. Make that *most* women. Not his ex-wife, who had emptied his bank account and ramped up his credit cards to max while he was lying in a hospital bed recovering from surgery to fix a broken collarbone, damaged while saving *her* dratted dog from the ledge it had fallen over.

'I put your beer in the fridge while you were gone.'

Back to practical things. Food and beer. Excellent. Not sex. Excellent. *Breathe.* 'The fish restaurant was the closest and I know they do fabulous meals, having eaten there often.'

'Would you prefer a glass of champagne now?' Alesha asked. Her glass sat on the bench nearly empty.

'I'll take a pass, thanks. Shall we eat outside? There's a table under cover around the corner, and the wind's dropped. I like getting out in the fresh air after a day at work.' He didn't like the idea of being cooped up in this small inside space with Alesha. Not now he'd begun noticing more things about her best avoided. As lovely as she was, a short fling was probably not a wise move. There again, why not? Because she'd very recently been dumped. That was why. She was hurting, didn't need a rebound affair.

'Outside's good. I'm warm after my shower.' There was a slight slur going on in her speech.

He set plates and forks on either side of the table and opened the container from the restaurant. 'After you,' he said, indicating the chair opposite.

When she pulled up a chair next to the one he was going to use his first instinct was to move to the other side, but she'd be affronted and he didn't want that. After the day he'd had and spending the last hour sorting out Alesha's problem, he craved peace and quiet to eat and then he'd go back to his mother's house, hopefully for an uninterrupted night's sleep. Although that wasn't guaranteed—no one ever knew when the next child would arrive on the doorstep, brought in by the police or a distraught neighbour.

It was draining enough doing this work for a week at a time. How his mother coped year in, year out, he had no idea, except she was resilient and had come through a lot in her life, including putting up with his father's affairs to be there for her son until she finally couldn't take any more. He had nothing to complain about really and next week he'd be back in London working every hour available dealing with his scheduled list of patients that was endless.

'You've gone quiet,' Alesha commented as she loaded her plate with salad. Her shoulder bumped against his. Deliberate or accidental?

'Just letting go of the day.' He shifted his chair sideways.

'Tell me more about this place you're helping out at. It must be quite big to have an operating theatre.'

'Like I said, it's a shelter for neglected children. The operating theatre's tiny. Not a lot of operations are done there. Take today. A wee girl was found hidden in bushes under the Dubrovnik bridge, cold, hungry and with numerous injuries. She hasn't spoken a word, has had surgery, and faced strangers poking at her and asking questions, and just stands there staring around as though nothing's real.'

'Except the pain in her heart.'

'Exactly. One look in her eyes and you can see it, you know? It's huge, and everyone accepts it's going to take a long, long time to lighten it.'

'If they ever do.' A layer of sadness settled in Alesha's eyes and voice.

She really got it. Did that mean she'd been hurt badly in the past? Or was there a massive heart inside that chest that understood people? 'At least she's safe now, but what the future holds is anyone's guess.' Kristof needed air, space. That sadness was tugging at him when it shouldn't. Standing up, he walked to the other end of the deck to stare down at the harbour filled with cruise ships. Tourists flooded Dubrovnik during the day, turning the Old City situated behind these hills into a place most locals avoided until winter, when they got the city back to themselves. At night many of the tourists would be back on board their ship making the most of the entertainment put on free of charge.

He heard a movement beside him and Alesha was standing there, her hands on the concrete wall, leaning forward to peer in the same direction as him. 'It's stunning.' So she'd joined him but wasn't continuing the conversation that had him fidgeting to get away.

He usually managed to keep the kids he saw in his mother's clinic at a distance. But today Capeka had got to him. His shield had slipped. He didn't know why, but did know it wasn't a good look. And that it couldn't happen again. Not if he intended to maintain his barriers against being in a loving relationship. 'Yes, it's magic.'

'Very different from London.'

If she was digging for information about his life back there she would need a bulldozer. He commented, 'We don't get the wonderful weather, for starters.'

Her mouth flattened. Then turned up into a grin. 'Fair enough.' The grin was quickly followed by a yawn. 'Sorry. It's been quite a day on top of a long night. I didn't knock off work until eleven last night and since it was my last time on the ward there was a visit to the pub involved afterwards. Then today Luke's bombshell really sank in when I stepped out of the plane into Croatia.'

'I'll leave you alone, then.' Kristof's jaw dropped. He didn't want to go. He really didn't, instead wanted to hold her close, kiss away that hurt that had started going on in her eyes when she'd mentioned a big day. 'Are you going to be all right?'

Wipe your mouth out. You don't do personal questions. With anyone.

It brought people close when he learned what made them tick, meant he could no longer put them in a box.

Alesha blinked, hard. Her mouth flattened. He didn't like that. Nor that slumping that sloped her shoulders.

'Sorry, don't answer that. It's none of my business.' But if he could make her feel a bit happier, he would.

'We planned this trip at Easter. Then a couple of weeks ago I learned I was the only one flying to Dubrovnik. Luke has found someone else and they've gone to Paris for the weekend.'

That was appalling. Who did that? 'Can I swear?'

'Go ahead but it won't change anything.' She'd crossed her arms and those long manicured fingernails were digging into her biceps.

He'd prefer they were on his biceps. Kristof stepped closer so his arm touched hers. That was as close as he was getting, tantalising fingers or not. But hell, he wanted to pull her into his arms and kiss that sadness away. Even when the man she'd want kissing her wasn't him.

Alesha leaned into him, as though now she'd voiced what had happened the strength to stay upright had deserted her.

He couldn't resist. His arm wound around her shoulders, to give her support. Nothing more. Or was it? A heady mix of gentleness, need and friendship closed around him. A totally foreign sensation. He lost track of how long they stood there, both staring out across the harbour with a myriad lights winking from the ships and the wharves, he holding her, she trembling.

Then she knocked him sideways with a whisper. 'You don't have to go. I could do with some company.' When she turned to face him she was close so her breasts brushed against his chest. When her mouth touched his, those lips were soft and warm, exciting, just as he'd imagined. Talk about getting what he wished for.

Kristof lifted his chin and stepped back, his hands on her shoulders until she found her balance. 'Thank you for asking but you're feeling let down, unhappy, disappointed. Tomorrow you'll regret having made that suggestion.' He was already regretting not following through. As far as kisses went that one had barely got started, but every cell in his body was screaming out for more and for the follow-up rampant sex.

'That's a no, then.'

'Yes, Alesha, it is.' Give him strength, because the more he said no, the more he knew it was a lie, that he wanted to accept her invitation, to lose himself in her, give her a reason to let go the hurt plaguing her eyes for a few hours at least.

'I could beg.' Fixed on him, her eyes were enormous.

'It wouldn't become you.' His lips grazed her forehead. He breathed in apples from her hair.

Go, while you still can.

Dropping his hands, he stepped further away. 'Take care, Alesha. Whatever you do, enjoy your time in Croatia.' And on that dry note he left, feeling her eyes boring into his back until he reached the bottom step and let himself out onto the street. He didn't know if she watched from above as he walked up the road, wasn't looking back over his shoulder to find out. Alesha had come into his life with a problem. Now the crisis was fixed and with every step he took he was leaving her further behind, safe, out of his life, out of the way of temptation. He couldn't fix her bigger problem.

'Kristof, wait. Stop. Look up the road.' Alesha was running after him. 'I think there's a fire further up.' She had his arm now, was pulling at him and pointing towards the area where his mother's house was.

A red glow backlit a building. Not his mother's, but close. Someone's house was definitely burning. 'I'm calling the emergency services. You go back inside.' He didn't need to be worrying about Alesha while he tried to assess the situation.

'I'm coming with you. There could be people inside.'

Arguing wasted time. 'What can you do to help?' It was an honest question. If she was hanging around there might be something she could do to help.

'I'm a nurse, remember?'

'Come on.' There wasn't time to argue, and she was right, she might be needed. He began sprinting up the road. Hopefully she wasn't going to be required at the scene of the fire.

Puff, puff, from beside him. Not a fit nurse, then.

The emergency dispatch for the city answered his call, preventing him saying something he'd regret. Rattling off what he knew about the location, nothing specific but once the emergency crews got close they'd work it out, he punched the red icon and shoved the phone deep into his pocket, hoping it stayed there while he got on with helping out at the fire. Losing all his work contacts was not on.

You don't want to lose Alesha's number either.

Best if he did, then he couldn't be tempted into calling her, asking her to join him for a beer or a trip into town for a meal during the coming week.

Kristof really was trying to fool himself. Who needed a number when he walked by the apartment complex every day? Which reminded him. 'Did you remember your keys?'

She gaped at him, her eyes wide and filled with disgust. 'Guess it really isn't my day.'

They weren't going to call Karolina out a second time. 'There's a spare bed at my mother's.'

Laughter filled the now smoky air. 'I meant there went my opportunity to crash at your place. I have keys and phone buttoned into my back pocket.'

He looked. How could he not? Yes, there, on that smooth, curved outline of her backside, was the obvious shape of a phone and a bundle of keys. 'Well done.'

Damn.

CHAPTER THREE

ALESHA DREW DEEP breaths in an attempt to stop puffing so hard. Time to find a gym if this was what a short run up a gently sloping hill did. Beside her Kristof was barely breathing any faster than normal.

'Bystanders are saying there's a family of four inside,' he told her. 'I'm going to see how close I can get.'

'Be careful.' Look out for yourself, don't get injured. Clench, clench went her stomach for her new— What? Friend?

She couldn't hear any sirens. 'How far away is the fire station?' She picked her way through the crowd behind him.

'Ten minutes. Stay back here.'

'And if you find someone in need of medical attention?'

'We'll bring them out here and you can help me.'

'We?' That was when she realised two other men were pushing ahead on the same track Kristof was following. 'Fine.' She was wasting precious time, holding him back from possibly saving someone. 'Go.' Her heart sank. If there really was a family in that inferno their chances of survival were slim, and getting smaller by the second. When she was training back in Christchurch she'd worked in a burns unit and had hated it. The stench, the raw agony, the horror in her patients' eyes as they stared at their scars, had drained her emotionally in a way no other field of nursing had.

Around her people were talking as they gaped at the scene. Unfortunately she couldn't understand a word. Someone pointed towards the house and there was a shout as a burning piece from the roof plunged to the ground. Kristof towered above everyone, making it easy to keep an eye on his progress.

Be safe, please.

He was in charge. No doubt about that. He seemed the kind of guy who'd take note of the situation and still charge in to save whoever he could with little regard for his own safety. Not that she could explain why she felt that, she just did. He'd impressed her with the way he'd looked after her earlier. No one had ever gone out of their way for her before, and it made her feel special, as if she counted for something. Then she'd repaid him by coming on to him. It was a wonder he'd spoken to her at all after that.

'Does anyone know if the family was definitely at home when the fire broke out?' she asked without thinking, and got a surprise.

'The mother and son came home thirty minutes ago,' the woman beside her answered. 'The husband and other son are still out.'

'Two safe. That's a start.' Where had Kristof gone? There was no way he could get inside. Not and survive. It was a furnace in there.

'I hear sirens,' said the woman.

There was movement ahead, and the crowd parted. Kristof strode towards her, a body in his arms. 'Alesha?

I've got the lad. He's unconscious.' Kneeling down, he laid his precious bundle on the ground.

Running forward, she dropped to her knees, ignored the gravel digging into the earlier bruises. 'That's a nasty cut on his head.' Blood oozed through the lad's hair. Her fingers gently probed, touched swollen flesh. 'Something must've fallen on him. Where did you find him? You'd better not have gone inside.' What did that matter now? If he had he was out safe.

'On the back porch lying half out the door.' Kristof began checking the boy over, gently rolling him onto his right side. 'Burns to his back and left arm.'

'Don't pull that shirt off,' she warned. They didn't need to cause any further damage.

'Agreed.' Kristof was feeling the bones in an oddly shaped elbow, a competent doctor at work. 'Fractures for sure. He's got cuts as well as massive trauma bruising. Someone mentioned an explosion.'

'Do people here use gas for cooking?' That could explain the injuries and the fire.

'Yes.' He gave her a nod of acknowledgment. 'You know your stuff.'

'Worked in a burns unit. He has respiratory problems, probably due to smoke inhalation.'

'I'll check his heart.'

Cardiac arrest often followed respiratory failure. 'Will an ambulance come with that fire engine?' A defibrillator wouldn't go astray right now, just in case of the worst-case scenario.

'Of course. From what I'm hearing two fire trucks and one ambulance have just pulled up. The good news is the hospital is only a mile further up the road.'

'Knowing the lingo is a plus.' Never had she felt so

useless. Not understanding what was going on was disturbing. But she did understand this boy's dilemma and that was all that really mattered. He needed her help, not her doubts and frustration.

'Great nursing skills don't need interpreting.' Kristof underscored her thoughts as his hand touched the back of hers briefly. Except she hadn't thought *great* was true, just thorough.

Someone in uniform knelt beside her, asking rapid questions in Croatian. No doubt a paramedic. She locked eyes on Kristof. 'You take this.'

He was already talking to the other man. She continued taking the boy's pulse for a second time. 'Slower.'

Another person in ambulance uniform joined them and Alesha was nudged aside. Her back cricked as she stood up and looked around. 'What about the mother?'

Screams rent the air. Someone was pushing through the crowd. A woman. In her late thirties? The boy's mother? Alesha crossed her fingers. That would mean she was safe and not inside. The woman dropped to the ground beside the boy, crying and shouting, reaching to touch her son, being gently held back by Kristof and another lady.

Alesha stepped away. The woman's grief was personal, and heart-wrenching. On the other side of the road she stopped amidst the crowd to take stock. Around her voices were low and all eyes seemed to be on the mother and boy. Time to head back to the apartment. There was nothing else she could do to help here.

'He's going to be in hospital for a while but I think he'll be all right.' Kristof materialised out of the gloom. 'None of those injuries look life-threatening.'

'If you don't count the scars he'll have.'

'True.' His sigh echoed her own. 'I'll see you back to the apartment.'

'That's not necessary. It's only a few hundred metres down the road.'

'I don't care if it's next door. I'm coming with you.'

Nice. Especially when she'd all but thrown herself at him. 'Thanks.' Maybe this time she'd finally get to bed to catch up on some sleep. Alone, and right now that didn't seem as lonely as it should. It was a normal state.

A sound like a sweeping broom from outside her room penetrated Alesha's mind, bringing her to the surface of the sleep that had dragged her under the moment she'd dropped onto the bed after getting back from the fire. Judging by the smell of smoke, she should've showered but falling asleep under the water jet wouldn't have been a bright idea. Her shirt was rucked up to her breasts but it seemed she had managed to pull her jeans off.

The good news was she'd slept all night. Picking up her phone from the floor, she gasped. It was nearly one in the afternoon. Half the day had gone. What a waste when Dubrovnik was out there, waiting to be investigated.

Swinging her legs over the bed, she sat up and instantly dropped her pounding head into her hands. Too much sleep did that. And too many glasses of champagne on an empty stomach. The half-full bottle mocked her from the bench. Another waste, but thank goodness she hadn't drunk it all or she wouldn't have been able to help with that boy last night. Nor would she be feeling semi good to go today. What had she been thinking to have beer and champagne? It was so not her, but nothing about last night had been. On the other hand, last time she got dumped she might have packed a sad and had a few drinks, but she hadn't locked herself out in a foreign country or made a pass at a relative stranger. Throw in the fire and it'd been a drama-filled night.

How was that boy today? Hopefully he'd be heavily sedated to allow those burns time to settle down. Days, if not weeks, of painkillers and heavy doses of antibiotics were ahead for him.

Picking up her jeans, she grimaced at the not so white fabric. Dirt from kneeling on the ground by the boy looked as if it would never come out, but she'd throw them in the laundry in case she got lucky.

Heading for the shower, she tripped over a bag. Kristof's clothes. He'd forgotten them in his hurry to get away from her. Now what? Could she nail them to the wall outside the gate for when he walked home tonight?

Swish, swish. The sound that had woken her. Opening the wooden blinds showed Karolina sweeping the deck that covered the width of the property and right back to the table where she'd eaten squid with Kristof. Karolina would know where to find the children's home. It wouldn't be a problem to drop the bag off there on her way to the Old City. She also owed Kristof an apology for her untoward behaviour while they were eating. What had possessed her? Apart from feeling unloved and a teeny bit in awe of him?

With a towel wrapped around her waist, she snatched up her keys and headed outside. 'Karolina, hi.'

The woman turned, her long, thick ponytail flicking across her back. 'I hear we have you to thank for young Stevan surviving the blaze that destroyed his family's home. You and Kristof.'

'There were other people there more qualified to look

after him. How is Stevan today?' Knowing his name brought him closer.

'He's in—how do you say—Intensive Care?'

Alesha nodded. 'That's it.'

'Heavily sedated?'

Again, Alesha nodded.

'For the pain from the burns and the operation on his shoulder, or was it his arm? I'm not certain.'

'Probably shoulder from what I saw. He's going to be in hospital for a while.' Alesha drew a breath. 'Karolina, can you tell me where the children's home is? I've got a bag to drop off there.'

'It's easy. Come and I show you how to get there.' She headed for the wall that overlooked the street below and the harbour beyond. 'See that building at the bottom of the hill behind those shops? That's it. I will draw on your street map how to get there. It's not far, fifteen minutes' walking.'

'If I don't get lost.' Alesha laughed, ignoring the thrill of excitement in her veins. Here was a foreign town and she was about to go exploring. Travel was her favourite pastime when she wasn't nursing. At last she was behaving sensibly, accepting her lot and not getting in a pickle about it. 'Though getting lost can be fun in strange cities, as long as I find my way out again without getting into seedy places.'

'You'll be good down there, nowhere nasty. But with the map it is easy. Then where are you going after the refuge?'

'To the Old City to have a look around, maybe take a tour up to the lookout.' The tour took only a couple of hours and there was still plenty of time left today. If she hurried. 'I'd better get showered and dressed. I only just woke up.'

'It was an eventful night for you.' Karolina chuckled as if it was a huge joke.

'It sure was. And now I've wasted enough of the day as it is.' She turned for her apartment only to have Karolina follow.

'I'll mark the map for you. Have you had breakfast?'

'No. I'll get something on the way to the shelter. But a coffee wouldn't go astray.' She filled the kettle and plugged it in while Karolina found the map on the shelf where the city info brochures lay.

'There're two good bakeries on the road below this one.' She marked the map with two crosses. 'Here is Kristof's mother's place where the children stay.' She drew a big X over the spot with a circle around it.

'That's great. Thanks. Do you want a coffee?' Now why offer that when she was suddenly in a hurry to get moving? Because she liked this woman who hadn't gone ape at her for forgetting her keys last night, and was more than helpful today. Because this holiday alone wasn't how it was meant to be and she wouldn't mind a bit of company.

'A quick one. I have to be at work in forty-five minutes. I'll make it while you get ready.'

'You have another job as well as running this place?'

'Yes, because in winter there are not many guests so I need to keep the money coming.'

'Mortgages don't pay themselves, eh?' No wonder there were shadows beneath Karolina's eyes. 'I'll be fast. Milk, no sugar, please.'

After rubbing sunscreen on every bit of skin that might be seen by the sun and slapping her make-up on with less care than normal Alesha dressed in navy shorts and a snappy white shirt with thin darts down the front to accentuate her shape. There no hiding her height so she always aimed to draw attention to her breasts and hips.

'Out here,' Karolina called when she left the bathroom. 'On the deck under the umbrella.'

Where she and Kristof had sat last night. Only he'd taken up a lot more space with his long legs and large, muscular frame. Hard to imagine someone so big doing delicate surgical procedures, but she'd seen it before when she worked in Theatre, and knew men could be as careful and light with their sewing skills as a woman. How gentle would Kristof's fingers be on her skin?

Gasp. Stop thinking these random thoughts.

'If you like I can walk part of the way with you. My work is in the same direction.'

'That'd be great.' Alesha gulped down her coffee. 'I know you're in a hurry. I'll just get my bag.'

'And keys.' Another laugh.

'Not likely to forget them again.' At her side she crossed her fingers for good measure.

The sun beat down as Alesha walked down the steps that led from one street to the next further down the hill. After the previous wet, cool week in London the heat was heaven, and gave her another pang of nostalgia for summer at home. She was getting quite a few of those at the moment. Not that home was warm when she factored in her family, but she was not going there today when she was in paradise.

Her destination became apparent once she reached the harbour, a collection of low houses joined together with what must be corridors, and all tucked against the hill, bathed in sun. While it wasn't glamorous it was warm and welcoming. The front door stood wide open, and since no one was about she walked in, calling, 'Hello?' as she made her way to the desk at the end of the hallway. 'Hello?' The colours were bright: pinks, greens, blues, yellow. Done for children, not to win a prize in a homemaker magazine.

'Can I help you?' she was asked in a classy Croatian English accent.

Alesha looked back the way she'd come to see an older, tall woman coming towards her. 'Hello. I'm Alesha Milligan, a visitor to Dubrovnik.' Was this Kristof's mother? The eyes were the same mesmerising blue-grey shade. 'I'm the idiot who locked herself out of her apartment.'

'Now I know who you are.' The woman's face relaxed, her smile wide and friendly. 'You're the nurse who helped the boy caught up in the fire last night.' When Alesha raised an eyebrow at her, she added, 'My son mentioned you this morning.'

'He did?' There was a surprise. She'd have thought Kristof would have put her to the back of his mind the moment he'd seen her through the gate for the second time. 'I suppose everyone's talking about the fire. It was awful.'

'It could've been worse.' In the lady's face there was sympathy along with a load of acceptance for what life threw at people. 'The consequences of not using a gas tank properly.'

Had that been established already? Alesha wasn't getting into details. She didn't intend hanging around long enough to become involved in local events, other than what had happened last night. She shifted her balance, held up the bag of clothes. 'I'm returning Kristof's things.

I probably shouldn't have come here but I don't know where he stays.'

I'd like to touch base with him, apologise again for being too forward.

'You are most welcome here. Unfortunately, my son's in Theatre at the moment. Removing an appendix for a young girl. It gives her merry hell regularly, but isn't serious enough for the hospital to fix so he's doing it. It's our second appendectomy in two days.'

'Her family must be relieved you can help.' It was a shame she wouldn't be seeing Kristof. He'd been her saviour. 'Can you tell Kristof I said thanks, um, and sorry, please?'

'Sorry?'

Trust this woman to pick up on that. As astute as her son. 'I wasn't in a good frame of mind last night. Before we attended the fire,' Alesha hastened to add, not wanting anyone to think she'd done something wrong by attending the boy.

'Kristof won't be long. Would you like to look around our establishment while you wait?' The woman was already walking towards a door, as though Alesha was expected to follow.

'I'm on my way to the Old City to take a mini tour up the hill and to some tiny waterfall near the border.'

'It'll still be there tomorrow.' Mrs Montfort glanced over her shoulder. 'I'd really like to show you what we are doing here.'

Why? 'I'm only in town for a few days.'

'So Kristof tells me.' She held a door open. 'By the way, I'm Antonija.'

Certain she was being played, but with no idea what for, Alesha gave in and followed, partly because she hated saying no, and partly because her interest had been piqued last night when Kristof talked briefly about his work here. 'Tell me how the place operates. Do some of the children stay long term?'

'We have permanent children, though we're always trying to find families to adopt those. Then there are others who are brought in by strangers or the police who've been abused, abandoned, or have run away from who knows what.' The older woman's voice darkened. 'Some go home again, or to relatives; some into state care, and others become our temporary residents.'

'That's so unfair. How do you cope with this day in, day out?' Alesha's heart was breaking and she hadn't met any of the children.

'With dignity, love, and difficulty.'

Talk about honest. How many people would admit to a stranger that it was tough doing what she did? Alesha smiled. 'You must be a very special lady.'

The smile she got back was soft. 'Thank you, dear. I'm not alone. There are a lot of kind people out there, some of whom come here to help.' Then she turned brisk. 'Come and meet some of the children. This is the classroom.' Judging by the racket when she opened the door, the teacher was as much in charge as a sheepdog rounding up a herd of cattle. 'They might be a bit nervous but don't let that stop you being at ease with them.'

This woman didn't know her. 'I won't.'

Alesha stepped inside and smiled. There was nothing particularly unusual about the room or the children. They were all dressed in mismatched clothes, and their faces and hair shone. Most of them sat at desks with books open, books they were ignoring, until one by one they became aware of Antonija and quietened down.

Alesha bit down on the urge to laugh. Undoing Antonija's effect wasn't on if she wanted to get out of here in one piece. Because she had no doubt this woman could be fierce if needed, and when it came to disrupting the children fierce might be needed. She'd seen a similar determination to do what was right in Kristof's eyes when they approached that burning house. And when he'd backed away from her advances. Heat filled her cheeks and her arms tightened against her sides. What an idiot she'd been.

Antonija spoke to the children in Croatian before explaining to Alesha, 'I've told them your name and that you're visiting from London.'

How much had Kristof talked about her that morning? And why? He'd been all too happy to finally say goodnight when he'd returned her to the apartment so she'd thought he'd have all but forgotten her by breakfast.

The kids were all staring at her, some giggling. All except one. A skinny child—the long hair suggested a girl—stood stock-still in the far corner, one leg tucked behind the other, one hand gripped tight at her side while the other arm was encased in a sling. But worse than that, more heart-rending, was the blank expression on her face, closely followed by the incomprehension in her eyes. No one so young should ever feel that lost and confused. Except they could, and often did. And it was the most hideous place to be.

Alesha's heart heaved. She wanted to race across and bundle the child up into her arms and hold her until her eyes cleared—which would take months, if not years. She didn't move. Frightening the girl further would be the worst thing possible. That girl was putting it out there, 'don't come near'. 'The poor darling,' she whispered.

'Capeka is our latest visitor.

'Visitor?'

'For lack of a better word. I don't like calling them waifs or strays. She was found under a bridge by strangers, who brought her to us yesterday.'

Alesha nodded. 'Kristof operated on her.'

'He mentioned that? To you?' Surprise rippled off the woman. 'Sorry, that wasn't meant in an offensive way, but my son never talks about his patients. Especially not the ones he sees in here.'

'Guess he thought it didn't matter when we're not going to see each other again.'

'Really?'

Alesha had no idea what this lady was asking about. Kristof telling her about the girl? Or that she wouldn't see him again? It didn't matter, though disappointment rippled through her at the thought of not seeing him once more. Now that she was fully awake, not half naked and exhausted, nor feeling as let down as she probably should, Kristof would probably look like an everyday guy. One she'd not think about at unexpected moments. 'Does Capeka stand in the corner all the time? She doesn't join the other children?'

'Not yet. It's early days. Sometimes it takes for ever for a child who comes here to feel accepted. She's watching you, though. Interesting. Still, we'll leave her alone to make her own mind up about whether to join in or not. Come and see the rest of the centre.'

There went her sightseeing, but it didn't matter. She was more than happy to take a look around the home.

Nearly an hour later Alesha found herself wandering into the classroom again. This time she was alone, and the children were quiet, working on an exercise the teacher had set. Capeka remained in the corner, her eyes averted, and yet Alesha would swear the malnourished girl was aware of every move, every word uttered, by the children and the teacher. Nodding to the teacher, she went to sit on a chair at the back of the room, not intruding on Capeka but close enough to be there for her. Not that she had anything other than life skills to help someone with this child's problems, and that wouldn't be enough, but she wanted, needed, to be there for her. Wanted to send warm vibes across the gap between them, to let her know she wasn't alone, and was in good care now. That there were good people who'd never hurt her.

Picking up a children's book from the table beside her, she slowly turned the pages, not able to read the words, but murmuring her own version of the story. Not hard to do when the pictures suggested it might be a classic from her own childhood. When she reached the end she started again. And again. Until she felt Capeka's gaze on her. Then she read the story again. The child wouldn't have a clue if she was telling the story correctly or making up a load of nonsense but hopefully she heard the genuine empathy in her voice. As long as Capeka watched her she'd continue telling the same story over and over.

Kristof stood in the classroom doorway, flabbergasted. Alesha. What was she doing at the refuge? And in this room at that? Strange how there were nine children in here yet only one was fully aware of her.

Capeka was fixated on the woman reading a story out loud. Staring, unafraid of Alesha. Though there was no way the kid understood a word she was saying she seemed to understand the light, carefree cadence, the soothing facial expressions, the gentleness, the slow way

Alesha turned the pages and touched the pictures. If little Capeka was so taken with her that for the first time since her arrival she was actively watching an adult, then he'd go get a bed for Alesha immediately. She was needed around here.

There was still caution in the girl's expression as she listened, watched, standing in that awkward position. What that was doing to her leg muscles was anyone's guess. The tension was there in tight tendons, and that clenched fist. In the pain in her eyes. But those eyes were glued to Alesha. Interesting.

'I've never seen anything like it,' his mother whispered.

He flicked her a look. 'Bottle her.' He'd forgotten his mother had been behind him, and he never forgot when she was around. Keeping his guard up was automatic since his marriage imploded back when he believed in happily ever after. Before his father finished off that belief once and for ever. Before the guilt over blaming his mother for everything that went wrong in their family landed on his shoulders. He had to admit it, Alesha had intrigued him from the get-go with those beautiful eyes and that wonderful figure. Then there was her laughter and willingness to enjoy herself despite everything.

It seemed that around Alesha Milligan he had to be doubly vigilant.

His mother said quietly, 'I'm going to ask her if she'll drop in every day to spend time doing this with Capeka until she goes home.'

'London, not home,' he countered automatically. Keeping things correct was another habit from the past.

'London? That's handy.' His mother looked up at him with a curious look in her shrewd eyes.

A look that paralysed him. Trouble was brewing and he wasn't going to like it. But forewarned gave him time to prepare—if only he knew what he was arming up for. Unless he was being precious and it wasn't him she was targeting at all, but merely getting help for Capeka from any source available. That was his mother to a tee. But the sneaking suspicion going on in the back of his head that this was about him couldn't be denied, not totally. He needed to stay prepared, ready for anything. 'Don't even bother,' he retorted just in case he was right.

She was impaling him with a smug smile. 'Fine.'

Stepping away from his mother, he carefully closed the door, effectively shutting her out, and leaned back against it. It was hard to ignore that chuckle from the other side of the door though. His eyes sought a diversion. Alesha. Without all that stress going on she was more beautiful than he remembered. Her skin was peaches and cream, English rather than the outdoorsy skin that the few New Zealand women he'd met at the hospital seemed to gain over years in the sun. The smattering of freckles on her cheeks was cute, and added to her intrigue, giving an air of innocence that the wariness in her eyes refuted. Her simple white shirt was the perfect contrast for her golden brown hair tied back loosely into a thick braid. No doubt the temperature was too high to wear it out, which was a shame. Last night her hair had been a mess, all over the show, and very compelling. It had taken strength not to run his fingers through those rampant curls.

Why did she do this to him? What was different about Alesha that fizzed his blood in a way other women didn't? Whatever, he wasn't going to waste time figuring it out. They weren't going to be a 'they'.

There was no denying the churning going on in his

belly, though, while Alesha looked the epitome of calmness sitting on that uncomfortable chair making up a story for a sad little girl. Too much so for his comfort. Because he didn't believe it. There was history in her face and expressions, last night and now, that spoke of knowledge of Capeka's pain. Knowledge gained from experience. Someone had hurt her, and he didn't believe it was just that man who dumped her unceremoniously before her holiday. That had hurt her, no doubt, but there'd been more anger than the deep, gutting pain that a broken heart would cause. He should know. He'd been there.

Maybe he should've taken her up on that offer she'd made by placing her mouth on his. He was not averse to a fling with a beautiful and willing woman. There was red blood in his veins, after all. Sex without strings. Add in a meal or two, sharing a glass of champagne, and it sounded good to him. Especially when he'd be heading back home to London next Saturday.

Alesha lives in London.

London was huge. They'd never bump into each other unless it was deliberate, and why would it be? He hadn't found out where she worked, and had no intention of doing so. She might be a nurse but there were many hospitals and medical service centres around the city.

Right then the woman causing his brain fade looked up and locked startled eyes on him, crimson creeping into her cheeks. 'Hello,' she said quietly.

He crossed the room and straddled a chair, his hands on the back as he studied her. 'Hello back.'

Her gaze dropped to the book and once again she began telling a story.

A quick glance showed Capeka wearing a frown and her head lowered. He'd wrecked the moment. 'Sorry,' he said as quietly as possible. 'I should've thought before I acted.'

It's your fault for getting in my head.

'It's okay. She's tiring anyway. It wasn't as though she was about to run across and crawl onto my knee. Unfortunately, that's going to take a lot of time and care so it won't be me she finally trusts enough to get close to.'

'You're starting the process though. That's good.' Last night he'd been thinking she was a bit of a loose cannon with her stress, drinking and that kiss. Though not at the fire. There she'd been calm and efficient, skilful and caring as she helped young Stevan. Nor did that describe the quiet, contained woman sitting opposite him now. Not even close. First impressions didn't always pan out. But usually he first got suckered into believing the woman was wonderful when really she was a conniving scheme wanting something from him. Could second impressions be just as wrong? Please no. So far all Alesha had wanted from him was a kiss and maybe follow-up sex. He couldn't argue with that. It certainly didn't appear to come with the *I'm taking all you've got* attitude of his ex.

You didn't see it with her until it was too late either, he warned himself.

Sweat broke out on his brow. It was time to get out of here, go find a kid who needed his attention, because right now his brain was on the blink, focusing on Alesha when it knew better. He wasn't in the market for a woman.

Hot and Alesha were suddenly in the same thought. His fingers dragged down his face. This was absolutely bat crazy. Get out of here.

Alesha stood up, unfolding her body slowly. 'I brought your clothes back.'

'I saw a bag on my mother's desk. Thank you.' He had to turn away or drown in the deep brown speckled pools fixed on him, full of nothing but friendship. Friendship was good. Even Alesha's wary version. It wasn't enough. Had to be more than enough. He wasn't about to add to her hurt. But he could alleviate it for a while.

'Easy. Our girl's watching you from under her eyebrows.' There was hope in Alesha's voice.

'Capeka. It means stork.'

'I heard.' Low laughter erupted from that sensuous mouth. 'It suits her. Not sure that's good, but if it works then what does it matter?'

'Capeka.' Kristof spoke softly in Croatian. 'Did you like Alesha's story?'

The girl nibbled her bottom lip and stared at the floor. Then slowly she nodded, once.

Alesha looked from the girl to him. 'What did you say?'

'She'd like you to come back and read to her again.' Sort of. What had possessed him to say that? He didn't want her hanging around here. Not when his belly knotted and his groin tightened just being in the same room. All very well to think a quick fling was a good idea, but every time he saw that darkness at the back of Alesha's gaze he knew he had to stay away. Adding to her pain was not happening on his watch.

'No problem. I'll drop in tomorrow.'

No surprise there. 'This could put restraints on your sightseeing.' He hadn't forgotten why she was here.

'I'm sure I can fit it all in.' Alesha closed the book and placed it on the table. Nodding at Capeka, she smiled.

'I'll be back tomorrow morning.' Then she headed for the door.

Kristof translated before following. And promptly wished he hadn't when his mother confronted him.

'Kristof, you said you couldn't find anyone to take as your partner to the fundraising dinner. I'd like you to take Alesha as a thank you to her for spending time with Capeka.'

'Mother,' he growled. 'There are reasons I am going alone.' Not that he could remember what they were right now, other than he hated charity functions with a passion. Sure, they raised the money needed for the cause, but he preferred to write a cheque any day. No palavering to be had. No smiling to people who'd done their damnedest to outbid everyone else just to prove they could.

'Alesha.' His mother had turned her shoulder on him. 'Tonight there's a dinner in the Old City to raise funds for the shelter and I'd like you to join us.'

Alesha would say no. So far she didn't seem to be the type who liked all that hype either. 'Really? That would be lovely, thank you. What time and where?'

Third impression—Alesha liked to socialise, and there would be her favourite champagne on tap too. He hadn't done very well at reading her at all.

His mother turned to him. 'Kristof will pick you up at seven.'

Thank you, Mum.

Short of looking and sounding unreasonable, he was stuck with bowing to her wishes and accompanying this woman to a dinner he did not want to attend. But he owed his mother. Always had, always would.

Bring it on.

CHAPTER FOUR

KRISTOF DIDN'T WANT to take her to the dinner. Alesha sighed her disappointment. There'd been no missing the annoyance that had flared in his face when his mother had told her he'd pick her up at seven. He was so obviously uninterested in her in any way, shape or form that it was going to be a long night having to sit side by side pretending they were comfortable with each other. To think she'd thrown herself at him last night. Thank goodness one of them had been thinking straight.

She really was a slow learner. To do that only weeks after Luke had dumped her, proving once again men weren't interested in her for anything but having a good time, a short good time at that, showed she'd hit rock bottom. Maybe she hadn't loved him as in completely and utterly, but her feelings for him had been strong and, she'd believed, growing. Could it be she hadn't loved him but loved the idea he might be the one? How long was she going to carry on believing there might be a man out there who could love her for all of her? Come on. She didn't truly, deep down, believe that. No, it was hope for the impossible that got in the way. Hope that had her taking chances that always backfired. Hope that because her parents stopped loving her didn't mean someone else would.

Alesha stared at her image in the small mirror in the apartment and twisted around to check the back of her fitted red dress. Red was this season's top colour and suited her well. Even if she said so herself she didn't scrub up too badly. Eat your heart out, Luke. Her shoulders slumped. Bet he was having a barrel of fun with *the one* in Paris, and hadn't thought of her once. Why would he when she was obviously yesterday's bread?

Stop it. She was going out to a dinner and auction with a gorgeous man in a city she'd never seen before. Take the positives and forget all about what might've been. A giggle escaped. She wasn't going to understand most of what went on so she could make fun filling in the gaps.

The zip had three inches to go and she couldn't reach it. She'd go knock on another apartment door if she thought any other guests were in, but she already knew they weren't. The complex had been eerily quiet when she returned from walking along Port Cruz.

Voices outside drew her attention. Karolina and—and Kristof. Bang on seven o'clock. Downing the last of the water in her glass, she picked up her keys and phone, shoved them in her clutch purse before drawing a deep breath and stepping outside. Almost into Kristof's arms as he reached to knock on the doorframe. 'Oh, hello,' she gasped, her gaze filled with an expanse of white-shirt-covered chest.

Kristof stepped back, taking that manly scent with him. 'You look stunning.'

Lifting her head, she stared up into warm eyes that didn't seem to be filled with a hidden agenda. 'Thank you.'

Don't let that go to your head.

It wasn't the first time a man had said the same, yet when Kristof spoke in that husky, warm voice that sent shivers down her spine she wanted to believe him more than she'd believed anyone before. Silly girl. Had she already forgotten her determination to be careful, and remain aloof from now on? If only she knew how to do that then she wouldn't get hurt. She turned to close her door.

'Stand still while I pull your zip up.' It was a command, not said with amusement or longing.

How had she forgotten the zip? Because Kristof stole the capability to think, to remember, to act normally. 'Sure.' Heat tiptoed into her skin where his fingers brushed, and even where they didn't. A quick tug and she was all done up, and free of him. This was going to be a very long night. She spun around. 'Let's go.' Being unpunctual was not her.

Kristof took her hand and placed it on his arm. 'Let's.'

On the short drive to the Old City Kristof pointed out landmarks and the quickest way for her to walk from the apartment when she wanted to go on the tour she'd missed out on that day. So far so good. The tension gripping her since he'd appeared at her door backed off, making it easy to chat with him. When she wasn't trying to ignore how handsome he was, or how sexy those black trousers, white shirt and black dinner jacket made him look, that was.

'You have to make time to wander around this city, day and night. It's special,' Kristof told her as they walked hand in hand—so she didn't slip on her heels apparently—down the sloping ancient road into the centre of the city where tables had been set up under large sun umbrellas outside a restaurant.

Stopping to stare around at the buildings and parapets, and the paved road, Alesha nodded. 'I can never get enough of these old towns. Back home old means weatherboard houses and simplistic churches. Nothing as beautiful as this.'

He laughed. 'I hear there are wonderful mountains and green hills for miles, and the sea is never far away.'

'Yes, there are those.' Another pang of homesickness knocked. Why? It wasn't as though she had family or close friends hankering for her return. But this going it alone meant being lonely at times, which was when she usually made the mistake of trying to get close to a man. Sucking her stomach in and tightening her shoulders, she got on with enjoying the evening with Kristof. 'Home is where the heart is—' though hers had gone AWOL '—and all that, but at the moment I'm having a great time discovering the northern hemisphere.'

Kristof nudged her towards the restaurant. 'So you're out to conquer the world? Or running away from home?'

Too close to the mark to acknowledge. 'Definitely conquering.'

'Let's find our seats and get a glass of your favourite tipple, then you can tell me about the places you've been.'

They were shown to the top table, and as Kristof held out her chair he was grumbling under his breath.

'Problem?' she asked.

A spark flared in his eyes as he leaned close. 'If we were seated at the back we could escape early. Now we're stuck to the bitter end.' His gaze seemed fixed on her, which didn't go with the bitter bit of his comment. That was a very heated gaze, stirring her in places that didn't need stirring, and twisting her stomach into knots that could make dining difficult.

Breathing deep did her sensory glands a whole load of

good and made her smile back at him. 'We'll have a good time regardless.' She was determined to. It wasn't often she got to go to a fancy dinner with a gorgeous man at her side to help raise funds for a worthwhile cause. Let's face it, she'd never done anything like this. Making the most of Kristof's mother's generous gesture wasn't going to be hard. 'Where's your mother?'

'Over the other side of the room working the crowd. When it comes to her strays, she's very good at getting people to put their hands in their pockets, or wave their credit cards over a machine.' Pride was mixed with resentment in his voice, in the tightness rippling off his shoulders.

What had he missed out on that he resented his mother giving so much of herself to those children? 'Has she always run the shelter? Or is it something she's started recently?'

Kristof took two glasses of champagne from the hovering waiter and passed one to her before sitting down. 'I thought we were talking about your travels.'

Shut down just like that. Go with it or up the ante? She glanced at Kristof's profile; his jutting jaw warned best to go with him if this evening was to be the fun she'd decided to have. Though that jaw was quite sexy with its implied strength and determination. 'I arrived in England two years ago with a six-month contract in the children's ward in Bristol's main hospital. While there I bought a car so I could get out and see places. At the end of that job I went to Wales for another short-term position.'

He listened with an intensity that seemed to cut out everyone and all the noise around them. Warmth stole over her. No man had shown such courtesy, or even interest, in her exploits before. Usually they only ever wanted to talk about themselves.

'Go on.'

It wasn't happening. His mother appeared between them and leaned down to kiss Alesha on both cheeks. 'Thank you for coming. I'm sure you'll have a wonderful evening. Now I'd like to introduce you to the other guests seated with us.'

When Alesha glanced behind this formidable woman she saw three couples waiting to be shown to their seats. She stood up at the same time as Kristof.

He placed his hand on her waist in a proprietary manner and nodded to everyone, taking over from his mother. 'Hello, everyone. This is Alesha, a nurse from New Zealand who's on holiday in Dubrovnik. Alesha, I'd like you to meet Filip and Nina Babic.'

As her hand was warmly shaken Alesha smiled and hoped everyone spoke a little English, but if not then she'd still enjoy the ambiance. Handshaking over, everyone sat and soon the noise level had increased to deafening.

Kristof leaned in close. 'Not sorry you came?'

She shook her head, breathed in his spicy aftershave, and smiled. 'If that's your get out of jail card, then sorry, but this is fun.'

'How much are you understanding?' He grinned.

'Very little but I'm fine with that, though I will need you to interpret the menu.' She could see it lying by her setting and it was impossible to read.

'Be nice to me or I'll extract revenge.' His breath was warm on her neck.

She could go with his revenge if that meant getting closer. Looking around, because looking at Kristof was too disturbing, she was shocked to find everyone with them was watching her and Kristof with indulgent smiles on their faces. 'Kristof,' she hissed into his ear. 'Sit up.'

He did, slowly, and gave her a wide smile before turning to talk to the woman on his other side.

On her right Filip asked, 'Have you come all the way from New Zealand to see our city?'

At least that was what she thought he asked in his scrambled English. His effort was appreciated. Any English was better than her Croatian. 'Not quite. I've been living in England for two years, visiting different European countries as work allows.' This was getting repetitive.

'You're fortunate you can do this.'

'I am,' she replied and sneaked a look at Kristof, who was watching her with a speculative gleam in his eyes. 'What?' A delicate shiver strolled up her spine.

'Nothing. Just keeping an eye out for you in what must be a strange setting.'

He had her back? She also couldn't remember anyone doing that for her before. She'd been mixing with the wrong crowds. Kristof was setting her a new benchmark. Not that she'd be getting any ideas regarding her and Kristof. Tonight was only about enjoying the moment, and this moment was with Kristof and his mother's friends. Turning to Filip, she told him, 'Having no ties back home allows me the pleasure of travelling wherever I choose.'

'You don't have family?'

She shook her head. Not really. Not one that acknowledged her, at any rate. 'No.'

'*Djèca?*'

'Pardon?'

'He means do you have any children?' Kristof spoke over his shoulder.

The guy was involved in another conversation and listening in on hers at the same time? She needed to be careful around him. Focusing on Filip, she said, 'I don't have a partner so no children.' Having children of her own would be wonderful and something she hoped for in the future. She'd love them unreservedly, never push them away or make them feel unwanted. Never.

Kristof turned his attention back to her. 'This guy who called off your relationship the other week? How serious were you about him?'

She preferred it when Kristof had his back to her. While this had nothing to do with him, she answered anyway. 'I wouldn't have agreed to come here with him if I wasn't.' But was that really true? It had been the romance of the occasion that had sucked her in, excited her, because no other man had ever promised such an exciting wonderful holiday for her, with her.

Kristof nodded. 'Fair enough.'

'Everyone has their way of showing their feelings,' she snapped, shaken at the idea seeping into her thoughts over the past couple of days. She was more angry about once again being shown she was unlovable than feeling as if her heart had been ripped out of her chest.

A large, warm hand covered hers briefly, those long fingers squeezing gently. 'You're right. I'm sorry.'

'Kristof.' She aimed for serous, half got it right. 'I'm not grieving for him. I'm angry he let me down, and for thinking there was more to our relationship than was real.' Startled, she dropped her fork. That was so true.

'Enough. Enjoy your entrée.' Kristof removed his hand, and picked up a fork. 'I hope you like lobster.'

Her mouth salivated. 'Do I what?' Grinning, she forked up a healthy mouthful. 'One of my favourite foods of all time. What else are we having?'

'Next course is rabbit goulash, followed by an apple and chocolate creation I'm sure you'll love.' His smile was wicked, sending her stomach into a riot of butterflies.

As the night progressed Alesha found it harder and harder to keep on track. Whenever Kristof looked at her as though *she* was his favourite course all her defence mechanisms came into play, at the same time warring with the need to have fun and follow her determination to enjoy each day as it unfolded. This latest version of her week in Dubrovnik had her blood racing and her nerves out of kilter. What if she made another mistake so soon after the last one? Was she throwing herself at Kristof?

Have a fling.

How did she start one if not by showing her intentions?

'We're only spending the evening together helping my mother out,' Kristof said in a tone that spoke loud and clear—there'd be no further dates. A reminder he hadn't been the one to invite her here.

Apparently she was an open book. 'I wasn't expecting anything else.' Although she might have been wishing for more. Disappointment tugged, because she was out with a handsome man in an amazing setting in a city far from any other she'd visited, and of course it would be fun to experience *everything* the city had to offer.

'Good.' This man did blunt well.

Time for a subject change. She shoved her chair back. 'I'm going to look at the gifts to be auctioned.' Bidding for something would be the right thing to do after Kristof's mother had so kindly invited her along.

Kristof strolled alongside her, his shoulder brushing

hers. Intentionally? After his warning? There were mixed messages coming her way. 'There's lots of art; paintings, pottery, and sketches. Most are too big to carry back to London.'

'Tell me what those vouchers are for.' Alesha pointed to a line of cards with photos of food, buses, views, and a beauty parlour, trying to ignore his tall, well-proportioned body. 'I get what most of them are about, but not where the service offered is situated. Like that one.' Her finger tapped a picture of an outdoor restaurant with the sparkling blue ocean as a backdrop.

'Cavtat, which is south of here. You can go by road, or, better yet, take a boat ride down there. It's a lovely town with a baroque church and the Rector's Palace to visit. The beaches are stunning, and there are lots of food choices.'

'You've sold me on the place. I'll visit one day this week.' She'd bid for that voucher, even though it was a meal for two people. She laughed. Perhaps she could use it twice. Or talk Kristof into going with her. Although, he'd made it clear, no further dates, remember? Was this even a date when his mother had invited her and demanded Kristof drive her?

'You could eat there every night this week for what you've just bid,' Kristof admonished an hour later when she held the Cavtat restaurant voucher in her hand.

'That's hardly the point of this auction.'

'I doubt my mother invited you along to spend your hard-earned money.'

'Then why did she?' Alesha asked, doubting she'd get an answer.

Kristof's face softened. 'She likes making kind gestures. Genuinely kind ones.'

And that was all Alesha was getting. She could ask until she was blue in the face but Kristof would not say another word on the subject. She knew that shut-off look already. She recognised the need to keep himself to himself, because it was the same with her. It didn't stop her wanting to wipe away that hurt flitting through his eyes, pain that he thought he had under wraps. 'Would you like to come to this restaurant with me?'

'I don't think that's a good idea.'

'I'm not asking you to do anything you wouldn't want to, just to share another meal with me.' So far she'd been in Dubrovnik two nights and had eaten with Kristof for both of them. 'Let me know if you change your mind.'

'I could drive you down to Cavtat after I finish at the children's centre, I suppose.'

Sound happy about it, why don't you?

'I'm going by boat so I get to see the coast along the way.' Sitting on a ferry was far more fun than in a car. 'Or don't you like being on the water?'

'You're persistent, aren't you?' He finally cracked a smile that sent fire throughout her. 'Okay, thank you. I'll go with you by boat to Cavtat. As long as we walk around the peninsula before eating. It's a spectacular spot with the water so clear you can see right to the bottom.'

'Done.' She wouldn't look smug, or excited, or grateful. Nope, just relieved, and happy, and—calm. Okay, that wasn't so easy to pull off, but she gave it her best shot. 'I guess we're going for dinner, not lunch?'

'Yes. If that's all right with you?' Kristof hastened to add, inexplicable excitement flashing across his face before he shut down again.

What was that about? Forget the fling idea. It wasn't

happening. They both had too many issues to let loose and enjoy each other. 'Absolutely.'

He stood up and reached for her hand to pull her gently upright. 'Let's say goodnight to everyone and get out of here. I've done my bit for this time.'

There it was again, that hint he was not happy about something to do with his mother. Or was it her charity he had issues with? Yet he gave her weeks out of what would no doubt be a hectic schedule back in London. Alesha smoothed down the front of her dress and looked at Kristof as he said goodbye to Filip and Nina. She'd probably never know what made this man tick. That wasn't such a bad thing. After this week she wouldn't see him again anyway. Getting to know more about him only meant getting close, involved with him, and she didn't need that. Nor, she suspected, did he.

Outside in the slightly cooler air Alesha stared around at the city so alien to anything at home. The night lights and shadows gave an eerie yet exhilarating feel to the place. 'Wow.'

'Come on. I'll take you down to the harbour edge. It's on the other side of these buildings.' Kristof reached for her hand.

The need to slip her hand in his was strong. As was the need to kiss him. She did neither. The champagne had been delicious at dinner but she'd refrained from enjoying too much, and she could do the same about holding hands. It would only be a gesture and she didn't need any more of those now that she'd made up her mind to be strong—and single.

Kristof pulled off the road outside the apartment complex, relieved he'd got Alesha back without giving into the temptation that was her scent, her beauty, the wondrous figure that skin-tight dress highlighted, her soft yet strong voice. He'd lost count of how many times he'd made to haul her into his arms so he could kiss her down at the waterfront by the boats tied up. Temptation usually came with written warnings, but there were no warnings about Alesha.

None other than the ones his brain kept throwing up. What really bugged him was that he never hesitated when a woman came on to him, and yet last night when Alesha had he'd hauled the brakes on fast. She overwhelmed him with her smiles, her frankness.

Oh, get real. She's so sexy in that little red number it's impossible to ignore her.

He wanted her, plain and simple.

Alesha opened her door. 'Thanks for a great time. I'll see you later in the week.'

Cavtat. Why had he agreed to go with her? How could he not when she'd looked at him with such candour in those heart-stopping eyes and said it was only for a meal? That felt like a challenge, and challenges were not to be ignored. 'I'll call to let you know what night works with my programme at the children's home.'

'I'm going to spend time with Capeka again so I might see you there.' She clambered out of the car. 'Goodnight, Kristof.'

No way. Alesha wasn't getting away that easily. The brakes were off. He wanted her. 'Wait.' He held his hand out for the keys. 'Let me.'

'It isn't necessary,' she quipped. 'I usually only make an idiot of myself once over any one thing.'

'Humour me, okay? One thing I did learn growing up was manners.' And to work hard at being different from his father. But that was another story, which had nothing to do with what was going on in his body.

'You just don't want to find me sleeping on the side of the road when you go to work in the morning.' Somehow she managed to pass the keys to him without touching his skin.

'I'll bring some toast in case.' The sorry dope he'd suddenly turned into had been hoping for a little bit of contact, an indication she might be a little attracted to him.

Her laughter tinkled in the clear air, drew him closer to her as they climbed the steps up to the apartments. His gaze fell to the curved, swaying backside in front of him, his groin tightening alarmingly. He should've stayed in the car. Then they were on the level and Alesha was waiting for him to open the door to her apartment, her back to him.

'Who's going to undo that zip for you?' The words spilled out. A logical question considering he'd had to finish doing up the zip in the first place, but it was filled with suggestion and hope and need that he couldn't hide. When had he last felt so awkward with a woman? Probably when he'd asked Melissa Stokes to his sixth birthday party.

'I could go door knocking,' she tossed over her shoulder as she stepped inside.

He followed her in and reached for her, hands on her shoulders. 'I don't like that idea.'

'Really? Then what are you going to do about it?'

Slowly he turned her around and lifted those long waves of golden brown hair with one hand. With the other he nudged the zip down an inch. And another inch. Another. All the way to the top of those curves he'd followed up the steps. The air stuck in his throat at the beauty before him. Soft, satin-like skin the colour of vanilla ice cream. The gentle flaring of those hips shaping her dress. The heat, the scent of summer. Everything about Alesha made his body hum.

Oh, so slowly Alesha turned. His hand spread across the width of the small of her back, the other cradling her hair, letting the silky texture slide through his fingers. The last of the restraints he'd placed on himself during the evening evaporated in an instant of heat and desire. Gone. All he knew was he wanted her so badly it hurt in places pain had no right to be. He leaned down so his mouth could caress Alesha's. It wasn't enough. Her soft lips melted into his so they became one where their mouths joined. It wasn't enough. His hands slid under the fabric of her dress, slid it down over her shoulders, while at the same time he kicked the door closed.

Alesha hesitated, pulled back to lock an unsteady gaze on him.

His lungs stalled.

Please don't say no.

Then she smiled and her lips were returning to his, her tongue making forays into his fevered mouth, driving him crazy. If this was what kissing Alesha did to him, then the next hour was going to be unbelievably erotic.

A low, slow groan escaped her mouth as she pressed her breasts against his chest, her taut nipples like beads of desire throbbing with the beat of his blood. He wound his arms tighter, brought her so close they moulded together. It was wonderful. The heat, the need coursing through his veins, and, he knew, hers too. It wasn't enough. His shirt and her dress were impediments.

Setting Alesha back only as far as necessary, he nudged the narrow straps from her shoulders. The dress fell away. Nothing held those pert breasts, no lace or silk, nothing but nature. His knees bowed. As he reached to bring her up against him she resisted.

'I want to see you.' Her hands were tugging his shirt free of his trousers.

He took his hands away from that warm skin for the moment it took to drag the offending garment over his head and toss it aside. Then he went back to touching, holding, looking. Feeling, aching, needing. And lifting her into his arms to place her on the beckoning bed where he could make love with this amazing woman all night long. Where he would give her everything she needed and wanted, first. Where the pleasure would be as much his as hers. Where he could lose himself in her heat, and her generosity.

CHAPTER FIVE

ALESHA ROLLED OVER in the rumpled mess that was sheets and pillows and the heady smell of a night making love with Kristof, and dragged her eyes open. Some time after the sun came up he had left to go back to his mother's house to get ready for a day at the children's home. He hadn't kissed her goodbye, hadn't uttered a word, just slipped into his shirt and trousers, slung his jacket over his shoulder and left. Message clear—this had been a one-off night.

It was surprising how comfortable she was with that. It might be too soon after being dumped but she'd gone into the evening eyes wide open and mind clear about having fun without any attachments. Her heart had not been involved, nor was it going to become so. Just because they'd both wanted to have fun without consequences that didn't make them a couple, or even best friends.

Shuffling up the bed and stuffing a pillow behind her, she leaned back and looked around. Sunlight snuck around the edges of the wooden blinds, teasing her to get up and make the most of another bright and sunny day. In a minute. It was relaxing to sit here with nowhere she had to be by a specific time. Freedom from work. Freedom from other people's expectations. Living up to her own for a change. Feeling hollowed out, yes, but that came with a sense of getting to understand herself as never before.

Looking back, she saw the nine-year-old version of Alesha—sad, bewildered, lost. Her parents suddenly didn't have time to talk to her about school or the games she played as they'd done before. They withdrew their love so she went looking for it elsewhere. Which was where this chasing men came from, she recognised now. She plucked at the sheet, unable to cry for the child who'd become the woman she was now, her heart heavy. Yet persistent hope pinged her. This time it was hope she'd get her life sorted in a way that fitted with her new dreams. Be strong and— She faltered. And single? Was it Kristof who'd made her see things differently? If so, she owed him, and not in a clingy, 'let's be together' kind of way.

There'd been a certain freedom about the evening, followed by that sexy, sensual night, with a man she'd only met the day before. Having never done anything so unrestrained before she'd have thought remorse would've been her prime emotion today, but no. For the first time in a long time she was completely relaxed, wasn't looking for hints of what might come in the future, what Kristof might expect of her today or next week or even when they were back in London. For once she wasn't getting ahead of herself.

Untangling her legs from the sheet, she leapt out of bed and stretched up on tiptoes, arms above her head, then bent to touch the floor with her fingers. While muscles everywhere ached, her body felt alive and ready for action. More action. Like a swim, breakfast, a visit to see Capeka, and then walk into the Old City to take a mini-tour up to the lookout on the hills behind the city.

'Morning,' Karolina called from the other side of the deck where she was sweeping the moment Alesha walked outside dressed in her bikini. 'You had a good time last night?'

How much did she know? 'I had a great time. The auction was a huge success.'

'So I hear.' Karolina's eyes sparkled with mischief.

So she knew more than how the dinner had gone. No need to confirm or deny though. Placing her keys and phone on a sunbed, Alesha then dived into the sparkling water and popped up at the far end. 'How often does Antonija organise auctions? I gather last night's wasn't the first.'

'Once a year. She says any more wouldn't bring in more money and double the cost of putting them on.'

'That makes sense.' As far as Alesha could discern, if ever there was a sensible woman Kristof's mother was her. 'The children's home must cost a bit to run.'

'I think so. Though Kristof arranges for doctors to come from England throughout the year free of charge.'

So he was happy to help out but had issues about his mother. She was not about to ask Karolina anything about him. That gleam in those knowing eyes would only increase and she didn't need that. She also wasn't going to explain she was having a week like no other where she'd be free and happy and take whatever was on offer, then go back to England, sign up for another job. Which reminded her—that job Cherry called about. She'd send in an application before she got on with this new way of life.

Oh, boy. She had plenty to think about. But not now. Job application, then a shower before heading down the hill for breakfast at one of those bakeries she'd spied yesterday on her way back from Port Gruž.

* * *

'Morning, Alesha,' Kristof called from the other end of the hallway as she entered the building. 'I didn't expect you here quite so soon.'

I didn't expect my pulse to go from slow to racing in two seconds flat just seeing you.

'Hi. Thought I'd spend some time with Capeka before I go sightseeing, if that's all right?' Had Kristof been looking out for her? Unlikely after his quiet way of leaving her apartment that morning. 'I'd like to try reading to her again, but only if you think it won't distress her when I'm leaving at the end of the week.'

'My mother was hoping you'd drop in for that reason, so she's not concerned about Capeka getting too fond of you in a short time.'

'That's good.' Alesha's heart rate sped up as she studied this man she'd been so intimate with before knowing much about him. But she had known he was kind, helpful, considerate, could laugh, and smiled like every woman's dream. What more did she need to know? He hadn't hurt her, probably wouldn't either. He certainly wouldn't if she didn't let him close. Did she regret last night? Not one bit.

'Got a minute first? I'd like to ask you a couple of things.' Kristof held a hand out in the direction of a door along the hall.

'Sure.' Nothing about last night showed in his straight expression. None of the passion or need or even the delight in sharing what they'd had. They were back to friendly without overdoing it. 'Sure,' she repeated.

She'd barely parked her butt on the chair by a desk when he asked, 'What line of nursing are you most qualified in?'

Definitely back to basics. That was fine by her. 'I've mostly worked on children's wards and in paediatric ICU. But as all nurses do in their training, I've covered everything and feel comfortable in most situations. Why?'

'Theatre work?'

So that was where this was going. 'Yes, some, but not for eighteen months when I worked for five weeks as a fill-in at one of the East London hospitals.'

Kristof locked his intense gaze on her. 'I know you're on holiday so this is asking a lot, but we're down a theatre nurse today and I have a tight schedule of small surgeries.' He paused. 'Would you mind helping with handing over bandages, suture equipment, things like that?'

Alesha rushed in. 'No problem.' The tour would be on every day so she wasn't missing out on anything and if she was needed here then that was fine with her.

'It's mundane, I know, but you haven't got clearance to work as a qualified nurse. I'd still like to check your credentials though.'

'I'd be leery if you didn't. Ring the nursing employment agency I am currently working through.' She tapped her phone for the number, and gave him a name to ask for. 'While you're doing that I'll go say hello to Capeka. Oh, and mundane doesn't bother me if I'm helping someone.'

Kristof was already picking up the phone, barely giving her a nod.

Okay. Definitely professional mode. Did that mean last night never happened? Or he wanted to forget it had? Or was Kristof afraid she was expecting more? Hearing him ask for the recruitment manager she'd referred him to, Alesha gave a mental shrug and left him to it. Whatever he thought about their night together wasn't going to change her plans.

Heading to the classroom where she'd met Capeka yesterday, she found a happy smile before entering quietly so as not to disturb the children who were all engrossed in their books. All, except one wee girl standing in the corner on one leg.

Alesha said hello to the teacher, and instantly Capeka lifted her head, a glimmer of hope in those big, sad eyes.

Oh, oh. This might not be a wise idea if the child was starting to look out for her. But Kristof said his mother was happy for her to drop by and if she could do even the smallest amount of good for this girl she would.

The teacher was holding out a book towards Alesha and she took it, relieved to see it was another classic that she could semi interpret into English. Not that it mattered if she made up the whole story since Capeka wouldn't understand a word, but it felt more right somehow.

Settling onto a small chair near without being too close to Capeka, she opened the book and dug into early childhood memories of sitting on her mother's knee to listen to this story. The words came readily. As did the warmth and security of being with her mother. Too readily. Her voice faltered. Deep breath, carry on. This was about a child in need right before her, not about *her*. Nor was it anything to do with what had happened when she'd been a child. But for the first time in a long time Alesha admitted to herself that she had a longing for those days when she'd been safe and loved and totally secure in her little girl's life.

Read, damn it. *Just* read. As in make up words to fit the pictures on the pages.

A small hand touched her arm, withdrew immediately.

Raising her eyes, Alesha saw an understanding in the brown eyes staring at her. An understanding no child this age should have. It was desperately hard not to reach out and hug this girl tight. Capeka had heard her pain in her voice and reacted. In the kindest way.

How am I going to leave her at the end of the week?

It might be kinder never to see her again than do that.

The girl stood in front of her, closer than she'd been before, one leg tucked tight behind the other, her arms folded across her waist. Her face was blank, but in those eyes a score of emotions swirled. Good, bad and probably the ugly. Then Capeka dipped her head as though to say, 'Come on. Keep reading.'

So she did.

Until the sound of a man clearing his throat interrupted. Kristof stood near but not so near as to frighten Capeka, watching them both. His eyes were unreadable.

Alesha asked, 'Did I pass muster?'

An abrupt nod. 'Of course. When you've finished that book I'd like to get started in Theatre. There are things I'll need to explain and show you first.'

'I'll be five minutes.' Returning to the story, she noted he didn't leave, merely stood there, watching and listening, and in a glance she saw just as unfathomable as he'd been earlier. His professional face. The one he seemed to use all the time around here. Thank goodness he hadn't used it last night or they'd never have got far.

Kristof's professionalism continued throughout the day. 'First up is a tonsillectomy. Mila is five and has had constant throat infections for the last nine months as far as we're aware. They probably go back a lot further but we only met her last September. Other children I'm operating on today have come in from the surrounding country towns where there are no hospitals. By coming to us they're avoiding the long waiting lists in the cities.'

'Does the children's home get funding for these operations?' she asked, without thinking she was probably overstepping the mark with such a question.

Kristof gave her one sharp shake of his handsome head. Scrubbed up and dressed in clean operating garb, he still looked as sexy as it was possible for a man to be. More than.

Alesha smiled behind her mask, let the heat that thought caused absorb into her, went with the job on hand, helping the other nurse as required. Stepping up to the table where Mila lay anaesthetised, she said, 'She's a little cutie, for sure.'

'A vast improvement on the day she came to us,' Jacob, the anaesthetist, informed her. An older man who worked part time at the local hospital, he was apparently always available for operations in this Theatre.

'Then I'm hoping Capeka will one day be happy too.'

'There's a long way to go before that's possible,' Kristof muttered, glancing her way, a snap heatwave blasting the air between them. Not so professional now, was he?

Gotcha.

She grinned behind her mask.

His gaze dropped to the top of her scrubs where her breasts resided, his eyes widening.

Her nipples tightened. Oh, boy, trouble in scrubs. Alesha grabbed the box of wipes the other nurse was indicating and dragged her eyes away from the man who'd given her the night of her life. Today was going to take for ever to end.

Kristof lifted a scalpel. 'Here we go.'

Alesha was in awe of the surgeon from that moment on. Not just the man under the scrubs. Kristof was focused on one thing and one thing only, removing Mila's tonsils with as little trauma as possible. He was thorough, tidy, neat with his suturing, fast to keep the time under anaesthesia to a minimum. In other words the best surgeon she'd ever had the privilege to observe in Theatre.

No surprises there, she realised as she donned another set of scrubs for their next patient—another tonsillectomy. Followed by the breaking and resetting of a small boy's fractured arm that had not been put in a cast at the time the injury occurred three months earlier. That made Alesha shiver. Even though she'd come across a similar case years ago it was still hard to believe a child could go without medical help. A child deserved all the kindness and care available out there, no matter where they lived or who they lived with. But that was being Pollyanna-ish, and she knew she wasn't about to change the world. At least she was helping a few youngsters in Dubrovnik.

When they stopped for a quick cup of tea and sandwich Kristof read files and absently put food in his mouth.

Alesha watched him from under lowered eyebrows, though she probably could've stared hard at him and he wouldn't have noticed.

Then he looked up and she realised he knew she'd been studying him. He nodded and returned to his notes.

Soon they returned to Theatre for an appendectomy, followed by other small but essential surgeries. The worst came in as they were wrapping up for the day. A boy had been attacked by a dog, his arm torn apart as he'd apparently tried to hide his face. In that, he'd succeeded, with only scratches on his cheeks. But the trauma they had to deal with was hideous and it would be a long time before the lad would be using his arm to full potential again, if ever.

'Why wasn't he taken to the main hospital?' Alesha asked.

'I don't know,' Kristof replied, not looking at her.

But he was guessing, and not liking what he was coming up with. She wouldn't probe any further. They'd been there to help the boy and that was all that mattered. Since this seemed to be the only room to change in, she slipped out of her scrubs pants and stepped into her sky-blue capris. 'I'm glad you could put him back together.' The odds on the boy's recovery being good were vastly improved having had Kristof operate on him.

'So am I.' Kristof had taken both pieces of his scrubs off and was pulling on khaki knee-length shorts, followed by a white tee shirt.

She tried not to gape at the array of muscles filling her vision with only the boxers to cover some of them. She quickly gave up and enjoyed the view. After all, he could've waited until she left the room before stripping down to his underwear, but, then again, she'd seen it all anyway. Did this mean professional Kristof was back in his box and the fun guy was joining her? Letting her hair free of the thick band she'd tugged it into earlier, she dragged a brush through the tangle. 'I'm going to see Capeka before heading out into the sunshine.' She presumed it was still sunny outside.

'I'll walk you back to the apartments when you're ready.' Kristof was studying his fingers. Then he raised his head and hit her with an irresistible smile. 'Can't have you getting lost or locked out.'

Right then she'd have done anything he asked. *Anything.* That smile should be bottled and sold to raise funds for this place. Her knees were incapable of bending, her head spun, and as for her heart—it had obviously forgotten what it had been put inside her chest to do. 'As if,' she croaked through a mire of happy shock.

'We'll go to Cavtat tonight.' He checked his watch. 'How about you have half an hour with Capeka then we'll head up the hill to get ready, and I'll pick you up at six?' That smile just got wider and warmer and—oh, where was the professional guy when she needed him?

'Umm, yes, I suppose so.' Wasn't she the one with the restaurant voucher? 'I thought I'd like to go by boat, remember?'

'I do. I'll arrange that. But we'll drive down to the Old City. It's a bit of a walk home from the boat after a late night.'

Alesha's face was worth a thousand pictures. Kristof had watched as excitement followed by irritation then resignation vied for supremacy. All because he'd taken charge about when to go to Cavtat. 'I figured since it's looking like being a beautiful evening we should make the most of it.' The chances of rain any time throughout the week were non-existent, but still. He hadn't been able to get any part of the previous evening and night out of his blood, out of his head, so the sooner they had this dinner together, the better. By the end of the night he'd either be over Ms Alesha Milligan or hanging out for more time with her. He had a sneaking suspicion which it would be after feasting his eyes on her most of the long day in Theatre.

Glancing at his watch, he grimaced. How long did thirty minutes take?

Apparently for ever. It wasn't as though Alesha had dragged out her time with Capeka. In fact it'd been bang on half an hour when she'd put aside the book she'd been using to make up a story to go with the pictures and left the room. 'Ready when you are,' she told him.

Was she as keen as him for the evening to begin? He hadn't felt this excited about a date in so long it was ridiculous. It had to be the air, or the sun, or the fact he was away from London. Yeah right. Try the red bikini, or that stunning figure, or the generosity in Alesha's lovemaking. Any one of those would do it. Put them all together and what chance did he have to remain sane and sensible around her? But he had to try. 'The boat ride's booked.'

'I'm looking forward to it,' she replied, sounding less excited than him.

'You're sure? We could make it another night.'

Don't dare say that's a good idea.

Was he rushing her? Into what? A dinner date that she'd asked him on. That was all. Relief softened his worry. He hadn't signed up for life. Didn't have to face the consequences of being tied to a woman for ever. The relief increased. He was just showing her some of the sights of his second hometown, as any decent person would. She'd been let down by the man who'd arranged this trip. In his book she deserved better than that. It wasn't as though he intended spending a lot of time with Alesha. Come Saturday he was on his way back to London.

As Alesha would be, he reminded himself. So what? They wouldn't have anything to do with each other there. They moved in different circles, professionally and privately. The only way they'd bump into each other would be if one of them deliberately got in touch with the other. And that was not happening. Not when he didn't trust women not to play around on him or rip him off or hurt him in some other way. He'd given his heart once, got it back flattened and broken. This wasn't only about Alesha. Most people he got close to just didn't seem able to give him what he wanted—honest to goodness friendship and commitment. Nothing more, nothing less. Not even his parents had done that.

'Tonight's good. I've got to grab the opportunity while I can. Who knows what I might find to do tomorrow night?' Alesha's smile was light and general, not aimed to knock him sideways.

But it did. He could live on Alesha smiles. They were warm, sometimes sexy, and always slapped his heart. Which wasn't good—but felt wonderful. 'Then let's head up the hill to get ready.' If she'd changed her mind about wanting to go with him to use her dinner voucher then she'd have to tell him. He wasn't going to make it easy for her to back off when he was looking out for her.

Tonight's figure-hugging dress was navy blue and as tantalising as the red one had been. More so now that Kristof knew what was underneath. For a guy who wasn't interested in getting close to a woman his body had other ideas, mocking his carefully held theories on how to live his life safely. 'You look beautiful,' he told Alesha as they strode along the wharf to their ride to Cavtat.

'Thank you.' Her tone was demure but her eyes were sparkling with pleasure.

'You also look happy.' She'd rallied quickly after being tossed aside for another woman. Or was she good at hiding her feelings? Except last night she hadn't held back in bed. He'd swear she'd made love to him with no thoughts for any other man.

'It's a wonderful city and I'm enjoying it, plus your company.' Then the smile dropped and she shrugged.

'You think I'm not acting how I should be after what Luke did to me.'

Kristof stopped and reached for both her hands. 'I'm thinking let's have a fling for the days we're both in Dubrovnik.'

The smile didn't return as her stunned gaze locked on him. 'Are you serious?'

'Yes.' Now that he thought about it, he was. Very. 'I know this week hasn't started out how you'd expected and I don't intend trying to make up for that. But last night was fun, and I like your company.' He shrugged. 'So why not? It can't hurt anyone.'

Her head flicked back, fell forward. 'As far as proposals go that's very sterile.' Then she lifted her chin, focused her gaze back on him. 'But I like that. It's perfect really. Originally I was coming here for fun and romance, instead I can have fun and—and more fun.' Her shoulders lifted deliberately.

'Hey, any time you're not happy say so and we'll call it quits.'

Finally she relaxed. 'Works for me.'

Worked for him and all. 'Then let's get on that boat before it leaves without us.' He kept one of her soft hands wrapped in his large one as he strode along the wharf. 'You're going to love Cavtat.'

Alesha wiped her mouth with the napkin and placed it beside her empty plate. 'That walnut torte is to die for.'

Kristof laughed. 'Told you. Like some more wine?'

She shook her head. 'No, thanks.' One night overindulging had been one too many. If they were going to bed together later on she wanted to be fully aware of everything, of Kristof. She did not want to miss a thing about that hard body and talented mouth, those sensuous fingers and cheeky lips. So she *was* having a fling. Who better to start this new lifestyle of having fun and no involvement with than a hunk who knew more about making love—sorry, having sex—than she'd have thought possible? Showed the kind of men she'd known before. They hadn't been up to scratch at all. Whereas Kristof had reset the line. Spoiled her for ever, probably. At least she'd have some amazing holiday memories. Just not the ones she'd expected.

'It's a pity you wore those shoes or we could've walked around the peninsula.'

'Isn't the path paved?' She'd forgotten about the walk when she'd been preening herself for the evening.

'Unfortunately not.'

'Then I'll have to come back in the day time because I do want to go around there and sit down by the water.' It would have been wonderful at night with Kristof, but this was a fling, not something romantic, so the shoes had saved her from getting her old hopes up.

'You should do that. There are also some buildings in the township to check out.' He didn't seem perturbed at having missed out on a night stroll with her. 'Are you into kayaking?'

'It's been a while but, yes, I could hire one and take a look at the town from out on the harbour.' Another day sorted. 'Tomorrow I am going to take that mini tour up the hill and on to the waterfall.'

'You'll love it.'

'Unless you need me at the children's centre again?' She'd be just as happy working alongside Kristof.

He stood up and reached for her hand, pulled her chair out as she rose. 'No, Alesha. You're here to see the sights and have already lost a day for the kids, so go out and make the most of the days you have left.'

Not mentioning the nights? 'I'll find time to read to Capeka though.'

'Don't feel bad if you find you're busy having fun and run out of time for a visit. She's still settling in and getting lots of attention from everyone else.'

So the reading times weren't important? Alesha thought otherwise. 'I'm sure I can find half an hour for her.' Unless she was causing more harm than good, but so far no one thought she was.

'Do you always let people close so quickly?' Kristof asked once they'd left the restaurant and were strolling down towards the harbour and their boat ride back to the city.

Did she? To a point, maybe. 'I like to be open with people.' Was he referring to Capeka? Or himself? 'Capeka needs people to care about what happens to her, and I want to give her some little thing to help her on that journey.'

She wasn't doing this for herself. Or was she? Could this be a way to avoid thinking too much about how much she'd hoped there was a future for her and Luke? But now she understood she hadn't been decimated by his news. She'd been hurt, angry, let down—all of the above. But heartbroken? Deep breath. Really gutted to the point she hadn't been able to get out of bed to face the next day? No, not even immediately after he'd told her. Kristof was probably rebound sex. But hey, if that was what it was so be it. It had helped, been fun, enjoyable, and she didn't feel ashamed at all. Kristof had made it all so easy. He'd had fun too, and that was that. Very civilised. Funny how bitter her laugh tasted.

'You need to guard your heart, or one day you're going to get hurt badly.'

Did he really just say that? Kristof, the man who was serious at work, and fun at play? She stared at him. He was wearing that professional look that grated, as though this was something he'd talk about but not on a personal level. So he'd been hurt in the past too. Find a normal adult who hadn't in one way or another to a varying degree. 'My heart's safe.'

'Then Luke didn't mean as much to you as I thought.'

'Maybe he's why it's safe.' Or the guy before him, or the one before that.

Kristof's arm was deliciously heavy over her shoulders, and she liked that she could tuck against his side and not look into those eyes that didn't miss a thing.

'What's your past, Alesha?'

Go for the big question, why don't you?

'Oh, I don't know. Unlucky in love?'

'A commitment-phobe?'

'It wasn't me who finished my last relationship. Or any of the others.'

'That doesn't really answer my question. You might be putting men off with a "you can look and touch but you can't keep" attitude.'

'And here I thought you were a surgeon.' Not an analyst who believed he could unravel her. 'Are you basing these questions on your past experiences?'

The muscles in his arm tensed on her shoulders. 'It's possible.'

They reached the jetty and joined the queue to board their return trip. There was no way they'd continue the discussion when surrounded by happy couples and groups laughing and making lots of noise. Instead they stood at the bow of the boat, Kristof using his body to shelter her from the cooler breeze created by the boat's forward motion, holding her close, his arms wrapped around her, his hands linked at her waist. Snuggling back against him, Alesha went with the moment, not thinking about tomorrow or next week or anything other than the lights on the hills they passed on the way back to Dubrovnik. Wasn't that the free and easy way to go?

Meandering through the Old City after disembarking, Alesha sighed with pleasure. A simple night out, no complexities, no one demanding more of her than she was prepared to give. There was something warming, and comfortable, and just plain lovely about it all. Something she didn't remember experiencing in any relationship in the past. Usually men expected more of her than they gave back.

Yes, and whose fault was that?

She'd gone along with them because she'd believed it was the way to a man's heart. Now she was starting to see how wrong she might've been. This going it alone wasn't such a bad idea at all. It meant she had begun standing up for herself. Another first.

When Kristof pulled his car into a park outside the apartments where she was staying it wasn't hard for Alesha to ask, 'Do you want to come in?'

'Yes.'

Her heart swelled and her body warmed. As far as flings went this was great. And they didn't have to talk, just hold each other and touch and feel and give and take…

CHAPTER SIX

IF THE DAYS sped past, the nights went even quicker. Alesha toured the city, the outlying environs, many of the islands nearby. She ate in bakeries, cafés, and at night enjoyed restaurants with Kristof. She told stories to Capeka every day, sometimes twice a day, and Friday, the day before she was leaving for London, the little girl gave her a smile filled with nothing but pleasure, which showed the lack of understanding of each other's language meant absolutely nothing. They were on the same page.

'Seeing her smile directly at me, her eyes meeting mine for the first time…it just blew me away,' she told Kristof over a quick coffee before heading into town. 'Now we need to get her to stop standing on one foot in the corner.'

'You're getting too involved,' he warned. 'Be careful.'

'Your mother's monitoring everything and I don't believe for one minute she'd let me visit if she thought it was detrimental for Capeka.' They still didn't know the girl's real name, or where she'd come from before arriving at the bridge. Apparently this wasn't unusual in similar cases. Alesha could understand the child not wanting to trust anyone with information about herself. People could use it in ways that hurt, and given how young Capeka was it was frightening to think she understood such danger.

While Alesha hadn't been in danger as such, when her parents had locked her out of their lives mentally she'd turned to her best friend and her family. They'd been kind at first, but after a few weeks her situation had begun to pall and soon the gossip had been flying around school about how her parents didn't want her so why should anyone else? The first time she'd heard that her parents couldn't face her now that their son had died and they wished it had been her, she'd confronted her girlfriend and asked why she wanted to tell lies about her. The blunt reply that she'd been speaking the truth had gutted Alesha so much she'd hidden in her bedroom for days, denying the truth slowly dawning on her for months. It was only when the school rang to ask her mother why she wasn't attending that she said she wanted to change schools, and when that happened she did make a few friends but never let any close enough to reveal her circumstances. Nor did her parents do anything to prove the stories untrue. That had hurt the most.

'I was thinking of you,' Kristof said, looking at her as though he were inside her head, seeing all her thoughts. 'You could get hurt in all this. There's a big heart in there.' He gently tapped her breastbone.

'I know how to look after myself.' Surely he couldn't see the hurt she'd fled from in the past. No, that was buried so deep it was invisible. Yet Alesha couldn't help wondering if he did understand that she'd been hurt because he had too. She'd like to talk to him about that, get to know a little more about what made him tick, but those weren't the rules of a fling. Certainly not theirs. So drawing in a breath, she eyeballed him. 'Are we fling-ing tonight?'

The surgeon face disappeared in a wide smile. 'Oh, yeah. After I've taken you to dinner at one of the best res-taurants in town. Not the best in food—though it won't be a dog's dinner either—but in location. It's on the coast where you can watch the lights coming on as darkness falls and feel as if you're in a dream world. It's magic.'

Who else had he taken there in the past? The green-eyed monster raised its head and she shuddered. The thought was unbecoming of her and their fling, and took effort to banish. 'Bring it on,' she said far more cheer-ily than she felt. This sudden sense of being just an-other notch for Kristof cooled her ardour. Then reality clicked into place. She hadn't had any expectations of Kristof other than to have fun with him for a few days. He owed her nothing, as she didn't him. 'It is our last night together.'

'Yes, Alesha, it is. And what a week it's been.' His finger now caressed her jawline, his eyes unreadable, and his face reverting to professional mode. 'I'd better get back to my patients. I'll see you at the usual time.'

But he didn't rush away, hovered, that finger stilled on her chin, those eyes wary but watchful.

When Alesha was around this man her heart always thudded unusually hard. As though he could become something special. Or was already beginning to. But she had a track record of failed relationships, and this one wasn't being given the chance to become one of those. This one had a finite end date. Tonight being it. It'd be the first time she'd walk away without that sucker-punched feeling in her tummy, because she'd agreed to the terms, had wanted them. This time she'd been in control of her emotions, and hadn't fallen even halfway in love—hadn't even come close to wanting to. Yet she was going to miss Kristof more than any man she'd known. There was something genuine about him. He was loyal, had integrity, was fun. A load more things she'd appreciated, and liked in a person. Wanted, even. But more than that, she cared about him, would like to see more of him because she enjoyed his company. That wasn't love. That was too ordinary for love. Wasn't it?

With a little shake of her head, she stepped away from that beguiling touch. 'See you at six. I've got an island to visit.'

The sea was blue and she could see all the way to the bottom where tiny fish darted back and forth impervious to the boatload of tourists above them. The sky was clear and blue with not a breath of wind to jimmy up clouds. The air was hot as though they were already into full-blown summer. The coastline was beautiful, magical, and she couldn't take her eyes off the hills and brightly painted houses and the boats tied up at wharves.

She didn't want to go back to London in the morning. Back to a life without her fling partner. Except if she stayed on here Kristof wouldn't be around anyway. He was heading to London too. Different flights, different times, same destination. From now on London wasn't going to feel the same big city where she never intended putting down roots. Now there was a man living there whose company she adored. A man she'd enjoy hanging out with in their respective spare time. Not a man to get close to, or to share her fears and needs with. She'd done that in the past and had them thrown back in her face. She'd hate Kristof doing that more than anyone before, so she wasn't giving him the opportunity.

The boat nudged the wharf, bringing her out of her reveries. Time to go back to the apartment and get ready for the night ahead. The last night with Kristof, because tomorrow, despite all the thoughts whirling around her head, they were going their separate ways. The finish of their fling, of anything between them. End of getting to know each other. As she'd accepted from the beginning, and as she knew was still the right thing to do, because at the conclusion of any relationship they had she'd still wind up alone, and possibly in this case far more hurt than ever before. Best to get out while unscathed, and happy to have known Kristof without the baggage. Except a part of her still wanted to know what made him tick, what was responsible for those deep, dark looks that sometimes filled his eyes, tightened his face into serious responsibility. If she wasn't careful, she'd be wanting to help him move beyond whatever ate him up on the inside.

So, one more night. *Go, get ready and make the most of it.* Tomorrow was another day.

But as for going back to London tomorrow, where she had nothing planned to fill in the coming three weeks?

Alesha veered away from going up the hill and headed in the direction of the children's centre again to ask Antonija, 'If I stayed on for a little while would I be of use to you around here?'

'Tell me why you want to do this?'

Expecting Antonija to simply say yes, Alesha dug for a simple answer. 'If you think I could harm Capeka, then I withdraw my offer.'

Shrewd eyes studied her. 'Is this about you?'

Too shrewd. But she had a new approach to life, remember? 'I could return to London, drive through south England, hang out in cafés and bars. Or I can be useful.'

She paused. 'And I believe this is the right thing for me at the moment. I need to know where I'm headed in the future.'

'Enjoy the weekend and join us on Monday.' Welcoming arms wrapped her up in a hug. 'And thank you.'

'No, thank you.'

And thank you, Kristof, for showing there are other ways to form relationships of all kinds.

Those couldn't be tears threatening. She didn't do crying.

The restaurant was intimate and stylish. Alesha looked around and felt a pang of longing. Not for the wealth that went with dining in a place like this, but for the week she'd had. Raising her glass to Kristof, she said, 'Thank you for a wonderful few days. You've really made my holiday.'

Worry rose in his face. 'Tomorrow you go back to reality. You'll be all right?'

Yes, she would, again thanks to Kristof. Maybe she should give herself a pat on the back for getting out there and not sitting around sulking in the apartment. 'Relax. I am not going to come knocking on your door in London demanding more attention. I only hope you've enjoyed these few days half as much as I have.'

His glass lifted towards her. 'I have. Thank you back. Not that it's over just yet.' His mouth softened into a smile that sent threads of warmth right down to her toes.

'Thank goodness.' She grinned back. Another night of passion to top off the week was exactly what she required. Who'd have thought on Saturday that she'd be feeling so relaxed and happy? Certainly not her. It seemed being strong and not getting involved suited her after all. 'I'm not going back to London tomorrow. I hadn't made any fixed plans to fill in the weeks other than apply for jobs through the agency, and now that's sorted with a six-month position on a paediatric ward starting in three weeks.' She grinned. 'I had a video interview with the recruitment officer at the hospital yesterday and got an email this morning saying the job is mine.'

He tapped the rim of her glass with his. 'Congratulations. You never mentioned anything about this.'

'Didn't want to jinx my chances. Anyway, I got to thinking about what I'd do for the weeks in between and suddenly it all seems ridiculous bumming around visiting places, wasting time, when I could be making myself useful.'

One black eyebrow rose. 'Next you'll be signing up for a permanent job somewhere.'

Alesha sipped her wine before nodding. 'You know what? That wouldn't be the end of the world. I've been drifting too long, looking for something to come along I might like when in fact I probably should settle and turn my life into what I want it to be. In other words, I need to stop relying on other people to set the standard.'

The serious face was slipping into place. 'Is that why you weren't broken-hearted when Luke pulled the plug?'

'I was never in love with him, desperately or otherwise.' How embarrassing was this? Though putting it out there was like letting a heavy weight go. And letting Kristof know where she stood. 'I liked him a lot and wanted something more—to have a chance at a future together. At least I thought I did. We seemed compatible, but it could be that wasn't enough.'

'And now?' There was an edge to Kristof's question she didn't understand.

Alesha didn't rush her answer. It needed considered

thought. After this week she finally understood she did want to go for the whole love package where she loved and was loved in return, but she didn't want second best. Did not want to wait for a man to condescend to love her a little bit. Not any more. Staring around the room, she sipped her wine, not really seeing anyone or anything until her gaze came back to Kristof. 'I'm ready to move on alone, to be the person I want to be without anyone else's input.' Then she'd have more to offer to the right man.

His head tilted to the side as he studied her. Then the happy face returned and he grinned. 'Then let's finish the week with a bang. We'll take a bottle of your favourite champagne back to the apartment and sit by the pool watching the city below before I take you to your bed for one last night of pleasure.'

'I can't argue with that,' she replied, setting her glass aside. No way was she drinking too much. She wanted to remember every word, every touch, every moment. And she wanted them to be the best ever.

Three-forty. Kristof rolled towards the sleeping, warm and curvaceous body beside him and wrapped his arms around Alesha, brought her butt up against his manhood, and snuggled his face into the soft place between her shoulder blades. It had been a wonderful week. Filled with pleasure and passion, fun and laughter; no grating barbs, no nasty moments. And now it was over. Within a couple of hours he'd climb out of bed and walk up the hill to get ready to head to the airport and home.

No regrets. No ties. No demands made on him. A perfect end to a perfect week.

And yet... It wasn't as easy as it sounded. If ever there

was a woman he might consider settling down with, falling in love with, Alesha rang all the bells. She was beautiful inside and out. But she wasn't ready. There were a lot of issues holding her back. She mightn't have talked about them but they were there if a guy knew where to look. He'd seen a hint of pain that first night when she'd admitted to being set up for the holiday of a lifetime that didn't happen. The pain that wasn't about being dumped but about lots of other things. Almost an acceptance because it had happened before and she seemed to expect it to happen again.

His lips brushed her silky skin, his nose breathed in the scent of woman. His woman. No, not his. Not once the sun came up. That was not reluctance to let go churning his gut. That was reality and practicality. Loving a woman was not on his to-do list. Even if it happened he'd never do anything about it. Loving people meant setting his heart up for danger, to be sliced up piece by piece and tossed aside. To be vulnerable again. He'd be a damned slow learner if he let that happen. His ex-wife had proved how right his father had been. Love was relative to the effort someone wanted to put into it. He'd given his all to his father, and to Cally, and got only scraps back. His mother might've forgiven him and still loved him fiercely, but that didn't make it any easier to go out there and fall in love again. He carried a weight of guilt over not believing his mother would never deliberately hurt him.

But if he'd ever feel free enough to try marriage he knew he'd found the woman to take the chance with. Except he wasn't going to. The consequences could be catastrophic.

Rolling onto his back, Kristof brought Alesha with

him so that she was sprawled across his chest, his belly, his rising manhood.

'Mmm…' she muttered sleepily. 'What time is it?'

'Time enough for me to make love to you again.' Make love? Or have sex? What did a name for it matter? They'd come together, share a moment, take and give pleasure. Call it what he liked, that wouldn't change the sensations, the need and the caring. This was one special lady and he was going to miss her. Far too much. But he'd get over her eventually. He had to.

'Oh, goodie.' She wriggled over so that she was facing him, her hands reaching for his shoulders, a simple touch ramping up the heat pouring through his already hot body.

Clasping her hips, he lifted her to straddle him, and lowered her over his manhood. Groaned as her moisture encompassed his throbbing need. She was always ready for him, a turn-on if he wasn't already turned on. Touching Alesha sent waves of desire rippling through her, and made her cry out. As she shuddered and gripped him he lost himself within her for one last time.

Dressed in hurriedly pulled-on shorts and shirt, Alesha hung over the parapet at the far end of the pool and watched Kristof striding up the hill as he had every day she'd been here. Confident, relaxed, ready for whatever came his way. Solid, strong, more masculine than any male had the right to be. That dark-blond hair, those wide shoulders, the long legs—only a start to the whole package.

Her heart sank further with every step he took away from her and their week. She had no right to be sad. They had agreed on a fling with a finite duration, and that was what they'd had. What she hadn't expected was the intensity of their lovemaking, or the way she'd begun to hang out for Kristof's voice at the end of the day, or how, when he was with her, she was his focus—as though he cared about her and what *she* did. She was going to miss that. Miss *him*.

But…

It was time to let go, get out in the world and make a life for herself that didn't require trying to find a compatible man who could once and for all prove to her she was lovable. So far no one had come along to love her in the only way she now accepted she needed—as in for ever, regardless of the stuff-ups she made. She'd been looking too hard, and probably chased away the men she'd known with her need for constant reassurance.

Whereas Kristof hadn't been chased away simply because they'd agreed to one week together and then to go their own ways. It had worked, despite the sadness pulling at her now.

As he disappeared around the corner at the top of the hill the sadness engulfing her grew heavier. 'Bye, Kristof.' She'd never see him again. It was how it was, and part of her was glad they wouldn't get the chance to fall out. She didn't want to be hurt by Kristof, nor to hurt him back. A bigger portion of her head, her heart, her need, wanted him to spin around and come racing down the hill to bang on the outside door leading into the complex as he yelled for her to let him back in.

It wasn't going to happen.

It was time to move on.

Starting with packing her bag and having some breakfast. Later she'd walk up the hill, following Kristof's tracks to his mother's house, and unpack her few belongings in a spare bedroom that was to be hers while she stayed on in Dubrovnik. Later, when there was no chance of bumping into Kristof. He'd made it plain when he left her bed they weren't going to see each other again, and she'd give him that. He'd done so much for her this week. And to see him one more time would be dragging out the sadness. It was time to let go. Not that she was supposed to have been caught up with him anyway. But like a great holiday, a seriously wonderful fling didn't evaporate into dusty memories within minutes.

Wrapping her arms around her waist, she smiled. It was unlikely she'd ever forget this past week. They'd made such magic memories, how could she?

Antonija welcomed her like a long-lost friend even though it was less than twenty-four hours since they'd talked about her staying on to help at the children's home. 'Here's a set of keys to my house. Come and go as you please. I've given you Kristof's room as it's got the best view.'

Kristof's room? Oh, no, that wasn't going to help with putting last week in its place. 'Thank you. I will spend most of my time down with the children though.'

'We have a busy schedule. Kristof's friend's coming across from London for a week. He's a paediatric specialist and will see each child during his visit for general medical check-ups. I intend for you to help him. But you must get out and enjoy the city as well.'

'No problem.' Kristof's room. Kristof's friend. This woman was missing her son already. Maybe she never stopped missing him when he headed back to London.

Alesha could relate to that. She was missing him too, and she hadn't spent the days in his sphere, except when she'd worked in Theatre with him that once. But those nights... 'I know you said take the weekend off but I'd prefer to see the kids today.'

'That'd be lovely. Some of them want to go to the park and an extra pair of eyes would help the staff no end.' The older woman gave a weary smile. 'The children do like to run wild a bit. It's often because of their background and being left to their own devices too much. Some of them, anyway.'

'Then they find you.' Alesha felt for this kind woman who, from what she'd seen, gave and gave of herself. 'When did you open the refuge?'

'Fifteen years ago when I returned home from London. I felt I'd had a good life and wanted to do what I could for those less fortunate. I never expected there to be so many children wanting a little love and support. That's all most of them want really. Not many are ill.'

'So the surgeons and other visiting specialists are for the general population?'

'The very poor at the end of the waiting list.'

'Right, let's get cracking.'

Alesha dropped her bag in the room that was Kristof's. Looking around, she found nothing to remind her of him. The décor was simple. No photos adorned the walls or the top of the dresser. No discarded jacket or shirt. Impersonal about described it. His idea of home with his mother? Or his mother's way of keeping her son at arm's length? That didn't explain the loneliness in the older woman's eyes. Kristof hid his feelings, though he had indicated he was not interested in a permanent relationship. Did that include one with his mother? Something had gone wrong for these two, and still Kristof came to Dubrovnik to help his mother out with her project, *and* he sought help from other qualified people for her children. Interesting.

The walk to the park with seven kids aged between eight and eleven was fun and kept Alesha on her toes the whole time. Two other staff members accompanied them, taking a soccer ball with them. The game was hilarious and no one took it seriously. Until one girl started gasping for breath. 'Marija? What's happening?'

Not understanding a word the child said had Alesha tensed up and extra vigilant as she assessed the situation. Then the man who was with them pulled an inhaler from his pocket and pushed it towards the girl, saying something that Alesha could only hope was to breathe deep with the puffer.

'Asthma?' she asked one of the staff and got a nod.

The girl was banging her chest and Alesha caught her hands and held them gently. 'Don't hurt yourself.' Her chest would be painful as the airways would've filled with mucous. Alesha took the inhaler and pressed it carefully between the girl's lips and squeezed it to express the bronchodilator into her airways to ease the tightness. 'Breathe in slowly,' which was really all the girl could manage anyway. Breathing out was a struggle. 'That's the girl.' With one hand she rubbed her back slowly, quietly. If only she spoke Croatian, this would be so much easier. Let's face it, learning Croatian wasn't on most people's to-do list.

The other children had gathered round to watch and Alesha shooed them away, administered more puffs of

Ventolin. Now what? The girl was not in any condition to walk the two kilometres back to the centre, especially since the temperature was around thirty. Her breathing was not settling, giving Alesha cause for concern. When she looked to the other two adults they shrugged as if to say they didn't know what to do.

Alesha sighed. Only one thing for it. Try to walk slowly as far as possible and then piggyback the girl if she had to. She pointed to herself and the girl, then in the direction they'd come from. 'I'll take her back.'

They nodded, said something which could've been acknowledgment or an order for takeout food for all she knew.

Taking the child's hand, Alesha set out. The girl's breathing had improved marginally but she didn't feel confident Marija was up to much walking. Soon she had hauled her up on her back and was trudging the pavement along the roads back to the children's home and a general check-up with the local trainee doctor putting in some hours over the weekend. All the way she kept up a monologue about anything that came to mind. Twice she stopped to administer another puff from the inhaler.

Urgency drove her to get back to the home. Running wasn't possible. She had too much weight on her back and it was far too hot. Her brisk pace had to do.

By the time she dragged her load up the front steps of the shelter she was exhausted, and soaking in sweat, especially where the child lay sprawled across her back.

'Alesha? What's the matter?' The doctor rushed out of a front room where he must've noticed her arriving.

Thank goodness he spoke English. 'Asthma attack. At least that's what I'm presuming the problem is. I can't get it under control out in that heat.'

'Give her to me.' The young man lifted the girl away and took her straight into the treatment room.

Alesha rolled her cramped shoulders, grimacing as muscles protested, and then followed her charge. 'The inhaler we used is empty.'

The doctor said, 'There're more in the storeroom. You have a key?'

'Not yet.'

'I'll be back.'

Alesha took the girl's hand in hers. 'You'll be right soon.'

The girl blinked and tears spilled down her cheeks as she tried to force air out of her lungs. Then the doctor was back and this time the inhaler started having an effect almost immediately.

'What you did for Marija today was over and above,' Antonija told Alesha over dinner that night.

'It was fine. We had to get back and it was the only way I could think of.'

'We do have taxis in town.' Kristof's mother laughed. 'One of the others could've told the driver where to go.'

'I did look for one but guess they all had better things to do down at the Old City.' Every time she'd been down there taxis were doing a roaring trade and wouldn't be bothered with cruising the back streets where they were unlikely to get a passenger.

'Are you going out tonight?'

'I don't think so.' Funny, but she didn't have the energy. Nor the inclination. It seemed that spending most of the night making out with Kristof had used up her energy stores. Throw in carrying Marija those couple of kilometres and the idea of walking down to Port Gruž or anywhere else didn't appeal. Nor did going alone. 'I'll have an early night instead.'

On Sunday afternoon Kristof headed into his office to go through patient notes for tomorrow's surgeries. One hip replacement for a sixty-two-year-old man, and a knee replacement for a thirty-one-year-old woman. All straightforward, except the woman had a heart condition that needed a cardiologist on board in case anything went wrong in that area. He'd tried to do the knee replacement three months ago but the woman had gone into cardiac arrhythmia while being prepped for Theatre. He did not want that happening again. For one, it had stressed his patient out to the max, and for two, she desperately wanted this new knee so she could start walking and getting fit and lean again so that her heart could settle down and play nice.

Tomorrow would be a challenge, but he loved those. As long as the outcome was satisfactory. He strived for perfection, hated settling for less when his patients put so much trust in him. In Theatre, being in charge of an operation, was the place where he knew he was in control. Where he had the knowledge and skills patients needed, where he was top of his game. But... But there were the days when a body didn't do as it was supposed to, like this woman's heart. At least that had happened before he'd begun the procedure. He hadn't even arrived in the hospital. Not that he'd felt any happier. The last time he'd struck a massive problem in Theatre the patient, a youngster of seven, had haemorrhaged all over the show from an aneurism no one had seen coming.

Kristof sighed and banged his feet down on his desktop. There were days he hated his job. The days that no amount of training and knowledge and skill could do any good. Days that just turned out to be ghastly for no apparent fault of his or anyone's. It didn't stop him feeling guilty though. Picking up the woman's file, he began reading the details he knew off by heart. No such thing as taking anything for granted when her life might depend upon him.

'Welcome home. I see you're operating on Maggie Shattersgood tomorrow.'

Kristof's head flipped up and he eyeballed his mate, Harry. 'Yes. Just going over everything.'

Harry pulled out a chair and plonked his butt down. 'So how was Dubrovnik?'

'Same as usual.'

Except there was this woman who'd been special.

'No scandal, no rampaging parties? Man, you're getting dull.'

'Says the guy who goes home to his wife and three kids every night, sober as a judge.' Kristof grinned, ignoring the sense of loss that gave him. Why did he want that now? He never had before. Not even back when he and Cally were a couple had he thought they might possibly get to that stage where he'd feel comfortable enough to bring children into the world.

'Yeah, well, I kind of love it.' Harry might *sound* sheepish, but he didn't look it at all.

And I'm not jealous.

Kristof sucked his lips in. They'd certainly had some heavy nights partying in the past, way back when there had been just the two of them to think about, but they'd barely been out of nappies. Now, older, not necessarily wiser, but supposedly serious and professional, they didn't do any of that any more. 'Fill me in on the gossip.

There must've been plenty happening while I've been gone.'

'How long have you got?' Harry's feet hit the other side of the desk top. 'Any beer in that fridge?'

The tiny, one-shelf cooling box. 'Yep, a couple. Pass me one while you're at it.'

Harry grunted and got back on his feet. 'So if you were being all proper and no parties what did you do when you weren't operating?'

Having unbelievable sex with an amazing Kiwi woman.

'Attended a charity dinner to raise money for the home.'

With an amazing Kiwi woman.

'Took a boat to Cavtat for dinner, visited the Old City.'

Did more than I've done in Dubrovnik in years. With an amazing...

Yeah, well. That was last week. Now he was back into his real life where surgery and patients and colleagues were the order of the day, and often a fair whack of the night.

'Alone?' Harry was studying him, but then the guy was a haematologist so studying specimens was his trade.

'Why wouldn't I be?'

'Because maybe it's time you weren't.'

Here we go again.

Only weeks before he'd left for Dubrovnik Harry and his wife had given him a speech about living alone and not finding a partner. They'd gone on and on about how he was becoming more solitary by the day. How he was turning into a serious surgeon twenty-four-seven, never letting up for fun. 'I already read that memo. It doesn't pertain to me.'

Just like that, an image of Alesha lying on the bed half covered in a sheet sprang into his head and he couldn't breathe. There was so much to like about her. So much to remember. To want to revisit. He could be in trouble here.

'Here, get this into you.' A cold, moist bottle was forced between his fingers. 'You look like you could do with something more powerful than cold H2O.'

Thanks, Harry.

Kristof lifted the bottle to his lips and drank deep of the cool, refreshing beer. Which did nothing to banish that picture from the front of his skull. She was so beautiful, so tantalising. And broken in some way.

Don't forget that. That's what will keep you away, if you choose to step back into her world for another week of passion. She was broken, he had been: they'd never make it work. If he even wanted to, which he didn't.

'Want to tell me something?' Persistence was Harry's middle name. Sometimes it was even his first name.

'I ate squid at the charity dinner.' Sitting beside Alesha, feeling at ease with all the socialite types for the first time, not feeling as though his father was breathing over his shoulder to make sure he did everything correctly so as to impress everyone. She'd been relaxed, despite telling him she wasn't used to rubbing shoulders with the wealthy. She'd charmed everyone seated at their table with her accent and her ability to laugh at herself. 'And drank champagne.'

Now that was a mistake. Harry was going to pick up on it straight away.

Yep. 'You weren't doing that alone.'

'I shared the bottle with the whole table.' He had, and ordered another so that Alesha didn't run out of her favourite drink. Though she'd been circumspect, barely touching her glass. He'd picked that was because she didn't want to do something like come on to him again in front of his mother's guests. Because while she hadn't come on to him again all evening, she'd sure responded when he'd turned the tables and kissed her.

The ringing of Harry's phone cut across his thoughts and brought him back to reality. 'You'd better get that.'

Alesha wasn't real? Wasn't warm and friendly and gorgeous?

Sure she was, but she didn't belong in this picture of him at work with his mate talking the breeze.

'Hi, Scallywag. How was it at the pool?' Harry's eyes were soft and dewy as he spoke to one of his daughters. 'You swam how far? That's amazing, you clever clogs.'

This picture of sitting with Harry having a beer just got complicated. Harry had pulled on his father cape, while *he* still sat here as the surgeon frantically denying Alesha access to his brain—and her ignoring him. He shoved to his feet. 'Time I headed home.' To his pristine apartment where everything stayed in the place he put it until he wanted it again. No shoes with six-inch heels lying around. No discarded clothing leading a trail to his bedroom. Paradise. Or so he used to think. When had that changed? Prior to or post Alesha? Or somewhere in the middle?

Harry looked up and flapped a hand at him. 'See you tomorrow,' he mouthed before returning his full attention to his daughter.

Tomorrow and the surgical list that'd keep him busy and focused, and in a zone he understood and needed.

Not a place where a certain woman interrupted his thoughts.

Not in his office while his mate sank into the love of his children excitedly talking to him and asking when he was coming home for dinner because they were starving. Yep, he'd heard all that, and just had to get away. It was too much.

It was not the lifestyle he endeavoured to get.

It was the one he'd dreamed of having if only Cally hadn't walked all over his love in hobnailed boots.

CHAPTER SEVEN

'HOLD THIS FOR ME, will you?' A doctor held out a saline bag to Alesha.

'Sure.' She took it and waited patiently while the young woman inserted a needle into the back of their little patient's hand to give the boy much-needed fluid after a severe bout of vomiting that had left him dehydrated.

On the other side of the bed the boy's father watched, his face ashen, and his eyes bleak with worry. 'I hope it wasn't the chicken he ate for lunch that's made him so sick. He started throwing up not long after and hasn't stopped since.'

It could very likely be food poisoning. Undercooked chicken was always risky. 'Was the chicken bought from a takeout place, or home-cooked?'

'I was cooking it last night for dinner when my mother phoned to ask us to go round for a meal. I turned the element off and left the pan with the lid on to cool down, and put it in the fridge when we got home.'

The doctor looked up. 'How late was that?'

The man winced as though he was about to get told off. 'About one in the morning.'

The temperature had been unusually high yesterday. 'You wouldn't have had air-conditioning running while

you were out, would you?' Alesha asked and got a nod
from the doctor.

'If only I had it.' The father reached for his lad's hand,
wound his much larger one around it. 'Sorry, Charlie.
Your dad's such a fool.'

Alesha felt for him. 'Don't say that. You made a
mistake, but that doesn't make you a fool. It's just that
chicken has to be cooked right through, no pinkness at
all.'

'I'm still learning to cook since my wife died. She was
a champ in the kitchen, could make the dullest of foods
tasty. I've got a long way to go to be half as good.' The
poor guy had more than enough to deal with without
beating himself up over his cooking skills.

'Sounds like you're trying and that's what counts.'

The doctor had the needle in and was attaching the
tubing to it that led from the bag Alesha held. 'I think
your boy is going to be fine once we get some liquid
into him as well as all those nutrients that come with it.'

Alesha took a quick glance at her watch. The day
couldn't go any slower if it tried. She hung the bag from
the steel frame and smoothed the damp curls off Charlie's
forehead. 'There you go. You'll be chasing your football
before you know it.'

'I'm going to run some blood tests,' the doctor said.

'I'll get the kit.' Alesha slipped around the curtain and
walked the length of the children's ward to the storeroom.

'How's it going?' Cherry asked as they passed in the
hall.

After five weeks Alesha already loved this job, and had
been hoping the nurse she was covering for really didn't
want to return at the end of her maternity leave. Though
today that idea felt tiring. 'I'm looking forward to knock-

ing off.' Half an hour to go and she'd be able to give into the exhaustion dragging at her. Never had she felt so debilitated by it. She was sounding geriatric. 'Can't wait to get home and put my feet up.' And try not to think about Kristof. Why had one week of fun together come to mean so much? It had been two months since they'd said goodbye in Dubrovnik. She should've moved on by now, not be thinking about him at all hours of the day and night. Just because he'd inadvertently made her see she needed to be strong and not let just any guy in close didn't give him the right to take over her thoughts and emotions.

'You really wore yourself out in Dubrovnik, didn't you?'

Oh, yes. That heady week with Kristof used up a lot of energy. Add in all the walking around the city she did every night after finishing work at the home. Staying on in Dubrovnik had turned out to be the right decision. Working full time with those children had made her believe she could actually settle down somewhere and become a part of a community, get a permanent job instead of taking slots all over the show. To make herself a home where she might finally integrate herself and become a part of the local picture. As much as she loved travelling it had palled in the light of what she'd done with those sad and needy children. So much she'd stayed on right up to the day before she was due to report here. And now... Well, now everything was about to change in a way she'd never foreseen.

Cherry had turned to follow her to the storeroom. 'Want to go to the pub tonight for a game of pool and a beer or two?'

'I've got to see someone tonight.' But a game of pool

was tempting. It'd be an easy option with no conflict, no arguments or disappointments, no professional façade glaring at her. And wouldn't solve a thing.

Her stomach clenched, sent a wave of nausea roaring up her throat. She held her breath, willed her body to behave. What was a bit of tiredness anyway?

But at seven that night, when Alesha finally found the address she needed and no one answered the bell she jabbed, her body all but dropped to the step. Tightening her spine, she turned and walked back the way she'd come to the bar she'd seen on the way in. The barman smirked when she ordered a cup of tea. Too bad. It was written on the blackboard.

At eight she tried the bell again with the same result. This time she couldn't fight the sagging of her knees and hit the step hard. Shuffling around, she made her butt as comfortable as possible on the concrete and clasped her knees to her chest, and waited. And waited.

'Alesha?' It was a soft question. Or was it a dream?

She blinked her eyes open. And blinked again. Kristof towered above her, concern lacing the puzzlement in those beautiful eyes.

Bang. Her heart tightened. And she knew. No doubt at all. She'd gone and fallen in love with Kristof in the space of that intense week. Not the maybe love, or a tentative, 'see how it worked out' love. Nor the *'had a great time and then goodbye'* kind. No, this was a full-on, 'involve the head, the body and the heart' love. A deal breaker.

She gasped. There was the problem. They had to make some sort of deal tonight, and she'd gone and got her side all messed up.

'What's wrong?' he asked in his professional voice.

* * *

When Kristof strolled up the road to his apartment from the parking garage, relieved another day was over and his patients were getting through post op as well as they should be, he'd been thinking how he could shuck off the clothes of his profession and pull on shorts and a casual shirt to relax with a cold one and think of nothing more difficult than what to have for dinner.

He'd been whistling under his breath, not expecting anything to change his plans as he turned towards his front door.

Then the whistle died. His feet slowed. While his eyes locked on the sleeping form sprawled across his front step.

'Alesha?' His heart skittered around in his chest. Alesha was on *his* doorstep? Why? Something cracked open a tiny way inside him. He slammed it shut with a deep breath and pulled back into work mode. 'What's wrong?' A pebble jabbed his knee when he knelt beside her. *Please be okay.* What had brought her here? Her long eyelashes were black against her pale skin. In his chest worry stabbed hard. Alesha had to be all right. She just had to be. He couldn't imagine her any other way, did not want anything bad to have happened to her. So much for being calm about this.

'Kristof?' She lifted her head, blinked at him. Then her eyes widened. 'I fell asleep.' Her voice was thick with sleep and surprise, as if she'd forgotten why she was here.

He had *no* idea why she was here. Alesha was the last person he'd expected to find tucked up on his doorstep. Not that he was used to finding anybody here. When they'd said goodbye in Dubrovnik that had been the wrap-up they'd agreed on. The end of a wonderful week, and not even the memories, and, yes, the longing for more in the middle of the night, had been going to change a thing. Yet here she was: the woman who wouldn't get out of his head. 'Are you all right?' Standing, he held a hand out to pull her to her feet.

She rubbed her arms and stared up at him, caution glittering out of those brown eyes. 'Why wouldn't I be?'

'How about because you're sleeping on a front step in a busy central London location? Or because you're outside my home, which I guess means you're wanting to visit.' He didn't add, *When we'd agreed not to get in touch.*

Ignoring his outstretched hand, she scrambled to her feet, then pushed back against the door, the rumpled blouse reminding him inexplicably of the night he'd found her pacing outside the apartments dressed only in a bikini and towel. As it wasn't her clothing that was the same it had to be the look of apprehension in her face that brought back that scene so clearly.

'It's good to see you. I've been wondering how you were getting on since coming back to London. Mum said you'd enjoyed your time working with her.' Now he was prattling like a teen on a hormone high. Clamping his mouth shut, he watched Alesha and waited.

'It was great. Those kids are so resilient they could teach most of us a thing or two about surviving life's hazards.' Her breasts rose and fell.

Yes, he remembered them all too well. Warm, soft, skin like satin.

Alesha continued, hopefully unaware of where his mind had strolled. 'I need to talk to you, but I won't stay long. Promise.' Did she just begin to cross her fingers then stop?

Stay as long as you like if I can touch you, hold you close, kiss that worry away. Make another memory.

He dug into his pocket for his keys. 'Let's go inside. Feel like a beer? Sorry, I don't have any of your favourite champagne.'

'Can I have a cup of tea?' Her teeth were chattering.

Tea? Apprehension trickled down his spine. 'No problem.' He hoped. 'Come through.' He led the way to his kitchen and plugged the kettle in before snatching a bottle of beer from the fridge. 'Sure I can't tempt you with one of these?' She had enjoyed a beer on a hot evening in Dubrovnik.

Alesha shook her head as she stared around. 'Wow. This is state-of-the-art.'

'Shame it doesn't get used as much as it should.'

'You don't do swanky dinner parties, then?' There. A glimmer of that wonderful smile that always created knots in his gut.

'Afraid not.' Kristof sipped his beer before getting a mug and a teabag.

'You really do stand alone.'

It was a statement, not a question. Seemed Alesha had seen more of what made him tick than most people ever did, and that was all in the space of a week. He must be slipping. 'I'm too busy most of the time, and when I do stop working I like to chill out without having to put my best face on.'

'Oh, boy.' She slumped, reached for a bench stool and sank onto it.

Apprehension grew, expanding and nudging aside the need for her that had begun pushing through. 'Why are you here? I'm presuming this isn't a social call to talk about the weather.'

Cool it. Don't upset her without good reason.

Alesha wouldn't be here if it wasn't necessary. Or would she? Did she want to go back on her word and continue their fling until it petered out—or became something more? Even if she did, it wasn't happening. He wasn't about to change his mind over trusting someone with his heart. Not even Alesha, as much as she intrigued him and had got under his skin.

The kettle whistled and clicked off. He poured boiling water over the teabag, his focus entirely on Alesha. Exhaustion was undoing her usually straight posture, while her hands fidgeted at her waist.

'Stop pouring,' she said in a surprisingly strong voice. 'Water's going everywhere.'

Sure was. A puddle crept towards the edge of the bench. Grabbing the cloth, he wiped it away. 'You're good at distracting me.'

Brain-slap. So not the thing to say. What if she did want to get together again?

He'd just fed into that line.

She stood up, straightened her body, and locked a steady gaze on him.

And the bottom fell out of his world. He had no idea what this was about, but he did know his life was about to change. For ever. 'Out with it.'

'I'm pregnant.'

'Really?' That was such an old line, and not what he'd expected from Alesha. Showed how little he knew her.

'Really,' she said quietly, with dignity.

'Hang on. Not so fast.' She was pregnant. *They* were having a baby. Alesha had said so. Whether it fitted in with his plans or not. What the hell was going on? He wouldn't, *couldn't*, be a parent. Kristof sank onto the stool next to the one Alesha had vacated. 'You walk in as though you belong here to tell me I'm the father of your baby? When we always used condoms.' Didn't they? He couldn't remember not using one. But they had got carried away to the point he'd known nothing but her body and the desire crashing through him.

A slow, wary nod was her reply, as she sank back down onto the stool.

'What are *your* plans for this baby?'

What little colour was in her cheeks disappeared. 'I'm keeping it. I will love it so much it won't grow up sad and lonely like me.' Her finger jabbed her thigh. 'Don't ever ask me that again. Got it?'

In spades. 'What do you want from me?' He had to start somewhere.

Her body jerked on the chair. 'To acknowledge you are the father, and to take part in his or her life.'

'That's it?' Disbelief whacked him. Pull the other one. 'It's a lot, but what about the other things? Money, somewhere to live.' His hands slapped his hips as he charged across to the window to stare out, unseeing. The breath he drew was ragged and bitter. 'What about marriage? You want me to commit to that as well?'

'No-o.' The chair crashed on the floor.

Kristof spun around to see Alesha running for the door. 'Wait.'

'What for? More insults?' Then she was tripping, sprawling across the hall carpet, her hands automatically protecting her belly. Her baby.

His baby. 'Alesha.' His knees hit the floor with a crack. 'Alesha, I'm sorry.' He bundled her into his arms and held her tight.

She fought him. 'Let me go.'

He didn't want to. He wanted to soothe her, make her feel better. Instead he rose and steadied her on her feet. 'Don't go. Not yet.' He'd behaved appallingly. 'You came to talk to me. Let's start. I promise not to be unkind again.'

She sank against the wall, her bottom lip trembling, her eyes filled with torment he was responsible for.

His heart stopped, and he hated himself. How monstrous had he been? No, he didn't want a baby, a child, in his life. But if one was on the way he had to man up and get on with accepting his fate. It didn't mean he had to like it.

'Call me when you've had time to get used to this,' Alesha whispered, and pushed upright.

'You're not going out on the street in this condition. Come and have that tea you wanted. I'll make you a fresh one, that first one will be ruined. We'll talk if you still want to.' He'd do all in his power to get across to her he was sorry for his reaction.

'That depends.' At least she was walking in the right direction.

'On my behaviour? I get it.' She'd shocked the pants off him. A baby. No way. Not him.

'Seeing the positive test knocked me over too.' Her mood wasn't lightening. Why would it after his outburst? 'But it was positive. I am pregnant.'

Kristof switched on the kettle, for want of something to do. He was going to be a father, one job he'd never put his hand up for. The only example he'd had of that role had turned out to be false and the biggest let-down of his life. But there was no avoiding that the unforeseeable *had* happened and he was going to be a dad. In some capacity at any rate.

Where did a guy start? How did he know what to do apart from the obvious like feeding and changing sodden nappies, things he'd learned training to be a doctor, not from his family? What if this child had high expectations of him, as he'd had of his father, and he let it—her or him—down? No, that would not happen. At least not before he'd poured everything he had into making certain he was doing his best for *his* child without getting too close emotionally.

An elbow nudged him out of the way. 'I'll get that.' A small hand took the packet of teabags from his fingers. 'Otherwise I could be here all night.' Apparently she didn't want that. Couldn't blame her at all.

Which wound him up in a flash. 'Why don't we eat and talk, and then you can stay the night instead of catching the train home afterwards since you're so tired? Sleeping past your stop late at night is not safe.'

The boiling water went into the mug without overflowing this time, but it came close. 'Because you don't really want me here. Another reason is that my morning sickness is evening sickness and I don't eat dinner at the moment.'

His protective instincts flared, cancelling the annoyance of a moment ago. 'All the more reason for you not to leave. There's a spare room with the bed made up.' He looked at her wan face and felt a squeeze in his chest for this woman he knew and yet didn't know. 'Please.'

A solitary tear leaked out of the corner of her right eye and tracked down her cheek.

Kristof caught it with his forefinger before it dripped onto her shirt. 'We'll make this work. You're not on your own.'

'No one's ever said that to me before.' Alesha coughed.

Seemed he'd opened a floodgate, such was the torrent that poured over her face now. Reaching for her, he tucked her against his body, her wet face pressed into his chest, her arms snaking around his waist to hold on tight. Stroking her back, he felt such a tenderness for Alesha it frightened him. Somehow they'd work their way through this and be there for each other in the future. Somehow. So much for remaining removed from her. Right now, she needed him, or his support, and damned if he wasn't going to oblige. Not just because it was the right thing to do, but because he couldn't not.

Run, man, run, while you still can. Get away, protect yourself.

But he couldn't. They had to sort this. A baby, for pity's sake. Him and a baby. Alesha and a baby, yes, he could see that was no problem. But him as a dad? Poor little kid.

It was going to take some accepting that he could no longer walk away from a relationship when he'd had enough without feeling he was missing out on something essential to life. A child was for ever. He or she had ended up with Kristof as a dad and that wasn't great.

What would it be like to hold his own baby? Would his heartstrings sing? Or would the fear of letting down the child outweigh the joy that Harry had often told him came with the first sight, the first touch, the first hold of your own baby?

He so wasn't ready for this. Who was?

But there was nothing for it. He had to step up to the mark. Alesha needed him and he would not let her down.

'I've never cried so much as I have these past days.' Alesha finally pulled out of Kristof's arms and picked up her cup of much-needed tea, though her hands were so shaky she was losing most of it over the rim as she crossed to the stool. Sitting down, she gripped the mug with both hands, took little sips, holding her breath after each one. Throwing up so wasn't a good look.

Kristof asked, 'Does this mean you'll be heading back to New Zealand?'

What? The whole point of telling him about the baby was so he'd have a part in his or her life. 'No, I'm not.'

'How long can you stay on in England on your visa?'

They really knew nothing about each other. 'My mother is British so I can come and go as I please. Getting work is not a legal problem.'

'We're both from multinational families, then.' Kristof was watching her as he asked, 'Won't you want to go home now to be close to your family when the baby is born?'

Close to her family? There was a joke, albeit a sour one. 'I won't be returning to New Zealand.'

A question formed in his eyes.

She hastened to avoid it. 'I like working in some of the large hospitals in London, and lately I've been thinking of buying my own place in a small town on the edge of the city, somewhere I can make into a home and feel like I belong.'

'In other words, settle down. Did this come before you found out you were pregnant, or after?'

'While I was helping at the children's home. The work was fulfilling in a different way from what I'm used to and I got to thinking about how I never stop anywhere for long. Yes, I've been in London now for two years, but I've spent a fair proportion of that time travelling or working in hospitals in other cities. I'm a bit like a stray cat looking for somewhere to get food and warmth before moving on.'

Too much information, girl. He's starting to look scared.

Kristof sipped his beer. 'You won't be working once the baby's born.'

She needed to correct that fast. 'Not at first, no, but eventually I'll have to go back to something.' There was money in the bank thanks to her grandmother's will. More than enough to buy a small property with a tiny backyard, and to keep her and the baby fed and clothed in reasonable comfort, because one thing she'd learned from her parents, about the only thing apart from how to abandon your child, was saving and being sensible with money, so she'd invested wisely.

'I'll support you financially so don't worry about that.'

Tea had never tasted so sour. 'I don't need that from you. I've got a nest egg back in New Zealand.' Time to start arranging for it to be transferred to a local bank.

'I'd prefer you don't touch it. For now at least.'

This was crazy. She was having their baby and they were talking about money. She never talked about that. Though yes, she could see that at some stage this discussion was probably necessary, but tonight when Kristof was still getting used to the idea he was going to be a father? 'Right. I won't. For now.'

Move on. Talk about what's really biting you. If you can.

'I will look into finding you an apartment near enough so I can visit daily.'

Her heart sank. Though why, when she'd known he'd never offer for her to move in with him? That wouldn't work when he didn't seem to want involvement on a permanent basis. It was why she was here. 'Why don't you ever want to settle down?' The question was out before she'd thought it through. Now he'd send her to the underground and her train. Forget not allowing her to go home.

'Are you asking why I haven't instantly begun plans for setting up house *together*?'

Did he have to sound so appalled? 'If you think that it was my intention to get that from you then think again. These days I am as wary as you of getting too close to someone. All I want, and I've had a few days to think about this, is for our child to be able to see as much of each of us as possible, and that we both have input into their life; with the decisions about education, sports, friends, where to live.' All the things that had stopped for her when she was nine and her parents had forgotten they had a daughter.

'Exactly. Where to live. In an apartment close by, or in a semi on the outskirts of the city that'll take time to get to and from.' Kristof stepped across the kitchen to stare out at whatever was outside. His hands were jammed in his pockets, his shoulders tense, his feet slightly splayed.

'For you.'

'Yes, for me working at Harley Street and in the hospital all hours.'

'Right, this is a problem already.' She waited. Sipped some more tea. And waited. And hardened her heart. This man had got under her skin, and she might've woken up to the fact she loved him, but she was not going to allow him to knock her off her feet. She had a child to fight for. Any relationship she got into had to be sincere and loving, so that child was safe and happy. A relationship bound up with doing the right thing and not letting hearts follow their course would not provide what her child needed.

And a life lived with parents who forgot more about their child than their own issues wasn't worth much.

Finally Kristof turned and leaned back against the window sill. 'I'm sorry. I know you're not a conniving woman. I know you'll only ever want the absolute best for your child.'

'Our child.'

He nodded. 'Our child. I will want the same. Just give me time.' His chest rose as he breathed in. 'I have been married. It was enough of a disaster that I never want to repeat the experience.'

Her heart softened—only a weeny bit. She couldn't afford to let it go all mushy on her. 'Kristof, I don't believe we know each other well enough after only one week together—a week that involved more action than talking—to consider marriage.' It was true, and at the same time it was a big, bad lie. Being married to Kristof had never occurred to her before she'd found out she was pregnant, but since then, in the dark of night when she was unable to sleep, the idea nudged her. But it wasn't happening so he was safe. *They* were safe.

The relief flooding his eyes still hurt though. Presuming his response and seeing it for real—yeah, well, that stung like a swarm of bees. Only guessing about that, mind.

'She played around on me. Often. Apparently our marriage was supposed to be an open one. Shame she didn't get around to telling me or I'd never have made that walk down the aisle in the first place.'

The man was still hurting. Did he still love this selfish woman from his past? Or was it that his heart wasn't ready to let go the pain of being abused? *That* she could understand all too well. 'Why marry you in the first place?' Bad question. Now he'd think she didn't consider him worthy of being a husband. Which so wasn't true. But it was one way of keeping him at a distance, and a distance she created was something she could control when everything seemed so up in the air. The space he kept between them was never going to shrink so she was protecting her heart, right?

'The lifestyle, my career, my family name and money, and, to be fair, me. She declared she loved me in all honesty and I believed her. Our parameters were poles apart, that's all.'

That's all?

That was huge, and not something never to be discussed before that final commitment at the altar. No wonder a darkness crept into his eyes when he was tired or facing decisions he didn't like. He had history that had made him wary, solitary, and downright sad at times.

She wanted to touch him, brush away that wariness with a kiss. Or two. To wind her arms around his waist and hold him close; to show he wasn't alone.

But that would be risking her own need to stand tall and strong. She had a baby coming who would need all her love and support, should never feel abandoned as she'd been. She needed to go for another option, get this back on track and away from the deep and meaningful stuff before she got sucked in and started begging for what she couldn't have. 'So, you mentioned dinner. What were you planning on?'

His mouth tightened, then softened into a facsimile of a smile. 'Thought you got night sickness.'

'And morning, afternoon, and all times in between. I have to eat for baby's sake so I go for small helpings often.'

'Lamb chops should go well with a Kiwi.' He crossed

to open the fridge. 'I can even throw a salad together. There're new spuds in the pantry. We're good to go.'

Go nowhere, she hoped. Right now that darned exhaustion was snagging her again, making her body heavy and her eyelids heavier. She slid off the stool before she fell off and went to sit on a chair by a table at a bay window, letting her chin rest on her breastbone.

Kristof scooped Alesha off the chair and held her against his chest as he strode down to his bedroom. Her only movement was to snuggle closer, her cheek pressed against his chest. Those eyelids did not lift one iota.

While his heart brimmed with tenderness. Damn it all. This wasn't meant to happen, this protectiveness and strange sense of belonging. But that was what Ms Alesha Milligan was doing to him, unravelling all the locks and chains on his heart, and she wasn't taking it slowly.

Lying her on his bed, he pulled a light cover over her and went to turn on the bathroom light in case she woke needing it in a hurry. He wasn't sure how much control she'd have over the nausea and she hadn't been here before. Wasn't meant to ever be here.

Pregnant? Who'd have believed it? Not him. How could he have been lax in protection when so much was at stake? As a result, his life would never be the same. The routine, the security in knowing how his days would pan out—gone.

Back by the bed he watched over her, like a warrior guarding his woman and his child. The dark shadows on her cheeks did not detract from her beauty, and those long black lashes enhanced it while at the same time making her appear fragile.

That was a myth. Alesha was strong in all the right

areas. She did seem to have men issues though. A chill settled on his heart. Not with him, she didn't. He would always be there for her now. They were joined together over this child. No way was he going to walk away even when the urge to run kept sneaking up on him.

Kristof kissed his fingertips and brushed the hair off Alesha's cheek. 'Sleep tight.'

Out in the kitchen he began putting lettuce in a bowl before chopping tomatoes, cucumber, avocado, and more. It was cathartic and he took no notice of what he was doing. His mind was focused on Alesha's news.

A baby. He was going to be a dad. An honest father who'd never deceive his son. He'd say the same for his wife, if he had one, but he didn't, and wouldn't.

His mother would be stoked. She'd never hidden the fact she'd like grandchildren some day, and sooner rather than later. She did not accept that he should forgo a happy family because the last attempt had gone belly up. *She* did not agree that his father should affect how he lived his life. *She* refused to acknowledge his guilt over how her love for her son had kept her shackled to her husband until her son was old enough not to need her there all the time.

Butt out, Mum. You're getting a grandchild. Be happy about that while I try to let the rest go.

Because he had to. He'd been screwed over—twice— and who put their hand up for a third crack at it? But it seemed that had happened when he was looking the other way.

Salad done, he scrubbed spuds and put them on to boil, snatching a sprig of mint from a plant growing in a pot by the back door. Waiting for the water to come to the boil, he popped the top on a beer and stood in the doorway staring out at the minuscule patio with its wooden outdoor furniture. It was his go-to place at the end of a hectic week or when he had a mess in his head that needed sorting. Like now.

This area was too small for a child wanting to play or chase a ball.

His head jerked up. So? The baby was only weeks old in the womb, had a long way to go before chasing a ball became part of the picture.

The beer was cool and moist on his dry throat. His eyes were moist as he visualised that scene of a boy running around shrieking as he chased the ball. A boy? Was that what he wanted? A son and heir? Or a little girl with her mother's sparkling eyes and sassy smile? Warmth stole into his chest, dried his eyes. A little girl who'd love her daddy and he'd love her back—so much. The dampness returned to his eyes. He wasn't supposed to be considering love. Standing out here was doing him no good. Time to put the chops on and go see if Alesha was still dead to the world or this was a catnap she'd wake from starving hungry.

The mobile phone rang as he was adding oil to the pan.

'Mr Montfort, it's Gabby from the ward. Jeremy Walbank has developed chest pain and shortness of breath. One of the registrars is with him but I thought you'd want to know.'

Mr Walbank had had bowel surgery for cancer that morning.

'On my way. Fill me in on everything now.' Kristof listened as he turned off the gas elements. 'Sounds like a pulmonary embolism. Take bloods for haematology, coagulation and biochemistry. I'll fill out the form when

I get there. Give Radiology the heads up that we'll be needing imaging.'

Quickly he scrawled Alesha a note.

Sorry, got called in to see a patient. Help yourself to anything you want. I'll be back as soon as possible to continue our discussion.
Kristof

He refrained from adding an *X* at the end, though as he drove towards the hospital he kind of wished he had put it there. It might go some way to getting back on side with Alesha. Then again, why complicate an already complicated situation? Alesha might read more into a simple penned kiss than he meant. Or she might do a runner, head for the train and the Friday-night revellers that would be on board. She'd better not leave. If she was adamant about going home later he'd drive her.

Or she might not wake up until he got home and climbed into bed beside her.

What? Why not? He could hold her, in the most innocent way, as a comfort, as support.

Oh, yeah, as if Alesha would accept that quietly. Somehow he felt cuddling was off the agenda for now, if not for ever.

That shouldn't sadden him; he should be ecstatic she wouldn't complicate things in that respect. It did, and he wasn't.

Go figure.

CHAPTER EIGHT

ALESHA WOKE AND stared around the semi dark room.
'Where am I?'

Then nausea struck and she leapt off the bed, followed
the light source to what was a fully equipped bathroom.
Grateful for en suite bathrooms, she sank to her knees
in front of the porcelain and let her baby rule.

Her head pounded and her eyes were filled with sleep
grit. Her body felt like a well-worn car tyre, and she
couldn't focus on anything except feeling so bad. Looking around the room, she saw a familiar shirt on top of
the laundry basket and it all tumbled back into her mind.

She was at Kristof's and they'd been discussing the
baby when she'd fallen asleep. That made her look enthu-
siastic, didn't it? But nowadays when the need for sleep
hit there was no stopping it. Unless she was at work she
usually grabbed half an hour on the couch and was good
to go again. At work she put matchsticks under her eyelids and carried on regardless, triple-checking everything she did.

Laying her hand on her belly, she drew up a smile.
'Hello, little one. You're being a wee bit tough on your
mum, you know? I could do without all this sickness

stuff. But then I suppose it's part of the deal and if it keeps you safe and comfy then I'll manage.'

Panic gripped her. What if she got what she wished for? At the cost of her baby? Pushing to her feet, she stared at her image in the mirror. 'Stay aboard, whatever you think. I love you already. Got that?'

Raising her blouse, she regarded her flat stomach. Not a hint of what lay inside. Turning side on, she changed her mind. 'A slight curve going on.' The panic backed off as fast as it had struck. 'I can't wait to meet you. Are you a girl or a boy?' If only she could be heard and understood, she'd love to feel a kick in answer to her questions.

Then her stomach groaned. Hunger was gathering strength. Kristof had mentioned chops and salad. Her mouth salivated. She had to find the kitchen. Which proved to be interesting. The apartment made the house she shared with three others look like a shoebox. There weren't many rooms but they were all very large, furnished elegantly and tastefully. It matched Kristof's professional look, not that sexy, have-fun man who only came out after everyone else had been seen to.

Not the sort of furniture for little children to climb all over.

That was Kristof's problem, not hers. So far she didn't have any furniture, not even a bed, but if she bought a place she'd have fun selecting things to make it look pretty and comfortable and *usable*. It could also be a disaster considering her lack of experience in decorating. But learning would be exciting. She'd do the baby's room first, sleep on the floor in the meantime if necessary. This settling down was sounding better by the day.

But now she had a father-in-waiting to talk to.

Except all she found was a note. And the smell of

minted potatoes, which were cooked to perfection. Sitting in the hot water must've finished them off. A delicious-looking salad in the fridge made her mouth water. All that was needed was one of those chops Kristof had mentioned. Would it be rude to cook herself one? Make that two, if the growling going on in her stomach was an indicator.

Rude or not, she couldn't wait until he came home. If he came home this side of midnight. Getting called in to a patient often meant long hours. Kristof might be in Theatre again, and even a short operation took time to prepare for, to undertake, and then hang around to see how the patient fared. The chops definitely couldn't wait a moment longer.

As Alesha slid two chops, slightly pink in the middle, onto a plate, she heard keys being dropped on the table by the front door. 'Well timed,' she called. Then hoped it was Kristof. Someone else might live here for all she knew. Someone who'd object to finding a stranger in the kitchen making a mess. She might be able to appease them with a chop.

No, her stomach growled. *I need both those.*

'Smells wonderful,' the gruff, sexy voice relieved her of that worry, but only set in motion all the other concerns about what role he'd finally decide on in the baby department. Her baby not having a father who loved and cared about him *could not* happen.

'I'll put some more on. We can start with one each.' She was acting as if she was in charge in Kristof's kitchen. Finally she was learning not to let other people dominate her. Not that this man did that.

Stay the night.

Not too much anyway.

He stood right beside her, watching as she added more oil to the pan, swirling it as it expanded with the heat. Then he picked up one of the cooked chops and bit into it. 'You know what you're doing.'

'Hey, I need that.' She grabbed the other before he could lay claim to it.

Kristof nodded. 'Salad and spuds after the protein?'

Alesha waved her chop between them. 'Only because I don't trust you not to steal this when I'm spooning salad onto my plate.' Was he in a good mood? Or still in shock? That raw denial seemed to have disappeared from his eyes, but she couldn't read what had replaced it.

'Come on, now. Would I do that?'

'Yes. You stole two of my deep-fried squid at the charity dinner.'

'I made up for it later.'

With the most amazing sex she'd ever experienced. Yep, she got it. Making light of a grave situation must be Kristof's way of coping. She backed away, sank onto a chair. 'We're not having sex tonight, not any night. The fling is over.'

'You're right.' Not even a hint of a smile now.

Kristof filled his plate with salad and sat down beside her at the small table. 'We did get on well when we didn't overthink things.'

Yes, but they hadn't had a baby in the picture then. The tomato was surprisingly sweet on her tongue, giving her hope other things could be too. 'Let's try to keep it that way. There's a lot at stake.'

'I agree.' His eyes were thoughtful. 'Have you told anyone else?'

She tried for a smile, but exhaustion got in the way. 'No. You had to be the first person who knew.'

'Thank you. That's important to me.'

Because she put him first? About to slip one finger across the back of his hand, she hesitated. Best not. 'I won't ever deliberately hurt you, or abuse your trust in me.'

His chair legs squeaked as they were pushed across the tiles. 'You don't know me well enough to trust me with something as important as your baby's future.'

Alesha drew herself up and locked her eyes on his. 'There are a lot of things I haven't a clue about when it comes to you, but I do know in here—' she tapped her chest '—that I can trust you to be considerate and to care about me in regards to our child. Actually, make that I trust you totally.' She really did. There were no grounds for this, and while every man she'd spent more than a couple of dates with had hurt her in one way or another this beggared belief. But she did believe it. Kristof would not do the dirty on her. How often had he watched out for her during their fling week? Attended her needs before his? That had been wonderful, worth gold.

Now she just had to prevent her heart thinking it was winning and that she was about to throw herself at Kristof. Because trust was well and good, but it wasn't the whole picture. Discovering she loved him didn't mean he reciprocated; didn't allow her to stop fighting for what her baby needed; wouldn't make the coming months a breeze to get through. Only if they could find common ground, fall in love together, make a real go of being a family.

In your dreams. Alesha.

His head came down, close to her, then his lips caressed her forehead. Inside, her temperature rose and her muscles softened, her stomach turned to goo. This was beautiful. It made her feel special. Which it shouldn't. She should back away now. Before he told her he wasn't interested in her or their baby.

Kristof beat her to it, pulling away and picking up their plates to take them to the sink. 'It's getting late. Tomorrow's Saturday. I think we should postpone further discussions until then. Go out for breakfast at the market and start making some plans.'

He expected her to stay when she hadn't agreed to. 'What time shall I meet you there?'

'Don't do that,' he growled. 'You're pushing me away.'

Was she pushing him away? If standing up for herself and showing she wouldn't be told what to do meant that then, yes, she was. 'I'm looking out for myself.'

'I get it, but staying here isn't going to prevent you doing that, and it makes sense not to go home on a train loaded with drunks and who knows what else. You'd only have to return in a few hours, hours that could be spent catching up on sleep you so desperately need if those shadows darkening your cheeks are any indication.'

'Fine. I'll stay.' What else could she say when her blood was humming with gratitude and something she'd rather not identify? Her head *was* nodding with fatigue and her legs really didn't have the strength to walk to the nearest station. 'Which bedroom shall I use?'

'Mine. It's got a bathroom within dashing distance.' His smile was strained, as if reality was finally catching up in a hurry.

All she could hope for was that she didn't wake up on the front step with a note attached telling her to go away, that he wasn't interested in becoming a parent. But he wouldn't. She trusted him. If that made her an idiot, then sorry, but once she'd allowed him in it seemed there wasn't any way he was leaving. 'Goodnight, Kristof.'

He had his phone out. Finding out how his patient was? Or was there a significant other person in his life? She'd never asked, believing he wouldn't have had that fling if there was. 'Goodnight, Alesha.'

'Is there someone special in your life you have to tell about the baby?' She couldn't help the squeak that accompanied her question, the need to hear him say no suddenly important.

'I'm single, without anyone regular in my life. In fact you've been the only woman I've been intimate with in months.'

Good. She wouldn't ask why. That'd be pushing too hard. 'Goodnight, Kristof.' She headed down the hall, a spring in her heavy footsteps.

They were definitely like two people who'd had a hot fling and moved on to become—what?—friends with a baby on the way? Friends was good, but nowhere near enough. Though until they'd worked their way through the issues surrounding baby then it could be that friendship was the way to go. Also, far better than fighting one another every step.

Down, disappointment, down.

This was what she'd come for, before she'd realised she loved the man.

Slipping out of her blouse and skirt, Alesha slid under the sheet in her underwear. It probably wasn't wise but it was all she had, and anyway she was as well dressed as the night she'd first met Kristof. Since then he'd seen it all. Smiling, she closed her eyes and instantly fell into a deep sleep where dreams of what they'd done together, followed by other dreams of what they could do next, skidded through her night.

Kristof stood in the doorway of his bedroom watching the gentle rise and fall of the sheet covering Alesha's breasts. He wasn't leering or even thinking sexy thoughts. No, his head was full of images of her holding their baby, of crooning to a crying little one, of kissing his or her forehead and pressing him or her to her swollen breast for milk. Don't ask him how, but he believed she was going to make an excellent mother.

As for him? An excellent father? Yes, he could be, would be, as long as he didn't get it all wrong. The child had better be strong, and depend more on his—or her— mother than him. Just in case Kristof made poor judgements and hurt them all. He'd misread his father, and blamed his mother for leaving them when she'd been struggling with Dad's infidelities. If only he'd known about those before he'd shouted at her, 'If you leave I never want to see you again.' He'd believed his father to be nigh on perfect, had never once considered the man he tried to emulate might be the one transgressing the marriage boundaries. Not that he'd been able to picture his mother having an affair either. His mother had been quick to brush away his apologies when he'd learned about the mistresses but it had been too late. He'd said those awful words and there was no taking them back. She'd returned to her home town of Dubrovnik before his father had died, and he'd missed her so much, but male pride had got in the way and kept him firmly in London, until he'd finally gone to apologise, and they'd slowly started to rebuild their relationship.

Then there was his marriage. Cally had wanted for ever with him, just not only him.

He'd never hurt a woman like that, or his child, but he'd also never risk his heart again.

One week was all it had taken to turn his world around, to change his direction for ever. Was he happy about it? Honestly? No. But there was no undoing what had happened. Alesha certainly had found the right man to accidentally get pregnant with. He'd stick by her throughout and beyond, as a friend, as the father of her child.

Kristof spun away to head to his TV room. A mindless programme would help quieten the questions and let him relax enough to fall asleep. The answers were there, under lock and key, waiting for a time he was able to look at them. He wanted to believe he'd get this right. He really, really did.

Because if he was lucky enough for his child to adore him he didn't want to crack his son's world wide open to disbelief and pain; to the acknowledgment his father had made a mockery of everything he'd been raised to believe.

As *his* father had done. Had his dad gone and died quietly and with dignity? Hell, no. A massive heart attack while in his mistress's bed had been the final chapter in what had turned out to be a double life right from the day he'd married Kristof's mother and been unfaithful with the bridesmaid.

At least according to the gossip and stories at the funeral and for months afterwards.

TV wasn't distracting him.

A brandy might. But he had to be ready to return to the hospital if called.

So checking out the property market in central London was an option.

Alesha didn't want to live in the city with her baby.

There had to be give and take. Alesha had to understand he wanted to be near but that he couldn't live too far from the hospital.

Another option would be to keep this apartment and buy a larger house where she wanted and go stay there at the weekends.

Just like your father.

He wasn't having a mistress in the city and Alesha waiting for him somewhere else. That wasn't the idea. Anyway, he and Alesha weren't a couple.

Just as well he wasn't on call tomorrow. He'd be next to useless.

A light knock on the bedroom door warned Alesha she was no longer alone. 'Hello?'

'Will a cup of tea make waking up easier?' Kristof stood in the doorway, that thick dark-blond hair with a very slept-in look and a line of stubble highlighting his jawline.

Her tongue roved over her lips at the gorgeous sight. Until her stomach warned her there were more important considerations right now. Gulp. 'Excuse me.' The bathroom door slammed behind her. This was not something she wanted to share with Kristof. That was going too far. She preferred he remembered her looking half decent at least.

The man didn't take the hint. Or was too thick to understand. The door opened and he was there, holding her hair away from her face, rubbing her back, and, when it was over, handing her a warm, moist face cloth.

While her stomach cringed at Kristof seeing her like this, there was no denying the tenderness flowing through her at his kindness and concern.

'Here.' He held out a thick white robe. 'Far too large, I know, but you look cold.'

Dressed in bra and knickers, she certainly wasn't overdressed. 'Thanks.' The soft fabric smelt of Kristof as she snuggled into the garment. She blinked rapidly to banish the sudden tears. All these tears. Pregnancy seemed to mess with her hormones quite a bit.

But when was the last time anyone had done something so ordinary and yet so endearing for her? No answer came to mind, unless she went back to when she was seven and her mother cuddled her after falling off a horse. Mum.

Don't go there.

But what would her mother say about the baby?

Forget it.

Her parents had had no time for her after Ryan got sick; they weren't going to find any for a grandchild. Especially since they were on the other side of the world. Her heart sank. It was so unfair. She was used to the abandoned feeling she'd known from the day her brother was diagnosed with acute leukaemia catching at her in unexpected moments, but it never got any easier. The sense that her parents should want to see her, talk to her, know what she was up to would not go away permanently. Sometimes that made her angry, mostly it made her sad.

'Ready to try that tea?' Kristof asked.

She nodded, her gaze lingering on him. His size filled the bathroom, his presence stole the air and her sense of gravity, made her head swirl. This man was the father of her baby. Unbelievable really, that he'd been keen enough to make love to her every night for a whole week and then welcome her into his home here in London when they weren't supposed to see each other again. A soft breath trickled over her lips. If only he could see her as a woman to spend his future with. If only she hadn't gone and fallen in love with him.

A steady hand took her elbow, and she was led out to the bedroom. 'Get back into bed until you're feeling one hundred per cent again. I'll bring your tea here.'

'I should be all right now. One bout at a time seems to be how it plays out for me.'

'Bed. Now.' There was a thread of command in his husky voice.

Alesha obeyed. She was quite liking having someone in charge for a few minutes. It gave her time to get her strength back and stop thinking about Kristof as anything other than the father of her child.

His head appeared around the door. 'Are you ready for a piece of toast? Dry or buttered?'

She shook her head. 'Just the tea. I'll eat when we get to the market.'

'You still want to go?'

Yes, she wanted to have that talk about how they were going to deal with being joint parents in separate homes, and it would be easier on her to do that away from this opulent apartment that needed knocking into comfortable, used shape. The atmosphere intimidated her at moments when she relaxed too far. She could not imagine a small child crawling around the place getting slobber on the carpet or a chair leg. 'I adore markets.'

One dark eyebrow arched and his mouth twitched. 'Should I hire a trailer for the morning's shopping?'

'A very large one.'

'You a shopaholic by any chance?' The question was laden.

'Nope. I like browsing and daydreaming but I don't usually buy up large.' Though there was a baby growing in her tummy. 'Though I might be tempted to get a teddy bear today.'

'Alesha.' The laughter had gone from his voice. 'Don't rush it. You're only a few weeks pregnant.'

Her skin tightened. 'You think I'm tempting fate?'

'I'm being super-cautious.'

'You're frightening me, is what you're doing.'

Immediately he was beside the bed, reaching for her hand to squeeze it gently. 'Sorry. I don't mean to.'

'Then why did you? Do you always look for the bad in things?'

Her hand fell from his as he stepped back. 'I'll make that tea.'

'Why are you avoiding my question?'

'I'm trying to come up with an answer.'

Looking back to their nights in Dubrovnik, she realised there'd been other times when he had changed the subject if she'd asked something personal. Oh, he'd have answers all right, just not ones he wanted to share. Great. Worked well for a relationship even of the kind they were planning—*not*. 'I would like to learn more about you.'

But he'd gone. Alesha huffed as she sat on the bed and leaned back against the headboard. Bet it took longer than usual to make the tea. Kristof wouldn't be in a hurry to talk to her now.

'So much for breakfast,' Kristof commented when they got to the market. The place was humming and the food cart had a queue to Africa. He'd thought the cooler weather might've kept people indoors, but apparently not. 'I should've made you something at home.' But then he'd have had to face up to some of Alesha's questions. She might've only asked one that morning, but answer it and there'd be more.

'I'm going to the bread stall to get something. I'm starving,' she told him. 'Then I'm grabbing a coffee. What about you?'

'Suits me perfectly. You meant to drink coffee?'

A look of annoyance lashed him. 'Okay, tea. You can't avoid talking about our baby just because we're not sitting down to breakfast. We've got all day.'

He winced. 'Actually we haven't. I've got a wedding to attend this afternoon.'

Rocking back on her heels, Alesha glared at him. 'Thanks for telling me.'

'I didn't see the need. We've got a few hours this morning.'

'Really?' She shoved the sleeve of her thick jacket up and held her wrist in front of him so he could read the time.

Another wince. Not hours, barely an hour before he had to get home to spruce himself up. 'Right, food first. We'll take it and the coffee over to one of the park benches.'

She didn't move. 'Are you trying to get out of this discussion by any chance?' One hand gripped a hip.

A hip he remembered kissing all too well. Which was totally inappropriate right now, and clouded the issue between them. 'No, but the morning did get away on us.'

With you being sick and me taking my time making your cup of tea so you might forget what you'd asked.

'Alesha, I understand you want to know where we're at and what the way forward might be.'

She did a funny twisty thing with her head as she continued that stare. 'Good. Then let's get down to it—while we're munching on food.'

'Surrounded by crowds and having to shout to be heard?' He shook his head before taking her elbow and leading her to the bread stall. 'What would you like?'

'Two chocolate croissants.'

Hardly healthy food for junior, but he daredn't comment, merely ordered said croissants and a bacon butty for himself. At the stall next door he got a long black and a tea before they walked across to a bench, only to lose it when they were yards away. 'Blast.'

Alesha placed her tea on the path between her feet and began devouring a croissant, chocolate smearing across her upper lip.

He itched to wipe it away with his finger, or, better yet, lick it up. Instead he bit into his butty and chewed and chewed. Bacon was his favourite morning kick-start, but nothing was happening today. Sipping the over-hot coffee added to his woes when it burned his tongue. 'At least we can be thankful you don't have to return to New Zealand.'

There was that despairing look again. 'We covered this last night.'

Just kicking off the talk. 'Are you sure you're happy settling down in England? I mean, why don't you want to go home to have your baby?' It was imperative he knew. Suddenly he couldn't imagine what it would be like if she did up sticks and return home, where she must have some friends, if not family. Not to have Alesha near was beginning to worry him. And this wasn't about the baby.

This was a leftover from their time in Croatia. Or was it? He didn't know. Didn't understand a thing that had happened, or been said, since those words had spilled out between them.

I'm pregnant.

'The baby's father lives in England.' The reply was too quick, as if she didn't want to say anything about what or who was—or wasn't—back in New Zealand. 'Are you afraid I'll take the baby away from you?' Now there was concern—*for him*—in her eyes.

He preferred the despair. 'I'd like you to be happy with where you are, secure in the knowledge you're doing the right thing by you and the baby.' Could he ask about her family without upsetting her too much? He would have to know some time.

'If I go south you'll take visiting rights twice a year. Fly in for a few days, have a great time at the amusement park with your child, and fly out again.' Despite the tartness in her voice that concern was still there; growing even.

He had to stop it, which meant not asking the big questions—yet. 'I want the best for you both. That's all.'

'Who hurt you, Kristof? Not your mother, surely? She worships the ground you walk on.'

You're right. She didn't.

But she was right about one thing. 'I hurt her.' Too much information. In his haste to stop this conversation he'd added fuel to the fire.

'That explains it.' Alesha was nodding as she bit into her second croissant.

Now he was in for it, if he didn't stop her in her tracks. 'Let's go look for that teddy bear.'

She sagged forward. 'I've got a better idea. Why don't

you head home and get yourself ready for the wedding
and I'll do my own thing?'

'Alesha, I'm…'

'You know what? I don't care what you're about to
say. We'll have this conversation when you've had time
to think about what you really want and in the meantime
I'll get on with preparing for motherhood.' Hurt dripped
off every word. The paper cup of tea spilled across the
path as she turned to throw the remains of her food in the
nearby bin. 'See you another time.' Her back was tight
as she stalked away.

Kristof ached for her, but his feet were glued to the
path. He'd achieved diversion—and hated himself for
it. But telling her the truth about his sorry background
and how he'd hurt his mother by believing his father? It
was never going to happen. He never talked about that
to anybody, and wasn't about to start.

So best he did what he was told and go get ready for
his friend's wedding, *his* day of happiness.

His eyes were fixed on the back of Alesha's head as
she pushed through the crowd. Admiration for her standing up to him grew. She was a fighter, in her own way.
By walking away she'd handed the ball back to him.
What better woman could his child have for a mother?
None that he could think of. But then his thinking was
all askew since he'd met her, so what did he know?

Only that she was better off without him in her life,
and now he had to remain on the outside looking in, sup-
porting her without touching her in any way, shape or
form. He hadn't taken up the opportunity of having affairs when Cally had revealed hers, but what if he had

his father's genes, those ones in particular? Even the best marriages had times when they didn't run smoothly. Was that when he'd show his true colours?

CHAPTER NINE

ALESHA THOUGHT ABOUT that week in Dubrovnik, how it had started out so badly and finished on a high. Her sigh was bitter sweet. If Luke had gone with her as planned her life would be so different right now. There wouldn't be a baby on the way. Love wouldn't be contracting her heart. She'd never have spent time at the Croatian children's home and found she was ready to settle down instead of planning her next trip for when this current contract ended.

'The bedrooms are small but there's lots of light,' the estate agent told her. 'And there's a little yard at the back with a patio where you could grow a few shrubs.'

The house did nothing for her. Neither had the previous two she'd seen. 'I'm sorry.' A backyard in New Zealand was huge compared to this postage-stamp-sized one.

You don't live there any more.

How true.

'Well, I don't have any more properties to show you at the moment.' The woman strode through the house. 'You might have to rethink your prerequisites or come up with more money to get what you want.'

Best to sort out other things first. 'I'll think about those options.' The woman wasn't overly friendly, not like the two sales people she'd been out with during the previous few days. They hadn't given up on her yet, had more viewings for next week. 'Thank you very much for showing me these houses.'

'She doesn't believe I can afford a property,' Alesha told Kristof over the phone that evening when they connected for a chat as they'd done every couple of nights since their disagreement in the market over two weeks ago.

'Didn't she ask you pertinent questions before taking you viewing?' Kristof's voice was always warm and sexy over the phone, almost as if their disagreement hadn't happened, and reminding her of what she couldn't have. If only she could see his face, his eyes.

No wonder she got little sleep at night. Kristof's voice was always there, reminding her of the boat ride to Cavtat, the charity dinner where she'd bought those vouchers, the walk around the Old City, and the lovemaking—sorry, sex—in her snazzy little apartment. Exhaustion had become a part of her day, and baby wasn't responsible for all of it.

'I filled out a fair amount of paperwork, yes. But a part of me thinks I'm being negative without trying.'

'You might not be ready to make a decision like this.' He drew a breath. 'You can stay with me when you stop work if that'll give you breathing space while you make up your mind. Or I can buy that apartment around the corner from here. If it doesn't work out it will still give you time to come up with an alternative.'

Then she'd be beholden to him. Buying an apartment in high-end London wasn't exactly like getting the fish that was on special for dinner. Or maybe it was for Kristof. How wealthy was he? His home, clothes, his car, all spoke of money, but what would she know coming from her background where clothes came from chain stores? As for cars and houses, she didn't know what her parents had now. When the world tipped upside down because of Ryan's illness the car had been an average family wagon, and the house middle class newish in Christchurch. She'd gone to see it before leaving for England but it'd been wrecked in the earthquake and bowled over by bulldozers. Seemingly, her parents had walked away with the insurance pay-out in their pockets.

'Alesha?'

'That's a lovely offer but I'll keep looking.'

'You pushing me away again?'

'No. Again.' Or was she? 'Kristof, can we take things one at a time? The house issue is not urgent…'

'Do you understand how long it can take for a purchase to go through?' he interrupted.

'Anything from a few days to a few weeks.'

'That might be the case where you come from, but not here. There are months involved with this.'

'Up the pressure, why don't you?' But she should've thought to ask about that. Showed how mixed up her brain was these days. 'About taking things one at a time, I'm having a scan tomorrow.'

'I've got surgery.'

He hadn't asked what time her appointment was. 'I see.' She really did. The blinkers had been lifting, now they were wide open. For all his offers of help regarding most things to do with the baby, he did not want to be a part of the pregnancy. So he was going to remain remote when it came to interacting with the baby. Her heart broke for their child. She knew all too well what that felt like, the hurt and bewilderment that followed her through life, the questions about what she'd done to earn the brush-off. Wasn't she good enough? For them? Her baby would not know that. Would not. Her heart also snapped for herself. They were not going to become a 'couple'.

'Kristof,' she snapped. Then swallowed and took a calming breath, though it went nowhere near to slowing her angry pulse rate. 'Are you sure you do not want to see your baby for the first time at the scan? Are you telling me this doesn't matter to you at all?'

Silence. Long and awkward.

She waited, holding her breath. Then had to draw in air, and wait again. In the end she said, 'Think about it. Goodnight, Kristof,' and hung up.

Gutted. That was how she felt. Hollowed out and stomped on. The man she loved was dodging the important issues involving his child. Every parent she knew had said that first scan was exciting beyond description. Even a man with commitment issues would want to be there. Wouldn't he? It was why she'd mentioned the appointment, not wanting to have him feel he was missing out. She'd got that wrong, hadn't she? It wasn't as though she'd been asking for something for herself.

'Why?' she cried as tears streamed down her cheeks. She hadn't asked for a marriage proposal or the signing over of all Kristof's assets into the baby's name. Only involvement.

Her phone rang. 'Kristof' flicked up on the screen.

This had better be good. 'Yes?'

'What time?'

'Five-thirty.' She gave the name of the hospital.

'I'll be there.'

'I'm glad. For your sake.' She wasn't saying it would be nice to have him with her for this important appointment. He'd pull out. Instead he had to do it for himself and the baby.

Alesha ended the call and stared at the mess on the kitchen bench. Everyone had left in a hurry that morning, leaving dishes and empty bread bags lying around. For once she didn't care.

She'd done it. Kristof was coming. Because she'd pricked his conscience? Or because he'd taken a minute to rethink his instant refusal? It didn't matter. She'd stuck up for her baby. She, who spent most of her life trying to please people rather than create waves, had put her baby before her own needs. While having Kristof there during the scan would help her, it was the baby she needed to be able to tell later 'when your father and I first saw you', not have to dodge the question of why Dad wasn't there.

Kristof was late through no fault of his own. 'I'm five minutes away.'

'I'll try to get the radiology tech to hold off, but she's wanting to finish for the day.' Alesha sounded peeved, as well she might.

But welcome to his world where patients came first, and often second and third. Often? Always. Things were going to have to change if he took this fathering thing seriously. Why wouldn't he? He was not going to be *his* father. No kid deserved that.

So you're going to buy a house outside the city and ask Alesha to marry you so you can all play happy families?

He tripped up the steps leading into the unit. Trying to do the right thing by the baby and Alesha was impossible when they were at odds. The baby needed all he could provide without him getting close; Alesha did not need him as a husband who was only there to provide the basics. He wasn't marrying without involving his heart. Back to the beginning. Full circle. No marriage. His mouth dried, and his heart slowed.

'Hi, you made it.' She was waiting outside the entrance to Radiology, relief beaming out of those beautiful eyes.

And drilling into his gut. Reminding him of how well they fitted together. Not only physically, but also they seemed to agree on the most important things. Suddenly the stress of getting here, of even having to be here, fell away and he reached for her hand. 'Let's go do this.' He wanted the first glimpse of his son or daughter more than anything.

Her fingers slipped between his; warm, soft, Alesha.

'Now, there's a surprise.' The girl pushing her scanner into Alesha's stomach grinned. 'There are two in there.'

'What?' The word exploded out of Kristof. 'Twins?'

'Two?' squeaked a stunned Alesha. 'Two babies. Oh, my.'

The girl nodded as she studied the screen in front of her. 'That explains your exhaustion, I'd say.'

Alesha murmured, 'Are you sure?'

Kristof wrapped an arm over her shoulders, held her tight. This was colossal. One baby in their situation was big, but two? They had a lot to consider. Not that anything had really changed. 'Do we know what we're getting?'

'Do you want to?' The girl looked from him to Alesha.

Alesha nibbled her bottom lip. 'I think I do. When it was only one baby I thought I'd like to be surprised, but two? I want to know.'

The scanner pushed against her belly and the images on the screen showed two tiny figures. 'How can you tell whether they're boys or girls?' Kristof asked. A dumb question. The woman was well qualified for this, but right now that picture seemed fuzzy to him and those babies so tiny they blurred before his eyes. He rubbed them and his hand came away damp. He was crying? Hadn't done that since he was a kid. He slashed harder at his face. It didn't do to be seen sniffling.

Alesha had no problems with crying. Buckets were needed to collect her tears. The tissues the girl passed her were quickly turned into a sodden ball and another box had to be found. Then she turned into him, buried her face against his shoulder, and saturated his shirt as well.

A boy *and* a girl. It was as though fate had caught him out and was playing a full hand in case it didn't get another chance. His lungs weren't coping. His heart had lost the ability to do slow and steady. Those images told him what Alesha hadn't been able to, what he hadn't been able to grasp fully. 'I'm going to be a dad.' As in raise, mentor, play with, cherish for ever, those babies. *Love* them regardless. 'Want to share those tissues?'

'I might have to agree to that apartment around the corner,' Alesha told Kristof over a cup of tea back at his place. 'Two babies are going to be a handful and if you're close by that'd help.'

'We'll get a nanny.'

Oh, Kristof. 'No, we won't. I am going to bring up my children. I will not leave them in someone else's care.' All the angst over being abandoned roared up through her and she was on her feet staring into Kristof's startled eyes. 'Never.'

'Whoa. Take it easy. I was only trying to make things better, not worse.' He sank onto a kitchen stool so he was at her level when she returned to her seat.

'Well, you weren't. Never, ever, suggest that again. You hear?'

'I think the whole street heard.' Then his lips flattened. 'Sorry. Not the right time for flippancy. But I'm out of my depth here. What do you want?'

He was trying to help. She had to drop the anger. It wasn't his fault her parents did what they did. 'My turn to apologise.' She retreated to her stool and tried to pick up her cup without sloshing tea everywhere. That was a fail.

'Talk to me, Alesha. How are you going to manage? Financially, for one. Raise two children while working, for another. There's something more going on here that I have no clue about.'

'I have my grandmother's money. She died when I was eleven and I couldn't touch the money till I was twenty-one. The lawyer she appointed invested very wisely for me.'

'There's more to this. Someone's hurt you, haven't they?'

As if he told her things about his past? But they'd get nowhere if they both kept this up. One of them had to start letting go and revealing what made them tick. It wouldn't be Kristof. He was too tight, too removed once the fun stopped. But could she talk to him about her family? Could she not? Her babies were depending on her getting things sorted before they arrived. Sorted properly, not doing a shoddy job that they'd all live to regret.

This time the tea didn't go over the edge of the mug when she picked it up, though it was now lukewarm. Guess she couldn't have it all. Sipping, she hoped her stomach didn't choose now to make a nuisance of itself. 'My brother died of AML when I was ten.' She hesitated. Took another sip. 'It was horrible. My parents couldn't deal with it.' She blinked, stared all around the room but not at Kristof. If his eyes filled with sympathy she'd fall apart.

His hand covered her one on her thigh. He didn't say a word. She still nearly fell to shreds.

More tea, more deep breathing. Then, 'They were lost in their grief, and I—from the day Ryan's bone-marrow result was delivered I didn't have parents any more. Not ones who were there for me. I was nine.'

'Who took care of you?'

'I did. I ate when I was hungry, shopped with the money Dad left lying around when the cupboards were bare, attended school to get away from the gloom pervading our house. I didn't go without, but it wasn't fun either.' No one asking how did school go, or questioning why she wanted to change schools. No acknowledgment she existed.

No love.

She could've handled everything else if her parents had only shown her half what they gave Ryan, even after he died.

Were those swear words spilling from Kristof's mouth? For her?

Finally Alesha looked at him. A mix of anger and sorrow twisted his mouth, darkened his eyes. He leaned closer, both hands held out to her.

It would be so simple to lean in against him and let go of her own anger and disappointment, let Kristof take charge. Too easy. Because ultimately she had to be strong for herself, and those babies. Leaping up, she paced across the room, back and forth, back and forth.

'Alesha, go easy. Let me help you. Now, and later with the babies.'

Babies. Not one, but two. She'd thought it would be hard raising one, now there was another one to think of. Could she do this?

She had to. *Wanted to.* But now she was afraid. Double trouble was what people said of twins. Double worry that she'd get it right. Twins. 'Are there twins in your family?' As far as she was aware there weren't any in her family.

'I don't recall any. Guess we managed them all by ourselves.' His light tone was forced, as though trying to pacify her.

It wasn't working. The agitation churning her insides got faster, harder, meaner. She had to get out of here. 'I'm going home.' Slinging her bag over her shoulder, she headed for the front door. Until her stomach warned it had other ideas. A quick detour took her to the bathroom.

Kristof left Alesha alone, knowing full well he was not welcome this time. But he was biting to get in there and hold her. Except no amount of caressing or soothing was going to work. Her story about her family appalled him. They'd done a lot of damage to Alesha, back when she was a child, and again tonight as she'd laid out the bare basics.

He was furious for her. How could parents do that to their daughter? Grief could paralyse a person, but to cast their child adrift? When she was so young? Actually, it didn't matter what age she was; it was wrong, and horrid, and totally incomprehensible. No wonder she never talked about her past.

Ten minutes ticked by. He couldn't stand waiting any longer. A light tap on the bathroom door and he let himself in. His heart hit his boots.

Alesha looked so forlorn he felt as though he'd been

slapped by a raging elephant. Having lowered the lid of the toilet she sat huddled with her arms around her knees, drowning in tears. Silent ones streaming all over her face and onto her arms.

She didn't raise her head when he said, 'You are going to be the best mother ever.'

Not a movement, not a whimper. Just those blasted tears.

Kristof sank down onto his haunches beside her and held the tissue box at the ready. How he hated tears. He didn't know what to do about them. How to stop them. How to obliterate the pain that caused them. He was useless. He waited some more.

Until a shaky hand reached for the box and tugged out a handful of tissues.

He watched as Alesha began mopping up her face, her chin, the backs of her arms. He handed her more tissues and removed the sodden ball from her hand.

She yawned. Her eyes were swollen and dull, exhaustion drew at her cheeks. Another yawn made up his mind.

'Come on. You're going to bed.' Leaning down, he lifted her into his arms, ready to put her down gently if she tried to get away.

Instead she snuggled into him, surprising the breath out of his body. Hope soared. She'd turned to him, not away. They might be able to work something out where Alesha had all the help she needed and he was there in the background to look out for her and the babies. She was right. Everything had got harder now that there were twins on the way. Solo parenting, even with him there for her, was hard, and that was with one child.

In his bedroom he toed the bedcover aside and laid Alesha down.

Another of those enormous yawns pulled at her.

Pulling the cover up to her chin, he kissed her hot cheeks. 'Get some sleep.'

Her hand snatched his. 'Twins. It's too much. I won't cope.'

'It's okay. *We'll* cope.'

Shuffling up the bed, she leant back against his headboard. 'No. *I* have to. I have to fight for my children. I can't fall apart when the going gets rough. I have to fight for them, no matter what tries to knock me off course.'

'You don't think you're already doing that?' He parked his butt on the edge of the bed and reached for her hands again.

'I don't know.' She pulled them away and tucked them on her stomach under the cover. 'Maybe I should go home.'

'You want to ride a train now?' What was wrong with staying here with him for the night? Disappointment slayed him.

'Back to New Zealand.'

Forget being disappointed. Try shocked. Hadn't she been adamant there was nothing for her back there? 'Why?'

'Smaller city, a health system I understand.'

'No family or friends to support you. No father of the babies you're going to have there to take his turn at feeding and changing nappies.' She couldn't take his children to the other side of the world. Could she? *Would* she?

Her smile did nothing to lift the chill settling over him. 'How often do you think you're going to be doing that? You'll be at work all day, dashing back to the hospital to check on a patient even when you do come home. Get real, Kristof. We're not going to be playing happy families. It might start out all right, but what happens when you've got a girlfriend in tow? Is she going to want to be second fiddle to bottles and potties?'

Go for the throat, why don't you? 'I don't have girl-friends. Only occasional enjoyable flings. Nothing permanent.' The words were out before he'd thought them through. 'As we had,' he added as his brain scrambled to rectify his blunder, only making things worse.

'There you go. A fling. Not a relationship. Not a life-long commitment.' Alesha tossed the cover away and her feet hit the carpet.

'This is different. We've got a lifetime commitment.' It felt as if they were going round and round with neither one of them saying *exactly* what needed to be said. Standing up, he reached out, placed his hands on her shoulders. 'Alesha, look at me.'

Instantly her face lifted and those big, sad eyes locked on him. 'Yes?'

'Marry me.' The words were out before he knew he was going to say them.

Take them back. Can't. Won't. I don't want to marry again, especially when there's no love between us.

Something like a rock nudged him. Wasn't there? No, of course not.

'Say that again,' Alesha demanded.

'It makes sense. That way we can make this work as a proper family. We'll get a bigger house with space for the children and our own rooms that the kids can go be-tween as they want.'

All colour drained from her face. 'I…' Gulp. 'That's not a marriage. That's a contract to keep the kids happy, except they won't be when they realise their parents don't share a life like their friends' parents do.'

'I thought we were trying to come to a workable arrangement where the children will be safe and happy.' Got it wrong again?

'You seem to have forgotten your reaction to that idea the night I told you I was pregnant.'

No, he hadn't. He'd had to time to weigh it all up and see there were positives about being married in this situation.

Nothing to do with loving Alesha?

He did not love her. Did he?

Sure this feeling of being turned inside out by Alesha isn't love?

It couldn't be. He'd been in love once, and that had been different.

Yeah, and she turned out to be the wrong woman for you.

What if he did love Alesha? Was in denial about it? His heart slowed as that thought took up residence in his head. No. That wasn't possible. He'd feel different, light, happy, excited. Not worried and concerned for Alesha and the babies, not trying to get everything right for them all. No, he'd be leaping in, boots and all, and to hell with the consequences. Wouldn't he?

Bending down, she picked up her bag from the floor and headed for the door. 'I know you really care about these babies, and maybe even me, but I do not want to add a half-hearted marriage into the mix.' In the kitchen she slipped her feet into her shoes. 'Thank you for the offer, but it's a no from me.'

His heart returned to his toes, and it had only just managed to climb up from there.

I want this.

Shock jerked him backwards. To have Alesha as his

wife. In his life. All the time. 'Would you at least think about it?'

She paused, cupped his cheek with her palm. And sent shivers of need rattling through him. 'Thank you for asking. I know it means a lot to you, but it isn't right for us.'

Even in a moment like this he wanted her, could feel the desire ramping up and overtaking all else. Act on that and he was a dead man. Or an idiot, which he doubted. 'We'll leave things as they stand for now.' When her hand dropped away he wanted to snatch it up and place it back against his skin. 'I'm not pushing you into anything you don't want. It's another option, that's all.'

'An option?' She shuddered. 'I understand.' Did she say 'all too well' under her breath?

'I don't think you do.' He didn't, so why would Alesha? All he knew was he'd proposed when the idea had not been there minutes before. She'd given him a reprieve— one that he did not want now he'd put the idea out there. She was the reason he'd turned down the blatant offer one of the bridesmaids had made at the wedding two weeks ago. The woman had been hot and willing, and he'd said no, thanks. Which said more than just about anything could about his state of mind. Confused, worried, and also waking up.

I want to marry Alesha, and not for the babies' sake.

He was ready to try again. Because of Alesha and her beautiful nature, her sense of right, her fun, her—her everything. 'Alesha?'

Sadness softened her lips, dulled her eyes further. 'I'm going home, London home, that is. I need to be alone.'

'I'll give you a lift.' He wasn't taking any argument

on that score. Alesha was shattered and upset. Riding a train was not on tonight.

'I appreciate the offer.' That came with a small, wry smile.

There was no understanding this woman. Seemed he could never get it right with her.

'Kristof proposed.' Alesha swallowed the lump in the back of her throat. 'I turned him down. How mad was I? I love him so much I hurt and I said no.'

It was the right thing to do.

He didn't love her, would one day come to regret it, especially when he met a woman he did want the whole commitment shebang with. Then he'd thank her for tonight.

Her stomach growled. Nothing to do with nausea though. It was hungry. The last thing she'd eaten had been hours ago in the canteen at work. Lunch had been a bread roll with salad and cheese—and a distant memory.

Padding out to the kitchen, she put a pan of water on and dropped in two eggs to poach, popped some bread into the toaster.

Somehow she'd managed to walk away from Kristof when her heart had been crying out to accept his proposal. She'd been strong. For her and the babies. They didn't need to grow up in a loveless family. Her love for Kristof overwhelmed her sometimes, it was so big and wonderful. But it hurt not to get any love back. Men had always dropped her when she got too serious about them.

Yeah, and this time was different. Kristof wants to marry me.

The toaster popped and the toast flipped onto the

bench. Not waiting for it to cool, she plastered a good dollop of butter over it.

I pushed him away, just like he said I did with others.

Hardly. Other men left her, not the other way round.

Why did they back off? Why hadn't Kristof? That was easy. She was having his babies. He was a stayer, took responsibility seriously. Look at how he wanted to buy her a place to live near his apartment so he could be there for them all. He'd always make sure she had everything she wanted.

All she wanted was for him to love her.

With a draining spoon Alesha lifted the eggs out of the water and slid them onto the toast. Any moment now her stomach was going to let her know it was kidding, it didn't want food at all, just another trip to the bathroom. A gentle rumble told her she was wrong. Food was required. Pulling a stool up to the bench, she plonked her butt down and dosed the eggs with enough salt and pepper to keep her taste buds happy.

There was something in Kristof's past that held him back. Something more than that failed marriage. Unless that was his problem and by proposing a loveless marriage he wasn't setting himself up to be hurt again. He'd said he loved his wife so it made sense his heart had been broken.

Egg yolk dripped down her chin. Wiping it away, she took another mouthful, chewed thoughtfully.

They'd both been hurt in the past. In different ways, but hurt was hurt whichever way it struck. She couldn't trust anyone to love her unconditionally. Yet she wanted to try. To give Kristof a chance. What if it didn't work out? It was better to give their relationship a chance than never knowing.

Which was good thinking except for one thing. Two things. Two children. They'd be the ones to suffer if the marriage failed. If Kristof never fell in love with her.

They might also suffer if she didn't marry the man she loved.

She was back to the beginning again. Darn but she was sick and tired of going round and round with all this.

Sick and tired. Her stomach had behaved for hours now. Wow, things could be looking up. But there was a beat going on behind her eyes that wasn't letting up. Her eyelids were heavier than her handbag. It was time for bed.

Tomorrow might bring some answers to all the questions floating around in her skull. Fingers crossed.

Kristof went to work the next morning. What else was he supposed to do? In his office he dropped into the chair behind his desk and stared at the files neatly stacked in the centre. He didn't want to look through them. Which was a first. Nothing in that pile was urgent, or even needed his attention until Monday morning. So why was he here? It was Saturday and there were plenty of other things needing his attention at home.

He'd phoned Alesha again and again. She wasn't picking up. Asleep still? Or avoiding him? It didn't matter. The result was the same. He was lost. Unable to decide how to make her see marriage was the best idea for their situation.

'Hey, man, you're looking about as happy as a dog whose bone got stolen.' Harry dropped into the opposite chair. 'What's up?'

'Nothing.' Kristof studied the files.

'Woman trouble.'

'You think?'

Harry laughed. 'I've never seen you look so glum, like you have a problem you don't know how to fix.'

'Could mean my shower's stopped working and I can't get a plumber at short notice.' The trouble with friends was they saw too much and had no compunction over talking about it.

'This the woman you met in Dubrovnik?'

When had he told Harry about Alesha? 'If I say yes will you go away?'

'She dump you?'

Considering it was well known he didn't do relationships, where had his pal got that idea from?

It's the truth.

So? Didn't mean he had to admit it. 'Sort of.'

Zip your mouth.

'Why?'

'Who the hell knows?' He didn't. Or maybe he did have an inkling. 'She lets people get so close then pushes them away.' And that was all he was saying. Kristof stood up.

'You free to join our tribe for dinner tonight? It's your goddaughter's birthday.'

A kick in the gut wouldn't hurt half as much. Kristof swore. 'I totally forgot.'

'Which is why I figured something was wrong. We'll be seeing you, then?'

'Of course. I'll go shopping now for that bike I promised her.' That'd keep his mind busy.

'Want to ask your lady friend to join us too?'

Yes, he did, but a man could only take so many knockbacks. 'She's busy.'

'Or you don't want to risk her saying no.'

'When did you get so clever?' Kristof sank back on his chair, suddenly unable to move forward. As if he were stuck in a groove between what he had and what he wanted. 'I'm going to be a father to twins. A boy and a girl.'

'You're pulling my leg?' Harry shook his head. 'Of course you're not. Twins? Talk about playing catch-up in a big way. Man, you are in for some fun and a heap of responsibility.'

Responsibility he could do. Fun he wanted, but wasn't sure where to start.

Harry hadn't finished. 'The fun means letting go and diving right in, becoming a hands-on dad, and that's scaring the pants off you.'

Kristof didn't say a word. What was the point?

Harry's hand slapped the desktop. 'Duh, how stupid of me. That's not the problem. It's the kids' mother putting that sour look on your face. You are worried about letting your feelings show, or how to act on them.'

Knew he'd get there in the end. 'So?'

'So take a chance. Stop hiding from the past. Go risk your heart for them all. I am right in presuming you love her?'

Kristof froze. Couldn't have blinked if he'd tried. Love Alesha? He cared for her, a lot. Wanted what was best for her. Needed to protect her, look out for her. But love her? Crack. A sharp pain stabbed his heart. Another crack opened it further.

Was this love? This all-encompassing, debilitating sensation filling his chest was the real deal? It wouldn't go away because he expected it to? Another stab hit his chest. 'I have totally screwed up,' he admitted.

Harry stood up. 'Then go fix it.'

'What if I'm too late?' Agony lanced him. Alesha had to give him a second chance. She just had to.

'I'll tell Katie you won't be there for her party for a very good reason. But, man, you'd better deliver on this. No one gets these chances very often. Don't wreck it before you've crawled on bare knees across hot, sharp coals.'

'Thanks.'

The door closed with a resounding click and Kristof stared at the paintwork. Katie's birthday and he'd forgotten all about it. What sort of godfather did that make him? The uninvolved kind. The kind of father he'd been hoping to avoid becoming. Leaping to his feet, he made for the door, hauled it back so hard it slammed the wall. 'Harry? If it's all right with you I'll pick Katie up after lunch and take her to choose her own bike. We'll have time together.'

Harry started back towards him, a smile on his dial. 'Now you're talking like a real godfather. What about your woman? Don't waste time there, either.'

'Alesha. Her name's Alesha.' His lungs expanded. 'I'm going to see if she likes buying bikes and having dinner with strangers.' And if she didn't, he'd call tomorrow and see if she wanted to go to the farmers' market. On Monday? He'd come up with something because as of now he was not giving up on winning her over.

Alesha arranged the two teddy bears, one pink and one blue, on her dresser and smiled. It didn't matter how hollowed out and sick she felt, excitement was in her belly, warming her heavy heart. She was having two babies, and, despite all the problems waving at her, she was excited.

'Hey.' Shelley stuck her head around the door. 'You've got a visitor.'

Alesha's smile fell away. There was only one person who'd be calling on her. Kristof. She didn't have a line-up of close friends who dropped in and out at the week-ends. It had to be the man who continuously played havoc with her head. 'Kristof?'

Shelley nodded. 'He said you might not want to talk to him but he looks so forlorn I had to come check with you.'

'He's right. I don't want to go near him.' She wanted to rush at him, wind her arms around his waist and never let go.

'This the father of your babies?'

It'd become impossible to keep her pregnancy a secret here when she was being sick so often. 'Yes.'

'Then what are you waiting for? Give the guy a chance to say whatever's making him look like he ate rotten fish for breakfast.'

That description did not bring a pretty picture to Alesha's mind, but it did trip the guilt button. Shoving herself up off the edge of the bed, she growled, 'All right, then. Just to shut you up, you understand?'

Shelley surprised her by wrapping her arms around her. 'You've been miserable for days. I'm thinking the other side of that coin is standing out in our lounge, hat in hand, waiting for you. Give yourself and your babies a break. Take a chance on whatever it is he's come to offer.'

How she wanted that. More than anything. As long as it came loaded with love.

'Are you up for bicycle shopping and a family din-ner?' A sombre smile highlighted Kristof's mouth. It didn't quite reach the sad eyes. Make that a sorry gaze. 'It's my goddaughter's birthday and I promised her a bike. Today I realised she needs to choose it, not old man Uncle Kristof.'

Goddaughter? He did have people close to him that he loved. Alesha looked closer. There was a struggle going on over his face. He hadn't thought to share the experience with the girl. Until now. There was love in his eyes when he mentioned the child, love he hadn't been able to share or acknowledge out loud? What had changed? Not anything to do with her and their babies, surely? 'You'd pick a plain-coloured one while she'll want fairies or out-of-world creatures.'

'You're onto it. Want to come and watch me forget how I like being in charge of everything?'

Did she? Yes, but where would it lead? To more heart-break? Or a settling-down time between them so they could start over on planning the future? Guess there was only one way to find out. 'Give me a minute to put my face on and grab my bag.' Only now did Alesha remember she hadn't bothered with make-up this morning, thinking no one would see her.

'You don't need any of that stuff on your skin. It's beautiful as it is.' If he hadn't sounded so genuine she'd have laughed in his face and told him to go find another woman to cajole. Ah, no, she wouldn't.

'Without make-up I feel naked.' She smiled when his eyes widened. 'Don't go there. We've got a bike to shop for.'

But as she smoothed make-up over her face her smile faded. What was this about? He didn't need her to go shopping with him and his goddaughter. So why was she being included in the trip to the mall? Hope rose. She squashed it. It came back stronger. This was going to end badly.

Or really, really well.

Out in the lounge she nodded to Kristof. 'Let's go,' she said as she held her breath.

Out on the street, he pinged the locks open then placed his hands on her shoulders to draw her close. 'I'm so sorry, Alesha. I struggle with letting those nearest and dearest know how I feel. My mother has suffered because of that. I was brought up in the stiff-upper-lip brigade. My father never showed us much love, though I believe he loved me. He probably loved Mum in his own way, not totally and solely, but enough to be furious when she left him.' He paused and looked skyward. His Adam's apple bobbed. Then he locked those beautiful eyes on her. 'What I'm trying to say...' Swallow. 'I want to tell you that I love you. I've taken for ever to come round to believing it, but it is true. I love you with all my heart, Alesha Milligan. Will you share my life? Raise our babies together in a loving way?'

She gasped. Her head was light. While behind her ribs there was a lot of pounding going on. Kristof loved her? As she loved him? Looking into those blue-grey eyes she saw nothing but love, genuine, deep love—for her. Oh, my. She gasped again. Was this really happening to *her*? Had she finally found what she'd been looking for all her life? She loved him so much, and this love was like nothing she'd thought possible. It meant everything, was all-encompassing.

He cleared his throat. 'Alesha?' Fear tripped through his gaze.

'Kristof, I'm—' She stopped. About to say sorry, which he'd have taken the wrong way. 'Yes,' she said quickly to dispel his fear. He had put his heart on the line without knowing how she really felt. It was probably

obvious, written all over her face when she wasn't dis-
agreeing with him. Kristof needed to hear those words as
much as she had. Rising on her toes and placing a hand
on his cheek, she answered, 'I love you, Kristof. It's the
for ever kind of love. The "dealing with everything that
life throws at us" love.'

Relief and love rose in his eyes. 'I know there are lots
of things still to work out.'

'I think we've just made that easier.' She smiled with
everything that was in her heart before her mouth found
his.

Kristof pulled her close, his hands holding her waist,
his mouth owning hers. 'I love you so much it hurts,' he
growled against her lips.

'I like that.' She kissed him back.

As the kiss deepened, Alesha sank in closer and closer
to that hard, caring, sexy body of her man, and let her
heart believe what it had heard, felt everything right itself inside.

*Hey, babies, looks like we've got ourselves a loving
future.*

Kristof pulled back only enough to stare into her eyes.
'So will you marry me now? For love and family and all
the wonderful things we both want?'

A phone ringing broke into the moment. Annoyance
and humour warred on his face as his hand shoved into
his pocket.

'Yes,' Alesha said. 'I will marry you.'

His hand hesitated as he leaned in for another kiss.
'Thank you. You've just made me the happiest man ever.'

'You'd better answer that call. It could be important.'
As happiness expanded throughout she couldn't even
find the smallest grudge against whoever had interrupted

her most important moment. If she let that happen she'd never be fully happy.

'Hey, Katie, we're on our way to pick you up. I'm running late but it is for the best reason. See you in a little while, okay?' Kristof listened to his goddaughter with love in his eyes.

Love for Katie? For her? For both of them? What did it matter? He had more than enough to go around, and now that he recognised it there'd be more where he found that. Alesha snuggled against her man and waited for him to finish the call. They were going out, on a date that included a little girl, and later to a dinner with Kristof's friends. Yes, it was all coming together nicely.

On the way back to Kristof's home late that night Alesha was suddenly enveloped with sadness and a fierce longing for *everything* to be made right in her life. Possibly she was asking too much but she had to try.

'What's up?' Kristof asked as he parked in the garage.

See? The man could read her too easily. 'I need to tell my parents we're getting married.'

He turned and took her hands in his. 'You do. And if you don't get the reaction you're obviously hoping for, then remember I'm here, that I'll love you more than enough for everyone.'

Right then her heart melted, the last little doubt that he might not love her enough for long enough dissolving into the pool lying behind her ribs. 'I know.'

The follow-up kiss was tender, filled with love, and with the acceptance they had finally got it right. What one week could do to change her life was beyond description.

When they went inside Kristof led her to the lounge

and sat down on the couch, pulling her onto his thighs. 'My father was my hero when I was growing up. He could do no wrong, and when my mother was sad, or angry with him, I blamed her for not loving him enough, blamed her for their marriage bust-up.' He swallowed hard. 'Then my father died and the truth came out. He'd cheated on her throughout their marriage. A lot of what he'd taught me about being a man was a lie.'

Now she understood those dark moments. 'You feel guilty for how you treated your mother.'

Kristof nodded. 'I married someone like my father in the fidelity stakes. That undermined my ability to believe in my feelings, my love. Which is why I became so focused on medicine where I knew I was good and couldn't be hurt by other people taking advantage of my feelings.'

'Pull the other one, Kristof. You think all those weeks you've spent helping out at the Croatian children's home wasn't about showing how you felt for your mother?'

His smile, when it came, was the most relaxed and happy he'd ever given her. 'Now I understand why I love you so much. There's no hiding anything from you.' He kissed her, which led to making love on the couch, and then heading for the bedroom to fall asleep in each other's arms.

As her eyes drooped shut Alesha whispered, 'I never knew I could be so happy. I love you.'

EPILOGUE

EIGHT WEEKS LATER Alesha walked up the pathway of the beautifully manicured gardens to the wedding venue.

Katie proudly strode ahead, a basket of rose petals in her hands, ready to sprinkle across the lawn right up to the marriage celebrant.

Alesha gripped a small bunch of peonies, the rose-pink colour lovely against her cream wedding gown that fitted tight over her breasts, and gathered over the babies tucked inside. Her face was split wide with a smile solely for the man who'd given her so much already. Yet tears streamed down her cheeks. Seemed that once she'd learned to cry she couldn't unlearn it.

She walked alone, but she wasn't alone. The people who mattered the most were here, smiling and rejoicing in her and Kristof's occasion. Cherry and Shelley had offered to walk her up the short path, but she'd declined. She didn't want to be given away—by anyone. She was going to Kristof, to be his wife and partner and lover. She was not giving herself to him to the point she didn't recognise herself again.

During the three phone calls she'd had with her parents her father had hesitatingly suggested he might give her away. She did not want that either. They had a long way to go to fix their relationship, if they ever could. As it happened her parents hadn't been able to get here for the wedding since her mother had fallen and broken her hip. They were all talking, and trying to move forward. It would be a long journey, but at least they'd started.

As she passed Antonija she saw her soon-to-be mother-in-law also crying, along with an enormous smile. Little Capeka watched solemnly from beside her adoptive grandmother. For a while Kristof and Alesha had considered bringing her to London for a new start in life, but she was struggling to find her feet and it had been decided the little girl should stay in Dubrovnik for now, at least, and, as no one had come forward to claim her, Antonija had taken her into her home permanently.

Glancing around, Alesha saw Harry's wife blink and surreptitiously wipe her eyes. What was with all these tears? It was the happiest day of her life and everyone was crying. Suddenly a laugh rippled out of Alesha's throat. Happy tears were afloat everywhere. 'This is wonderful. I am so happy to be marrying the man of my heart.' And she stepped up beside him. Kristof, he was all that really mattered. With him she'd found what she'd been looking for most of her life, and he was generous with his love. That was so special she had to keep pinching herself to make sure she hadn't fallen asleep in the sun somewhere.

Then Kristof was taking her hand and kissing her cheek. Love shone out of those blue-grey eyes she adored. 'I love you, darling.'

The celebrant chuckled. 'You're getting ahead of yourself, Mr Montfort. I think I'd better get this under way quick smart.'

Kristof's words of devotion and love were a blur for Alesha, yet she felt them deep in her heart. And when it was her turn to pledge her love she saw him open up more than ever to accept her promises of love.

'I pronounce you man and wife. Kristof, now you can kiss your bride.'

Amidst laughter and lots of sweet-scented petals, Alesha reached up and kissed her husband.

* * * * *

COMING SOON!

We really hope you enjoyed reading this book. If you're looking for more romance, be sure to head to the shops when new books are available on

Thursday
23rd August

To see which titles are coming soon, please visit
millsandboon.co.uk

MILLS & BOON

Coming next month

THE NURSE'S PREGNANCY MIRACLE
Ann McIntosh

Nychelle tried with all her might to say they shouldn't
go any further, but couldn't get the words out. Knowing
she needed to tell him the rest of her story battled with
the desire making her head swim and her body tingle
and thrum with desire.

'Tell me you don't want me,' he said again, and she
knew she couldn't. To do so would be to lie.

'I can't. You know I can't. But...'

He didn't wait to hear the rest, just took her mouth
in a kiss that made what she'd planned to say fly right
out of her brain.

Desire flared, hotter than the Florida sun, and Nychelle
surrendered to it, unable and unwilling to risk missing
this chance to know David intimately, even if it were just
this once. Was it right? Wrong? She couldn't decide —
didn't want to try to.

There were so many more things she should explain
to him, but she knew she wouldn't. Telling him about
the baby when she knew he didn't want a family would
destroy whatever it was growing between them. It was
craven, perhaps even despicable not to be honest with
him, and she hated herself for being underhand, but her
mind, heart and body were at war, and she'd already
accepted which would win.

She'd deal with the fallout, whatever it might be, tomorrow. Today—this evening—she was going to have what she wanted, live the way she wanted. Enjoy David for this one time. There would only be regrets if she didn't.

His lips were still on hers, demanding, delicious. She'd relived the kisses they'd shared over and over in her mind, but now she realized memory was only a faded facsimile of reality. The touch and taste and scent of him encompassed her, overtaking her system on every level.

Her desperate hands found their way beneath his shirt, and his groan of pleasure was as heartfelt as her joy at the first sensation of his bare skin beneath her palms. His hands, in turn, explored her yearning flesh, stroking her face, then her neck. When they brushed along her shoulders, easing the straps of her sundress away, Nychelle. arched against him.

Suddenly it was as though they had both lost all restraint. Arms tight around each other, their bodies moved in concert, their fiercely demanding kisses whipping the flames of arousal to an inferno.

Continue reading
THE NURSE'S PREGNANCY MIRACLE
Ann McIntosh

Available next month
www.millsandboon.co.uk

LET'S TALK
Romance

For exclusive extracts, competitions
and special offers, find us online:

 facebook.com/millsandboon

 @millsandboonuk

 @millsandboon

Or get in touch on 0844 844 1351*

For all the latest titles coming soon, visit
millsandboon.co.uk/nextmonth